The

BATHING
WOMEN

A Novel

TIE NING

Translated by Hongling Zhang and Jason Sommer

SCRIBNER

New York London Toronto Sydney New Delhi

SCRIBNER
A Division of Simon & Schuster, Inc.
1230 Avenue of the Americas
New York, NY 10020

Originally published in Chinese by People's Literature

First Scribner hardcover edition October 2012

SCRIBNER and design are registered trademarks of The Gale Group, Inc.,
used under license by Simon & Schuster, Inc., the publisher of this work.

For information about special discounts for bulk purchases, please contact
Simon & Schuster Special Sales at 1-866-506-1949 or
business@simonandschuster.com.

The Simon & Schuster Speakers Bureau can bring authors to your
live event. For more information or to book an event contact the
Simon & Schuster Speakers Bureau at 1-866-248-3049 or
visit our website at www.simonspeakers.com.

Book design by Ellen R. Sasahara

Manufactured in the United States of America

1   3   5   7   9   10   8   6   4   2

Library of Congress Cataloging-in-Publication Data is available.

ISBN 978-1-4516-9484-0
ISBN 978-1-4767-0426-5 (ebook)

The song on page 7 is adapted from a Tibetan folk melody
with new lyrics by Ma Zhuo.

THE

BATHING

WOMEN

❧ ❧ ❧

Prologue

❀ ❀ ❀

*T*iao's apartment had a three-seater sofa and two single armchairs. Their covers were satin brocade, a sort of fuzzy blue-gray, like the eyes of some European women, soft and clear. The chairs were arranged in the shape of a flattened U, with the sofa at the base and the armchairs facing each other on two sides.

Tiao's memory of sofas went back to when she was about three. It was in the early sixties; her home had a pair of old dark red corduroy sofas. The springs were a bit broken, and stuck out of their coir and hemp wrappings, pressing firmly up through a layer of corduroy that was not very thick. The whole sofa had a lumpy look and it creaked when people sat down. Every time Tiao hauled herself onto it, she could feel little fists punching up from underneath her. The broken springs would grind into her delicate knees and sensitive back. But she still liked to climb up on the sofa because compared to the hard-backed little chair that belonged to her, it allowed her to move around freely, leaning this way and that—and being able to move freely this way and that makes for comfort; ever since she was small, Tiao pursued comfort. Later, and for a long time, an object like a sofa was labeled as associated with a certain class. And that class obviously wanted to exert a bad influence on the spirit and body of the people, like a plague or marijuana. Most Chinese people's behinds had never come in contact with sofas; even soft-cushioned chairs were rare in

1

most homes. By then—probably in the early seventies—Tiao eventually found a pair of down pillows in a home that only had a few hard chairs. The down pillows were from her parents' beds. When they weren't home, she dragged the pillows off, reserved one for herself, and gave one to her younger sister Fan. They put the pillows on two hard chairs and settled into them, wriggling on the puffy pillows, pretending they were on sofas. They enjoyed the sheer luxury of reclining on these "sofas," cracking sunflower seeds or eating a handful of hawthorn berries. Often, when this was going on, Quan would wave her arms anxiously and stumble over in a rush from the other end of the room going, "Ah-ah-ah-ah."

Quan, the younger sister of Tiao and Fan, would have been two years old then. She would stumble all the way over to her two sisters, obviously wanting to join their "sofa leisure," but they planned to ignore her completely. They also looked down on her flaw—Quan couldn't talk even though she was two; she would probably be a mute. But the mute Quan was a little beauty, the kind everyone loved on sight, and she enjoyed communicating with people very much, allowing adults or almost-adults to take turns holding her. She would toss her natural brown curls, purse her fresh little red lips, and make all kinds of signs—no one knew where she picked up these gestures. When she wanted to flirt, she pressed her tender fingers to her lips and blew you a kiss; when she wanted to show her anger, she waved around her bamboo-shoot pinkie in front of your eyes; when she wanted you to leave, she pointed at the sky and then put her hands over her ears as if saying: Oh, it's getting dark and I have to go to sleep.

Now Quan stood before Tiao and Fan and kept blowing them kisses, which apparently were meant as a plea to let her join them in "sofa leisure." She got no response, so she switched her sign, angrily thrusting out her arm and sticking up her pinkie to tell them: You two are bad, really bad. You're just as small as this little pinkie and I despise you. Still, no one spoke to her, so she started to stamp her feet and beat her chest. This description isn't the usual dramatic exaggeration—she literally stood there beating her chest and stamping her feet. She clenched her hands and beat the butter-colored, flower-bordered bib embroidered with two white pigeons, her little fists pounding like raindrops. Meanwhile, she stamped on the concrete floor noisily with her little dumpling feet, in her red leather shoes. Then, with tears and runny nose, she let herself go entirely. She lay on the floor, pumping her strong and fleshy legs vigorously in the air, as if pedaling an invisible wheel.

You think throwing a tantrum is going to soften our hearts? You want to blow us kisses—go ahead and blow! You want to hold up your pinkie at us—go on and hold it up! You want to beat your chest and stamp your feet—do it! You want to lie on the floor and pedal—go pedal! Go ahead and pedal, you!

Through half-closed eyes, Tiao looked at Quan, who was rolling around on the floor. Satisfaction at the venting of her hatred radiated from her heart all over her body. It was a sort of ice-cold excitement, a turbulent calm. Afterward, she simply closed her eyes, pretending to catnap. Sitting in the chair next to her, Fan imitated her sister's catnap. Her obedience to her sister was inbred. Besides, she didn't like Quan, either, whose birth directly shook Fan's privileged status; she was next in line for Fan's privileges. Fan was unhappy simply because she was like all world leaders, always watchful for their successors and disgusted by them.

When they awoke from their catnap, Quan was no longer in sight. She disappeared. She died.

The foregoing memory might be true; it could also be one of Tiao's revisions. If everyone has memories that are more or less personally revised, then the unreliability of the human race wasn't Tiao's responsibility alone. The exact date of Quan's death was six days after that tantrum, but Tiao was always tempted to place her death on the same day that she beat her chest and stamped her feet, as if by doing so she and Fan could be exonerated. It was on that day that Quan had left the world, right at the moment we blinked, as we dozed off into a dream. We didn't touch her; we didn't leave the room—the pillows under us could prove it. What happened afterward? Nothing. No design; no plot; no action. Ah, how weak and helpless I am! What a poisonous snake I am! Tiao chose to believe only what she wanted to believe; what she wasn't willing to believe, she pretended didn't exist. But what happened six days later did exist, wrapped up and buried in Tiao's heart, never to be let go.

Now neither of them sits on the sofa. When Tiao and Fan chat, they always sit separately on those two blue-gray armchairs, face-to-face. More than twenty years have passed and Quan still exists. She sits on that sofa at the center of that U as if it were custom-made for her. She still has the height of a two-year-old, about sixty centimeters, but the ratio of her head to her body is not a baby's, which is one to four—that is, the length of the body should equal four heads. The ratio of her head to her body is completely adult, one to seven. This makes her look less like a two-year-old girl and more like a tiny woman. She wears a cream-colored satin negligee, and sits with one thigh crossed over the other. From time to time she touches her smooth, supple face with one of her fingers. When she stretches out her hand, the bamboo-shoot tip of her pinkie curves naturally, like the hand gesture of an opera singer, which makes her look a bit coy. She looks like such a social butterfly! Tiao thinks, not knowing why she would choose such an outdated phrase to describe Quan. But she doesn't want to use those new, intolerably vulgar words such as "little honey." Although "social butterfly" also implies ambiguity, seduction, frivolousness, and impurity, the mystery and romance that it conveyed in the past can't be replaced by any other words. She was low and cynical, but not a simple dependent, stiffly submitting to authority. No one could ever know the deep loneliness behind her pride, radiance, and passion.

Life like falling petals and flowing water: the social butterfly Yin Xiaoquan.

Chapter 1

❀ ❀ ❀

Premarital Examination

1

The provincial sunshine was actually not much different from the sunshine in the capital. In the early spring the sunshine in both the province and the capital was precious. At this point in the season, the heating in the office buildings, apartments, and private homes was already off. During the day, the temperature inside was much colder than the temperature outside. Tiao's bones and muscles often felt sore at this time of year. When she walked on the street, her thigh muscle would suddenly ache. The little toe on her left foot (or her right foot), inside those delicate little knuckles, delivered zigzagging pinpricks of pain. The pain was uncomfortable, but it was the kind of discomfort that makes you feel good, a kind of minor pain, coy, a half-drunk moan bathed in sunlight. Overhead, the roadside poplars had turned green. Still new, the green coiled around the waists of the light-colored buildings like mist. The city revealed its softness then, and also its unease.

Sitting in the provincial taxi, Tiao rolled down the window and stuck out her head, as if to test the temperature outside, or to invite all the sun in the sky to shine on that short-cropped head of hers. The way she stuck out her head looked a bit wild, or would even seem crude if she overdid it. But Tiao never overdid it; from a young age she was naturally good at striking poses. So the way she stuck out her head then combined a little wildness with a little elegance. The lowered window pressed at her chin, like a gleaming blade just about to slice her neck, giving her a feeling of having her head under the ax. The bloody yet satisfying scene, a bit stirring and a bit masochistic, was an indelible memory of the story of Liu Hulan, which she heard as a child. Whenever she thought about how the Nationalist bandits decapitated the fifteen-year-old Liu Hulan with an ax, she couldn't stop gulping—with an indescribable fear and an unnameable pleasure. At that moment she would always ask herself: Why is the most frightening thing also the most alluring? She couldn't tell whether it was the desire to become a hero that made her imagine lying under an ax, or was it that the more she feared lying under the ax, the more she wanted to lie under the ax?

She couldn't decide.

The taxi sped along the sun-drenched avenue. The sunshine in the provinces was actually not much different from the sunshine in the capital, Tiao thought.

Yet at this moment, in the midst of the provincial capital, Fuan, a city just two hundred kilometers from Beijing, the dust and fiber in the sunshine, people's expressions and the shape of things as the sun struck them, all of it seemed a bit different from the capital for some reason. When the taxi came to a red light, Tiao started to look at the people stopped by the light. A girl wearing black platform shoes and tight-fitting black clothes had a shapely figure and pretty face, with the ends of her hair dyed blond. This reminded her of girls she'd seen in Tel Aviv, New York, and Seoul who liked to wear black. Whatever was trendy around the world was trendy here, too. Sitting splayed over her white mountain bike, the provincial girl in black anxiously raised her wrist to look at her watch as she spat. She looked at the watch and spat; she spat and then looked at her watch. Tiao supposed she must have something urgent to do and that time was important to her. But why did she spit, since she had a watch? Because she had a watch, there was no need for her to spit. Because she spat, there was no need for her to wear a watch. Because she learned the art of managing her time, she should have learned the art of controlling her spit. Because she had a watch, she shouldn't have spit. Because she spat, she shouldn't have a watch. Because she had a watch, she really shouldn't have spit. Because she had spit, she really shouldn't have a watch. Because watch . . . because spit . . . because spit . . . because watch . . . because . . . because . . . The red light had long since turned green and the girl in black had shot herself forward like an arrow, and Tiao was still going around and around with watch and spit. This obsession of hers with "if not this, it must be that" made people feel that she was going to run screaming through the street, but this sort of obsession didn't appear to be true indignation. If she'd forced herself to quietly recite the sentence "Because there is a watch there shouldn't be spit" fifteen more times, she definitely would have gotten confused and lost track of what it meant. Then her obsession was indeed not real indignation; it was sarcastic babble she hadn't much stake in. The era was one during which watches and spit coexisted, particularly in the provinces.

Tiao brought her head in from the car window. The radio was playing an old song: "Atop the golden mountain in Beijing, / rays of light shine in all directions. Chairman Mao is exactly like that golden sun, / so warm, so kind, he lights up the hearts of us serfs, / as we march on the socialist path to happiness— / Hey, *ba zha hei!*" It was a game show from the local music station. The host asked the audience to guess the song title and the original singer. The winner would get a case of Jiabao SOD skin-care products. Audience members phoned in constantly, guessing titles and singers over and over again in Fuan-accented Mandarin, but none of them guessed right. After all, the song and the old singer who sang the song were unfamiliar to the audience of the day, so unfamiliar that even the host felt embarrassed. Tiao knew the title of the old song and the singer who sang it, which drew her into the game show, even though she had no plans to call the hotline. She just sang the song over and over in her head—only the refrain, *"Ba zha hei! Ba zha hei! Ba zha hei! Ba zha hei! . . ."* Twenty years ago, when she and her classmates sang that song together, they loved to sing the last line, *"Ba zha hei!"* It was a Tibetan folk song, sung by the liberated serfs in gratitude to Chairman Mao. *"Ba zha hei!"* obviously isn't Chinese. It must be because it was not Chinese that Tiao used to repeat it with such enthusiasm, with some of that feeling of liberation, like chanting, like clever wordplay. The thought of clever wordplay made her force herself to stop repeating *"Ba zha hei."* She returned to the present, to the taxi in the provincial capital of Fuan. The game show on the music station was over; the seat in the quiet taxi was covered by a patterned cotton cushion, not too clean, which resembled those shoe inserts handmade and embroidered by country girls from the north. Tiao always felt as if she were sitting on the padding over a Kang bed-stove whenever she sat in a taxi like this. Even though she had been living here for twenty years, she still compared everything to the capital. Whether psychologically or geographically, Beijing was always close to her. This would seem to have a lot to do with the fact that she was born in Beijing, and was a Beijinger. But most of the time she didn't feel she was a Beijinger, nor did she feel she was a provincial person, a Fuaner. She felt she didn't belong anywhere, and she often thought this with some spite, some perverse pleasure. It was almost as if she made herself rootless on purpose, as if only in rootlessness could she be free and remain apart from the city around her, allowing her to face all cities and life itself with detachment and calm. And when she thought of the word "calm," it finally occurred to her that the person sitting in the taxi shouldn't be so calm; she was probably going to get married.

She had never been married before—the sentence sounded a little odd, as if others who were preparing to get married had all been married many times. But she had never been married before—she still preferred to think this way. She thought about herself this way without any commendatory or derogatory connotations, though sometimes with a touch of pride, and sometimes a touch of sadness. She knew she didn't look like someone who was approaching forty. Often her eyes would moisten suddenly and a hazy look would float over them; her body had the kind of vigor, agility, and alertness that only an unmarried, childless mature woman would have. The drawers in her office were always stuffed with snacks: preserved plums, eel jerky, fruit chocolate, etc. She was the vice president of a children's publishing house, but none of her colleagues addressed her as President Yin. Instead, they called her by her name: Yin Xiaotiao. She looked smug a lot of the time, and she knew the person most annoyed by her smugness was her younger sister Fan. Particularly after Fan left for America, things became much clearer. For a long time, she was afraid to tell Fan about her love affairs, but the more she was afraid, the more she felt driven to tell Fan about every one of them. It was almost as though she could prove she wasn't afraid of Fan by putting up with Fan's criticism of what she did in her affairs. Even right now she was thinking this, with a somewhat sneaky bravado. It was as if she'd already picked up the phone, and could already imagine the troubled, inquiring expression that Fan had on the other end of the overseas line at getting the news, along with the string of her words, delivered with a nasal tinge. They, Tiao and Fan, had suffered together; they'd felt together as one. What made Fan so contemptuous of Tiao's life? It was surely contempt—for her clothes, her hairstyle, and the men in her life. Nothing escaped Fan's ridicule and condemnation—even the showerhead in Tiao's bathroom. The first year Fan came back to visit, she stayed with Tiao. She complained that the water pressure in the showerhead was too weak to get her hair clean—that precious hair of hers. She complained with a straight face, showing no sign of joking at all. Tiao managed to conceal her unhappiness behind a phony smile, but she would always remember that phony smile.

Maybe she shouldn't tell her.

The taxi brought Tiao to the Happy Millions Supermarket. She bought food enough for a week and then took the taxi home.

The heat in her apartment wasn't on, so the rooms felt shadowy and cold. It was different from a winter chill, none of that dense stiffness filling the space; it was uncertain, bearing faint traces of loneliness. On such an evening of such a season, Tiao liked to turn on all the lights, first the hallway, then the kitchen, the study, the living room, the bedroom, and the bathroom, all the lights, ceiling light, wall light, desk light, floor light, mirror light, and bedside light . . . her hands took turns clicking the switches; only the owner of the place could be so practiced and precise. Tiao was the master of the house, and she greeted her apartment by turning the lights on. She lit her home with all these lights, but it seemed as if the lights lit themselves to welcome Tiao back. So lights illuminated every piece of furniture, and every bit of dim haziness in the shadows contributed to her sense of security and substance. She walked through every room this way until she finally came to a small corner: to that blue-gray satin brocade armchair, which seemed to be her favorite corner when she was not sleeping. Every time she came home, returning from work or a business trip, she would sit in this small armchair, staring blankly for a while, drinking a cup of hot water, and refreshing herself until both her body and mind felt rested and relaxed. She never sat on the sofa. Even when Chen Zai held her in his arms and asked to move onto the more comfortable sofa, she remained uncooperative. Then, in a desperate moment, finally feeling she couldn't refuse anymore, she simply said, "Let's go to bed."

For Chen Zai, that was an unforgettable sentence because they had never gone to bed before, even though they had known each other for decades. Later, when they sometimes teased back and forth about who seduced whom first, Chen Zai would quote this sentence of Tiao's, "Let's go to bed." It was so straightforward and innocent and it caught him so off guard that he almost missed the erotic implications. It made Chen Zai think again and again that this lithe woman he held in his arms was his true love, and always had been. It was also because of this sentence that they didn't do anything that first night.

Chen Zai was not home tonight. He had gone to the south on a business trip. Tiao ate dinner, sat back in the armchair, and read a manuscript for a while. Then she took a shower and got into bed. She preferred to slip into her quilt nest early; she preferred to wait for Chen Zai's phone call in there. She especially liked the words "slip into her quilt nest," a little unsophisticated—poor and unworldly-sounding. She just liked the words "slip," "quilt," "nest." She never got used to hotels and the way foreigners slept—the blanket tucked in at the foot of the bed, stretched tight over the mattress. Once you stuck your legs and feet into the blanket, you felt disconnected, with nothing to touch. She also didn't like quilts made of down, or artificial cotton. The way they floated lightly over your body made you more restless. She always used quilts made of real cotton; she liked everything about a quilt nest folded with a cotton quilt, the tender, swaddled feeling of the light weight distributed over her whole body, the different temperatures that hid in the little creases of the quilt nest. When she couldn't sleep because of the heat, she would use her feet to look for the cool spots in the soft creases under the quilt. When she needed to curl up, the quilt nest would come along with her, clinging to her body. So unlike those bedclothes pinned down by the mattress, where you wouldn't dream of moving, but would have to yield to the tyranny, forced into an approved sleeping posture—by what right? Tiao thought. Every time she went on a business trip or traveled abroad, she would intentionally mess up those blankets. Cotton quilts always made Tiao sleep well. But unpleasant thoughts pressed in on her after she woke up in the middle of the night. When she turned on the table lamp, tottered to the bathroom to pee, and returned, when she lay back in her bed and turned off the light, at that moment she would feel the intense loneliness and boredom. She began to think about things in a confused way, and the things that people tend to think, awakening after midnight, are often unpleasant. How she hated waking up in the middle of the night! Only after she truly had Chen Zai did she lose the fear. Then she was no longer by herself.

She curled up in her quilt nest and waited for Chen Zai's phone call. He kissed her through the phone and they talked for a long time. When Tiao hung up, she found herself still not wanting to sleep. This evening, a night when Chen Zai was far away from Fuan, she had an overwhelming desire to read the love letters locked in her bookcase. They were not from Chen Zai, and she no longer loved the man who had written her the love letters. Her desire now was not to reminisce, or to take stock. Maybe she just cherished the handwriting on the paper. Nowadays, few people would put pen to paper, especially not to write love letters.

2

There were sixty-eight letters altogether, and Tiao numbered every one of them in chronological order. She opened number one, a white paper whose edges had yellowed: "Comrade Yin Xiaotiao, the unexpected meeting with you in Beijing left a deep impression on me. I have a feeling that we will definitely see each other again. I'm writing to you on an airplane. I will arrive in Shanghai today and will leave for San Francisco tomorrow. I'll seriously consider your suggestion about writing a childhood memoir—only because it was a request of yours." The letter was signed by Fang Jing, the date was March 1982.

It was more like a note than a letter. The words, scrawled on an oversized piece of paper, seemed big and sparse. The words looked like they were staring stupidly at the reader. Strictly speaking, it was not a love letter, but the thrill that it brought to Tiao's soul was much stronger than what those real love letters of his gave her later.

The letter's author, Fang Jing, had been very hot in the movie business at the time. He'd written, directed, and acted in a movie called *A Beautiful Life*. After an endless run in theaters around the country, the movie also won quite a few major awards. It was a movie about middle-aged intellectuals who'd suffered horrendously during the Cultural Revolution but still managed to survive, optimism intact. Fang Jing played an intellectual imprisoned in a labor camp on the border. He was a violinist whose imprisonment gave him no chance to play the violin. There was an episode in the movie that showed how, after the hero endures heavy labor with an empty stomach, when he straightens up in the wheat field, catching sight of the beautiful sunset in the distance, he can't help stretching out his arms. His right arm becomes the violin neck and he presses on it with his left hand, fingers moving around as on the strings of a violin. There was a close-up of this in the movie, the scrawny scarred arm and that strangely transformed hand. The arm as the violin and the hand playing on it broke people's hearts. Tiao would cry every time she watched this part. She was convinced that Fang

Jing wasn't performing but reliving his own experience. The scene might seem sentimental now, but back then, at a time when people's hearts had been repressed for so long, it could easily bring an audience to tears.

Tiao never thought she would come to know Fang Jing personally. She had recently graduated from university and, through connections, got a job as an editor in the Fuan Children's Publishing House. Like all young people who admired celebrities, she and her classmates and colleagues enthusiastically discussed the movie *A Beautiful Life*, and Fang Jing himself. They read all the profiles of Fang Jing in the newspapers and magazines and traded information with each other: his background, his life experience, his family and hobbies, his current project, what movie he entered in a film festival and what new award he won there, even his height and weight; Tiao knew all the details. It was by chance that Tiao and he got to know each other. She went to Beijing to solicit manuscripts for books and ran into a college roommate. The father of this roommate worked in a filmmakers' association, so she was very much in the know. The roommate told Tiao that the filmmakers' association was holding a conference on Fang Jing's work and that she could get Tiao in.

On the day of the conference, her roommate slipped Tiao into the meeting room. Tiao has forgotten now what was said in the conference; she remembers only that Fang Jing looked younger than he did in the movie and that he spoke Mandarin with a southern accent. He had a resonant voice, and when he laughed, he frequently leaned back, which made him look easygoing. She also remembered he held a wooden tobacco pipe and would wave the pipe in the air when he got excited. People thought that was natural and charming. He was surrounded by good-looking men and women. When the conference ended, the attendees swarmed forward, held out their notebooks, and asked him for autographs. Her roommate grabbed Tiao's hand, wanting to rush forward with the crowd. Tiao rose from the chair but backed away. Her roommate had no choice but to let go of her and push forward on her own. In fact, the notebook in Tiao's hand had been turned to a new page, a blank page ready for Fang Jing to sign his name. But she still backed away clutching the notebook, maybe because she was a bit timid, maybe because an incongruous pride inhibited her. Even though she was so insignificant compared to him, she was still unwilling to play the airhead autograph hound. She backed away, all the while regretting the lost chance. Right then, Fang Jing stretched out an apelike arm from the midst of the swirl of people and pointed at Tiao, who stood apart, saying, "Hey, you!" as he parted the crowd and walked toward Tiao.

He came up to her and grabbed her notebook without asking, and signed his famous name in it.

"Happy now?" He looked directly into Tiao's eyes with a faintly condescending attitude.

"I guess I would say that I'm very grateful instead, Mr. Fang Jing!" Tiao felt surprised and excited. Emboldened, she started to forget herself. "But how do you know what I want is your autograph?" She tried to look directly into his eyes, too.

"Then what do you want?" He didn't understand.

"I want . . . it's like this, I want to solicit a manuscript for a book project—" she said, on the spur of the moment, confronting Fang with childlike seriousness, distinguishing herself from the autograph hunters.

"I think we should trade places," Fang Jing said, fumbling in his pocket and taking out a wrinkled envelope. "Think it's okay to ask you to sign your name for me?" He handed the envelope to Tiao. Tiao was embarrassed, but she still signed her name, and, at Fang Jing's reminder, left her publishing house's address and number. Then she took the opportunity to talk further about the idea for which she was soliciting manuscripts, even though she had come up with it on the spot a few minutes before. She said she had submitted a proposal and the publishing house had approved it. She intended to do a series of books featuring the childhoods of celebrities, including scientists, artists, writers, scholars, directors, and professors, aimed at elementary and middle school students. Mr. Fang Jing's work and harsh life experiences had already attracted so much attention, if he could write a memoir about himself for children, it would definitely become popular with them, and would benefit society as well. Tiao talked quickly while feeling ashamed of her reckless fabrications. The more ashamed she was, the more in earnest she pretended to be. It was as though the more she talked, the more real it seemed. Yes, it felt quite real. How she hoped Fang Jing would turn her down while she rattled on. Then she would feel relieved, and then everything would be as if nothing had happened. It was actually true that nothing had happened. What could happen between a big celebrity and a common editor from the provinces? But Fang Jing didn't interrupt her or turn her down; those TV journalists interrupted them, swarming over him to bring him to his interview.

Not long after the conference, Tiao received the first letter from Fang Jing, written on the airplane. She read the letter numerous times, studying, analyzing, and chipping away at the words and lines to reveal what they meant or did not mean. Why did he have to write a letter to me on an airplane? Why must he reveal so carelessly to a stranger his location in Shanghai or San Francisco? In Tiao's mind, everything about a celebrity should be mysterious, including his whereabouts. Why would he only consider the idea seriously because it was a request of Tiao's? Did that make sense? She turned those thoughts over and over in her mind, unable to think clearly, but unable to resist puzzling over them, either, letting a secret sweetness spread in her heart. At least her little vanity got an unexpected boost and her job would probably get off to a wonderful start as well. She'd have to take that offhand, improvised plan seriously. She would make a feasible, deliberate, and persuasive presentation to her editor in chief, trying to get the plan approved by the publishing house just because a celebrity like Fang Jing had promised to consider writing for her. Everything sounded real.

A few days later, Tiao received Fang Jing's second letter from San Francisco.

This was number two in Tiao's file:

Tiao:

   You don't mind me leaving out the word "comrade," do you? I feel very strange. Why do I keep on writing to you—a girl who wouldn't condescend to ask for an autograph from me? When a large group of beautiful girls leaped at me, you backed away. Please forgive me for such a silly, conceited sentence. But they have been leaping at me constantly, which I've enjoyed for the last two years, half reluctantly, and yet with a feeling that it was my due. Then you appear, so indifferent and so puzzling. Right now, on the West Coast of the United States, thousands of miles away, your face on that day appears before me constantly, your eyes like an abyss that no one would dare to look into, your lips mysteriously sealed. I don't think you came to me on your own; you were sent by a divine power. When I left for America, I brought a map of China along as if compelled by a supernatural force. It was a little pretentious, as though I were showing off how much I love my country and what a fanatical patriot I am. Not until later did I realize I brought it because I wanted to carry with me on a map of China—Fuan—your city, where you live, small as a grain of rice on the map, which I constantly touch with my fingertips—that grain of rice just like . . . just like . . . I think, although we have only met once, we actually don't live far apart, only two hundred kilometers. Maybe sometime I will go to the city where you live to visit you. Does that sound ridiculous? If it's not convenient, you don't have to see me. I would be happy just to stand under your window. Also, after serious consideration, I believe the topic of your proposal is very important. I've made up my mind to write the book for you; I can write during downtime between scenes on set.

   I went to the famous Golden Gate Bridge this afternoon. When I stood beside the great bridge to look at San Francisco in the sunset, the dream city created with its man-made island, I got a clear idea about this city for the first time. If I had misgivings or prejudices about cities before, San Francisco changed my perception. It made me realize the heights human wisdom and power could reach and what a magnificent scene the human and the city create together out of their striving. I don't know your life experience, and have no idea how much people your age know about Western cuisine. Here at Fisherman's Wharf, they sell a very interesting dish: a big, round, crusty loaf of bread with a lid (the lid is also bread). When you open it, there is steaming-hot, thick, buttery soup inside. The bread is actually a big bowl. You have to hold the bread bowl carefully while eating. You have a bite of bread and a mouthful of soup. After you finish the soup, you eat the bowl, which goes down to your stomach. When I stood in the ocean breeze eating my fill of the bread bowl, I recalled the years I spent in the labor camp. I was thinking even if I exhausted all the creativity in me, I couldn't have invented such a simple and unusual food. Oddly, I also thought about you. For some reason I believe you would love to eat this.

Of course, most of the time I was thinking about our country; we're too poor. Our people have to get rich as soon as possible. Only then can we genuinely and frankly get along with any of the cities in the world, and genuinely rid ourselves of the sense of inferiority hidden in the depths of our hearts, the sense of inferiority that usually reveals itself strongly in the form of pride. It also exists in me . . . I think I've taken too much of your time. I'll save many things for when we meet; I'll tell you more later, little by little. I've been feeling that we will have a lot of time together, you and I.

It's very late at night now. Outside my window, the waves of the Pacific Ocean sound like they're right in your ears. I hope you receive and read this letter. I'll be returning to China within the week. If it's possible, can you please write me back? You can send the letter to the movie studio. Of course, this might well be too much to hope for on my part.

Wishing you happiness,
Fang Jing

_____, _____, 1982

3

When she was a senior at a university in Beijing, her roommate in the upper bunk, the one who took her to the conference on Fang Jing's work later, often returned to the dorm late at night. Everyone knew she was madly in love. Miss Upper Bunk was a plain girl, but love gave her eyes an unusual brightness and made her whole face radiant. One night, when she returned to the dorm on tiptoe in the dark, she didn't climb into her upper bunk as usual. That night, Tiao in the lower bunk was also awake. From her bed, Tiao quietly watched her roommate walk into the dorm room. She saw Miss Upper Bunk take out a small round mirror from a drawer, raise the mirror toward the window, and study her own face by moonlight. The moonlight was too dim to allow her a good view of her own face, so she tiptoed to the door and gently pushed it open. A beam of yellow light from the hallway shone on her roommate's body. She stood in the doorway and angled her head and the mirror toward the light. Tiao looked at her face; it was a beautiful face with a hint of drunken flush. She must have been content with herself at that moment. This girls' dorm, deep in sleep then, had become rich and peaceful. Tiao was touched by the sight, and not just because of her roommate, but why else, then?

Another late night, her roommate tossed and turned in her bed after coming back. She leaned her head down to Tiao's lower bunk and quietly woke her up. Then she climbed down and lay side by side with Tiao, and began to speak in urgent tones. She said, "Tiao, let me tell you—I have to tell you—I'm finally no longer a virgin. A man loves me, and how wonderful a thing it is you couldn't possibly understand." She wanted Tiao to guess who the man was, and Tiao guessed a few boys from their class. Miss Upper Bunk said condescendingly, "Them? You can't mean them!" She said she never would have anything to do with the men on campus. She said they didn't have brains and she admired men with avant-garde ideas and a unique insight on society, those forward-thinkers who could enlighten people. She had fallen in love with a forward-thinker and that forward-thinker liberated her mind and body, turning her from a virgin into a . . .

a woman. "A woman, do you understand or not, Tiao? You have a right to enjoy this, also, and you've had the right for a long time, without realizing." Her upper-bunk roommate described the experience of being with that forward-thinker. She said, "Do you know who he is? You'll be shocked if I tell you his name." She paused as if to let the suspense build for Tiao. Tiao was really excited by her words and couldn't help asking, "Who is he, who is he?" Her upper-bunk roommate took a deep breath and then breathed out a few words gently as if she were afraid of frightening someone away. "The author of *Zero Degree File.*" The name was indeed breathed out, barely formed on the lips. To this day Tiao still clearly remembers the nervous hot breath of her roommate when she said the words: *"Zero Degree File."*

Zero Degree File was a work of fiction, representative of the "Scar Literature" school, particularly popular among young people, with whom the author of course had made his reputation. At the time, people followed a novel and author with great sincerity and enthusiasm. The enthusiasm might be naïve and shallow, but it had an innocence and purity that would never come again. Tiao would certainly have envied Miss Upper Bunk had she stopped right there, but she couldn't. She felt compelled to share her intimate happiness with others. She said, "You have to know he's not an ordinary person but a writer, a writer overflowing with talent. Tiao, you know, only now do I truly understand what 'overflowing' means." She said, "This writer, overflowing with talent, is so good to me. One night I couldn't fall asleep and I suddenly had a craving for dried hawthorn berries, so I shook him awake and asked him to go out and buy some for me. He actually got up and biked through the entire city looking for dried hawthorn berries. A writer, overflowing with talent, went to buy me dried hawthorn berries in the middle of the night! Did you hear that, Tiao? Did you hear that? Are you still a virgin? Tiao, are you still a virgin? If you are, then you are really being cheated. Don't you realize how late it's getting? You're really good for nothing until you . . ."

Tiao didn't know why her upper-bunk roommate had to associate dried hawthorn fruit with virginity, as if she didn't deserve to eat dried hawthorn fruit if she were still a virgin. The statement "I'm finally no longer a virgin" jarred Tiao, and made her confused and agitated. In any case, that "finally" shouldn't be the highest expectation that her upper-bunk roommate should have for her own youth. Maybe she exaggerated. When one era urgently wanted to replace another, everything got exaggerated, everything, from novels to virginity. But the frenzied enthusiasm of her upper-bunk roommate still affected Tiao. When her roommate chattered, she felt like an ignorant moron of a country girl, completely uncultivated, an idiot who'd fallen behind the times and whose youth was flowing away downstream with the current. It was indeed an era of thought liberation, liberation-liberation, and liberation again. The trend swept over Tiao and she felt like she were being dragged along, accused, and ridiculed by her upper-bunk roommate. Her body seemed to be filled with a new and ambiguous desire. She must do something, but even the "must do" was a kind of blind exaggeration. What should she do? She wasn't dating; there was no man on campus worthy of her attention. Then she should look beyond the campus. One day her roommate said she was going to introduce her to someone. She said, though the guy was neither a writer nor a poet, he was pretty close to poets, an editor for a poetry magazine. She said he was fun to talk to. She said at a literary gathering he read a poem called "My Ass": "O my ass and this ass of mine, why would I sit down beside the bourgeoisie when I sit down? Stool of the working class, I beg you, I beg you to receive my ignorant ass—even if you are a neglected stool . . ." Tiao didn't think it was a poem. Maybe the author was imitating those who did crazy self-denunciations in the denouncement meetings. The "poem" just reminded Tiao of her own butt, making her think about the secret, happy times when she pretended the down pillows were a sofa. She had never realized that one could talk about asses so openly in poetry; after all, very few could have the imposing manner of Chairman Mao, who wrote about asses in his poems. But she went on a date with this editor, deliberately looking for some excitement. After all, she was only a student and the man was the editor of a poetry magazine. An editor was no more than a step below a writer; barely lower than a writer, a tiny bit.

They met on a cold evening in front of the art museum and shook hands with a little stiffness. After the greeting, they began to stroll back and forth. With the thick down jackets and tightly fitting jeans both wore, from a distance they must have looked like a pair of meandering ostriches. Tiao had never gone on a date alone with a man, particularly a man so "close to poets." As they started to walk around uncomfortably, Tiao was struck with the meaninglessness of it all: What was she doing here? Where did she want to go? Didn't her roommate tell her that the editor was a married man when she set them up? She meant this to indicate that Tiao could relax; they could date or not, no pressure—can't a man and woman meet alone, whether they're on a date or not? In eras like the sixties or seventies it might have seemed absurd, but things were different now. From her roommate's perspective, only when a single female student dated a married male editor could an era be proved open and a person be proved free. And at this moment, her theory was being put into practice with Tiao's help. Unfortunately, neither Tiao's body nor her mind felt free; she was very nervous. When she felt nervous she just babbled. She talked about the boys and girls in her class, the food in their cafeteria, and how their professor of modern literature walked into the classroom with a misbuttoned shirt . . . she went on and on, quickly and at random, so her conversation wasn't at all intellectual, clever, fun, or witty. Her mind went completely blank, and her blank mind soberly reminded her again and again how ridiculous her meeting with this "ostrich" beside her was. By spouting endless nonsense, she was simply punishing herself for going on this most absurd date. She rambled on and on, full of anxiety because she had no experience in ending a meeting that should have ended before it began. She even stupidly believed that if she kept on talking without a pause, she could hasten the end of the date. Finally the editor interrupted her, and not until then did she discover how nasal his voice was. She didn't like men with nasal voices. People who spoke that way sounded pretentious, as if they were practicing pronunciation while speaking. The editor said, "Do you plan to go back to your hometown? Your hometown is Fuan, right? Even though it's an ancient city, it's still provincial. I suggest you try and arrange to stay in Beijing for your graduation assignment. It's the only cultural center. Of this I'm very sure."

Tiao was a little bit offended by the editor's words. What right did he have to keep saying "your town"? Her upper-bunk roommate said he'd just been transferred to Beijing from Huangtu Plateau a few years ago, and now he talked so patronizingly to Tiao as if he were some kind of master of Beijing. Where was he when she was sipping raspberry soda in the alleys of Beijing?

Images from the past were still vivid for her: all those things that happened long ago, how she suffered when she first entered the city of Fuan as a young Beijinger. She'd felt wronged as well as proud. She'd tried hard to blend into the city, and maybe she had. The way she did blend in gave her energy, and allowed her, along with several close friends, to keep her Beijing accent bravely in that ancient, xenophobic city. Beijing! Beijing had never known there were several young women like this who had tried in vain to bring her culture to a strange city. Even though Beijing had never needed and would never need their sacrifice, Tiao and her friends insisted on such devotion. But the man in front of her, this man, what had he done for Beijing? He already considered himself a Beijinger. Besides, his mention of her graduation assignment annoyed her. How could she discuss personal business like her graduation assignment with a stranger? In short, nothing felt right. She resented the attitude of her roommate and her own silliness—she very much wanted to use this word to describe herself. She felt a bit sad, for the way she had thrust herself forward without any idea of the direction she should take; she also felt a bit awakened: she suddenly realized that her youth wasn't flowing away in the current, that what she herself treasured was still precious, and she felt lucky to be able to hold on to it. She was as good as her roommate in many ways, and if she couldn't keep up with her in this way, she was content to "fall behind."

As she waited for the last bus to come, her thinking became clearer and clearer. There were many people on the bus. She flashed a farewell smile at the editor, ran to catch it, and then tried with all her might to force her way onto the already packed bus. The editor had followed her, apparently not wanting to leave until he made sure she'd gotten on. She turned around and yelled at him, "Hey, can you give me a push?" He gave a push, and she got herself crammed on board. The door shut behind her with a swoosh.

Standing in the last bus, she suddenly smiled to herself. She realized "Give me a push" was actually what she most wanted to say tonight. She also realized the editor was a nice, honest man. But just as she wasn't attracted to him, he also wasn't at all attracted to her.

4

It wasn't as though she didn't want to write Fang Jing back; she put off writing because she didn't know what to say. Maybe everything had happened too quickly. In any case, she couldn't treat Fang Jing's letter from San Francisco as a casual note. She carefully read the letter over and over, and time and again it brought her to tears. She'd never read such a good letter, and she had no reason to doubt the author's sincerity.

So she started to write back. "Mr. Fang Jing, how are you?" she wrote. Then she would tear the letter up and start over. He was so important and she was so insignificant. She lacked confidence and was afraid of making a fool of herself—but how could she write a letter of the same quality as a celebrity like Fang Jing? It was impossible; she had neither the writing talent nor the emotional maturity his letter displayed. Just based on the letter alone, Tiao felt that she had already fallen in love with him. And she had to fall in love with him because she believed he had fallen in love with her—and it was her good fortune to be loved by him, she thought selflessly. At her age and with her lack of experience, she couldn't immediately tell the difference between admiration and love, or know how quickly a feeling driven by vanity might get the better of her. Maybe at those times she thought about her senior-year roommate. Compared to Fang Jing, who was that writer of her roommate's, with his "overflowing talent"? How could her love affair match Tiao's secret life now? College life, the flare of red-hot emotion that came and went quickly.

Once again she started to write a reply to him, but finally could only come up with those few words, "Dear Mr. Fang Jing, how are you?"

She went out and found a second-run theater to watch a movie of his, to meet him on the screen. She listened to his voice, studied his features, and savored his expressions. She tried very hard to memorize his looks, but when she returned home and lay in her bed, she found she had completely forgotten. It frightened and worried her, and seemed like a bad sign. The next day she took the opportunity to watch the movie again. She stared at him on the screen, as if she had found a long-lost family member. She still couldn't compose the letter. Then she received his phone call at her office.

He phoned at a time that everyone was in the office. The chief editor said to her, "Tiao, your uncle's calling." As soon as she walked to the phone and picked up the receiver, she recognized his southern-accented Mandarin. He said the following paragraph in one breath, with some formality and a tone that left her no room for contradiction: "Is this Comrade Yin Xiaotiao? This is Fang Jing. I know there are a lot of people in your office. You don't have to say anything. Don't call me Mr. Fang Jing. Just listen to me. I've returned to Beijing and haven't received a letter or phone call from you. It's very likely that you're laughing at me for being foolish. But please let me finish. Don't hang up on me and don't be afraid of me. I don't want to be unreasonable. I just want to see you. Listen to me—I'm at a conference at the Beijing Hotel. Can you arrange to come to Beijing to solicit manuscripts? I know editors come to Beijing all the time. You come and we'll meet. I'll give you my phone number for the conference. You don't have to respond to me right away, though of course I want to have your immediate response, your positive response, very much. No, no, you should think it over first. I have a few more things I want to ramble on about, I know I don't seem very composed, but I have somehow lost control of myself, which is very unusual for me. I would rather trust my instincts, though. Please don't be in a hurry to refuse me. Don't be in a hurry to refuse me. Now I'm going to give you the number. Can you write it down? Can you remember it . . . ?"

She was very bad at memorizing numbers, but she learned Fang Jing's number by heart even though he said it only once. She went to Beijing three days later, and saw him in his room at the Beijing Hotel. When she was alone with him, she felt he seemed even taller than when she had first met him. Like so many tall people, he stooped a little. But this didn't change his bearing, that arrogant and nonchalant attitude he was famous for. Tiao thought she must have appeared affected when she walked into his room, because Fang Jing seemed to catch an uneasiness from her. He gave her a broad smile, but the easy, witty manner of the conference was gone. He poured her a cup of tea but somehow managed to spill the hot tea, scalding Tiao's hand as well as his own. The telephone rang endlessly—that was the way the celebrities were, always pursued by phone calls. He kept picking up the phone, lying to the callers without missing a beat: "No, I can't do it today. Now? Impossible. I have to go see the rough cut in a minute. How about tomorrow? Tomorrow I'll treat you at Da Sanyuan . . ."

Sitting on the sofa listening quietly to Fang Jing's lies, Tiao sensed an unspoken understanding grow between them, and in herself a strange new feeling, dreamlike. She was grateful for all those smooth lies, thankful that he was turning those others down for her, with lies made for her, all of them, for the sake of their reunion. She started to relax; the phone calls were precisely what she needed to give herself the time to regroup.

Fang Jing finally finished the calls and came over to Tiao. He crouched down right in front of her, face-to-face. It was a sudden movement, but the gesture was quite natural and simple, like a peasant tending crops in the field, or an adult who needs to crouch down to talk to a child, or a person who crouches down to observe a small insect like an ant or beetle. With his age and status, the crouching gave him an air of childish naughtiness. He said to Tiao, who was sitting on the sofa, "How about we go out? Those phone calls are pretty annoying."

They left the room and went to the hotel bar. They chose a quiet corner and sipped coffee. He was holding his pipe. After a short silence, he began to speak, saying, "What do you think of me?"

She said, "I respect you very much. Like so many people, I admire your movie *A Beautiful Life*. Like me, a great many people hold your talent in high regard. In our editors' office, you're often the topic of discussion. We—"

He interrupted her and said, "Are you going to talk to me in this sort of tone all night? Are you? Tell me."

She shook her head and then nodded. She'd wanted to restrain her excitement in this way. She already found herself liking to be with him very much.

Then he said, out of the blue, "You stood apart from the crowd at the conference, naïve but also seeming to have a mind of your own. I saw at a glance that you were the person that God sent to keep an eye on me. I can't lie to you; I want to tell you everything. I . . . I . . . I . . ." He puffed on his pipe. "Do you know that what I wrote you was what was on my mind? I had never written to a woman, never. But I couldn't help it after I saw you. I am well aware of my talent and gifts, and I am also well aware that they're far from being fully developed. I will be much more famous than I am now. The day will come. Just wait and see. I also want to talk about my attitude towards women; I simply don't reject any women who approach me. Most women want me for my fame, maybe my money, too. Of course, some don't want anything from me, just want to devote themselves to me. They are especially pathetic, because in many respects . . . I am actually very dirty—I hope I am not frightening you with my words."

His words did frighten her quite a bit. All exposed things are frightening, and why would he treat her to such an exposed view of himself? She felt sorry for him because of that "dirtiness." She'd thought what she was going to hear would be much more romantic than this. Just exactly what kind of man was he? What did he want from her? Tiao was puzzled but knew well she didn't have the ability to take the initiative in their conversation. She was passive; she had been passive from the very start, and she could have no idea that the passivity would later produce something evil in her.

"Therefore . . ." He took another puff of his pipe and said, "Therefore, I don't deserve you. It looks like I'm pursuing you now, but how could I possess you? You're a woman who can't be possessed—by anyone. But I'll be with you sooner or later."

She finally spoke. She asked, "What leads you to such a conclusion?" His directness made her heart race.

But he ignored her question completely; he just continued, "You and I will be together sooner or later. But I want to tell you that even though someday I will be madly in love with you, I will still have many other women. And I will certainly not hide that from you. I'll tell you everything: who they are, how it happened . . . I'll let you judge me, punish me, because you're the woman I love the most. Only you deserve me to be so frank, so truthful, and so weak. You're my goddess, and I need a goddess. Just remember what I say. Maybe you're too young now, but you'll understand me, you definitely will. Ordinary people might think I'm talking like a hooligan. Well, maybe I am and maybe I'm not."

Hearing such words from Fang Jing, Tiao didn't want to label them the language of a hooligan. But what was it exactly? Should a married man with a successful career say those things to an innocent girl? But Tiao was lost then in the labyrinth created by his nonsense, as if under a spell. She strained to understand his philosophy and rise to the state of consciousness he had attained. A strange charisma came from the arrogance he projected and his domineering manner. The hints of coldness that occasionally strayed from his passionate eyes also drew her deeply in. She couldn't help beginning to question herself just to keep up with his thinking: What kind of person was she? What kind of person might she become? What was her attraction to this celebrity anyway? . . .

Strangely, he did not move closer to Tiao as he talked. He leaned back instead, putting more distance between them the more he spoke. His hunger for her was not going to end in a simple, impulsive touch and physical closeness. The way he kept proper physical distance didn't seem to be the behavior of an experienced man who was so used to being spoiled by women.

It was not until very, very late that Tiao left the Beijing Hotel. Fang Jing insisted on walking her back to her small hotel.

The evening breeze of late spring on broad Changan Avenue made Tiao feel much more relaxed. At that moment she realized how exhausting it was to be with him. It would always be exhausting, but she would be willing to be with him for many years to come.

He walked at her left side for a while and then at her right side. He said, "Tiao, I want to tell you one more thing."

"What is it?" she asked.

"You're a good girl," he said.

"But you don't really know me."

"True, I don't know you, but I'm confident there is nobody else who understands you better than I do."

"Why?"

"You know, after all, this is a matter that has been decided by mysterious powers, but you and I have a lot of things in common. For instance, we're both sensitive, and below our surface indifference, we both have molten passion . . ."

"How do you know I have molten passion? And what do you mean by describing me as indifferent? Do you feel that I didn't show you enough respect?"

"See, you're starting an argument with me," he said with some excitement. "Your arrogance is also coming out—no, not arrogance, it's pride. I don't have that sort of pride; the pride is yours alone."

"Why is it mine alone?" She softened her tone. "If you didn't have pride at your core, how could you be so outspoken—those words you said a little while ago at the hotel?"

He suddenly smiled with some concern. "Do you really think that's pride? What I actually have at my core is more like insolence. Insolence, you understand?"

She couldn't agree with him, or she couldn't allow him to describe himself this way. Only many years later when she reflected on this did she understand that his self-analysis was really quite accurate, but she resisted him fiercely at the time. She started to tell him about all of the feelings she had for him—as she read his two letters, while she watched his movie again for fear of forgetting what he looked like. She spoke with a great deal of effort, sometimes worried she might not be expressing herself well enough with her words. When she mentioned his heavily scarred arm in the movie, she couldn't help starting to cry. So she paused until she could hold her tears back. He didn't want her to continue but she insisted on speaking, not to move him but to move herself. She had a vague sense that the man before her, who had suffered more than enough, deserved everything he wanted. If he were sent to a labor camp again, she would be his companion in suffering all her life, like the wives of those Decembrists in Russia, who were willing to go into exile in Siberia with their husbands. Ah, to prove her faithfulness, bravery, nobility, and detachment, she simply couldn't help wanting to relive the era that had tormented Fang Jing. Let an era like that be the measure of her heart—but who the hell was she? Fang Jing had a wife and a daughter.

They arrived at her small hotel while she was talking. She immediately stopped speaking and held out her hand to him. He looked into her eyes while holding her hand and said, "Let me say it one more time: you're a good girl."

They said goodbye and he turned around. She walked through the hotel gate but immediately came back and ran into the street. She called out to stop him.

He knew what she wanted to do, he told her later.

Now he remained where he was and waited for her to come to him. She ran over, stopped in front of him, and said, "I want to kiss you."

He opened his arms to hold her loosely, so loosely that their bodies didn't come close. She went on tiptoes, raising her face to kiss him, then immediately let him go and ran into the hotel.

Fang Jing could never forget Tiao's first kiss, because it was so light and subtle, like a dragonfly skimming the water. It could not actually be considered a kiss, at most it was just half a kiss, like a flying feather gently brushing his lips, an imagined snowflake melting away without a trace on a burning-hot stove. But she was so devoted and shy. It was impulsiveness caused by too much devotion, and too much shyness that caused . . . what did it cause? She just about missed his lips.

Maybe it was not only that. When Tiao ran so decisively toward Fang Jing, her heart had already started to hesitate. All by herself, she felt she had to run to this man. She responded to her own prompting in one moment, but letting her lips slip away from the unknown in the next. It was hesitation caused by fear, and caution caused by discretion.

It was the solemn and hasty half kiss, so pure and complicated, that prevented Fang Jing from returning her kiss. He didn't dare. And when he loosely encircled her slim and supple waist with his arms, he knew his heart had been captured by this distant and intimate person.

5

The letters he wrote to her usually ran very long, and his handwriting was very small. He used a special type of Parker fountain pen to write, which produced extremely thin strokes, "as thin as a strand of hair," as the saying goes. This sharp pen allowed him to write smaller and more densely packed characters, like an army of ants wriggling across the paper. He wrote the tiny words greedily, wrestling them onto the white paper. He used those tiny words to invade and torture the white sheets, leaving no breaks for paragraphs, and paying no attention to format and space. He was not writing words; he was eating paper and gnawing on paper with words. It looked as though he were driven to use those tiny black words to occupy every inch of the paper, to fill all the empty places on every sheet of white paper with those tiny black words, transforming pieces of thin paper by force into chunks of heavy dark clouds. He couldn't help shouting at the sky: Give me a huge piece of white paper and let me finish writing the words of my entire life.

No one else wrote to her like that before or afterward. Ten years later, when she read those letters with critical detachment, the patience he took in writing pages of tiny words, the vast amount of time he spent on writing such letters, the hunger and thirst with which he fought for every inch of paper with his words and sentences, could still move her somehow. What she valued was this meticulous patience, this primitive, sincere, awkward, and real dependence and love between paper and words, whether it was written to her or some other woman.

He wrote in his letter:

Tiao, I worry about your eyes because you have to read such small writing from me. But still I write smaller and smaller, and the paper gets thinner and thinner because I have more and more to say to you. If I wrote in big characters and used thick paper, it might not be safe to send it to your publishing house. People might think it is a manuscript from an author and open it for you.

He also talked about his absurd experiences, in some of the letters.

Tiao:

You're not going to be happy to read this letter, but I must write it because you're watching me anyway even if I don't write it. You have been watching me all the time. A few days ago, I was on location at Fang Mountain—you know what I'm talking about, the place where I shot Hibernation. *I was making love to actress so and so (she is even younger than you are, and not very well known) but I felt terrible. Maybe because everything was too rushed, and she was too purposeful and too blunt. She had been chatting me up for the last few days, not that she wanted to angle for the part of the heroine in this film—the heroine had been cast long ago. She was maneuvering for the next role. She was hoping I'd give her a juicier part in my next film. Clearly, she has some experience with men. She is straightforward, not allowing a man to retreat, but my male vanity made me hope she at least had some feeling for me. Unfortunately she had none. She doesn't even bother to flirt with me. To girls of her age, I might just be a boring, dirty old man, even though I'm not fifty years old yet. But she wanted to make love to me badly. I admit her body attracted me, but I kept my attitude toward her light, only kidding with her. Later I was turned on by my contempt for her but I didn't understand why I was thinking about you at the time. It was because of you that I so yearned to get a kiss from her. Nothing else but her kiss, wholehearted, passionate, a kiss that risks a life, like the kind I want from you, although I have never gotten it. The only thing you granted me on that evening I can't forget, after which I couldn't sleep, was utmost power, the power of "not daring."*

There was nothing that I didn't dare to do to so and so. I stopped her when she rushed to take off her clothes. I told her to kiss me and she did as I said. She pressed against my body and wrapped her arms around my neck, kissing me for a long time, often asking, "Is that enough, is that enough?" She kissed me deeply and thoroughly, her tongue going almost everywhere she could reach in my mouth, and yet she seemed distracted. I closed my eyes and imagined it was you, your lips and your passionate kisses. But it didn't work. The more she kissed me, the more I felt it was not you. And she apparently grew impatient—it was precisely because she became impatient that I insisted on having her continue to kiss me. I held her around the waist with my hands, not allowing her to move. We two looked like we were struggling with one another. Later, everything finally went in a different direction because she snuck her hand from my neck and started to touch and fondle me. She was nervous and I could understand her nervousness. She didn't know why I wanted her only for kissing; she must have thought it wasn't sufficient, that the kissing alone was not going to satisfy my desire and therefore her desire was even less likely to be satisfied.

She fondled me anxiously as if to say, even though my kisses didn't seem to satisfy you, there is something more that I'm willing to give you . . . we started to make love, but you were everywhere before my eyes— I'm so obscene, but I beg you not to throw away the letter. In the end I felt horrible. On the one hand I imagined it was you who lay under me, my beloved, but when I did, the guilt I felt was so strong that it kept me from achieving the pleasure I could have had. The guilt was so strong that I couldn't tell who exactly lay under my body then or exactly what I was doing after all. Eventually I had to use my hand to . . . I could only get release with my own hand.

I'm willing to let you curse me ten thousand times. Only when you curse me does my empty soul find a peaceful place to go. Where can my soul rest safely? Maybe I demand too much. Why, when I kept getting those prizes I dreamed of—success, fame, national and international awards, family, children, admiration, beautiful women, money, etc.— and the rest . . . —did my anxiety only deepen?

I had a woman before I was married. She was a one-legged woman, fifteen years older than I was. She was a sadist. I took up with her because even though I was the lowest of the low I still needed women. Or you could say she took up with me. But I never guessed that she didn't want me for the needs that a man could satisfy. She had only one leg but her physical strength was matchless. I certainly couldn't match her, with that body of mine weakened by years of hard labor and starvation. She often tied me up late at night and pricked my arms and thighs with an awl, not deep, just enough to make me bleed. What shocked me even more was the time she lifted up the blanket when I was dead asleep, and began frantically plucking my pubic hair . . . she was crazy. She must have been crazy. But I didn't go crazy and I think it must have had something to do with the mountains I saw every time I went out. When I stepped out of the low, small mud hut and saw the silent mountains, unchanged for more than ten thousand years, when I saw the chickens running helter-skelter in the yard and dung steaming on the dirt road, the desire to live surged in me. I developed a talent: even when she tortured me until my body was bloodstained and black and blue all over, as soon as she stopped, I could fall back asleep immediately, and without having a nightmare. But today, I have to ask myself again and again: What do you want in the end, what do you want after all?

I don't want to pollute your eyes with the above words, but I can only ease my heart by writing to you. I have such desire to be with you, so much so that this desire has turned into fear. And moreover, I have the uncouth and unreasonable fear that you are with other men. From my own experience of men and women, I know extremely well the power you have. When we were drinking coffee at the Beijing Hotel, you probably didn't notice two men sitting at the next table who stared at you the whole time. There was an old Englishman sitting across from our table—I'm certain he was English—that old man also stared at you constantly. You didn't notice any of this; you were too nervous at the time. But I noticed; it didn't take much to figure out; glimpses from the corners of my eyes were enough. I'm very sure of my judgment. You're the kind of woman who can capture a man's attention; there is something in you that attracts people. You have the power to make people look at you, even though you are not polished at it yet. I think you should be more aware of this: you need to learn to protect yourself. Has anyone said this to you before? I believe I'm the only one who has. You should always button up your clothing; don't let men take advantage of you with their eyes. Don't. Not that the men who admire you would actually do something to harm you. No, I have to admit those who stare at you have taste. They are not hooligans or perverts. And I'm more nervous exactly because of that. I don't want them to take you away from me, though I still don't know how you truly feel about me. I've said before it was very likely that I would go to your city—Fuan, that tiny grain of rice that I caressed with my fingers when I was in the States. I will figure out a way to disguise myself in the street. Someday I will do that.

Now let me talk about the book you asked me to write. I tried to write the beginning and finished fifteen hundred words. It was very difficult because I couldn't find a direct, uncluttered tone. If the readers are kids, the writer should first get himself an open heart. My heart is open—at least to you, but not very clean. I feel very guilty and challenged by it. I plan to focus on writing the book after I finish shooting Hibernation. *I'm curious to find out my potential as an author. Will you think I'm too wordy? But wordiness is a sign of aging. Do you know what else I'm thinking about? How I look forward to you getting old quickly. Only when you get so old that you can't get any older, and*

I also get so old that I can't get any older, can we be together. By that time we'll both be so old that people won't be able to tell what sex we are: you might be an old man and I might be an old woman. We'd lose all our teeth, but our lips would still be all right so we could still talk. The human body is so strange, the hardest things, like teeth, disappear first, but the softest things, like tongues and lips, will come along with us to the last moment of our lives . . .

6

One day in the fall of 1966, Tiao, as a new student in the first grade of Lamp Alley Primary School in Beijing, participated in a noisy and confusing denouncement meeting on the school's sports field. It was an assembly that the entire faculty and student body attended, where many desks were brought together and stacked to make a tall stage. In front of the stage, students from all grades sat on their own little chairs that they brought out of the classrooms.

It was new to Tiao, who had just become an elementary school student a few days earlier. Back then she didn't have a clear idea about what having such a meeting meant. She thought sitting this way on the field was like having class in the open air, and felt freer than having an ordinary class. During class, teachers required children to sit straight with hands behind their backs; only correct posture would help their bodies grow healthily. But today, on the sports field, their class teacher didn't ask them to put their hands behind them; they could keep their hands wherever they wanted. Maybe, with the atmosphere so serious and subdued, the teachers couldn't bother about the students' sitting positions. Tiao remembered the senior students leading them in the continuous shouting of slogans. No one told them to clench their fists and raise their arms when they shouted, but somehow they all figured it out by themselves. They raised their little arms over and over and vehemently shouted those slogans, even though they had no idea what the slogans meant. As some of the slogans slowly began to make sense to her, she started to understand what they were and at whom they were directed. For instance, there was the slogan "Down with female hooligan Tang Jingjing!" As Tiao shouted, she knew Tang Jingjing was a female teacher who taught senior students math in their school. She also heard boys from other classes behind her talking: "So, Teacher Tang is a female hooligan."

Teacher Tang was escorted to the stage by several senior girls. She had a big white sign around her neck, hanging down over her chest, with words in ink: "I am a female hooligan!" The first grade sat in the first row, so Tiao saw the words on the sign very clearly. She recognized three characters, "I am woman," and figured out the last word must be "hooligan," based on the slogan they'd shouted a moment before. The sentence terrified her because, in her mind, "hooligan" didn't just mean bad people, but the worst of the worst, worse than landlords and capitalists. She was wondering how an adult could so easily admit "I am a female hooligan" in the first person. That use of the first person to declare "I am ***" made Tiao extremely uncomfortable, although she couldn't explain why.

Sitting in the front row, Tiao also had a clear view of Tang Jingjing. Tang Jingjing was about thirty years old, fair-skinned, and thin; so thin and white that with the pointiness of both her nose and close-cropped head, she resembled a toothpick. Toothpick would be how Tiao described her after she grew up. She indeed looked like a toothpick, not a willow wand. She appeared thin and weak, but she was very tough and strong. She stuck herself into the stage like a toothpick and refused to bend or lower her head no matter how the senior girls pushed her around. Tiao at the time wouldn't have been able to come up with the description "toothpick"; she simply had a natural sympathy for Teacher Tang, because—it was funny that Tiao didn't know where she got the idea that the word "hooligan" only referred to men—how could a woman be a hooligan? She sympathized with Teacher Tang also because Teacher Tang was pretty. Pretty, that was the reason.

Since Teacher Tang refused to lower her head and bend her back, both on stage and off, people appeared excited and a little out of control. The senior girl students apparently didn't know what to do,

and other teachers just shouted the slogans. None of them personally seemed willing to grab their colleague's neck and force her to
lower her head. Just as the scene looked like it was about to run out
of gas, a middle-aged woman in a moon-white shirt rushed onto the
stage (only later did Tiao learn she was the director of the Lamp
Alley Street Committee) and pointed at Teacher Tang. "Did you feel
wronged because we said you were a hooligan? Then let me ask you:
Are you married or not? According to the information we've collected, you've never married. Why do you have a child, then, even
though you were never married? You have to confess truthfully the
identity of the person with whom you had the child!" The chanting arose again: "Tang Jingjing must confess the truth! If she doesn't
confess, we revolutionary students will not stop!" Then a group of
even older students jumped up to the stage; they came from a nearby
middle school, all wearing red armbands, to assist their little brothers'
and sisters' revolutionary action.

These middle schoolers were good at fighting. One of them went
behind Teacher Tang and swung a leg at the back of her knee and
she immediately knelt down with a thud. The audience cheered; the
die-hard Teacher Tang was finally subdued by the revolutionary students. The denouncement meeting continued. Several young teachers went onto the stage to speak one by one. With great emotion
they accused Teacher Tang of hiding serious corruption in her life
in order to deceive her colleagues, school, and students into trusting her. Just imagine, everyone, what a terrible thing it is! A woman
with such a degenerate morality and corrupt lifestyle could get into
our school and become a teacher . . . The slogans arose again: "Tang
Jingjing must leave Lamp Alley Primary School! We successors of
the revolution demand she leave Lamp Alley Primary School!" The
middle-aged woman in the moon-white shirt continued to expose
Tang Jingjing's crimes: According to her neighbors, Tang Jingjing
pretended to live simply and plainly, but at home she always lived
a bourgeois lifestyle—she had a cat, and treated her cat better than
people. One day she even dared to kiss her cat right in the courtyard—in the name of heaven, kissing a cat!

The audience first broke into laughter at this and then switched to even angrier shouting. "Down with female hooligan Tang Jingjing!"

How insufficient it seemed just to allow Tang Jingjing to kneel there listening to people shouting while more and more of her disgusting actions were revealed. The intractable hostility on her pale, skinny face particularly made people on the stage burn with anger. A boy student with a red armband suddenly stuck out his rubber army overshoe into Tang Jingjing's face and said, "If you can kiss a bourgeois cat, can't you kiss a working-class shoe?" He kept his foot in Tang Jingjing's face as he spoke. A girl ran over and pressed Tang Jingjing's head down to force her to kiss the boy's shoe. More dust-covered shoes were extended to force her to kiss them.

The field seethed and the stage gave way to chaos. The students in front of the stage could no longer sit still, some knocking over their chairs, some standing on them, and others pushing their way to the front in order to see more clearly. Dust flew around and choked Tiao until she coughed. She also stood up and wanted to see more clearly. But unlike some of the boys in her class, she didn't step on her chair; she instinctively thought it was improper, something that a student shouldn't do. But she felt so small in the midst of the crowd and could see nothing on the stage, which made her anxious. Just then a stink wafted over. Someone brought up a cup of shit, and then a voice rang out, "Tang Jingjing isn't worthy of kissing our shoes; her mouth simply deserves to eat shit!"

"Right, right," others chimed in. "Let her confess to the revolutionary teachers and students. If she doesn't confess we'll make her eat shit."

Make her eat shit.

The emergence of shit suddenly calmed the boiling crowd, and the smell also made people hold their breath and concentrate. The shit was carried to the stage openly in a teacup, which played on the ugliest nerve hidden in the depths of the human mind. The terrorizing power of shit came onto the stage. The ones who had crowded to the front backed away, and the ones who stood on the chairs sat down. It was just like at a concert, when there's some opening act during which the audience can raise as much clamor as they want, and only during the star's big number will they sit straight and properly appreciate the performance. Making Tang Jingjing eat shit might well be the big number of the day's denouncement meeting.

The shit was placed in front of Tang Jingjing, only a meter away from her. She kept that ghostly pale face of hers still. Everyone is waiting for you to confess, why don't you just open your mouth? . . . Tiao's heart contracted as if clutched by a hand, and she could hardly breathe. She hoped Teacher Tang would open her mouth immediately so that she didn't have to eat shit. But many people might not have thought like Tiao, and they might not have been so eager to hear Tang Jingjing's confession anymore. When a person is given a choice between confessing and eating shit, what others are eager to see may not be her confessing but her shit-eating.

She didn't open her mouth, nor did she eat the shit. So a boy student ran to the middle-aged woman in the moon-white shirt and whispered something in her ear. He then returned to Tang Jingjing and spoke to the entire audience. "If Tang Jingjing refuses to confess or eat shit, we have another method. We revolutionary masses will not be frightened by her hooligan's arrogance. We will bring her daughter to the stage and let you look at her. Let everyone take a look at her daughter. Her daughter will be the evidence that stands as proof of her hooligan activities."

Tang Jingjing finally lost her poise. Tiao saw her quickly move two steps in a kneeling position toward the teacup. Those urgent and determined "kneeling steps," which came like a thunderclap exploding before anyone could cover their ears, left a lifelong impression on Tiao. She moved with her "kneeling steps" to the teacup and stared at the cup for a while. Then, under the gaze of everyone, she grabbed the teacup with two hands and drank down the shit and urine in one swallow . . .

The first thing Tiao did after returning home was brush her teeth and rinse her mouth; she couldn't resist the urge to eat all the toothpaste in the Little White Rabbit tube that only she and Fan used. Brushing her teeth made her vomit and after vomiting she continued to brush her teeth. Once she had finished brushing she continued to reach into her throat with the toothbrush. Then she began to vomit again. She vomited some food until at last only sticky sour fluid came out. She finished vomiting and brushing and then cupped her nose and mouth with her two hands—she cupped them very tightly, careful not to leave any space—and then she exhaled in big breaths—as she learned to do in kindergarten. She could smell her breath this way. Finally she could relax and she should relax; there wasn't any taste in her mouth. She looked at herself in the mirror numerous times; she saw that her lips were white, like they'd been dyed white with the toothpaste, but they were even whiter than the toothpaste. She rubbed her lips hard with a towel until they became hot and red and almost bled, until they throbbed with pain. She locked herself in the bathroom tormenting herself for a long time.

Then she came out of the bathroom with red eyes and a heavy head. Fan came over, and she embraced Fan and kissed her. Fan kissed back and they kissed each other loudly. She then went to kiss her father, her mother, that pair of old corduroy sofas at her home, her little chair, and the ice-cold radio/tape recorder made in the Soviet Union. Believing that she must be sick, her father and mother told her to go to bed. There she saw her folded handkerchief. She opened the handkerchief, at whose center was a white, yellow-eyed cat. She stared at the white cat and swept the handkerchief to the corner of the bed, but later she reached out to get it back. She opened the handkerchief and stared at the white cat. She put her mouth on the cat's mouth and cried.

Chapter 2

❦ ❦ ❦

Pillow Time

1

Like everyone else arriving at the Reed River Farm, Wu and Yixun were placed on male and female teams. Located in the alkali salt flats southwest of Fuan, the farm was where the provincial Architectural Design Academy congregated its own intellectuals for isolated labor reform.

The couple's transfer from Beijing to the provincial capital Fuan in the late sixties already had an undertone of punishment: as an engineer in the Beijing Architectural Design Academy, Yixun had aired his dissatisfaction with Beijing's urban planning. He was young and aggressive back then, often speaking bluntly. A piece of history most people might not be aware of: when the country was just established, Chairman Mao invited Mr. Liang Sicheng to the Tiananmen Tower to discuss the future urban planning of the new Beijing. Not knowing much about cities, Chairman Mao might well have been in the grip of his own excitement at having won the revolution, or he might actually have had an in-depth understanding of the urgency of rapid industrialization, if the country were to be strong and prosperous.

In either case, he stood on the Tiananmen Tower and looked down, sweeping that great-man's arm of his toward the gray misty distance and saying to Liang Sicheng, "In the future, chimneys should be visible from here in every direction." The great leader's declaration must have terrified Liang Sichang, the great architect so devoted to preserving old Beijing. And Yixun, an undistinguished young architect, immediately expressed his own doubts on hearing this piece of privileged information. He thought it was absurd and inconceivable to make chimneys appear everywhere in the view from the Tiananmen Tower. How could Beijing, a city famous for culture, which had survived so many dynasties, be turned into a huge factory? A few years later, when Yixun's sympathetic comments to Liang Sicheng were reported, both he and his wife, Wu, an English translator in the reference room, were transferred to Fuan.

This transfer didn't set off panic in their hearts. The Cultural Revolution had already started by then, and one city was much like another. Most people at the Beijing Architectural Design Academy were headed for a farm located somewhere in the south for concentrated labor and thought reform. The revolution was not going to give up on any of its revolutionary targets easily.

They brought their two daughters—Tiao and Fan—to the provincial capital, Fuan, only to have to leave it behind as soon as they got used to it. They hastily settled their daughters and gave Tiao their residential card, rice ration book, clothes coupons, bankbook, and a small sum of money. After emphasizing over and over again to Tiao the great responsibility she would have as head of the household, they took their bags and left for Reed River Farm with most of their colleagues. It had been suggested that the period of labor might have no definite end, it wouldn't be a week or a month; it could be several years, perhaps, so they prepared themselves for a long stay. They were put under the leadership and management of the working class, and the first thing they were asked to do was to separate—husbands and wives must separate in order to help them temper their revolutionary willpower and strengthen their dedication to the labor. They lived in big collective dormitories—men in a male dorm and women in a female dorm—and inside, lines of plank beds stretched out toward the vanishing point. They were assigned to work in the brick factory. Every day, Yixun hauled the bricks in a big cart, originally pulled by a horse, and Wu wore coarse cloth gloves to load the bricks into the cart.

Those intellectuals who labored at the Reed River Farm—the

male and female teams—didn't object to the Cultural Revolution. They had plenty of time when they were not laboring to study or to criticize each other, to attend denunciation meetings or to do self-criticism. They diligently tried to use these methods to remove the nonproletarian marks imprinted on their bodies, rolling in the mud and stepping into cow dung, fervently hoping to be reborn. But at the same time they were weak and easily distracted by fantasy. For instance, their hearts and minds didn't always remain at peace. At the end of a day's work, when they returned to their separate dormitories, stinking of sweat, their faces all dusty, husbands always longed for their wives, just as wives always longed for their husbands.

If you were to look at Reed River Farm from the point of view of someone who appreciates landscape, ignoring the atmosphere and mood of the time, you would find it a boundless and magnificent place. The farm was surrounded by thousands of acres of reeds, like the passionate, tender petals clustering around a sunflower. Especially in autumn, the golden reeds, taller than a person, with the white, fluffy flower on their heads, would suddenly grow and swell, releasing a spirit overpoweringly fierce and deeply peaceful, as if they wanted to take over the world and withdraw from it at the same time. Because the reeds blocked the view and smothered all sound, only the wild dark brown ducks could play freely and nest in the thicket of reeds, laying eggs that no one could collect. Walking in, you would be awed and dumbstruck by the stillness of the ten thousand acres of densely packed reeds; you would also be cleansed by the noble, pure spirit of the ten thousand acres of reeds and feel renewed. At nightfall, clusters of reeds would seem more crowded in the autumn wind, like groups of women in white kerchiefs and skirts holding their breath and walking one after the other in mincing steps. Unfortunately, the farm separated the people from the reeds behind an enclosing wall. At the time neither Wu nor Yixun were in the mood to appreciate the grandeur of the reeds outside the wall. Compared to the charming sweep and vast stillness, the farm seemed very plain and drab, with identical low red-brick buildings everywhere. There was only one attractive place, a small house on top of a hill. Yet how could it actually be a hill? Here, it was an endless plain. The hill was a small slope at the end of a vegetable field slightly higher than the farmland; ordinarily it wouldn't pass as a hill. But on the plain, even the most modest elevation could be considered a hill. The flatness of the plain made any rise stand out as individual and unique. No matter how small, as long as people were willing to, they could call it a hill. The small house on the hill.

On Sundays, only on Sundays, it was open to the couples who lived in the collective dormitories. It was locked and left unused on other days. Wu and Yixun hadn't counted how many couples there were among the male and female teams—probably at least eighty. Anyone in a couple would need to use the small house on the hill sooner or later. There was only one house and one day of the week, so people had to wait in line. This type of line was different from the kind they waited in to buy rice and vegetables. Although they were husbands and wives openly, they couldn't openly wait in line one after another to use the small house. The implication of the word "use" was so direct and obvious that people felt excited and embarrassed on hearing it. Therefore their waiting in line had about it a bit of the intellectuals' reserve, a modesty, the result of their upbringing, and maybe the careful calculations of the powerless. Early Sunday morning, you wouldn't see a distinct group milling in front of the house, but you could see men and women in couples scattered randomly around, far and near. They were either under a tree, on a vegetable patch, or sitting on bricks, apparently engaged in tête-à-tête. They looked calm and relaxed, but their eyes were fixed intensely on the tightly closed door of that small house. Every time the door opened and a couple walked out after finishing their business, the next couple to enter would be the one closest to the door, and the next couple after them would take a definite step closer. This "step" was very discreet, maintaining a distance of at least fifteen meters. Who would be heartless enough to wait right outside the door? Couples who came late would judge with care which spot to take. Latecomers never rushed past those who were already there to get to the door. The couples were all very precise about the order. It almost looked like they were scouts—in groups of two—slowly outflanking the small house; the scene also resembled a round of confused chess, unintelligible to laymen, with those anxious couples as the pieces on the board. The chess game only appeared disorderly; it was the unexpected that led to trouble, which happened once in Wu and Yixun's memory.

The door high above had finally opened and a couple emerged. Wu and Yixun, as the closest couple, knew that it was their turn and immediately, in unspoken understanding, walked toward the small house. But right then another couple also approached from the opposite direction. The two couples had arrived almost at the same time and their distance from the small house was also about the same. If you used a diagram to illustrate the situation, the relationship of the two couples to the small house could be presented as an equilateral triangle. While they simultaneously headed toward the small house, they simultaneously realized the awkwardness of the situation. When they realized that awkwardness, they may all have hesitated briefly— a pause as tiny as a blade of grass, a product of their polite upbringing. But the reality was so powerful that their footsteps immediately left the tiny mental hesitation behind. Wu felt her legs hurry more urgently than the moment before because the couple coming from the opposite direction seemed to be moving with increased speed and agility: they seemed to be striding in bigger and bigger steps. So she began to extend her stride, too . . . and the twenty-something meters where the two couples raced with quiet ferocity seemed endless. They kept adjusting their stride and glancing over at each other, calculating how they could arrive a step ahead. Their eagerness made them ignore the way they appeared as they walked; certainly ugly, since they were race-walking without even following a race walker's form. The only thing they didn't do was run, but they didn't run because after all they still couldn't accept the fact that they would have to run in order to do their conjugal business. Actual running would have damaged the collegiality between the couples, although in their hearts they were running wildly.

Wu swung her waist and hips to stride forward, intent on occupying the small house first. She was a bit embarrassed about her big steps because they were the sign of her desire. Her desire was originally intended solely for her husband, Yixun, but now she had to announce to reeds, trees, bricks, and tiles, and all these irrelevant things, in broad daylight and with her inelegant way of walking, that she wanted to make love to her husband. She took big steps, unsure of whether she was being shameless or simply had no choice. When they finally reached the small house first, and pushed the door open, she felt very sorry for the couple who would be shut outside.

The race left her and Yixun short of breath and distracted. They neither kissed nor talked, but tried to finish as soon as possible. Because they'd gotten in first, they felt they shouldn't take too much time in the small house. They didn't even look at each other, as if they were afraid to face the crudeness of their current situation, or were embarrassed about winning the race of a few moments before. Most couples behaved similarly in the small house; they knew how to discipline themselves. No one dawdled endlessly behind the door. Even so, not every couple got a chance. The ones who didn't would have to wait quietly for next Sunday.

Two kilometers' walk from the farm, Reed River Town had roasted chickens for sale. On Sundays, only on Sundays, could the people on the male and female teams go to the town to satisfy their craving. Women always have more cravings for food than men. After Wu and Yixun occupied the small house, Wu would immediately think about the roasted chicken in Reed River Town. Unfortunately, she could not have both at the same time; she couldn't have the small house and taste the chicken simultaneously. People also needed to set off early on Sunday to buy roast chickens, which were prized then. Since the farm had so many people like Wu, the limited supply of chickens in the town would be sold out in no time.

There was one couple who did try to have both on the same day. As soon as the gate opened, early on Sunday morning, they left the farm and went deep into the vast, dense reed thickets. They gave up on the wait for the hill house and planned to do their business there in the reeds and hurry to the town to buy a roast chicken as soon as they'd finished. But they got caught in the act by the farmworkers and were made to do numerous self-criticisms at various meetings as typical examples of weak revolutionary willpower and low-life behavior.

When Wu reminisced about the past many years later, she would try to avoid the part about the Reed River Farm. She couldn't bring herself to imagine it was because she couldn't have both at the same time that she became really sick: half a year later, she had attacks of severe dizziness on the farm. She fainted twice beside the stacks of bricks. She was finally allowed to rest in the dorm for a few days, but had to attend the study group every evening—studying was more relaxing than laboring.

She participated in the study group, but unfortunately she fainted again in the meeting room, twice. She was sent to the farm clinic, but the doctor there was unable to diagnose the cause of this strange dizziness. Her blood pressure and pulse were normal, but she would sweat profusely and her whole body would feel like a puddle of mud after she regained consciousness. She always looked discouraged when she opened her eyes, as if she regretted coming back to life again. Only when she saw Yixun's weary and anxious face did she try to make herself more awake. She loved her husband, but when she caught sight of her cracked hands, smelled the moldy damp of the straw bed, took in the little wooden box used as a makeshift desk, the porcelain cup whose handle was broken by a scurrying rat—that cup with a broken handle made everything seem so shabby . . . she looked at all this and thought boldly that instead of the endless shabbiness, she might be more than willing to submerge herself in dizziness. It was surely a kind of submergence. She would hide herself in dizziness and never reveal the truth to anyone until the day she died, not even to her husband.

2

How nice it was to lie, with her head and neck buried in a big fluffy feather pillow, her disheveled short hair down over her forehead! No one on the Reed River Farm could reach her. She slipped her hands under the quilt, too; she didn't want to stuff her hands into the rough cloth gloves anymore or stand in front of the stacks of bricks, inhaling the never-ending red powder.

Wu woke to find herself in her own home, lying on her own big bed, and resting her head on her own pillow—this pillow, this pillow of hers. She couldn't help swiveling her head a few times, languidly and with some coy playfulness. She rubbed the snow-white pillow with the back of her head, playing with the real pillow that she had missed so much. She remembered her laziness as a small child. Every morning, when it was time to get up, Nanny Tian had to stand by that little steel-springed bed of hers and try again and again to waken her. She was like that in those days, rubbing the back of her head against the pillow until her hair was a mess. Meanwhile, she'd kick her legs and feet under the quilt and turn her head to the side, pretending to sleep on. Nanny Tian didn't give up, but kept calling her from beside her bed.

Wu then would pry open her eyes and ask Nanny Tian to make faces for her, to do cats and dogs and copy the way the mynah bird spoke. Nanny Tian first undid her apron, folded it into a triangle, and tied it onto her head to play the wolf grandmother in "Little Red Riding Hood"; then she tensed her voice to imitate the cat; leaving the best for last, she imitated the mynah: "Nanny Tian, get the meal ready; Nanny Tian, get the meal ready." Nanny Tian smacked her thick lips and held her neck stiffly to mimic the bird, which made Wu laugh heartily. Nanny Tian did such a good impression of the mynah, which was kept in the kitchen as company for her. Wu loved to get into the kitchen whenever she had the chance. Her favorite thing was listening to that mynah talk, but she knew, whether it was the mynah imitating Nanny Tian or Nanny Tian imitating the mynah, both would deliver a great performance. Even when she went away to the university, she couldn't help wanting to bring Nanny Tian along, though not for waking her up in the morning, of course. But it seemed to have become a habit to listen to Nanny Tian nag at her every morning, a part of Wu's peaceful, languid sleep.

Wu rubbed the snow-white pillow with the back of her head; she finally could snuggle into her pillow again. The farm approved her return to Fuan for a week to treat her mysterious dizziness. She was overjoyed, and Yixun was also happy for her, making a special trip to town to buy a pair of roast chickens for her to bring back to the children. Although Tiao always said, "We're doing fine," in her letters, Yixun still felt it wasn't a good idea to leave two children alone at home. It was simply not a good idea. "It would be great if you could stay home longer," he told Wu. He didn't expect his words to become the main excuse for Wu to stay on in Fuan. "Isn't this what you were wishing for, too? Didn't you want me to stay at home?" Later, she would say this to him in a loud voice, but with some guilty feelings.

A week was so precious to Wu that she first buried herself in the pillow and slept for three days. It was the sleep of oblivion, a three-days-without-leaving-the-bed sleep, a making-up-for-half-a-year's-lost-sleep-in-one sleep. She opened her eyes only when she was thirsty or hungry, having Tiao bring water and food to her bed. After she finished eating and drinking she dropped her head and fell back asleep, snoring gently. It was Tiao who discovered that her mother snored. She believed her mom must have picked up the habit at the Reed River Farm.

At last she opened her eyes. After getting up and doing some stretches to loosen her muscles, she felt wide awake. Her limbs felt strong, and her insides felt clean and clear, ready to be filled with food. Where was her dizziness? Just as she started to feel lucky that she was no longer dizzy, a fit of panic gripped her: When will the dizziness come back? If she was no longer dizzy, how could she get a diagnosis from the hospital? And she must get that diagnosis. The whole purpose for the week of sick leave was for her to go to the hospital and get a diagnosis. When she returned to the farm, she would have to submit a diagnosis from the hospital.

She sat on the side of her bed trying very hard to locate the dizziness in her. Fan, nesting by her legs, grabbed her pants with one hand and asked: Mom, are you still dizzy? Then Wu really did feel a little dizzy—if even Fan knew about her dizziness, how could she not be dizzy? She tried to make herself dizzy and took a bus to People's Hospital.

The hallway of the clinic at People's Hospital was noisy chaos. A draft of chokingly sweet fish smell, mixed with the unhealthy breath of the waiting patients, made Wu almost leave a few times. Finally the registrar nurse called out her number. Just as she sat down in front of the doctor, an old fellow from the countryside squeezed in, saying, "Doctor, you can't fool us country folk. I walked over a hundred *li* to come to your hospital, and you give me a ten-cent prescription? Can ten cents treat an illness? You people tell me, isn't this a boondoggle?" He yammered on, pestering the doctor for a more expensive medicine, demanding and pleading until the doctor had no choice but to rewrite his prescription.

"Next, please. Name?" the doctor said without raising his head. Wu gave her name and the doctor lifted his head, taking a look at Wu and then listening to her complaint. She didn't know why, but she felt a little nervous, and gave the account of her symptoms in a dry and hesitant way. She seemed to have some difficulty meeting the doctor's direct gaze, although she knew it was just his professional manner. He was a man of about her age, with a clean, long, thin face under a clean white cap. His eyes were small and very dark, and when he stared at her with his small, dark eyes, they seemed to be bouncing over her face like lead shot. Like most doctors, he made no small talk. He listened to Wu's heartbeat, ordered several laboratory tests for her, routine tests like blood sugar and fat levels, EKG, etc., and he also asked her to get an X-ray of her neck at the radiology department.

Some test results came back the same day and some wouldn't be ready until the next. So, the following day, Wu returned to People's Hospital. She registered at internal medicine first, collected all the test results, and then waited quietly to see Dr. Tang—she had learned from the forms that the doctor's family name was Tang.

When she sat across from him again, she immediately sensed on her face the bouncing of his lead-shot eyes. She handed her test reports to him; he buried himself in them for a while, then looked up and said, "You can set your mind at ease. You're very healthy. There is nothing wrong with you. I thought you might have cervical vertebra disease or a heart problem, but I can assure you now that there is nothing wrong with you."

What was he talking about? she thought. Was he saying that she wasn't sick at all? If she wasn't sick, why would she come to the hospital? If she wasn't sick, how was it possible for her to leave the Reed River Farm? That's right, leave the Reed River Farm. Just then Wu at last completely understood her heart's desire: to leave the Reed River Farm. She really didn't want to go back to that place, so she had to be sick, and it was impossible that she was not sick.

"It's impossible," she said, and stood up, forgetting herself a little.

Gesturing for her to sit down, he asked, somewhat puzzled, "Why don't you want yourself to be healthy?"

"Because I'm not healthy. I'm sick." She sat down, but insisted on her opinion.

"The problem is that you're not sick." He took another look through the stack of test results, along with the EKG report and neck X-rays. "Your symptoms might be mental in origin, caused by excessive nervousness."

"I'm not nervous and I was never nervous." Wu contradicted Dr. Tang again.

"But your current state is a manifestation of nervousness," Dr. Tang said.

She then told Dr. Tang again that it was not nervousness but some disease. "It is really a disease." She realized she had already begun to act a little irrationally. Her confrontation with the doctor not only didn't convince the doctor, it didn't convince her, either.

Dr. Tang gave a helpless smile. "Certainly, mental nervousness can be an illness, a condition. But as a doctor of internal medicine, I have no authority to give a diagnosis in this matter. I can only . . . I can only . . ."

His conclusion brought her up from the chair again. She began to ramble and repeat herself like a gabby old woman. "I'm not only sick, I also have two kids. They're so small. My husband and I both work on the farm and can't take care of them at all. You know the Reed River Farm, quite far away from Fuan. Ordinarily we can't come back. My two daughters, they . . . they . . . because . . ." At this point she suddenly leaned her face in to Dr. Tang's and lowered her voice, desperately whispering, "You can't . . . you can't . . ." The next thing she felt was the spinning of the sky and earth. Her dizziness came to her rescue just in time and she lost consciousness.

She was hospitalized in the internal medicine ward and Dr. Tang was the physician in charge.

The first thing that came to her mind after she woke was actually Dr. Tang's small, dark eyes. She also remembered her whispered pleading before she fainted—it was a sort of pleading, and how could she have spoken in that whispering voice to a strange man? She could explain it as her fear of being overheard by others in the clinic, but then, wasn't she afraid this strange man would throw a woman who tried to fake an illness out of the hospital, or report her to her work unit? Then, during the Cultural Revolution, doctors also basically took on the responsibility of monitoring patients' thoughts and consciousness. She was afraid, but maybe she was willing to risk her life to win over with whispers this man who controlled her fate. Her dizziness had rescued her in the end. Coming from a woman who might faint at any time, no matter how pitiful and helpless compared to an earthshaking howl, those eerie, frail whispers still hinted at things, either serious or playful, and offered vague temptations. Maybe she hadn't at all meant to stir up hints of temptation around her, but it was the hints of temptation that stirred her.

As she lay on the white bed of the internal medicine ward, her body never felt healthier. She told Tiao and Fan later that she was so healthy because of the superb nutrition she received as a child: fish oil, calcium, vitamins . . . the fish oil was imported from Germany and her grandmother forced her to pinch her nose and take it. Tiao looked at her face carefully and asked, Why are you still dizzy, then?

Lying on the white bed of the internal medicine ward, she also had a feeling that she had been adopted—Dr. Tang adopted her, keeping her far away from the Reed River Farm, far away from the brick factory, and far from the revolution. Revolution, that was her required course of study at the farm every day. Chairman Mao's quotations about revolution were to be memorized every day; they were also made into songs, which Wu had already learned by heart and could sing from start to finish: "A revolution is not inviting friends to dine, not writing, not painting, or needlepoint; never so refined, so calm and polite, so mild and moderate, well-mannered and generous. A revolution is an uprising, violence with which one class overthrows another."

Revolution is violence. Violence. Wu temporarily left the violence far behind. She longed to see the concentrated, calm dark eyes of Dr. Tang; she longed to have him extend the cold little stethoscope to her chest . . .

One night when he was on duty, she felt the dizziness again and rang the bell. So he came to her room, where Wu was the only resident for the time being, though there were four beds. She never asked Dr. Tang later whether he made the arrangements deliberately or it just happened that there were no other patients. It was late at night then. He turned on the light and leaned over to ask her what was wrong and where she felt the discomfort. She saw that pair of small dark eyes again. She turned her head to the side and closed her eyes, saying it was her heart that pained her. He took out his stethoscope—she could sense that he had taken it out. He extended it toward her and when that ice-cold thing touched her flesh and pressed down over her heart, she reached up her hand and pressed down on his hand—the hand that held the stethoscope—and then she turned off the light.

In the dark they remained locked like this for a long time, as if their breathing had also stopped. That hand of his, pressed down by hers, remained motionless, although he suspected motionlessness was not what she had in mind for him. She didn't move, either, only the heart beneath their overlapped hands raced wildly. They remained motionless, as if each was feeling out the other: Is he going to call a nurse? Is she suddenly going to scream? They grappled and stalled, as if each were waiting for the other to make the first move, whether it was to attack or to surrender.

Her palm began to sweat, and the sweat of her palm wet the back of his hand. Her body started to heave in the dark because a hot current was surging and circulating in her lower belly, burning down right between her legs. She began to repeat to him the whispers of the other day in the clinic. Her voice grew quieter and more indistinct, accompanied by wild panting. The panting clearly had some elements of performance about it and was also mixed with some reluctant sighing. She repeated her whispers: "You can't . . . you can't . . . you can't . . ." He didn't know if she was saying that he couldn't withdraw his hand or that he couldn't go further. But just then he pulled his stethoscope free, tossed it aside, and put his hands on her breasts, calmly and with resolve.

When he pressed his long, lean body on her ample body, she suddenly felt an unprecedented sense of liberation. Yes, liberation, and she didn't feel guilty at all. Only then was she convinced that she would truly be adopted by Dr. Tang. The floodgate to her pure desire was thrown open. She clutched his waist with her hands, and she coiled her legs high, hooking her feet tightly around his hips. She didn't stop and didn't allow him to stop. Still in motion, she took a pillow and put it under her hips. She wanted him to go deeper and deeper. Until maybe it wasn't about going deeper anymore; it was about going through her entire body, to pierce her body entirely.

3

The night arrived like this: right in the middle of her boredom and brazen anticipation. She inhaled the smell of the laundry room from the pillow, along with the special smell of disinfectant from the hospital ward . . . laundry room and disinfectant. A healthy woman put in an isolated room and the mix of these two smells producing a crazy arousal in parts of her body.

At this time, in this moment, Wu was suppressing her excitement, waiting in the dark. The night before, as he was leaving her room, Dr. Tang told her that maybe she should have rheumatic heart disease. He would provide her certification of the diagnosis and a note for sick leave, a note that would allow her to rest for a month, which was the longest time that a physician in charge at People's Hospital could prescribe. She didn't want to concentrate on the thought that this was what she was waiting for, this note that would allow her to stay at Fuan and at home; that would make her seem degraded. The implication of exchange was all too obvious. She preferred to think she was waiting for the fulfillment of her sexual desire. She had experienced a feeling with him that she had never felt before. It seemed to be a kind of pleasure brought on by a nervousness and secrecy, and also a kind of submission to fate as thorough as if she were falling into an abyss.

He arrived, and when he put the note into her hand, she turned off the light again. This time she had the urge to caress him; it might be the female's most primitive physical expression of gratitude. She stroked his hair and his face, which she was not really familiar with; she lay down on him and looked for his lips. She hadn't touched his lips and he hadn't touched hers, either. She discovered he didn't like her to get near his face. When her hair brushed the corner of his mouth, he reached out his hands to hold her head, as if to avoid her. He held her head and pushed it all the way down, down. Her head, mouth, and face slipped farther and farther down, over his chest and stomach, then to that thicket of thorns, dense and a little scratchy. She didn't remember when he left the room. When she calmed down and was about to wipe her body, she noticed that she was still clutching the sick leave note.

She left the hospital and returned home. She announced to the sisters that she could stay home for a month, a month. After she said that, she lay back on her bed. She remembered she had rheumatic heart disease, so she needed to lie in bed. She leaned back against that big wide feather pillow and wrote separate letters to Yixun and to the farm leader, enclosing the certificate of diagnosis and the sick leave note. She asked Tiao to go out to mail the letters for her. Tiao held the letters and asked her, "Mom, what do you want to eat?"

What do I want to eat? Wu listened to Tiao's question and looked at her eleven-year-old daughter. The question obviously showed her daughter's concern for her, and it was unusual for a girl at such a young age to know how to take care of people, but the closeness between mother and daughter also seemed to be missing. Tiao never played cute with her, nor did she ever throw tantrums. And Wu never knew what was in Tiao's small head. Fan, who had just turned six, seemed to be under her older sister's influence. She stood next to Tiao and asked Wu in an adult way, "Mom, what do you want to eat?" As if she could cook anything her mom wanted to eat. Looking at her daughters, for a moment Wu felt like she had become a guest in the house, and the two sisters were the hosts. But she still gave serious thought to what she wanted to eat. She said, "Mom wants to eat fish."

Tiao mailed the letter at the post office, then went to the grocery store and bought a big live carp. The grocer tied the fish's mouth closed with a string of iris grass and handed it over to Tiao. She always remembered the price of that carp: ninety-five cents. She would forget many things over the years but not the ninety-five-cent carp. Her mood at the time was also memorable: she walked home carrying the swinging fish, straining a little bit, but feeling happy, confident, and proud. She liked having Wu back to prop up the family; she also wanted Wu to see that Tiao was not an ordinary girl in her parents' absence. She wasn't only capable of buying things, but she also knew how to cook them. She returned home, put the fish in the sink, removed the scales, cut open the belly, rinsed the cavity, drained it, picked up the cleaver and made diagonal cuts on the fish's body, then patted a thin layer of cornstarch onto the fish and fried it . . . In the end she produced a braised carp and took it to Wu. Her little face was red from the heat of the greasy smoke, and the sweat made her bangs stick to her forehead; the sleeves of her shirt were rolled up, revealing her tiny arms.

Fan ran around and cheered; she was proud of her older sister. She also took the opportunity to show off her own cooking tips, saying, "Mom, do you know what to do if you accidentally break the fish's gallbladder when you're cleaning it? Right away you pour some white wine into the fish belly . . ."

Tiao's braised carp took Wu by surprise. She felt a lump in her throat, yes, a lump, and then she began to cry. It was the first time she had cried since getting home; the tears came from the kind of guilt that can't be eased with an apology. She realized then that she hadn't asked about the two children's lives since she came home, how school was, what they ate every day, and whether they were being bullied or not. She really wanted to hold them to her breast and hug them tightly, but she didn't seem able to. Not every mother is capable of loving her child, although every child in the world longs to be loved. Not every mother can give off the maternal glow, although every child in the world longs to be bathed in it. Tiao always guarded herself against possible closeness with Wu, including the occasions when her mother cried. When tears threatened to bring them closer to one another, Tiao got embarrassed. This would be their regret, as mother and daughter, all their lives: they almost never could laugh or cry at the same time; either the mother was half a beat slower, or the other way around. That was why Wu's tears now couldn't move and comfort Tiao; Tiao just tried her hardest simply to understand her mother, and felt proud of herself for the effort.

They began to eat the fish. Wu said, "I'm going to knit a sweater for each of you." She said it eagerly, as if knitting sweaters were another form of embrace. She couldn't hug them, so she was going to knit sweaters for them. Tiao said, "Knit a sweater for Fan first. Rose is the prettiest color, isn't it, Fan?"

Fan said, "Rose is the prettiest color and it's the only color I want." This loyalty of hers to Tiao, this enthusiastic response, made Tiao feel like it had been a dream whenever she recalled it later. Next, as if to go along with the pleasant atmosphere, Wu talked about her plan to invite a guest over for dinner. She said that during her hospital stay, she had been really fortunate there was this Dr. Tang . . . a Dr. Tang. So, to express her gratitude, she wanted to invite him over for dinner. She said, "You're both young and don't know how hard it is to see a doctor." If there hadn't been this Dr. Tang, her life might have been in danger, not to mention the sick leave. She deliberately said the words "sick leave " softly, under her breath, but Tiao still heard her. If there hadn't been this sick leave, she wouldn't be able to stay home for a month. Tiao said she didn't understand. "Didn't you get the sick leave because you were sick? Why was it because of the doctor that you got the sick leave?"

Wu said, "Not every patient could get permission to rest. To put it simply, Dr. Tang is important and someone we should thank."

So they thanked him. It was a Sunday and Wu broke her routine and got up early. She asked Tiao to help her in the kitchen and was busy for almost an entire morning. She hadn't cooked for a long time and was out of practice, and her sense about salt, sugar, soy sauce, and MSG was off. She was intimidated by the kitchen, the way she was by the Reed River Farm. But as she bustled around, the one tiny advantage of the Reed River Farm occurred to her: they didn't need to cook there; they ate in the canteen. She made several odd-looking dishes, asking Tiao over and over again where the seasonings were. Spicy soy sauce and fennel—she had completely forgotten where they were. Finally, she planned to make a dessert: grilled miniature snowballs. She mentioned it to Tiao and Tiao said, "That's my dad's dish. No one knows how to make it when he's not home."

"Why can't we make it? Aren't fresh milk, eggs, and sugar all we need?"

"We also need vanilla and citric acid. Without citric acid, milk will stay liquid. It won't become miniature snowballs."

Wu looked at Tiao with surprise and asked, "How do you know?"

"I've seen Dad make it."

Wu said, "Find citric acid for me and I'll make grilled miniature snowballs."

"We don't have citric acid."

Wu believed Tiao, but she had a vague feeling that Tiao wanted to keep the recipe for miniature snowballs to herself.

Later, candied apple was substituted for grilled snowballs. Tiao despised this dish from the bottom of her heart. She had never liked any kind of "candied" dish, thinking it was neither hygienic nor civilized for people to pull out the apples with their chopsticks, trailing syrupy tangled candied strings, and then everyone dipping them into the same bowl of cold water, meanwhile faking the same amazed and satisfied expressions as they ate. Besides, what was so amazing and satisfying about eating sugarcoated apple? Furthermore, when Wu made candied apple, she always overdid the sugar, so there weren't any sugar strings to be pulled no matter how hard you tried. There were just gooey pieces and chunks that would stick to your teeth and palate. Tiao would keep licking the roof of her mouth with her tongue and sometimes had to put her fingers into her mouth to pry the stuff free. However, it passed as a dessert. With the way Wu cooked, who could blame Tiao for telling her that they didn't have citric acid?

When the dinner was ready, Wu began changing her clothes, going back and forth between the few outfits she had, whose styles were almost all the same, but in different colors like gray, green, blue, etc. But Wu looked good, her face glowing with excitement. She kept looking at herself in the mirror and also lowered her head and asked Tiao to smell her hair. "Do you think my hair smells of grease? Smell it again. Maybe I should wash my hair."

Tiao sniffed at Wu's hair and smelled a little grease smoke, but wasn't in a hurry to say anything. She asked Wu suddenly, "Is Dr. Tang a man or a woman?" Wu was startled for a moment and then straightened her back, her hair falling over half of her face. She said, "It's . . . it's uncle. You should call him uncle. What's the matter?" "Nothing," Tiao said. For some reason she didn't want to tell Wu that her hair smelled of grease smoke; she didn't want Wu to wash her hair one more time for this thank-you dinner. She felt Wu had spent too much time preparing for the dinner and took it too seriously. She had never seen her mother so serious about anything, including Tiao's and Fan's business. Wu ignored Tiao's reservations and washed her hair once more, as if she'd known that Tiao hadn't told the truth. Her dark, shiny hair matched her fresh, lustrous face—with the two soft, delicate, faultless eyebrows—it all looked very beautiful to Tiao, but she never said so to Wu.

Dr. Tang arrived, a very reserved man speaking perfect Beijing dialect. He didn't have his white cap on, so it was the first time that Wu had seen his hair, brownish hair that made his small dark eyes look even darker. They exchanged some courtesies and sat down to dinner. Wu told Tiao and Fan to call him uncle, but Tiao insisted on calling him Dr. Tang and Fan followed her sister's lead. Fan had a white plastic set of doctor toys, which included a syringe, a stetho-scope, and a "kidney tray" for surgery. She showed these toys to Dr. Tang and said with regret that she didn't have a thermometer, for which she often had to substitute a popsicle stick. If she found some-one with a fever, she would give that person a shot. "If you have a fever, you need a shot, right, Dr. Tang?" She repeated the words "have a fever" in a high-pitched voice; for her all illness could be summed up in the words "have a fever."

Have a fever.

Dr. Tang and Wu talked for a long time after dinner. He handed Wu a hardback copy of *The Family Medical Encyclopedia* and told her that there was a chapter dedicated to rheumatic heart disease. When Wu took the book from him, she noticed a loose thread on one of the sleeves of his sweater. She thought, why would she be so quick to tell Tiao and Fan that she was going to knit sweaters for them?

She bought a pure light gray woolen yarn and started to knit a sweater, leaning back against her pillow. She usually knitted the sweater dur-ing the daytime, after Tiao went to school, and also in the evening, after Tiao and Fan fell asleep. That made her look a little underhanded and evasive because she didn't want her daughters to see her knit this sweater. But in a simple home like theirs, where could she hide the sweater? Tiao eventually found the light gray half-finished item.

She was a little surprised and asked Wu, "This isn't Fan's sweater, is it? Didn't you say that you were going to knit a sweater for Fan?"

Wu grabbed the sweater back. "I did say that I was going to knit a sweater for Fan, but I can knit one for myself first."

"This is not a woman's sweater. It's not for you." She stood beside Wu's bed and seemed indignant.

The next day, when Wu unfolded the sweater to continue her work, she found that the sleeve she had almost finished the day before had disappeared.

4

The sleeve had to have been taken apart by Tiao. The knitting needles had vanished, and each row of stitches was undone—Wu had put her heart and soul into those stitches. She was furious, but couldn't really allow herself to lose her temper. She clutched the unraveled sweater, kept her anger in check, and went to talk things over with Tiao. She thought it might take some effort to get Tiao to confess, and hadn't expected it to be so easy. Tiao admitted it as soon as Wu asked, as if she were waiting for Wu to question her.

"Was it you who took the sweater apart?"

"It was me."

"What did I do wrong, to have you unravel my sweater?"

"You said you were going to knit a sweater for Fan but you didn't keep your promise."

"Yes, I did say that. It was . . . I couldn't find the rose yarn in the shop. I saw this kind, which was nice but more suitable for an adult—"

"What adult? Which adult?" Tiao interrupted Wu.

"Which adult?" Wu repeated Tiao's question. "Me, for instance. Like me." She lowered her voice.

"But this is not for you. This is a man's sweater." Tiao's voice remained firm.

"How do you know this is a man's sweater? You don't even know how to knit." Wu's anger flared again.

"Of course I know. I've seen you knit before. I've seen you knit for Dad. Are you knitting it for Dad?" Tiao looked directly into Wu's eyes.

"Yes . . . uh, no." Wu seemed to be forced into a corner by Tiao. She knew if she continued saying that the sweater was for Yixun, she would look even more stupid than she already did. Maybe Tiao would immediately write to her dad and tell him that Mom was knitting a sweater for him. So she admitted that the sweater was for Dr. Tang. It was Dr. Tang who asked her to knit a sweater for him. Dr. Tang was not married yet and he needed someone to take care of him. So she agreed to knit this sweater for him. She was even going to try to find him a girlfriend . . . She didn't know why she was babbling all of this to Tiao.

"Then why did you say you were knitting this for yourself?" Tiao still didn't let it go.

Wu's guilt turned into anger. She said, "What do you want? What do you really want from me? Why do you upset me so much? Don't you know that I'm ill?"

"If you're ill, then why do you spend so much time knitting?" Tiao didn't back down.

"I spend so much time knitting because . . . because I hope to spend more time home with you. Does my doing this bother you? Look at the other children in the Architectural Design Academy. Don't they all have to stay home by themselves, pathetically wasting their lives? Not all parents are as lucky as we are: to be able to have one of us at home to take an interest in our children."

Tiao didn't say anything more. She was thinking Wu might be right, but mostly her mind was filled with doubt. Wu spoke about "taking an interest" but Tiao didn't see any of it from her. She was not concerned about the sisters; didn't notice Fan had lost her front tooth, and didn't ask once what they had eaten every day in the last half a year. The way Tiao was mistreated for not knowing how to speak the Fuan dialect—Wu had never asked about any of this. So Tiao was more skeptical than trusting. And she didn't believe that Wu believed her own words, either. Her years of suspicion crystallized into doubt at that moment. This was sad for both mother and daughter, and something that neither seemed to be able to do anything about, which made it feel even crueler to have to accept.

Wu didn't feel she had won just because Tiao didn't reply, but she preferred not to think about it any further. She was the kind of person who didn't like to think deeply, a lifelong escapist. Her mind was not large enough to accommodate either caring for others or self-analysis. She clutched the sweater and returned to bed and to her big crumpled pillow to resume knitting. By the lamplight, she used the bamboo knitting needles to pick up the loose stitches one by one and finished the sleeve and the entire sweater in a single night.

Then she bought some yarn to knit a sweater for Yixun. She changed the color to a cream. She knitted the sweater day and night, her hands flying and her eyes getting bloodshot, as if she wanted to work off her guilt with the unusual knitting as well as ease her nerves. She knitted with great skill and she herself was surprised by the speed: she took only seven days to knit sweaters for two men. Seven days; she had never come close to that mark, not before or afterward. Whether it was to punish herself for her fall or to ease the way for her to fall further, she didn't know. She had a feeling that her relationship with Dr. Tang had not yet run its course.

Neither had had their fill of each other. Almost every Sunday, Dr. Tang came to Wu's house for dinner. When Wu's month of sick leave was up, he renewed it for another month. If he continued to renew her sick leave without anyone noticing, wouldn't she be able to stay home for a long time? This was something she hardly dared to imagine but wished for with all of her heart. When the Cultural Revolution turned violent, she became what was known as a wanderer, and she really wanted to be one. "Wanderers" was the label given to the faction of people who avoided political campaigns and labor reform and refused to take a stand on matters of principle. This group—muddleheaded, backward—couldn't be brought onto the stage to play their parts in history. If a doctor were found to provide a false certification for a patient, the consequences could be very severe. They wouldn't merely say he was violating professional ethics, which wouldn't be a serious enough charge. They would accuse him of undermining the great revolution, that is, being antirevolutionary. And Dr. Tang might very likely get arrested as an antirevolutionary. Dr. Tang was in fact risking his life, for Wu.

Now Dr. Tang wore the sweater Wu knitted for him openly—it fit really well, that sweater. Wu liked to look at his mouth chewing in the daylight. The way he ate was very elegant; his mouth made small but accurate movements, adeptly dealing with difficult foods like fish heads or spare ribs. It almost looked like he used his mouth as a knife to perform a quiet operation on food. That mouth of his seemed to be of particular use for eating food and keeping silent—when he wasn't eating, he was very quiet. His words were rare, which seemed to make his mouth even more precious. Wu would try to kiss him when no one was around, but he would pull away. So she let him be. She didn't have to kiss him. In some respects, she was easily satisfied. She would confine herself to observing that mouth. From her limited experience of men, she believed he was shy. He was an unmarried man.

She kept telling the sisters that she was going to get a girlfriend for Dr. Tang, but that it was really difficult. Dr. Tang came from a politically tainted family, and was also raising his niece on his own. The niece, whom Wu had met, was an orphan, the child of his older sister. She kept talking about finding a girlfriend but never took action. Tiao had never seen her bring anyone home who looked like a girlfriend type. During this period, Yixun came home for the change of season and stayed for three days—he had only three days' vacation. He invited Dr. Tang home to drink beer with him. Back then Fuan didn't have bottled beer, so beer was sold only in restaurants. The restaurant employees would use a rice bowl as a measure, ladle out the beer from a ceramic barrel, and then pour it into the customer's own container. The beer didn't have any head and tasted sour and bitter.

The two men drank beer and ate a roast chicken together, one that Yixun had brought back from Reed River Town. Yixun inquired about Wu's illness, and when he asked about it, Wu remembered she was sick. She had to be sick, with rheumatic heart disease. Yixun asked about all the details thoughtfully, full of concern for Wu and gratitude to Dr. Tang. Dr. Tang said this type of heart disease was the most common in China, making up 40 to 50 percent of the various heart conditions. Most patients were young or middle-aged, ranging from twenty to forty years old, and the majority were women. It was a form of heart disease that was mainly valvular, caused by acute rheumatic fever, usually attacking the bicuspid and aortic valves, causing stenosis or valve insufficiency and blood circulation stasis that would eventually lead to overall heart insufficiency.

Yixun said, "So, do you think Wu's dizziness has something to do with rheumatic heart disease?"

Dr. Tang said it was possible because a minority of patients might have shortness of breath or faint when the symptoms got worse. As Dr. Tang was talking, he and Wu exchanged a glance, a quick one, barely noticeable. In the face of Yixun's careful concern, both seemed a little bit ashamed. They hadn't expected that Yixun would invite Dr. Tang for a beer and have such a friendly conversation with him. It was, of course, the normal attitude of a normal person: Yixun felt indebted to the doctor for his kindness—Wu described in her letter to him how Dr. Tang came to her rescue when she passed out in the clinic and how he managed to get her into the internal medicine ward. When Dr. Tang told Yixun that there usually wasn't great danger as long as the patient took care to rest and avoided intense physical activity, Yixun felt reassured.

Three days later when Yixun was returning to the farm, Wu packed the cream-colored sweater she had knitted into his luggage.

Their house went quiet for a few days. Wu lay quietly on the bed, often without moving, as if she were really afraid of intense activity. Tiao felt everything was fine, as if Dr. Tang had never appeared in their house—which was when she realized that she had never liked Dr. Tang, even if he had saved Wu's life a hundred times over. But the calm lasted only a few days, after which Wu started to get active. Apparently it had become inconvenient for her to invite Dr. Tang home anymore, or she felt embarrassed to invite him over so quickly—so soon after Yixun had been there. She didn't want the children to notice the obvious contrast; she already felt Tiao's awkwardness was harder and harder to handle, so she decided to go out.

She must be going either to the hospital or Dr. Tang's place, Tiao thought. Wu often went out after dark and didn't come back until very late. Before she left, she always spent a long time in front of the mirror, combing her hair, gazing at her reflection, changing clothes and practicing pleasant expressions, checking both her front view and side view. How wilted and spiritless she appeared when she was tossing around on her pillow, her hair disheveled and her eyes dull, with drool at the corner of her mouth, thin and silvery, like a snail track. Had Dr. Tang seen her this way? If Dr. Tang saw this side of her, would he still want her to visit him?

But when Wu stood before the mirror and prepared to leave, she seemed to have turned into a completely different person, enthusiastic and energetic, her entire body lit up like a candle. Sometimes she even brought one or two dishes along, food for Dr. Tang. For this reason she had to enter the kitchen, the place she had always hated. Clumsily, she'd make fried eggplant and beef-carrot stew. She would put up with Tiao's comments, believing Tiao was just being intentionally hurtful. Tiao made a point of saying that Wu's cooking was bland, that the beef-carrot stew wouldn't be tasty if she didn't use curry powder. Wu then humbly asked where the curry powder was, but Tiao declared happily she didn't have any and they just couldn't find curry powder in Fuan, that the curry powder they used to have came with them from Beijing. Wu never noticed that Tiao had been removing the seasonings little by little. She hid them so Wu wouldn't find them and use them, because they had all become too closely associated with Dr. Tang.

When Wu was not home, Tiao flipped through the pages of *The Family Medical Encyclopedia* that Dr. Tang had given Wu. She turned to the section on rheumatic heart disease, but unfortunately there were too many words she didn't understand. She looked at pictures of ugly human bodies, one of which was a woman with a curled, upside-down baby in her belly. Tiao wrote a line in pencil in the margin next to the baby: "This is Dr. Tang." Why would she pick a baby and make it into Dr. Tang? Was it because only a baby like that was less powerful than she was? She then could freely express her contempt for the adult Dr. Tang through this fetus.

Wu still went to see Dr. Tang, carrying her lunch box, offering Dr. Tang the food she cooked, and herself. One evening she left, and didn't come home the whole night. It was on that night that Fan had a high fever. Having a fever, having a fever. Precisely the words Fan always used when she was playing the doctor-patient game. Her entire body was burning hot, her face all red, and her nostrils flaring.

She said she was very thirsty and wanted Tiao to cuddle her. Tiao held her in her arms and let Fan's fever scald her. She gave Fan water and orange juice, but neither could lower her temperature. Where was Wu? Both of them needed her. When Fan's fever made her cry, Tiao cried with her. She patted Fan's back with her small hand and said, "Let me tell you a story. Don't you love to listen to stories?" But Fan was not interested in stories. She must have felt terrible. She kept coughing and threw up several times. Her coughing and vomiting made her sound both old and young, like an old man trapped in a child's body. Tiao's heart was broken into a thousand pieces; Fan's suffering gripped her with pain. She hated Wu, thinking how she would shout at her when she came home. She held Fan in her arms all night long. Young and small as she was, she took on the responsibility of caring for Fan, who was smaller and weaker than she. She didn't close her eyes the whole night, washing her face when she felt sleepy. She was determined to wait for Wu to come home with open eyes, letting Wu see for herself that Tiao had been waiting for her all night. At daybreak Wu opened the door and tiptoed in.

A big pillow flew at Wu as a welcome—Tiao had grabbed it from the bed and thrown it at Wu's face. She didn't know where she got the nerve for this rude behavior, which should never be used to deal with adults and parents. But once the pillow was thrown there was no way to take it back. She stared boldly at her mother.

Wu's mind went blank. Only when Tiao shouted at her that Fan was dying did she come to her senses and rush to Fan. Fan was half conscious with the fever, a pink rash covering her forehead and behind her ears. She probably had the measles.

Fan's illness worried and frightened Wu. But she had no time for regret right then. She just picked up Fan and hurried out.

"Where are you going?"

"The hospital."

Tiao asked which hospital, and Wu said People's Hospital.

"You can't go to People's Hospital!" Tiao stamped her feet like a little lunatic.

5

Adults are still adults. Even if you throw pillows at their faces, these somewhat confused people remain in charge. Wu ignored Tiao's stamping. She put Fan on the crossbar of her bicycle and pedaled directly to People's Hospital. Tiao followed the bike, running all the way. In the emergency room, while the doctor on duty took Fan's temperature, Wu went to the internal medicine ward and got Dr. Tang. It was not that she didn't trust the doctor on duty; she just trusted Dr. Tang more. In this unfamiliar city, when she had trouble, a doctor with whom she had an intimate relationship would naturally become her protector, even though he was not on duty in the emergency room and didn't know pediatrics. Tiao couldn't stop Dr. Tang from appearing. She watched Wu and Dr. Tang bustle around Fan and had a feeling she had been deceived. Yes, she had been fooled by this pair of hypocrites, this man and woman. She felt angry and sad. She didn't know the word "hypocrite" then. She wouldn't find this word for them until she was an adult looking back. But right then she thought about her dad. She felt very sorry for Yixun. She decided to write him a letter. She wanted him to come to save her, and Fan as well.

Fan had measles.

At home, later that day, Tiao began to write to Yixun behind Wu's back, using stationery with light green lines. In the upper right corner of the paper was a row of light green printing, the size of sesame seeds: Beijing Bus Company. They'd brought the paper along with them from Beijing when they moved. Tiao had bought it at a stationery store when she was still at Denger Alley Elementary School. At the time she never considered why the paper would have Beijing Bus Company on it. These light green words gave her a feeling that whenever she wrote, a bus would come to pick up the letter and take it far away, to the place where it belonged. Years later, when she worked in the publishing house and saw all kinds of letters and manuscripts, she recalled her childhood, and the Beijing Bus Company paper she had used to write letters. She understood then it must be letterhead from the printing house of Beijing Bus Company, but was still puzzled. Why would a bus company own a printing house? And why would its paper flood every major stationery store in Beijing? On Beijing Bus Company paper Tiao wrote to Yixun.

Dear Dad:

How are you? I missed you very much today because Fan had measles. She had a fever, coughed very hard, and even threw up. I think she also missed you very much, but you were not home. Next, I'm going to tell you something about Mom; I must expose her. Ever since she came home, she hasn't taken care of us at all. She either lies in bed sleeping or goes to the hospital to see a doctor. I told her about my school, how I was going to graduate from elementary school soon but haven't joined the Junior Red Guards yet. Besides me, there are only four other of my classmates who are not in the Junior Red Guards. Two of them have landlord grandfathers and one has a father who wrote to the Nationalist Party in Taiwan. There is one other classmate whose mom used to be the vice president of a university here and had been denounced. I think I'm different from them. I believe you two are good people, but why can't I join the Junior Red Guards? Is it just because I came from Beijing and have a different accent? I asked Mom and she said if I couldn't join the Junior Red Guards then just don't join. She also won't allow me to learn the Fuan dialect, saying it's an ugly accent. You see how backward she is! Dad, you probably don't know that we don't have classes anymore. Our teachers take us to dig air-raid shelters every day, telling us that this is to protect us from the invasion of the Soviet revisionists. Since I'm not a Junior Red Guard, I work especially hard, much harder than those Junior Red Guards. How I wish the teacher noticed my performance! Once, I was so tired that I fell asleep at the air-raid shelter. I used the wet, sticky dirt as a pillow, and my head got full of dirt. The teacher didn't find me until almost dark. She didn't praise me; maybe she thought she should praise those Junior Red Guards first and I was a lower creature than they were. I was disappointed and wanted to tell Mom all about this, but every time I tried to talk to her, she always said, I know, I know. Mom is busy and doesn't have time to listen to this . . . "Mom is busy" is what she says most often. What is Mom? Mom is "I know, I know, and Mom is busy." Mom is busy. How busy she is! She is busy knitting a sweater for Dr. Tang. She originally said she was going to knit one for each of us, but she ended up knitting a sweater for Dr. Tang. Dear Dad, I want to tell you that I'm disgusted by this Dr. Tang. I hate that he always came to our house and I know Mom sometimes went to his place as well. Fan is a big fool. Every time Dr. Tang came, she would talk about the doctor-patient game with him. She also showed him her toys. Mom would ask me to cook with her for Dr. Tang. Dr. Tang is not a part of our family, but she gave him all her time, which I really don't understand. Just a few days ago, on the night when Fan had measles, Mom didn't come home all night. Where could I find her on such a dark night? Why didn't she pay attention to us? Dear Dad, I am almost crying as I'm writing this. I remember when we lived in Beijing, you and Mom took us to the Forbidden City and the Beihai Park. You told us the Forbidden City was where the emperor lived. After a while, Fan saw a worker decorating the window in the palace hall, she ran back and told everyone mysteriously, I saw the emperor. The emperor was decorating the window. We also went to the Beihai Park to row the boats, eating barley buns and leaving the park after dark. It was you who carried me on your back the whole time. Mom held Fan. We fell asleep and I heard you tell Mom: Just look at how soundly they're sleeping. Actually I was not fast asleep. I could have walked on my own but I pretended to be sleeping so you would carry me a little longer. Now I beg you to come home as soon as you read this letter. If this can be tolerated, what else cannot be?

I wish you health,
Your daughter, Tiao

It was a long letter sprinkled with political phrases popular back then, such as "If this can be tolerated, what else cannot be?" and "expose," etc., a letter filled with accusation and tears. Continually looking up words in an elementary school dictionary, Tiao spent three days finishing the letter. At sad moments, tears soaked the paper, smudging some of the words and stippling the pages. Tiao wanted to copy the letter over one more time, but she was eager to send it out. Besides, even though the letter was a bit messy, it did reveal her real feelings, after all. She wanted Yixun to see her true feelings and anxiety.

She found an envelope and carefully wrote down the names and addresses for both the sender and receiver. She then hid the letter in her backpack and threw it into the first mailbox she saw on her way to school. It was a round, cast-iron pillar box that stood outside the gate of the Architectural Design Academy, only a hundred meters from Tiao's home, Building Number 6 in the residential complex. She stood on tiptoe to throw the letter into the mailbox, and her heart felt relieved as soon as she heard the gentle *pa* sound as the letter dropped to the bottom of the box, as if the mailbox liberated her right at that moment, setting her long-unhappy heart free.

When she came home in the afternoon, Wu had already cooked the dinner. It won't taste good, Tiao thought, but she ate her fill. She believed Yixun was coming home soon and things would change. Nothing would be a problem. Her change of mood started after dinner. At the time, Fan was lying under the covers of Wu's big bed with her eyes quietly closed, her fever down and her measles almost gone. Wu was leaning on the side of the bed knitting. This sweater was for Fan. She had followed Tiao's suggestion and bought the rose-colored yarn. Keeping vigil over Fan for several days in a row had made her thinner than before; her eyes were red and her hair slightly messy. She knitted with her head lowered for a while, then took a bottle of eyedrops from the nightstand and put a few drops into her eyes. The eyedrops must have burned, and she leaned against the pillow with her eyes closed, bearing it quietly for a while. Some liquid ran out of the corners of her eyes, which Tiao thought was a mixture of tears and eyedrops. She felt that the way Wu leaned on the pillow with her messy hair and teary eyes looked a little awkward and pitiful. How she clutched her knitting needles also touched Tiao with a kind of sadness that she couldn't explain. The room was quiet and peaceful, as if no stranger had ever entered and nothing had ever happened. In those few seconds, just in a few seconds, everything changed.

Why did she have to write to Yixun? Was everything she put in the letter true? What would happen to her family when her dad came home? Why would she expose Wu? Wasn't that a word that should be used only for enemies? All of a sudden Tiao felt pressure in her head as if a disaster were approaching—it must feel that way when a disaster approached. With the pressure building in her head, when Wu was not paying attention, she opened the door and sneaked out.

She passed several residential buildings in the Architectural Design Academy, going by the office building near the gate, the one pasted with all kinds of slogans and posters. In the daytime, the wind blew through layer upon layer of posters and tore them to shreds, making the building look like a giant wailing madman. Night silenced the madman and its body only made small monotonous rustlings, a bit lonely but not frightening. As soon as she crossed the pitch-black courtyard and walked out the gate, she saw the mailbox, faithfully and steadfastly standing in the shadow of the sidewalk trees. She rushed straight at the mailbox with hands outstretched. She anxiously groped for the mail slot: a narrow slot, which immediately made her realize the pointlessness of her fumbling, since she had no way to slide her hand into it. By the dim streetlight, she could read the two rows of small words below the slot: "Pickup time, 11 a.m. and 5 p.m."

Tiao clearly understood those two lines of words, but once again she reached her hands into the slot. She explored the narrow slot with her fingers one after another, hoping that a miracle would happen, that her small fingers could fish out a letter that was already gone. She had sneaked out of the house believing she could get the letter back as long as she found the mailbox. Now she realized that this belief of hers was just a pathetic, self-deceiving fantasy. Up and down, she studied the ice-cold cast-iron mailbox, taller and bigger than she was. She encircled it with her arms, holding its waist in hopes of pulling it up by the root, or pushing it over and smashing it. She wrestled with it, pleaded with it, and sulked at it; all the while she believed for no reason that as long as she kept working on it she could get that terrible letter back. She didn't know how long she tortured herself, not stopping until she was utterly exhausted. She then threw herself onto the mailbox and beat it wearily with her small fists. This seemingly faithful mailbox had refused to serve her. She leaned against the mailbox and started to cry, sobbing and beating it, not knowing where to find the letter that had gone. After a while she heard someone speak behind her: "Hey, child, what's the matter?"

She was frightened and immediately stopped crying, staring alertly at the one who had asked her the question. Although much taller than she was, he was not an adult, but three or four years older than she was, or four or five at the most. He was one of those high school students who, of course, were adults in Tiao's eyes because they normally treated elementary school students with arrogance, and liked to appear older than they actually were. That was why this boy addressed her as a child.

But there was nothing arrogant about him. His voice was soft and there was real concern in it. He stooped toward Tiao, who was still leaning on the mailbox, looked at her, and gently asked again, "Child, what's the matter?"

Tiao shook her head, saying nothing. Somehow the word "child" calmed her and brought back her tears; a vague feeling of having been wronged filled her heart, as if this "Child, what's the matter?" were something she had looked forward to hearing for a long time. She was entitled to be addressed that way and asked that question about many, many things. Now a stranger had done it, which made her want to trust him even though she shook her head and didn't say anything. She said nothing and just wanted to hurry home because she remembered the adults' warning: Don't talk to strangers.

He followed her to the gate of the design academy and asked, "Do you live in the design academy? Then we are in the same complex. I live here, too. I can take you home." He wanted to walk beside her, but she picked up her pace to get rid of him, as if he were a stalker.

Finally, she ran into the building and up the stairs. She heard him calling outside, "I want to tell you my name is Chen Zai and I live in Building Number Two."

6

Why do I always run into you when I'm at my lowest? Why do I run into you when I don't want to run into anyone? When I am basking in glory, all decked out, and pleased with myself, you're never there. That night, when I stood on the sidewalk hopelessly beating the mailbox, I was oblivious to the possibility that someone could see me and I might get arrested. Something like that happened in Fuan later; two bored young men lit a firework, threw it into a mailbox, and burned all the mail. They were sent to prison. I heard about it a year later. Luckily, throwing fireworks into a mailbox never would have occurred to me; luckily, that incident happened after I tortured the mailbox, otherwise I probably would have done the same thing out of frustration. I know it's a crime, and I must have looked like a criminal at the time; at least I showed criminal passion. It was you who observed the darker side of me, and how long had you been watching? Did you start to spy on me as soon as I walked to the mailbox, or did you approach as soon as you saw me? If it's the former, that would make me very unhappy, because if you'd been watching that long you would have figured out that I wanted to steal letters. That's the kind of thing others shouldn't know, that battle I had with myself. Maybe you just accidentally saw me, and that "Child, what's the matter?" really came out of concern, like that of a close family member. Maybe I just should have howled in front of you and begged you to smash the mailbox along with me. But you're not family. Besides, what's the use of pounding a mailbox? I didn't realize until later when I was calm that my letter was long gone from the mailbox. *Ai!* You said you lived in the same complex as I did, Building Number 2, three buildings away from us, which made me feel both trusting and uneasy. Trusting because living in the same complex felt like being "comrades in the same trench"—the catch-phrase at the time—uneasy because you might see me again, point me out to your classmates or neighbors, and gossip about me, telling them about the show I'd put on that night. Who knows? One day, an afternoon in summer, I was playing rubber-band jump rope in front of the building with the rope of rubber bands strung between two trees and slipped higher and higher; I always liked the game, from primary school right through to middle school—I had just started sixth grade. I'd been easily able to jump to the "middle reach" long before; I hoped I could kick my leg up to the "big reach," the highest height in the game. How high was the rubber-band rope then? It would have been the distance from my feet to the tips of my middle fingers when I stretched my arms upward over my head. My feet couldn't reach that high at the time, which I simply couldn't accept. One classmate of mine who was shorter than I was could jump to the "big reach." That could only mean that I was awkward, my legs not sufficiently flexible, and maybe my waist not supple enough. So, my rubber-band jumping on this summer afternoon was not just self-amusement but a strict training regimen. I hoped to jump to the "big reach" so that I could get back at those who humiliated me by making me the rubber-band-rope holder. I tied the two ends of the rope to a pair of poplar trees and raised the height gradually, one try after another. I jumped very smoothly and finally raised the rope to the "big reach." I gathered all my strength and kicked my right leg up toward the band, but unfortunately, I did it too violently, lost my balance, and fell to the ground. Maybe because the afternoon was so quiet, I heard the thump of my own fall.

Half of my face scraped on the ground and I skinned a knee. My vanity must have been considerable, because even when the pain made me grimace I remembered to look around, to check if anyone had witnessed my embarrassment. At first glance I caught sight of you, recognizing you as the person who said, "Child, what's the matter?" to me that night. You happened to be passing by on your bike and saw this tumble of mine. It made me very angry, at you and at myself as well. I was still angry as I hurried to get up from the ground, hiding the sharp pain and pretending to walk home calmly as if no one were around. I hummed a song as I entered the building. I had to show you that even though I fell down it hadn't hurt at all, that I didn't mind falling, that everyone fell while learning to do the "big reach" . . . I was so nervous that I forgot to untie the rubber-band rope from the trees. When I remembered it late in the afternoon and ran back to the poplars, someone had stolen it. The ten-foot-long rubber-band rope, which I'd put together by saving the rubber bands one by one!

Many years later, when I was an adult, during the winter Fang Jing left me, I wrote a letter to force him to come see me at Fuan. He agreed to come, but said he was very busy and could only talk to me at the train station. He bought a return ticket to Beijing as soon as he got off the train. We sat in the noisy, smoky waiting room— sometimes the noisiest public location can be the best place to have a private conversation. I asked why he had promised to get a divorce but kept putting it off. Why would he stay married while he forbade me to have a boyfriend? I said a lot and he said very little; he spoke one sentence after I said ten. He said, finally, "Falling in love with me was a mistake, and you should calm down and think about starting a new life on your own." Full of himself and absentminded, he stood up and got ready to leave while he was still talking. I seized his sleeve then, the sleeve of his ostrich-gray Brazilian leather jacket. This was what I'd most feared hearing; I would rather have had him say, "You can't have a boyfriend. I won't allow it." That would have at least shown that he cared about me. I held on to his sleeve, bowed my head, and started to cry, quietly but in surging waves. I didn't know when he disappeared from view, but I still held on to a bag of Fuan's local delicacy: honey twisted dough sticks. How would Fang Jing in his Brazilian leather jacket appreciate this sort of local specialty? But I sincerely wanted to please him with the dough sticks, even when I faced his impatience. I curled up on the wooden bench in the waiting room, not wanting to go home, my hand still clutching the bag of dough sticks and my heart as confused as a tangled bunch of twine. I must have been stupid to the extreme, because even after Fang Jing escaped my pestering (if that was what it was) and had boarded the train to return to Beijing, I still hated him and missed him—to hate is to miss. I stayed there and didn't want to leave because Fang Jing had just sat there, his breath and the warmth of his body lingering. Chen Zai, you arrived again, always showing up at moments like these. But I wasn't afraid of you anymore, nor did I pretend to be someone I wasn't, as I had the year I fell at rubber-band rope. We were all grown up and you were like an older brother of mine, not too close but not too distant, either. We lived in the same complex; we would smile and talk a bit when we saw each other. I sensed that you meant me no harm and had never intended to ridicule me. You walked over and sat next to me. You must have been going to Beijing also—I knew you were a graduate student of architecture. You said, "That man who was just talking to you looks very familiar. Isn't he the big celebrity Fang Jing?" I burst into tears then, burying my face in my hands without caring. Time slowly made me understand, that day in the waiting room, it was exactly because I was with you that I could be so free. Only you, no one else, could allow me to cry in public without restraint. You accidentally witness everything about me, my slyness, my falling, the love carved in my heart, and its loss. You've seen all of it. I held on to you as if I had grabbed a lifesaver, spontaneously telling you everything about Fang Jing and me, regardless of whether you wanted to hear or not. We sat in the waiting room for an entire day. You bought bread and water when we were hungry; neither of us touched the bag of dough sticks. You didn't return home with me until very late. You lied that you were going back to Beijing next morning; you told me only after we walked into the building that you had to take the train back to school that night. Only then did I realize you'd stayed just for me. I didn't know why I would load all my trouble and sadness on you, about whom I didn't know much. Time made me understand it was unfair to you, but it seemed fated.

Why do you always run into me when you're at your lowest? Why do you run into me when you don't want to run into anyone? On that windy night, I saw a delicate little girl holding the mailbox, sighing, and hitting it, although you didn't know you were sighing. I hadn't yet seen your face then, but from your body, from that small dark figure of yours, strangely I felt a deep pain like I'd never felt before. Later you turned your face toward me. It was too dark to make out your expression, but my own pain increased because you seemed so much in pain, although I couldn't see it in your face. Real pain is expressionless; real pain might well be a little girl holding a mailbox under the dim streetlight. I couldn't help being moved by you, moved in a way that will stay with me all my life, I thought. Yet what felt like a vow might have been a young man's impulse, a momentary instinctive sympathy for the weak. Back then I wasn't considered an adult yet, although I was five years older than you were. But I was wrong; my long love started when you were twelve, right from the night when you stood in front of the mailbox. How happy I was when I found out you and I lived in the same complex. You wouldn't know for many years how I'd find excuses to pass your building, Number 6. That summer afternoon, the afternoon you fell when you were jumping, I didn't pass by your building by accident; I'd circled the building many times on my bike. I didn't intend to see you fall; I just wanted to see your little face in the daylight. But you fell just as I came around. You raised your head, looking at me with a frown, half of your face smeared with sweat-soaked dirt. I wanted to say I loved your small soiled face. I loved the vain little trick that you played, pretending to be so casual even though you were limping. I loved your back as you hurried, where a little braid came loose. I even remember the song you hummed then: *Villages and kampongs, beat the drum and strike the gong, Ah Wa people, sing a new song* . . . with your knee bleeding, you sang "Villages and Kampongs" and went home, not leaving me the slightest chance of saying hello. It's my own business that I love you. When I was looking at your back, fluttering and dusty, I had a vague feeling that you would make me feel rich and full; you would always be the immovable center of my heart. But why does it matter? For many years I deliberately avoided telling you how I felt. I was especially surprised to have you tell me your story in the waiting room so suddenly. Your total trust of me was so unexpected and cruel; it mercilessly pushed me farther away. I couldn't express my love for you when you'd just lost your love; I would look like some rat trying to take advantage. You always controlled the distance between you and me; we could be only so close and no closer. I don't know how long I have to keep all this bottled up, but I don't want to stay far from you; I like to see you often, and to do my best to help you when you need it.

A week after the mailbox incident, when Tiao went to check for mail and newspapers, she unexpectedly found the letter she had sent out, the one to Yixun at the Reed River Farm. She'd been so eager that she'd forgotten to put on a stamp, and the letter was returned for "unpaid postage."

When Tiao, who had been on edge for a week, expecting Yixun to come home any minute and turn the house upside down, who often broke into a cold sweat at a knock on the door, finally got the letter, she almost laughed out loud. Ah, post office, how grateful I am to you! Ah, mailbox, how grateful I am to you! she shouted in her heart while she clutched the letter that had strayed for days, as if she were afraid it would fly away. The dark clouds cleared and the sunshine returned. This "lost-and-found letter" gave her a lifelong fondness for the post office and mailboxes, which always seemed to have some mystical connection of good luck for her.

She slipped the letter into her pocket and then opened the door. After handing the newspaper to Wu, she rushed into the bathroom and locked herself in. She sat on the toilet and tore the letter to shreds, until it was turned into snowflake-like bits. She dumped them into the toilet and flushed it again and again. Fortunately, Wu was not paying attention to Tiao's behavior, otherwise she would have thought Tiao was having diarrhea in the bathroom.

Tiao emerged from the bathroom completely at ease. She wanted to forgive her mother. She even thought if Dr. Tang came again, she would try her best not to object.

Chapter 3

❧ ❧ ❧

Where the Mermaid's Fishnet
Comes From

1

Dr. Tang came again, and this time he brought his niece Fei.

Tiao was immediately drawn to Fei, who was fifteen that year, but to Tiao she already appeared to have the body of a grown woman. Her dark eyebrows, red lips, and deep chestnut curls on her forehead lit up Tiao's eyes. It was a time when makeup wasn't allowed, so how were Fei's lips so brightly colored and gorgeous? It was also a time when perms were banned, so how did Fei get her curled bangs? How did she dare? The vivid lips and curled bangs made Fei look like a visitor from another planet; those slightly skewed eyes of hers gave her a touch of boldness and decadence. Tiao learned the word "decadence" from political posters. It was a bad word, but for some reason this bad word made her heart race. Even though she didn't completely understand the meaning of decadence, she was already sure it applied to Fei precisely. Perhaps by associating this word with Fei she unconsciously expressed her own attraction to evil: the female spy, the social butterfly . . . in the movies she used to watch, those women, constantly surrounded by men, always wore expensive and beautiful clothes, drank good wine, and looked mysterious. That would be decadence, but why were decadent people so pretty? Fei was decadent, and that vague decadence in her excited Tiao. She had never met a female before Fei who thrilled her so much. She felt that somehow she'd already started to worship Fei, this beautiful, decadent girl. Because of this, her loathing for Dr. Tang lessened somewhat.

Dr. Tang brought two movie tickets, distributed by the hospital, for an Algerian film, *Victory over Death*. "Let Tiao and Fei go, otherwise who knows how long they'll have to wait for the school to buy them group tickets," Wu said very agreeably, seemingly eager to please, which annoyed Tiao a little. Although she liked going to the movies, especially with someone like Fei, she didn't like Wu's tone. The more ingratiating Wu sounded, the more she heard a dismissal—she was sending Tiao and Fei off so she could be with Dr. Tang. So Tiao said she didn't want to go; she had to do her homework. She just wanted to make a little trouble for Wu.

Then Fei stretched out her hand to her uncle, not her entire hand, but two of the fingers: index and middle. She wiggled her fingers at her uncle and said, "Tickets. Tickets. Give me the tickets." Tiao wasn't surprised by her Beijing dialect; she believed a person with Fei's looks had to speak Beijing dialect. It would have been strange if she hadn't. The way she wiggled her fingers seemed indecent, and the tone in which she spoke to the adults made her sound impudent. Tiao had never come across anyone who behaved in this manner and spoke in that tone. She was probably stunned, so when Fei almost grabbed the tickets from her uncle's hand and gestured with her head, Tiao stood up and left with Fei as if she had received an irresistible command.

The movie was showing at Da Guangming Theater, three bus stops from Tiao's home. They didn't take the bus—they walked. For a shortcut, they wound through some alleys single-file. Fei walked very fast, pretending not to notice Tiao's quivering eagerness to follow her. She didn't talk to Tiao and didn't bother to walk beside her. She wore a plissé shirt, white background printed with bean-sized strawberries, and a pair of blue khaki uniform pants that perfectly hugged her swaying bottom. On her feet, she had on a pair of black T-strap leather shoes, which weren't for adults, but were hard for a middle school student to get. The shoes didn't just represent wealth, but also a style and taste beyond those of an ordinary Fuan family. Shoe factories in

Fuan didn't make leather shoes of this kind; one could immediately tell they came from a big city, even though they were just made of fine pigskin. Fei swung her bottom, raised her chin slightly, and stuck out her already-developed chest, walking in front of Tiao all the time. She rolled her plissé sleeves above her elbows, revealing the layer of soft, fine yellow down on her forearms, dazzling in the sunshine. She was so striking that there were always passersby who stopped to look at her: men, women, adults and children . . . Two young men in worker's clothes came toward them on their bikes. They swung around after passing and caught up with Fei from behind, purposely sandwiching her from both sides. Swaying and squirming on their bikes, they brushed their sleeves on her bare arms and then darted off. She didn't call them "Obnoxious!" or "Pervert!"—just walked more proudly, as if no one else existed. She didn't pay attention to them at all; they were not worthy of her spit or her curses.

At last they entered the narrow, quiet alley that led to Da Guang-ming Theater. Noticing there was no one around, Fei suddenly stopped, as if waiting for Tiao to catch up. Excitedly, Tiao caught up with her, feeling it was a gesture from Fei showing that she regarded Tiao as her equal and would finally walk with her side by side. Tiao rushed to her, only to be forced by Fei into a corner. Backed against the wall, face-to-face with Fei, Tiao thought she was going to tell her some secret, which sometimes happened when two girls walked together. But before she could react, Fei slapped her hard across the face. The crisp, loud slap, echoing in the alley, made Tiao see black in front of her eyes, followed by thousands of golden sparkles dancing around her head. It didn't hurt; she had no memory of pain. Maybe what Fei said blocked the pain that Tiao might have felt, or transferred the feeling to somewhere else in her. After she slapped Tiao, Fei got very close to her face and said something terrible with that pretty mouth of hers. She said, "Your mom is a bad woman, a whore!"

Tiao opened her eyes; the alley was still the same alley, and Fei stood before her, with her hands on her hips and sweat on her face, as if awaiting Tiao's counterattack. "Your mom is a whore." Tiao couldn't believe she had really heard it, that the vulgar, explosive words had really come out of Fei's mouth. She never wanted to hear those words again in her whole life, but she felt compelled to repeat them over and over in her mind. Her heart raced, every hair on her body seemed to stand up, and hot blood rushed to her face, the swollen face that Fei had slapped. Tiao was angry, but a terrible shame kept her from raising her head. For a moment, she was about to agree with Fei. She suspected that her mother's being a whore involved Dr. Tang, and the things she had written about in the letter to her dad. She now believed the only people who knew about Wu and Dr. Tang were her and Fei, but her instinct was to protect Wu. For a stranger to insult her mother this way was intolerable. She intended to retaliate but didn't know how; she felt guilty because what Fei had said was true, and she couldn't quite find the words for a reply. Tears started suddenly and she tried to turn around to walk back. The good things about home came to her mind and she wanted to go there. "Don't you dare leave!" Fei said behind her, and she stopped, compelled by Fei's voice. She really didn't know why she would listen to Fei.

Fei grabbed Tiao's arm and forced Tiao to keep going to Da Guang-ming Theater with her. She was very strong and Tiao was unprepared for such physical proximity to Fei. She was escorted to the movie theater and pushed into a seat. When the movie started and the the-ater was all dark, Tiao settled down a little bit. The dark made her relax and let out a long sigh, long but uneven: shivery and halting, as if she were restraining herself. She felt hurt, and reached up with her hand to touch the side of her face; it was numb. With a numbed face, she tried to focus on the movie, but Fei's words kept ringing in her ears. She couldn't concentrate on the movie until a good-looking woman guerrilla appeared on the screen. The movie was about the fight between Albanian people and the Nazis during the Second World War. Tiao kept imagining herself as the heroine, the woman guerrilla Mira, beautiful and strong. After a while, Mira's leader, a woman captain with a big black mole on her upper lip, appeared on the screen. The captain was interrogated and tortured after her capture. Blood trickled from the corner of her mouth; white skin was peeling from her cracked, dry lips. (Later, Tiao would learn the "white skin" was makeup, a layer of dried rice soup.) Then a pitcher of water was placed in front of her, the clear cut-glass making the water seem even more precious. The Nazi officer poured a glass and handed it to the woman captain. She swallowed her saliva, opened her puffed lips with difficulty, and sneered at the officer: "Thanks. Fascists' humanitarianism, I know!" This was really excellent, a once-in-a-lifetime retort; so witty and proud that Tiao was thrilled. At this point, she decided that she didn't want to be Mira anymore; she wanted to be this woman captain with the black mole on her upper lip, although she was truly ugly, and her thin, bow-shaped eyebrows, which seemed to have been drawn with a pencil, were particularly hideous. But she refused to surrender even under interrogation and torture and could also come out with heroic utterances. Tiao gazed at the screen with a numbed face; the slap in the alley never stopped reverberating in her heart. Who else could be the woman captain if she weren't? And the Nazi officer was Fei. She would hand Tiao a glass of water and Tiao would sniff at her and say, "Thanks. Fascists' humanitarianism, I know." Unfortunately, Fei hadn't given her a glass of water; instead she gave her a slap. What should Tiao say to a slap? "I'll fight you to the death!" Or, "I don't know. Even if I knew, I wouldn't tell." She tried to recall all the anti-Japanese movies she had seen before and make up all the lines that she should say when confronting a slap. She mixed up movies and life, her mind confused and her heart welling up with her sense of having been wronged.

When the theater lights came on again, the audience stood up one after another, whacking back the plywood seats, and Tiao realized the movie had ended. She didn't want to leave, especially not with Fei. She didn't want to go outside with the burden of that sentence, a shame that she couldn't throw off. She planned to stay here alone, here where people's eyes fix on the screen, not on each other. But Fei grabbed her arm and asked, "Are you leaving or not?"

"No, I'm not leaving." She answered Fei with a good measure of the revolutionary's determination, as if the movie that had just ended had injected some strength into her.

"Are you really not leaving?"

"What can you do about it if I don't?"

"You wouldn't dare!" Fei reached out with her other hand to grab the back of Tiao's collar as she was speaking. Tiao was in her grasp; she really couldn't believe such a pretty girl would grab people by their collars. She had never been slapped or seized by the collar in all her life, and now she had been treated to both insults on the same day. With Fei clutching her arm, she left the theater and entered the quiet alley. Seeing no one around, Tiao suddenly stopped, this time determined to take the initiative on whether she would go or stay.

"Why don't you keep walking? Want another good slap?"

Tiao collected her courage and said, "Puh—let me tell you, my mom is not a whore. Your mom is a whore."

"Unfortunately," said Fei, "I don't have a mom." She put out a foot as she was talking, turning her hip to one side and standing at ease, in a relaxed stance. "Allow me to repeat: too bad I don't have a mom."

This, Tiao hadn't expected. Since Fei didn't have a mom, obviously her eye-for-an-eye counterattack not only failed but also appeared crude. She also saw clearly, when Fei said "too bad I don't have a mom," how she grinned at Tiao. It seemed she wanted to make Tiao angry with this grin, to annoy her: I don't have a mom, so you've said something stupid. And Tiao couldn't do anything about it even though her insides ached and itched. But the grin made Tiao feel a little sad. Almost at the moment Fei grinned, Tiao forgave her fierce slap and her shouting.

The grin stayed on Fei's face, which made Tiao feel she should help relieve her of it with an apology. "I'm sorry, Fei," she said, "I didn't know you don't have a mom." The grin diminished but still lingered at the corner of Fei's mouth, as if she were not capable of withdrawing it completely. She hadn't reached the age where she could let it come and go at will; after all, she was only fifteen. "It doesn't matter. You don't have to apologize. You can talk about somebody else, for instance, my uncle. I don't have a mom, but I have an uncle. Try saying my uncle is a bad man. Maybe you can say my uncle is a hooligan. Say it. You say it." Fei started to tremble as she was talking, and the corner of her mouth, where the grin persisted, twitched strangely, making it hard for Tiao to tell whether it marked the end of laughing or the start of crying. Maybe there is no real difference between laughter and crying, and Fei's crying was born in the middle of laughter. She still kept her head high and chest out, but the bossy air she'd had most of the night was gone. She repeated the technique of backing Tiao, step by step, against the wall, but this time she had tears streaming down her face, and she whispered to Tiao, "I know you hate my uncle. You must hate my uncle, just like . . . just like I hate your mom. You can curse him in front of me, just one sentence, they . . . they . . . *ai*, why would I say these things to you? What do you know?" Fei wiped her tears with the back of her hand and stood against the wall with Tiao, side by side. She cocked her head lazily and squinted her tear-stung eyes, like the yellow cat with the long legs and thin face who sunbathed on the roof year-round.

Tiao couldn't say any bad words about Dr. Tang aloud to Fei. The fact that Fei was motherless touched her, and the way Fei cursed her own uncle comforted her. From now on she would no longer be alone. They were in the same boat. She felt that they understood each other and that part of the understanding could only be felt, not put into words. But they didn't have to put it into words.

"Can we talk about something else? Where is your mom?" Tiao asked.

"She died. She died in Beijing. We used to live in Beijing."

"As soon as I saw you I knew you were from Beijing. My family moved here from Beijing, too. I used to go to Denger Alley Elementary School."

"Me, too," said Fei. "My mom was a teacher at Denger Alley Elementary School. Teacher Tang."

Teacher Tang, Tang Jingjing. Tiao remembered that denouncement meeting—the smell—how Teacher Tang, thin and white as a toothpick, knelt to walk to the teacup that held shit. She thought that it had been because Teacher Tang didn't want Fei to be denounced with her that she ate shit. She had eaten shit because she didn't want Fei to be insulted in public. She also remembered how she rinsed her own mouth and brushed her teeth after she got back that day.

"There was a denouncement meeting," Fei continued.

"I attended that denouncement meeting," Tiao said.

"My mom hanged herself later."

"Were you there that day?" Tiao asked.

"I was."

Tiao had originally wanted to ask, "What about your dad? Where is your dad?" But she didn't. She recalled that at the denouncement meeting, which seemed so long ago, people with angry, pale faces demanded in harsh tones that Teacher Tang tell whose child Fei was. But no one knew who her father was because Teacher Tang had never married. Because she had never married, people were especially intent on identifying the child's father. She remembered the big sign hanging over Teacher Tang's chest, which read "I'm a female hooligan." If an unmarried woman who gave birth to a child was a female hooligan, then a married woman with children who had a man besides her children's father must be a whore. Whore or female hooligan, which was worse? Tiao thought hard about these sad things, but they only got jumbled up in her mind. She knew she couldn't ask anyone to untangle them for her, but that twelve-year-old head only came to one conclusion: that Fei was more unfortunate than she was. Although Fei had just slapped her, nothing could stop them from becoming good friends.

They stood there blankly for a while, and then it was Fei who broke the silence. She wiped her tears and waved her hand at Tiao. "Follow me. Let's buy something delicious to eat."

They went to Old Ma's Spiced Meat Shop. In the mid-sixties, the shop had changed its name to Innovations. Fei spent six cents on two marinated rabbit heads and handed Tiao one of them. Now the movie came back to Tiao, and she knew her chance had come. She curled her lips and said to Fei, "Thanks. Fascists' humanitarianism, I know."

Fei started to laugh, this time from her heart. "Go to hell with your fascists!" she said to Tiao. "I bought the marinated rabbits' heads for their ears—crispy, tasty, and crunchy when you chew on them. Listen. Listen to it."

Crispy, tasty, and crunchy.

"I have never eaten a rabbit's head and I'm not going to eat one now."

"Don't you dare refuse," said Fei.

Tiao looked at the rabbit's head, bit off half of the ear, and chewed. It was true; it was indeed crispy, tasty, and crunchy. Many years later, when Fei was sick and really wanted to nibble on a rabbit's head, Tiao searched all over Fuan in vain. The snack had gone out of fashion; its shape and surprisingly cheap price were like a dream. A rabbit's head for three cents, the price of a popsicle; had such a thing really existed in this world? They both chewed on the crispy, tasty, and crunchy rabbit ears; Tiao's mouth got extremely messy. She looked at Fei, whose lips were still so bright and clean. Anyone could see that she treated her mouth especially well and that she really knew how to eat. With anything that entered her mouth, she was very careful, but not with what came out, like what she had said about Tiao's mom.

2

Before she met Fei, Tiao was often lonely at school. Fuan was a different place from Beijing. The teachers here asked the students to use Mandarin in class, but after class everyone spoke Fuan dialect, including the teachers. Tiao, as a newcomer, had been called on twice to read aloud; the teacher complimented her standard, clearly pronounced Mandarin and fluent reading, which made a lot of girls jealous. She wanted to participate in their activities: hopscotch, rubber-band jumping, jump rope, sandbag toss, and sheep-bone grab, but they didn't let her. "What is that language that you're talking?" they asked. "We don't get it." They said "thayat" instead of "that" and "doan" instead of "don't." And even the "o" in "don't" sounded more like a combination of "ah" and "oh." So "don't" came out in a drawl. They talked to her in a thick provincial accent, pretending they didn't understand her even though they knew perfectly well what she was saying, and then they accused her of playing high and mighty with them. Although she was disdainful of the strange Fuan dialect, she feared being left out and was desperate to join the group. She tried to change her pronunciation, but it was awkward and strange, making them laugh in her face and discouraging her from talking at all. She kept to herself quietly, waiting for the days to drag on and the bell to ring at the end of the last class.

But even her silence didn't satisfy them. They saw it as a challenge that made them feel more uncomfortable than her begging to join their group. So they tried to provoke her. They often came up behind her suddenly when she was sitting at her desk staring into space and shouted, "Hey, do you have mung bean cake? Do you have mung bean cake?" She was confused and didn't know how to respond. But their expressions were urgent, as if they were expecting to grab a mung bean cake from her hand immediately. So she would hurriedly answer, "No, I don't have mung bean cake."

"Oh, really, now, you don't have mung bean cake!" they would exclaim.

"Do you have egg cake? Do you have egg cake?" they would ask immediately.

"No, I don't have egg cake," she would answer again sincerely.

"Oh, really now, after all this you don't have egg cake!" they would exclaim.

They were so pleased with themselves for making her fall for their tricks that they broke into squeals of laughter. It was so much fun that they kept it up all day long, repeatedly asking her for mung bean cake or egg cake. Tiao finally caught on, but she didn't really appreciate this kind of "cleverness" and didn't think their antics were funny. She believed this sort of clowning was low-class and she looked down on them, although she herself didn't have any highbrow jokes as a comeback.

She also didn't like the hairdo popular in Fuan then: two braids, tight and low, starting at the earlobe, and so short that, seen from the front, they seemed to stick out of the cheeks like the two legs of an alarm clock, which was why the style was called Little Alarm Clock. She wore the Little Alarm Clock style for a few days, so that she could look like her classmates, though her mother said this provincial hairstyle did nothing for her; it didn't make her look younger or older, nor did it make her look more like a country girl or a city girl. Wu hauled her in front of the mirror and said, "Look at yourself." She told Tiao to change her hair immediately, even if it meant wearing common pigtails, tied with rubber bands. Tiao shared her mother's opinion on the subject, puzzled at why such an ugly style would become popular in Fuan. She changed her hair from Little Alarm Clock to pigtails as if to announce her determination to be different, to stand on her own. Then Fei entered her life. Fei didn't wear the Little Alarm Clock hairstyle and didn't drawl. On the contrary, she grew out her hair to the maximum length allowed back then—shoulder-length. She wore her braids loosely, and had her bangs curling wildly on her forehead, giving her the look of a revolutionary fighter, a combination of languor and high spirits. She taught Tiao the trick to curling bangs—wetting the hair before bedtime, and then rolling it on black steel clips, around and around, one after another. When the clips came off the next morning, the bangs would be curled like a perm and last the whole day.

Tiao performed the experiment with her bangs and they did curl, and she looked at herself in the mirror and felt she resembled a doll she'd had in childhood, so cute and lively. She was afraid to go to school with curled bangs, so she could only demonstrate at home in front of Fan. Fan said happily, "Show off, new bride, / shake your butt from side to side. / Show off, foreign shrew, / hands on hips, strutting through." She said this children's rhyme in Fuan dialect, which was usually the way children shouted it at women who wore unusual clothes, something that people like Fei would often hear. In the middle school Fei attended, she heard worse words than these. Had such words been applied to Tiao, she would have killed herself, but Fei could scoff at words. She poked at her face and said to Tiao, "My skin is thicker than a city wall. Hmm, I would like to see them try that stuff on me." A loner with no friends, Fei played things light and loose, but she had a strength of her own, which attracted and inspired Tiao, making her feel there was something she could rely on. When she thought about the rejection of her classmates and their stupid pranks, she was glad to be left alone to drift around with Fei.

When Tiao graduated from elementary school, she and Fei happened to be in the same middle school. They grew closer and saw each other more frequently.

The families who lived in the Architectural Design Academy were doing a side job now, binding *The Selected Works of Chairman Mao*. The book was eight-by-ten and used high-quality, extra-white dictionary paper, and fine strong nylon thread. The families stitched the pages into covers with the nylon thread, and they were paid five cents per volume. The binding had originally been done at the printing factory, but since the book was in great demand at the time and the workload kept increasing, the factory outsourced part of the process, just as the foreign export trading units did in the nineties, giving embroidery and knitting to housewives. A woman in their complex worked in the factory, which was how the families got the job. They liked it very much; binding *The Selected Works of Chairman Mao* was a sacred task to begin with, not to mention the money they made. What's more, the sewing also enriched their drab lives. When the job came in summer, groups of sewing women were all over the place, in front of the buildings and under the shade of trees. Old women with poor eyesight kept trying to get their grandchildren, just back from school, to help them thread needles and mark places in the books' spines with the teeth of special small steel saws to make it easy to push the needles through. The scene was very peaceful, viewed from afar, a courtyard of women, old and young alike, burying their heads in sewing.

Women must embroider and sew, they must, to make a living, for their families, and even more, to suppress their wild natures. It served to kill spare time as well as to add color to their pale lives. So when the flatbed tricycle pulled the unprocessed books into the complex, the adults and the children would cheer. Even Fan would use the ugly Fuan dialect to shout at the top of her lungs in front of the building, "The job's here. The job's here." Really, what did the "job" have to do with her? Why was she always so enthusiastic about everything in the world? Was it because she was so enthusiastic as a child that she would become so angry as an adult, after she had gone to America?

Wu didn't take on work like this herself, nor did she allow Tiao to participate. She had contempt for this kind of thing, and she didn't plan to let her own children do child labor, which meant that Tiao had more free time. Whenever she passed the sewing crowds in the complex as she went to look for Fei, girls her own age or older were holding *The Selected Works of Chairman Mao* and attentively wrestling with needle and thread, along with their grandmothers, making asterisks of crisscrossed threads on the thick spines.

Tiao didn't sew this "treasured red book," nor did Fei. They were intent on other things, such as calling on pretty women. One day Fei said, "I want to take you to see the head nurse of internal medicine at People's Hospital. I bet you've never seen anyone as good-looking as she is." They went to the hospital and Fei pointed her out in the hallway of the internal medicine ward. She was probably about fifty years old then. A nun from the old society before 1949 who had worked in the church hospital, she had been suspected of being a spy and was no longer the head nurse. Her daily job now was to clean the hallway and the bathrooms of the ward. She wore old light blue clothes and was squatting by a wall to scrape saliva stains and spots of filth off it. When she sensed Tiao and Fei standing behind her, she turned her head to them.

What a beautiful face, Tiao thought, beauty from a bygone age. But what left a deep impression on Tiao was not the woman's beauty, but her unusually serene expression. In the noisy, messy hallway of the internal medicine ward, she assumed a humble squatting position and faced a wall full of saliva stains. Gray hair clustered around her face, but she didn't seem sad or worried. What made her treat spit stains with such care? Really such a beautiful face, looking up from the foot of a dirty wall, so serene and detached. Tiao never forgot that face.

They left the internal medicine ward and went out to walk in the courtyard. Besides having to work as a janitor, the woman often underwent denouncement. "But she doesn't look like a spy at all," Tiao observed.

"I don't want to believe she is a spy, either," said Fei, "but she confessed the passwords. They had passwords. My uncle told me that."

"What are their passwords?" Tiao asked nervously.

Fei said, "When someone came to contact her, the head nurse would ask, 'Where does the mermaid's fishnet come from?' The other one would answer, 'From the ocean.'"

Where does the mermaid's fishnet come from? That was it; that was exactly the sort of thing spies would say. Although neither Tiao nor Fei knew what a spy's passwords would be, they both felt the head nurse's passwords fit. The words were so mysterious and romantic, yet shadowy and frightening at the same time, so erotic and tender, but also having the scent of death about them. They couldn't help repeating them a few times. Fei lowered her voice and said to Tiao, "Where does the mermaid's fishnet come from?"

"From the ocean," Tiao answered immediately, also lowering her voice.

"Where does the mermaid's fishnet come from?"

"From the ocean."

They said the passwords back and forth several times, spellbound. Then they looked at each other and were suddenly frightened, as if they had turned into spies in the blink of an eye and would be drowned in the ocean of the people's war. They looked around—there was no one nearby, but they took to their legs and ran as fast as they could, as if saying a spy's passwords in a deserted place made them look suspicious and dangerous. They ran to the hospital's outpatient department, which was dense with people. They maneuvered through the crowd, but Tiao was not ready to leave yet; she wanted Fei to take her to see the head nurse one more time.

They came to the internal medicine ward again and the head nurse was still squatting by the wall, scraping with a small knife. Though this time Tiao's desire to see her was even stronger than before, she didn't dare get too near. The passwords proved the woman was an actual spy, and Tiao was a little panicked. She suddenly felt that the reason for them to keep coming to see her was to respond to the password. The head nurse would take them by surprise by turning that seemingly serene face to them and say, "Where does the mermaid's fishnet come from?"

They would answer: "From the ocean."

They eventually left before the head nurse turned around. Tiao sighed, saying she didn't believe the serene expression on the head nurse's face was fake. What she didn't know was that the head nurse had actually made up the passwords when the torture became unbearable, and she was willing to confess to anything to make her confession convincing. The passwords she made up were so poetic; she satisfied people's curiosity with these poetic fantasies and was regarded as a spy forever.

3

Then Youyou came into their lives. Youyou was not the mermaid's fishnet, and she didn't come from the ocean; she was in the same class as Tiao.

She'd gotten into trouble almost as soon as she entered middle school. She was called on by her language arts teacher to recite Chairman Mao's quotations by heart. Memorizing and copying Chairman Mao's quotations was a part of the language arts classes then. She had to memorize the part about revolution: "A revolution is not inviting friends to dinner, not writing an essay . . ." She stood up and recited by heart: "A revolution is inviting friends to dinner, is . . ." "Stop! Stop!" said the teacher. Youyou stopped and found her classmates were all covering their mouths and laughing. The teacher knocked on the desk with a bamboo pointer and said, "What are you laughing at? Meng Youyou, do you know you recited Chairman Mao's quotation wrong?" Youyou nodded her head and said she knew, but when the teacher asked her to start over she just couldn't open her mouth anymore. She was so afraid she might get it wrong again. Because she refused to open her mouth, the teacher had no choice but to let her sit down. What if she had gotten it wrong again? Who would be held responsible for such an incident? Probably not Meng Youyou; she was only thirteen. The teacher would have to take responsibility. From then on, the teacher never called on Youyou in class again; she believed the child was either stupid or actually retarded.

Tiao and Youyou took the same route home from school. Soon Tiao discovered that Youyou lived in the same complex as she did. They hadn't met before because they had not been in the same elementary school, and now that she found that they were in the same class and complex, Tiao wanted to make an effort to get to know her. She didn't look down on her at all, believing that even though reciting Chairman Mao's quotations wrong was dishonorable, Youyou hadn't done it on purpose. She was just a little careless. She also wanted to talk to her because Youyou spoke Beijing dialect, not Fuan. Tiao hurried after Youyou and called to her, "Hey, Youyou, wait a second."

Her greeting sounded like an old friend's, but the two hadn't spoken before. Youyou, who was walking ahead of Tiao, stopped after she heard the greeting, waiting for Tiao as if she were an old friend. Youyou stood there, a thirteen-year-old with a tendency to put on weight, or, one could say, she was already a fat young girl. She had skin as smooth and pale as butter, short hair, and large breasts. Yet nothing about her seemed sexual, perhaps because of her innocent, cheerful face.

From the very beginning, they communicated with ease and needed no small talk because they instinctively liked the look of each other. They started from "Revolution is not inviting friends over for dinner." Youyou said, "I'm actually not as stupid as the teacher thinks. Yes, I recited the quotation wrong, but think about it carefully: If revolution is not inviting friends over for dinner, what is revolution for?"

What is revolution for? This was a question that Tiao had never considered before. Now this Youyou who looked so carefree on the surface got her thinking. "Revolution . . ." Youyou said, "revolution at the very least ought to allow people to invite friends over for dinner."

"But Chairman Mao said revolution was an uprising," Tiao said.

"Exactly. If the people uprising don't have food, how will they have strength to rise up?" Youyou said. "I'm afraid of being hungry— it scares me more than anything. If someone gives me a mouthful of food, I call him Grandpa."

Tiao couldn't help smiling, because of Youyou's big heart, and because of her strange talk about revolution. Youyou pleased and surprised her. As they walked side by side, arriving at Building Number 6,

Youyou had already put her cool, plump arm around Tiao's shoulder. She whispered to Tiao, intimately and naturally, "Tiao, I really want you to know that I don't blame our classmates for avoiding me. I'm a backward person. I just think the best thing to do is to sleep when your eyes are closed, and to eat when your eyes are open. So, guess what I want to be when I grow up? I want to be a chef. How much good stuff is there for a chef to do? A chef spends the day either treating people to food or eating it. Have you seen the movie called *Satisfied or Not Satisfied*? It's about a chef. Someday I'll put on the tall white cap that the chefs wear! Don't tell anybody. I know you won't."

How clever and lovely you are, Youyou! Tiao thought. Although Tiao had never thought about becoming a chef when she grew up, her passion for food wasn't any less than Youyou's. She and Youyou shared the same dangerous tastes, but she could never express herself so thoroughly, so bluntly and truthfully, so . . . so corruptly and decadently. Right in the middle of a revolution that was an uprising, here they were, talking about giving a dinner party and wearing a chef's white cap. This was the pursuit of the corrupt and decadent lifestyle of the bourgeois; this was corruption and decadence itself. Tiao couldn't help agreeing with Youyou's philosophy while at the same time criticizing herself in her heart. She very much wanted to enjoy corruption with Youyou secretly, to experience decadence secretly.

They reluctantly said goodbye to each other. Although Youyou lived in Building Number 2, the same one as Chen Zai, only four buildings away from Tiao, they still felt reluctant to part, a feeling that Tiao would never again experience with a friend in her life.

Youyou was going to give a dinner party. One day early in winter, after school, she invited Tiao to come to a banquet at her house on Sunday. She chose Sunday because she would be the only one home. Her parents were in the Reed River Farm, like Tiao's father. Normally, her grandmother stayed with her, but Youyou's aunt had recently given birth to a child and her grandma had gone to look after the baby, so Youyou was the only one left at home.

She was happy to stay home alone; first of all, she didn't have to answer her grandma's gabby, irrelevant questions. Grandma loved to listen to the radio, but she often misunderstood what was on it. The radio always broadcast the news of whom the great leader had just met, and that "the meeting took place in a cordial and friendly atmosphere." Grandma would ask, "Youyou, how come this cordial and friendly meeting only lasted for seven minutes?" She also mistook Nixon for "onion" and said, "Youyou, how come they call a big shot like him an onion?" Now that Grandma was away, Youyou, with her intense devotion, could take over the kitchen.

People's food back then was simple and boring, so their kitchens were bare and basic. Although born with a passion for food, Youyou hadn't seen much by way of gourmet cooking, nor did she have much money. But even with a single yuan in her pocket, she had the confidence to invite friends for dinner.

She spent fifty cents to buy a piece of streaky pork. She sliced off the skin and cooked it on low heat for several hours. When the skin quivered and turned fluffy and soft and the juice thickened, Youyou added soy sauce and chopped scallions, set it aside to cool and congeal, and she had jelly from pork skin, a dish called pork skin aspic—done. She then diced the fatty pork, coated it in flour batter, and fried it in oil (the diced pork burned because there was not enough oil), and the crystal pork was done. To be eaten dipped in salt and pepper.

She fished out some dried wood-ear mushrooms and daylily buds from the kitchen cabinet, soaked them open, and used leftover pork to make muxi pork—another dish done.

She wanted to serve four dishes and a soup, so she spent two cents on a piece of pressed crabapple cake. She shredded white turnip and sliced the cake. White turnip mixed with red crabapple cake, delicious even to the eye. She then made a bowl of dried shrimp soup with soy sauce. Now the banquet, for which she had spent a total of fifty-two cents, was complete. Lastly, she grilled a handful of rice noodles on the stove for decoration. This was her own invention and ahead of its time—clear rice noodles that would puff up and whiten after being grilled, nicely crunchy, like the puffed food that would become popular in the eighties.

Tiao came for the banquet and brought Fei along. Youyou felt honored to have a great beauty like Fei at dinner. She believed the gourmet food she created was intended for someone like her, and only a great beauty was worthy of it.

The three of them sat down to enjoy Youyou's cooking. At Fei's suggestion, they even drank some wine, which was really water. When the girls heard that Youyou had spent only fifty-two cents on such a big table of gourmet food, they couldn't help praising her as a culinary genius, a genius who could turn lead into gold. Fei gulped the wine, gobbled up the pork skin aspic and the turnip, and munched on the crispy rice noodles. She ate and drank until her body slumped and her eyes went hazy. Youyou and Tiao helped her lie down on the bed. She lay on her side with her face propped up on an elbow and said, "Youyou, you have a really nice place, I wouldn't mind staying here forever." She looked so pretty at that moment, like a princess or a queen, that Tiao and Youyou, who stood beside the bed, were willing to serve her with all their hearts.

When every scrap of food was gone, they started to discuss the menu for their next banquet. Tiao said, "My dad knows how to do a dessert called grilled miniature snowballs." Youyou said, "Wait, wait, grilled miniature snowballs? That sounds wonderful. Just by the name I can tell it's unusual. Who would have imagined? Can snowballs be grilled?" She wanted Tiao to tell her every detail of the recipe for grilled miniature snowballs, but Tiao couldn't remember it all, so she promised Youyou she would look it up when she got home.

How exciting it would be to make grilled snowballs! It got Tiao enthusiastically searching for old magazines at home. Even though there were not many left, she remembered that when they moved from Beijing, Wu had kept a few copies of the Chinese edition of *Soviet Woman*, selling or discarding the rest. A magazine that Wu used to subscribe to, *Soviet Woman* introduced different styles of cooking, knitting, cosmetics and grooming, and fashion. Wu loved the knitting and fashion sections in the magazine—it was where she had found many of her sweater patterns—but had no interest in the food. When a holiday came, it was Yixun who created novelty dishes from the magazines. He successfully made the grilled snowballs, the magic of which Tiao would never forget. She came back to rummage through the books and magazines, taking advantage of Wu's absence. Wu must have gone to People's Hospital to see Dr. Tang, but Tiao found herself less concerned about that than she had been. It was definitely not because she'd gotten more accepting of Dr. Tang, but because she now had her own friends, friendships that were more important to her than the relationship between Wu and Dr. Tang.

She searched for the issues of *Soviet Woman* at home, and Fan, just back from school, helped her until they finally found them. Tiao knew that to carry around this kind of magazine was illegal, and that it would be subject to confiscation, which was exactly why she had the excitement and vigilance of a secret agent. She wrapped the magazines in newspapers, hid them in a big backpack, and then dragged Fan along with her to Youyou's place.

She came through the door and signaled Youyou to lock it behind her. Youyou bolted the door and tiptoed to sit beside Tiao, patiently waiting for her to show her the *Soviet Woman* magazines. Tiao opened the backpack, took one of the illustrated magazines out of the newspaper wrapping, turned to a page, and read aloud, word for word: "Nothing could be better than following your holiday lunch with a delicious, easily digested dessert like grilled miniature snowballs.

"Mix powdered sugar and citric acid into egg white that has been beaten into foam, then dip a soup spoon in cold water, scoop up the egg white batter, one spoonful at a time, and drop into the boiling milk. Don't let the balls stick together. These balls of egg white and citric acid will then absorb some milk and react chemically with it to form miniature snowballs. Cook the snowballs for three minutes, gently scoop them up with a straining ladle, and then put them in a colander. When the miniature snowballs dry, serve on a plate with syrup. Take care not to let them stick together.

"Syrup: Carefully mix egg yolk and sugar and beat well. Add a soup spoon of flour and pour the batter into boiling milk. Keep stirring as it cooks, until the syrup begins to thicken. Add vanilla, stir, set aside to cool.

"To make miniature snowballs, you'll need two egg whites, 30 cubic centimeters of sugar powder, 30 cubic centimeters of citric acid, and 200 cubic centimeters of milk. To make the syrup, you'll need 100 cubic centimeters of milk, 100 cubic centimeters of sugar, and one egg yolk. The quantity of vanilla will vary according to taste."

What Tiao read aloud struck Youyou with awe. Although many things in the recipe, such as vanilla, citric acid, and sugar powder, were mysterious to her, she had the superior intuition of the world's gourmets. Her intuition involved her sense of smell, taste, and touch, and allowed her to come to the conclusion that the grilled miniature snowballs must be flavorful, rich, mellow, and delicious. Her pork skin aspic and crystal pork were nothing compared to the snowballs; they were not on the same level—didn't belong in the same world. But she was not intimidated; she believed she could make the dish. She asked what a cubic centimeter was, and Tiao said one cubic centimeter was a gram. Now Youyou became more confident—an experienced chef always pays attention to details. Her other questions concerned where she could find the ingredients. Youyou didn't drink milk, and there were only egg, sugar, and flour in her house. Tiao said, "That's no problem. We still have citric acid and vanilla. We also have milk. Fan and I drink half a *jin* of milk every day, which we can save for snowballs. Doesn't the magazine say it takes only three hundred cubic centimeters? Three hundred cubic centimeters are three hundred grams, not even a *jin*, which is five hundred. Fan, what do you think?"

Fan nodded vigorously. She knew contributing half a *jin* of milk would be worth it, because they would definitely invite her to eat the miniature snowballs.

4

These copies of the Chinese edition of *Soviet Woman*, slightly dog-eared and hard to put down, were Tiao, Fei, and Youyou's spiritual food for a long time.

They used Youyou's house as a stronghold, reading and practicing recipes over and over without getting bored. With Tiao's help, Youyou successfully made grilled miniature snowballs. When they stood in front of the briquet stove, cheek to cheek, and watched the egg white batter drop into the boiling milk and absorb enough to form the snowballs, they almost wept with excitement. They felt like they had reached a new level, where they were not just display-ing craft, but art, great art. They held the spoons, gently placing the snow-white balls, along with light yellow syrup, into their mouths, onto their tongues, letting their tongues surround and taste them. They held their breath to chew and savor. They had a real feeling for it and it had feeling for them, as well. It gave fragrance to their mouths and stomachs and its rich flavor told them life could be very beautiful. Youyou would never go back to cooking those puffed rice noodles and crystal pork; her ambition now was to try out all the best recipes in *Soviet Woman.* Tiao went right along with Youyou's ambi-tion, generously providing all the ingredients that she could possibly find, items she had hidden from Wu, such as curry powder, cinna-mon, bay leaf, whole white pepper, spiced soy sauce, tomato sauce, citric acid, vanilla, etc. . . . Almost every one of them was put to use at their stronghold for eating and drinking.

They didn't spend their pocket money anymore; they saved it, one cent at a time. When they had saved enough, they shared the cost of buying fish, meat, fruit, eggs, and sugar. *Soviet Woman* calmed them, and they no longer minded the indifference of their teachers and classmates, the on-again-off-again classes, and the heavy physi-cal labor—after they entered middle school they often went to dig air-raid shelters, and sometimes mixed dirt and water into molds for no apparent reason. They would come home muddy and wet. After they washed, they went right to Youyou's house, where *Soviet Woman* was waiting.

They studied and then made Armenian grilled pork patties: Mix ground pork, egg yolk, salt, pepper, and chopped onions together and make patties; sprinkle flour on the patties and brush with egg. Then sprinkle bread crumbs on the patties, put them in the oven, and bake for fifteen minutes. Use meat broth to make tomato sauce, according to the recipe as follows: Add tomato sauce to the meat broth and boil. Add MSG, salt, and a little flour or cornstarch. Finally, put the grilled pork patties on a plate and pour the sauce over them. They didn't have an oven, but Youyou hit on the idea that she could substitute frying for grilling, spreading oil on the patties and using a low flame. They tasted very good.

There were also Tbilisi pickles, Italian wine fish stew, Hungarian cabbage stew, Ukraine red cabbage soup, Cantonese tomato barbecued pork, and Hangzhou barbecued pork. They felt particularly close to the Chinese dishes introduced in *Soviet Woman*. But for grilled and fried game, they felt totally at sea. Because they had no way to get game, they made fun of the illustrations in the cooking section: a rabbit holds a knife in one hand and a fork in the other, explaining to the readers how to cook and eat delicious game. It was like a person enthusiastically telling others how to kill him and make him as delicious as possible.

Once in a while, they would try to make some snacks: Russian sweet bread, sugar and honey pancake, and curry beef turnover. Some recipes required "marshmallow cream," and they immediately studied the instructions and searched for the ingredients to make it: cream, gelatin, egg white, sugar, caramel, water, and vanilla. To make marshmallow cream you mix these ingredients together and beat for a long time until it becomes fluffy. Cream, gelatin, and caramel were the things that were most difficult to find, and the stores in Fuan just didn't sell this kind of stuff. Youyou remembered that the mother of one of her elementary school classmates worked in a food processing factory, so she went to talk to her. Her classmate's mother said, "Our factory does have these things, but what do you need them for?"

Youyou said, "My grandma is sick and the doctor gave her this folk prescription, which requires only these three things. Just a little, a little bit of each of them." But even a little cost money. The food processing factory was government-run, so Youyou used her back-door connections and spent a vast sum of money, 1.40 yuan, to buy cream, gelatin, and caramel. She and Tiao took turns beating the mixture, using chopsticks, the way they beat eggs. It was really hard work. When Tiao thought about it years later, she felt that mixing these watery ingredients and beating them into a snow-white, fluffy cream was nothing short of a miracle. She'd kept at it with Youyou's encouragement. They beat the mixture for almost an hour, until their arms were sore and their vision was blurred, but, at last, they succeeded. The sticky fluid finally turned into fragrant cream! Ah, marshmallow cream!

There was a sumptuous spread in the "Home-Style Kitchen" section that particularly interested Youyou. Actually, it was only a few examples of cold dishes with fruit and vegetables. It read: The dishes you make should be both tasty and attractive. Using ingredients like fresh cucumber, green peas, sliced boiled eggs, green onions, and tomatoes, you can put together an attractive dish. In early autumn, vegetables are abundant, so homemakers can easily prepare a variety of delicious and appealing dishes.

Below are recipes from Vladimir Lepushin, head chef of Moscow's Metropol Hotel.

1. Festive Appetizer (Cold Dish): First, cut cooked wild fowl into thin slices, and then take fresh potatoes, green peas, cauliflower, and celery stalks, and dice after boiling. Thinly slice both cucumber and tomatoes into the same thickness, then combine all of these, adding salt and dressing (mix vegetable oil, egg yolk, and, according to taste, add mustard and vinegar, and whisk together). Then your appetizer is done. Next, arrange your appetizer in the following manner: In a tall, footed bowl, stack the ingredients in layers, making a tower shape, and drizzle with the dressing. Then on top of the tower place a hollowed-out chili pepper, and on its carved-out tip place an olive (or a small plum) and then surround the tower with olives (or plums), and around this arrange fresh apple and cucumber slices with their edges cut in a zigzag shape. On these slices place more olives, and finally around the outer edge of the bowl garnish with fresh lettuce leaves.

2. Apple Cup: Carve out most of the flesh of an apple to form a shell in the shape of a cup, then take the small pieces of carved-out apple, along with fresh cucumber, boiled carrot, green peas, and cabbage, and combine, adding dressing, and place back into the apple shell. Put the apples on a platter and surround with lettuce leaves, lemon slices, and rings of sliced chili pepper.

3. Little Basket: Take a large cucumber, scoop out the core, and carve into an oval-shaped basket. In the interior of the small basket you can add cold vegetables. Using a green onion, fashion a handle for the small basket. Around the small basket arrange cabbage leaves, and on top of the leaves you can place balls carved from carrots and fresh cucumbers.

Youyou attentively studied the three examples described and felt that the "Festive Appetizer" was not achievable. The wild fowl and olives would be impossible to get, and furthermore, the whole process seemed too complicated, like culinary acrobatics. The "Little Basket," however, was feasible. Cucumbers, green onions, carrots, and cabbage were all easy to find. She then started carefully sculpting the "Little Basket."

Tiao was not interested in any of the "garnishing" techniques in cuisine. As an adult, every time she saw those "realistic" peacocks and flowers carved out of carrots and turnips, or goldfish made out of preserved eggs on a banquet table, she would respond with disgust at the showy bad taste. She thought that for a chef to spend so much time and effort on these decorations was not only unnecessary but simply a useless sidetrack of culinary art. That was why she didn't applaud Youyou's "Little Basket," even though Youyou crafted an exquisite version with her inspired hands and a paring knife.

Fei had her own amusements at the time. She leafed through the pages of photos in *Soviet Woman* for the fashions:

> This coat, with gold print, has raglan sleeves and
> no buttons. The skirt and lining are made of pale
> mauve silk.

Gorgeous two-piece dress, waist-length, with form-fitting top.

Woolen dress with white and green stripes, set-in sleeves. Skirt pleated along the stripes.

Boating clothes. Tank top, pants made of pea-green waterproof material, and a deep blue jacket with black and white stripes.

Fei devoured the fashions in the magazines, sure she would look very pretty in any of the outfits, particularly the boating clothes. It was *Soviet Woman* that first informed her that boating involved special clothing. How professional and romantic it made a pastime like boating look! Fei told Tiao what she thought and Tiao agreed with her. During a period in which no one could tell women's clothes from men's, everything they saw seemed beyond luxury. They stared at those clothes obsessively, so absorbed that they couldn't help fantasizing that they could lift them right off the page and try them on. There was a black evening gown with flared skirt called "Cairo Night," worn by a model with bare shoulders and a slender waist, which Fei couldn't resist imitating. She put down the magazine, walked to the door, and took down a black raincoat that belonged to Youyou's father, conveniently hanging on the back of it.

She ducked into the bathroom with the raincoat. When she came out, she was "Cairo Night," her braids coiled on the back of her head and her beautiful, smooth shoulders exposed. She caught the black raincoat below her shoulders and above her breasts, showing off her sculpted collarbones. She clutched the clothes tightly at her chest to keep the raincoat from slipping down. Ah, "Cairo Night," both Tiao and Youyou clapped for her. Just then she played a little trick, suddenly loosening her grip and letting the raincoat fall. She stood naked in front of her two friends. Perhaps she hadn't really done it on purpose; or perhaps she wanted them to see that body of hers, so mature and worldly. How many secrets her body kept from them!

Youyou screamed and Tiao laughed. Smiling, Fei calmly put her clothes back on. Next, she did their makeup for dinner. It was accomplished very simply: the only thing necessary was lipstick. She tore off and moistened a small strip of red paper, telling them to take the paper between their teeth and press down with their lips. The red of the paper was printed on their lips. Their faces immediately radiated seduction. They sat down to dine with red lips, putting on pretentious airs. "I'll have the Ukraine red cabbage soup," Tiao said to Youyou. And Youyou, wearing a tall homemade chef's hat, waited on her attentively. Fei stuck out her pinkie and made a special request for Tbilisi pickles. She pinched a cigarette, a real cigarette, between her fingers while she ordered. They ate, drank, and then wanted to hear a story. Their stomachs had been tended, now it was their minds' turn. The storytelling was usually left up to Tiao.

Tiao looked at Youyou, and then turned to Fei. Ah, what a perfect arrangement, with her in the middle savoring the gourmet food and admiring the lovely chef on her left and the beautiful girl on her right. She was the perfect storyteller. What else did she need? She started to tell a story she had read in *Soviet Woman*, the issue that had the "Little Basket" recipe.

It was actually a very ordinary story. A girl named Genia is sulking and giving her fiancé, Mischa, a hard time on their outing. For the whole day, Mischa tries all sorts of things to cheer Genia up, but fails. One moment he's making faces, the next he's telling stories, and after that he's singing songs—songs that Genia loves, but still she pouts. So, during their dinner at a small restaurant, Mischa flirts with a girl sitting at the next table, to make Genia jealous. That was all that happened in the story, according to Tiao. She thought the story was boring; she was interested only in the jealousy part. From the story, Tiao got the impression that emotion sometimes had to be indirect: a man loves a woman, but occasionally he has to make the woman he loves jealous by flirting with another woman. If she gets jealous, it proves that she loves and values him. A man has to use this roundabout way, approaching other women, to love the woman he loves. This way of testing the feeling, Mischa's jealousy method, had a subtle attraction for Tiao. How troublesome and intricate the relationship between men and women could be! But what did jealousy feel like?

It took time and energy to get jealous and to make people jealous. Jealousy, this bitter, delicate, sharp feeling, perhaps had something primitive about it, an antique foolishness; an emotion out of the Era of Steam. Jealousy would have no place in the nineties. There would be no time for anything, no time to laugh or cry, to win or lose at love, no time for heart-to-heart talks, no time to get jealous or to work up the courage to duel. The nineties were an era without rivalry in love. This was what Tiao would believe as an adult. If rivalry in love didn't exist anymore, who could make you jealous?

But right then, in the seventies, the girls with red-paper-dyed lips still discussed jealousy.

"Would you get jealous, Youyou?"

"Would you get jealous, Tiao?"

"Would you get jealous, Fei?"

Fei said, "I won't get jealous, but I'll make others jealous of me."

5

Fei always seemed different from others, and she was different. When Tiao and Youyou talked about whether they would get jealous or not, Fei was thinking about making others jealous of her; when Tiao and Youyou sighed for lives like those in the movies, Fei told them, "I am a movie."

I am a movie.

I am a movie. A grand statement that only the bold and lovely could make. Nothing seemed to frighten Fei. Was it true that any woman who'd found love could be as arrogant and spoiled as Fei?

She liked men, and she liked to make men like her. Fifteen-year-old Fei already had a steady boyfriend, an upperclassman at her school nicknamed Captain Sneakers. The boy had several followers, all of whom shaved their heads and wore white sneakers and the same kind of clothing. They disrupted classes and gave the teachers trouble in school, and outside of school they ran riot, getting involved in gang fights. People called them the White Sneaker Gang.

Captain Sneakers got to know Fei through a sort of abduction.

One evening when Fei was on her way home, he and several of his gang members trailed her slowly on their bikes, and she couldn't get away from them. She pretended to walk calmly, aware of being stalked by these older boys. It was threatening even though they rode their bikes very slowly. Their speed was a warning not to try to escape by running because her legs couldn't outrun their wheels. So she dismissed the idea of running, and walked even more slowly instead. She glanced at Captain Sneakers out of the corner of her eye, his bald head and his strong body; she could hear his slightly nervous breathing. At school he was a figure of fear for everyone, and girls would lower their heads when they encountered him, as if he might immediately pounce. He had never pounced on any of them, and he actually liked Fei, sincerely. Fei walked slowly, not knowing what would happen but not really afraid; not knowing what would happen but eager for it, whatever it was. His nervous breathing puzzled her a little, her heart telling her that something should perhaps have happened already, but she didn't know what. They were about to reach People's Hospital. The streetlights were lit, but the darkness of the shadow-covered sidewalk seemed only to deepen. The gang members formed a half circle around her on the sidewalk with their bikes and he said, "Hey, get up behind me on my bike and let me take you somewhere."

His voice didn't sound evil or threatening, so she lifted herself onto his bike. The gang spread out in a line across the street and rode crazily as if they were flying. He roared back to Fei on the seat behind him, "Hold on to my waist." She reached her hands around and held on to his strong waist, feeling flashes of dizziness. It was the first time that she had held a man by the waist, a strange man, which made her seem brash and shameless, and she enjoyed the feeling. The crazy pedaling of the bicycle, the speed and the movement of the cyclist's waist and legs, all gave her an unexpected joy, a pleasure she'd never known. What would she be doing if she weren't doing this? She had been bored to death, already bored to death for so long.

The boys rode their bicycles wildly until they got to a gray, bare residential building. The rest of the gang stopped outside, but Captain Sneakers locked his bike and brought Fei upstairs. He opened an apartment door with a key and locked it as soon as they entered, leaving the light off. Then he lunged toward her, grabbing her, forcing her back, step by step—back through a small hallway, past the bathroom and the kitchen, into a room that looked like a bedroom, and into the corner. Her heart beat loudly with a *thud, thud, thud*, and his breath puffed on her face, exciting her beyond words. She was finding it difficult to breathe, so she opened her mouth, hoping to ease her breathlessness with words. "What do you want to do?" she said.

Suddenly he pressed against her hard with his body, grinding out the words through his teeth: "I want to fuck you. The first fucking time I saw you, I . . . you knew I wanted it for so long. Tell me, do you want it, too? Tell me you . . ." He sought out her mouth with his as he spoke, but she twisted and turned her head to avoid him. Even though those hot, naked obscenities of his dizzied her like blows to the head, she resolutely guarded her mouth. No man would ever kiss her mouth, as long as she lived.

He reached out trying to steady her head with his hands, growing more and more determined to kiss her, so she grabbed his wrists and put his hands on her breasts. He stopped trying for her mouth and began to tear at her blouse. Inexperienced with women, trembling, he ripped her blouse. Finally, he touched her warm, small, firm breasts and rubbed them, roughly making her hiss with pain. Unable to wait any longer, he pulled her to the bed and pushed her down. As he was taking off his clothes, he said, "Don't worry. Don't worry. This is my parents' bed and they're not home." After taking off his own clothes, he fumbled in the dark for hers. He was surprised to find she was naked already. When he reached out to her, he touched her smooth, slightly trembling thighs. He didn't despise her, then or later, for removing her clothes herself. On the contrary, he was grateful. He liked Fei's directness and honesty, compared to those phony girls who half refused and half went along. Unfortunately, at the age of eighteen, he didn't know how to show his appreciation.

Her desire had been truly stirred by then. Seduced by his wild excitement, and without fear, her body welcomed his weight and the hardness that made her sweat with pain. She didn't know what love was, and, in fact, she never loved Captain Sneakers. She just wanted him to handle her in this way, as if it made her more thoroughly degenerate, and meanwhile allowed her to raise her head more proudly.

The whole school soon became aware of her relationship with Captain Sneakers, so she sat on his bike holding him around the waist more naturally. She asked him for cigarettes, Big Wheels, seventeen cents a pack. The girls in her class wouldn't talk to her. They heard the rumor going around the other classes saying Fei was the human form of the fox spirit and had a big bushy tail hidden in her pants. They would go further. Then what about summer? Where would she hide her tail in summer? The one who spread the rumor responded that her tail could shrink as well as grow. In the summer she would simply shrink her tail and wrap it around her waist. So they got a malicious thrill out of following her to the toilet to spy on her, imagining they would see that tail hidden in her pants.

The boys in her class didn't talk to her, either. One of them, who lived in the same complex as Fei, would stick notes to the back of her chair with things like "bastard daughter" written on them. After she and Captain Sneakers started dating, she told him about these incidents, and Captain Sneakers beat the hell out of the boy, knocking out one of his front teeth. From then on, no one dared cross her. She wasn't somebody to be crossed; she made girls jealous and boys afraid.

She continued to tell her boyfriend to do this or that for her. One day, out of the blue, she got the idea of giving Tiao and Youyou a big surprise. So she told Captain Sneakers to have his gang break into the school's canteen at night, and they did, sneaking out a bottle of bean oil, several *jin* of marinated beltfish, a small bag of flour, twenty eggs, and some spices, like Sichuan peppercorn and aniseed. Fei led their procession of bicycles over to Youyou's house with the booty. Tiao and Youyou were so happy that they turned somersaults on the bed. They picked up the eggs one moment and sniffed at the Sichuan peppercorn and aniseed the next, and then they sifted the expensive enriched flour through their fingers and cradled the bean oil bottle, not wanting to put it down. In that era when eggs and oil were rationed, they were almost rich. They felt very rich. They felt like landowners, and even a landowner couldn't have felt richer than they did.

Grabbing a handful of the flour, Youyou announced that she was going to deep-fry the eggs and flour to make *sa-qi-ma*. Fei said, "You girls can make it and eat it. I won't join you because he and I have other things to do." She walked out as she spoke. Tiao and Youyou came out to see them off—Fei and Captain Sneakers—watching Fei wiggle her butt as she settled on his bike and put her arms around his waist. This couple, the beauty and the hero sitting together on the bike, attracted attention on the small road inside the residential complex. Back then, in all of Fuan, the entire province, or the capital and the whole of China, what girl had the nerve to sit on a boy's bike in public and hold on to his waist? It seemed only Fei had the nerve. Only she could be so scandalous and so fearless.

What boy doesn't want to show off in front of the girl he loves? What girl doesn't want her man to stand up for her and make her proud? But the word "love" didn't apply to the relationship between Fei and Captain Sneakers. They never said the word "love." The two bodies were attracted to each other by biological instinct, plus some youthful vanity and a hint of loneliness that couldn't be expressed or relieved. Observed closely, they were not really like lovers; they were careless with each other, never caressing or flirting. Most of the time they acted more like buddies than lovers, always expecting to stand up for each other when there was trouble. Their lovemaking was monotonous, simple, and crude, even though they had enough time together. Fei never got any pleasure in bed, and Captain Sneakers never satisfied her—the question of satisfaction occurred to her only later. At the time she didn't know that she could be happy and satisfied, just as she didn't know what love was. She thought this was the way things went: she looked forward to it, and then just had to tolerate it. She was a model of toleration. All she needed to do was tighten up her lips and open her legs and then she could begin her tolerating.

Was this the inexpressible mystery that people referred to? She would have preferred to put on clothes instead and hang around the street with him, where she could at least collect stares, envious, disapproving, or puzzled. She could, at least, let people know that there was a tough-looking man to protect her. She badly needed to be protected by a tough-looking man, whom she could boss around and manipulate and who liked the way she arched her eyebrows and widened her eyes angrily with her hands on her hips. The dull days started to have some flavor because of the way they were together, which seemed to be closely connected to sex and also seemed to have nothing to do with sex.

Both loafed around. Fei often stayed out at night, sometimes sleeping with him, sometimes asking to sleep over at Youyou's. One night, Tiao, Youyou, and she had dinner at Youyou's house, and Tiao was vividly telling a Shakespeare story called "Emilia." From an old comic book that she read recently, the breathtaking and soul-stirring story concerned a mistress who fell out of favor. Captain Sneakers came and asked Fei to leave with him, and Fei didn't want to, so he reached over and gave her a slap that jarred the warm, peaceful atmosphere and their tender hearts.

Tiao said angrily, "Why did you hit her?"

Captain Sneakers grabbed Fei's waist and said to Tiao as they were leaving, "You know fucking nothing!"

Tiao and Youyou stared after them as they left Youyou's home. They were thinking that maybe it was true they knew "fucking nothing," because Fei didn't seem to resent Captain Sneakers's slap. The slap reminded Tiao of the first time she and Fei met. That was the day she got a similar gift from Fei in the alley, in honor of their new acquaintance.

Fei and Captain Sneakers continued this way until he graduated from high school and was sent down to the countryside for peasant's reeducation. Then Fei met a dancer from the Fuan Song and Dance Troupe. The dancer had been invited to their school to teach dance—

the Propaganda Team of Mao Zedong's Thoughts was rehearsing a Tibetan dance, *Song of the Washing Girls*. Fei was not a member of the Propaganda Team of Mao Zedong's Thoughts. She wouldn't have qualified because of her corrupt lifestyle, and she didn't like singing and dancing, either. But as long as she was around school, she attracted attention. She caught the dancer's eye, and he caught hers, too. His handsome face won the girls' hearts and his easygoing manner attracted the boys, as well. But Fei believed that he noticed her alone, that Fei was the only one he wanted to get to know personally. That was what she imagined.

6

"Listen, you're in really great physical condition, why don't you join the Propaganda Team of Mao Zedong's Thoughts? I think you'd be the perfect lead dancer for *Song of the Washing Girls*. I've been watching you closely." The dancer stopped Fei at school and told her this one day.

He had finally spoken to her, which made her feel proud. Her guess had proved correct; by now she'd had some experience of men. She smiled at him and said, "My name is Tang Fei."

"I know your name is Tang Fei," he responded.

"That's right," she said. "A lot of people talk behind my back at school."

He seemed not to want their conversation to go in that direction; he was more interested in talking about things related to his profession. "Have you done any dancing?" he asked. She told him she hadn't. She'd never danced. She didn't like dancing and didn't plan to dance in the future. Confident in the power of her beauty, Fei deliberately put distance between herself and dance. She didn't need to attract this dancer by pretending she liked dancing, nor did she have to get close to him by saying that she had danced. She was right in front of him, the possessor of a wonderful body without ever needing to dance. But what a goddess she'd have become if she'd received some training. A goddess, really, Fei thought childishly.

He continued, "One of your parents must have been an artist. Otherwise, you wouldn't have emerged as such—such a beauty. Beauty, do you understand?" She was clearly disturbed at his mention of her parents, but his compliments pleased her, particularly his use of the word "emerged," which made her heart skip a beat. In her mind "emerged" formed an absolutely beautiful image, like a fresh, early sun rushing up out of the morning rays, a downy new chick pushing out of its egg, meeting the world innocently for the first time, or a lotus flower standing above the filthy mud, distinguished and free. And the images—touching and suggestive—was Fei truly worthy of them? She looked at the dancer and said nothing for some moments. She didn't want to respond to his comment about her parents, nor did she want to discuss the idea of beauty.

"Anyway," he went on, "I think with a little bit of training you should be able to dance well."

"You need to start out the training young if you want to dance. See how old I am. My waist and legs are too stiff now," Fei protested, turning at the waist as she spoke, and kicking her legs in a deliberately stiff way.

"Not necessarily true," the dancer said. "You're probably not seventeen yet, right? I can take some time to look at your waist and legs. How is Sunday? Sunday in your classroom."

"Just the two of us?" Fei asked.

The dancer said, "Just the two of us."

Sunday at the appointed time, Fei walked into the classroom, and the dancer was sitting on the lecture desk in front of the blackboard, waiting for her. She liked the way he looked as he sat on the desk with his long, agile legs dangling and arms folded in front of his chest. Her impression of classrooms was that they were always noisy and smelly. She didn't like being in them and had never remained in an empty one. As she entered today, she felt waves of vague anticipation. She liked the quiet classroom at this moment because the dancer was sitting on the lecture desk and there was no one else seated at the rows of desks.

At the sight of her, he jumped down, slipping off his watch and putting it on the desk. "Come, let's get started."

He walked up to her, asking her to lean against a desk in the first row and hold the edge for balance. Then he took hold of her ankle and raised up, little by little. The leg was not trained, after all, and before he pushed it too high, she said, "No, no, it hurts too much." So he let her leg drop, but his hand stayed on her ankle. She stood against the desk, and he knelt to caress the ankle, tentatively and gently, but at the same time firmly, showing no intention of letting go. His hand kept moving up, going up her calf, and reaching her thigh. He said, "I'm checking on the proportion of your calf to your thigh. Just right. Just right. And there is also this delicate kneecap." He held her delicate knee for a while, moved his hand up to touch her waist, and slid it smoothly under her shirt, which had been loosely tucked into a leather belt, pushing directly up to her breasts. She didn't know at what point she had been laid down on the desk, his head, with its luxuriant hair, bent over her breasts. He leaned down over, greedily sucking and biting her. Then the hand that had risen from her ankle slid down, down to her flat stomach and between her legs. His fingers were as nimble as his dancer's legs, making her body writhe involuntarily. The writhing invited him to go deeper and deeper. She longed for him to finger her and stab her, stab her moistness and destroy the trembling deep inside her . . .

Fei fell in love with the dancer, although their first intimacy stopped right at that point. She longed to see him day and night, so he took her home when his wife wasn't there. He was a married man, and she knew it, but she didn't want to think about that. She just liked to be with him, and liked to hear him whisper in her ear that she was his tender little cat, meaty little pigeon, shameless little slut . . . he had plenty of sweet talk, and he also combed and braided her hair, which made her heart swell. No one had braided her hair since her mother died. It was a service that she didn't expect to receive from such a handsome man. He stood behind her, and as she sat, absorbing his scent through the back of her head, she fantasized sitting like this in a trance and letting him braid her hair for her entire life, not leaving, even when his wife came home. She actually wanted to beg his wife to agree to let the three of them live together.

Later, she got pregnant and wasn't afraid at all. She naïvely believed, Now that I have your child you have to marry me. Marry me, and let me go away with you, leaving Fuan, leaving all that filthy gossip behind. Because she was with him, she started to pay attention to her reputation, trying to avoid the filthy gossip directed at her. She didn't really value herself; it was him that she treasured. She wanted to be worthy of him.

When she told him that she was pregnant, he was scared to death. "No, no, no, no . . ." he said, a series of no's in a single breath. After that he heaved a sigh and pulled her by the hand to make her sit down. He said, "That won't work. You should know you're still a child."

She asked him, "Then why didn't you think of me as a child when you laid me down on the desk?"

He said, "It's my fault. It's all my fault. What made me love you so much? What made you so lovable?"

She said, with tears streaming, "Then why don't you want me?" He then began to explain how law and marriage work. She had no concept of law; no one had ever spoken to her about law in such a serious way. She only knew if she killed someone she had to pay with her life, and if she owed someone money she had to pay it back, things even an idiot would understand. But she'd never thought about killing someone, nor did she owe anyone money. What did law have to do with her life? Now, as a sixteen-year-old, pregnant with this man's child, she had to listen to him babble about the law. According to him, they had violated some law, which scared her a little. She said, "Then what should I do?"

"I don't know," he said, "but, whatever it is, you'll have to . . . have to get rid of the child." She told him she was afraid to go to the hospital herself and wanted him to accompany her. He said that was impossible. The troupe had just given him an important assignment. He spoke about a faraway place in Sichuan Province. "There's a famous group of clay sculptures called *Rent Collection Yard* in Sichuan, have you heard of it? It shows how this big landlord Liu Wencai bullied and oppressed his tenant farmers. Our troupe is planning to base a dance drama around the sculptures. They want to send me to Sichuan to observe and come back and do the choreography. A dance drama out of *Rent Collection Yard*—think of it, maybe it will cause a big sensation around the country. It isn't just the usual dance show, but a political mission. Do you understand?" She didn't know anything about political missions, though she thought she'd heard of Liu Wencai and *Rent Collection Yard*. But none of that interested her; she just wanted to know when he would be returning. He replied vaguely that it might take some time, anything from ten days to three months. A political mission couldn't be concerned about time. He then mentioned Liu and *Rent Collection Yard* over and over like a broken record, as if to make Fei feel that if she needed to resent something, she should resent those two things. These were what took him away from her and prevented him from accompanying her to the hospital.

She lowered her head, no longer speaking. Then he slipped the watch off his wrist and handed it to her and said, "I want to give you this watch as a keepsake. It's a brand-name watch, a Shanghai Coral Jewel." He lifted her left hand and put it on her wrist. The men's watch, with a metal wristband, hung loose and heavy on Fei's delicate wrist. She remembered how their affair had begun that Sunday in the classroom with his slipping off his watch and walking to the desk. She remembered the way he slipped it off. Now she saw the gesture again and realized their affair would probably end here. She saw the end even though her brain was a little numb. She did not remember afterward how he gently maneuvered her out the door, gently but giving her no chance to resist. She remembered only that she opened the door one last time, asking him helplessly, "What should I do?"

He put his shoulder against that half-opened door and said in a lowered voice, "Doesn't your family live in the hospital? You should ask your uncle to come up with something."

Fei left his building and went back into the street, walking to the riverbank to sit down. The river wasn't polluted then, and the slow-moving water didn't stink as it would later. Although layers of paper, posters, and slogans covered the bridge, the river still flowed in its ancient way. Fei hadn't felt it was realistic when she saw characters in movies or comic books run to a riverbank when they couldn't solve their problems. Only now, as she sat down by the river herself, did she find it believable. If the city has a river, people will run to the riverbank when they have something they have to think through. A river is fair and calm. A river never classifies people by their social standing. A river can purify people's eyes and hearts. Fei sat there thinking for a long time. She thought about many, many things, and finally she remembered the scrap of paper that a boy in her class had put on the back of her chair: "bastard daughter." She was a bastard daughter herself, and she couldn't let this life in her belly become another. She didn't have the right, and she had to get rid of it. She was thinking that maybe the dancer had a point. Why didn't she ask her uncle for help? She'd almost forgotten that her uncle was a doctor and that she lived right in the hospital.

What time is it? she wondered. She looked at the Coral Jewel man's watch on her wrist and saw it was pretty late. Because of the watch, she had the luxury of asking herself the time. She took the watch from her wrist, wrapped it in a handkerchief, and put it in her pocket. Even in her saddest moment she never thought of throwing the damn watch into the river. She valued the watch, after all. Back then, a Coral Jewel watch was a considerable piece of property, even to an adult. Her hard thinking by the city moat was over. She'd sorted out her own thoughts carefully and simply. In the end, there were only two actions that summed up her relationship with the dancer. He slipped off his watch the first time and put it on the desk, and he slipped off his watch the second time and put it on her wrist. She smiled to herself ironically, dusted off her behind, and went home.

7

Fei came home with the watch in her pocket. As soon as she walked in the door, she put on a tough expression for the conversation with Dr. Tang. The tough look twisted her face, which was her strategy for hiding her intense fear. She wasn't sure how her uncle would respond. Maybe he would kick her out.

Dr. Tang was quiet for a long time after hearing what Fei had to tell him. He just stared with his dark bullet eyes at his niece, as if he wanted to read in her face whether she was talking nonsense or telling the truth. Finally, he was sure that she was telling the truth. By nature he was a quiet man and usually didn't have much to say to her, and now he had even less. He nervously clenched his hands tightly, his knuckles turning white. Fei said, "Uncle, say something."

"What do you want me to say?" he asked. "Have you ever thought about the difficulties that grown-ups have to deal with?"

Fei shot back at him, "How about you? Have you thought about the difficulties I face?"

"What difficulties do you face?" he said. "I took you from Beijing and offered you a place to live. I gave you food and sent you to school, and I think I've done all the things that I should have done for my dead sister. But look at what you've done! Do you have any self-respect?"

"No, I don't," she said.

"You don't have self-respect, but I do," Dr. Tang said. "Don't you see that I'm still alone because of you? Who would want to marry a man who lives with his niece? Do you understand?"

"I do. That's why I don't want to get you into trouble."

Dr. Tang said, "What do you mean by that?"

"If you help me with this surgery," she said, "I'll leave home immediately. I'm about to graduate from high school and I can support myself."

Dr. Tang said, "What? What did you just say? You want me to do the surgery for you? Me?"

"Yes, aren't you a doctor?"

"What nonsense are you talking? This is an ob-gyn's area, not an internist's. It's impossible."

"Why is it impossible?" she persisted.

Dr. Tang said, "If I say it's impossible, then it's impossible. I can't do it."

"Then I'll go to an ob-gyn myself," Fei said, "and I won't go anywhere else; I'll just go to the ob-gyn at your hospital—"

Dr. Tang immediately interrupted her. "Shut up, will you? Do you think I will let you do that and publicly shame us? Shame yourself and shame me? Shame our family? Now you must answer a question for me."

"What question?"

"Who is he?"

Fei didn't answer.

"Who is he?" Dr. Tang repeated. "You must tell me."

"What if I don't tell you?"

"Then I'll go to your school and find out."

"Okay, I'll tell you," Fei finally said, "but only if you answer a question of mine: Who is my father?"

"Why do you ask me this question now?" said Dr. Tang.

Fei went on, "Both of you, you and Mom, always hid it from me, but I have the right to know. I have even more of a right to know now. Who should be responsible for me, after all? Who else would it be if not my father? Will you tell me who my father is, and where he is?"

"Didn't we tell you that he was dead?" said Dr. Tang.

"I don't believe it," Fei insisted. "What is his name, how did he die, and where did he die? Why do I know nothing about it? And you try to force me to tell you my private business."

Fei's mention of her father stopped Dr. Tang from pressing her further, as if the deal had fallen through. He would rather give up on knowing the man who had taken advantage of his niece than tell her about her father. But the real problem hadn't been solved; the problem was Fei's surgery, something that Dr. Tang found thorny and irritating, which angered him but about which he could do nothing.

He couldn't come up with a better idea. He stood and paced back and forth in their two-bedroom apartment, subconsciously glancing at the partly filled bookshelf in the corner. Other than a plastic fluorescent portrait of Chairman Mao, which gave off a green glow in the dark, there were only clinical reference books on internal medicine. He didn't have any ob-gyn books. Fei said, "Uncle, are you going to do the surgery for me or not?"

"No, it isn't possible," he said. "I won't do it. It's dangerous. It's your life we're talking about."

Fei said, "I'm not afraid."

Dr. Tang sneered. "Hmmm, I know you're not afraid. Would you do it if you were afraid?"

Fei sneered back at him, something she probably picked up from a movie. "You're not afraid, either. Otherwise, you wouldn't have written a phony sick-leave note."

Dr. Tang's expression changed. He walked toward Fei and patted the table gently, "What sick-leave note? What nonsense are you talking?"

Fei said, "You wrote a fake sick-leave note for Tiao's mother. You and she also . . . have acted like hooligans. You thought I didn't know? I'm going to expose you. I'm going to the revolutionary committee of your hospital to expose you." She stood up as she was talking, and ran to the door like a wild animal. She was afraid she was going to cry if she stayed any longer. She felt very sad for her underhanded behavior and for bringing up her innocent friend, Tiao, although she did resent Tiao's mother.

Dr. Tang stopped his niece, saying, "You're getting hysterical. Don't be so hysterical!" He grabbed her arms to force her to sit, trying to maintain his adult dignity as much as possible. "Stop your hysteria. I will think about the surgery. Give me some time."

Dr. Tang racked his brain. He worked in a place where there were countless doctors, but he knew he couldn't get help from anyone because of the need to protect Fei's reputation, so he could only rely on himself. He must take the risk. He borrowed a few books to get an idea of the surgery and the instruments he would need. Then, during the day, he inspected an ob-gyn operating room. He decided to jimmy the door open at night to get in, block the window with a blanket to prevent the light from being seen outside, and then perform the surgery in secret. It took him about a week to finish the preparations. He knew he couldn't delay. The longer he waited, the more dangerous the procedure became.

They did it. To prevent Fei from making noise because of the pain, he gagged her mouth with gauze beforehand.

Dr. Tang, who was no stranger to human organs and had interned in the surgery department as a medical student, was not at all confident about this minor ob-gyn operation. But this was not the only reason that he'd tried so hard to avoid doing this for Fei. Even if he were an ob-gyn doctor, he would have been unwilling to perform such surgery on his niece. He felt that it was cruel, a humiliation that life had dealt him, and that Fei was ridiculing him. He couldn't imagine having to accept such a reality, but he had to. Fear forced him to accept the situation, and fear also saved him, leaving him no room for delay. Once he stood in front of the operating table, in his terror, Fei became neither a man nor a woman, neither a family member nor a stranger. She was simply not a living person. She was politics, and she was Dr. Tang's fate. He was not performing a surgery, either; he was praying for fate to help him survive.

Everything was finally completed in a stumbling sort of way. Fei couldn't help clinging to her uncle, and they embraced, weeping uncontrollably. In the tears, their unspoken trouble and sadness were expressed, and their feelings for each other were reestablished. There was forgiveness in the weeping. Their blood tie—that profound, ancient magic—connected them, body and soul. They were family, no matter how much they had neglected each other.

This would be the only surgery that Dr. Tang would ever perform, an ob-gyn surgery. When he stood at the top of a chimney near the end of his short, unhappy life, the last place he cast his glance was at the window of the ob-gyn operating room at People's Hospital. He reflected on his own life and felt there were too many areas where he had stinted on his orphaned niece. He had neglected her and resented her, seeing her as the stumbling block of his life. Only in thinking of her as an obstacle did he give her her due. He had risked arrest, dismissal, and prison to save her precious reputation with his mediocre surgical skills.

At the Spring Festival that year, Captain Sneakers returned from the countryside to Fuan for the holidays. Late one night, he and his former gang members broke into one of the apartments in the rows of one-story dorms and gang-raped the head nurse of internal medicine, the female "spy" who scrubbed the restroom, swept the hallways, and confessed the passwords "Where does the mermaid's fishnet come from?"

Captain Sneakers had planned to break into Fei's home to revenge himself on her. He had heard about her affair with the dancer. He took a knife with him, intending to slash her face to get even with her for his humiliation. When he lifted the woman, fast asleep, from the bed, he found he'd picked the wrong person. But he didn't spare her, the old beauty, the old beauty from the old society. He also let his gang members take turns with her. He held the knife to the old woman's neck, listening to them panting over her body in the dark. He was thinking that, after all, she wasn't Fei. If it were Fei, he wouldn't let them do this to her. He felt, as he listened to their panting, that at least he had a conscience when it came to Fei. Fei, you little piece of damaged goods. He cursed her in his heart. You have this old woman under our bodies to thank. Because of her you get to keep your pretty face. I really want to slash your fucking face . . .

The head nurse went to hospital security after daybreak to report the attacks on her. But who would pay attention to her? The victim of the rape was not a decent woman. An old female spy got raped. An old female spy who was born to be raped. Who else should be raped if not her?

Where does the mermaid's fishnet come from?

From the ocean.

Chapter 4

❦ ❦ ❦

Cat in the Mirror

1

There is no such thing in the world as a never-ending banquet. The more sumptuous the banquet, the sadder and lonelier the aftermath. Tiao, Fei, and Youyou had had their secret celebrations, with the grilled miniature snowballs, the Ukrainian red cabbage soup, the sporty boating clothes, and the mysterious "Cairo Night," in which they submerged and isolated themselves. Tiao even believed that she would never have to worry about anything anymore, not school or family. She already had a world of joy. It was Quan who ruined that joy. Quan's presence was like crows' wings, whose flapping and flying made her heart feel gloomy and heavy.

Tiao was deeply unhappy about Quan's birth. To express her unhappiness, she completely ignored her youngest sister and lavished attention on Fan. She loved Fan, and Fan loved her. Fan obeyed her unconditionally in almost everything, and the foundation of their love was indestructible. Even when Fan had barely learned to talk, she would cheer enthusiastically for her sister, Fan's clumsy tongue spitting out incomprehensible words. When Tiao tried to kill a fly with a fly swatter, no matter whether she hit it or not, killed the fly or not, Fan would simply make the same loud announcements, "Shmashed. Shmashed." She praised and encouraged her sister, making Tiao believe that even if the world stopped turning and the seas ran dry, she and Fan would still be inseparable.

They had depended on each other when their parents were away at the Reed River Farm. Fan loved to eat apples and beltfish and Tiao would try to buy them for her whenever possible. She knew their money was not enough for both of them to eat these treats every day, so she taught herself to dislike eating apples and beltfish. She would just watch Fan eat. It was fun to watch Fan eat fish because when she finished a piece, she would use the fish skeleton to comb her hair. "This is a comb," she told Tiao happily. Tiao stopped her even though she liked her cleverness and imagination. She didn't want Fan to get her hair dirty. She washed Fan's hair and feet. They washed their feet every night before bed, sitting on small stools, face-to-face, with the washing basin between them. Tiao liked to smell Fan's toes, fat and slightly sour-smelling. She washed very carefully, reaching in between every one of Fan's toes. Sometimes she forgot to keep a towel handy, so she used her own pants instead, letting Fan rub her feet on them. She could have left the basin and gotten a towel, but she liked to have Fan dry her feet on her pants.

"I'll wipe them," Fan would say. "I'm really going to wipe them hard." Tiao then placed both of Fan's dripping feet on her knees and let Fan playfully kick her feet on her knees, so foot-washing became a game, a shared silliness between them.

If they were walking on the street and Tiao had a basketful of groceries, Fan would always lend a hand. The lending a hand was precisely that, Fan putting her hand on the basket without lifting any of the weight. She just held on to the edge as if she were carrying the basket along with her sister. She loved to help with the work because she loved her sister.

If Fan was bullied by someone in the complex, Tiao would stand up for her against the bullies faithfully to the end. She put aside any shyness or reserve she had. Once, a boy, at the entrance to the building, held out a piece of soap that looked like a rice ball, and he said to Fan, "Lick it. Lick it. It's a rice ball and tastes very sweet." Fan stuck out her tongue and was about to lick it. Tiao happened to be passing by. She grabbed the soap and forced it into the boy's mouth. She actually did that. She stuffed his mouth with soap until he began to cry. He bent over, squatted on the ground, and threw up over and over. Tiao took Fan by the hand and went home with her head high. As soon as she entered the house, she told Fan, "That was soap, not a rice ball. Besides, even if it was really a rice ball, you still shouldn't eat it. You can't just eat other people's stuff like that without thinking. Will you remember this?" Fan kept nodding her head. She would never forget any of Tiao's words.

Then Quan was born a year after Wu's return from the Reed River Farm. By then, the discipline at the farm had slackened quite a bit, and many people in the academy had found excuses to come back and stay at home. Wu simply raised Quan in plain sight of everyone. She no longer mentioned her rheumatic heart disease, and the baby in her arms was the most convincing reason for her to be at home. As a nursing mother, she had the right to stay home with her baby.

The house was a mess, and Tiao had to do a lot of chores. Wu made her warm up Quan's milk one moment and wash her diapers the next. Tiao slammed the milk pot and dented it. She wouldn't wash the diapers carefully—just dipped them into the water quickly and then snatched them out. She favored Fan and let Fan drink all the orange juice that Wu bought for Quan. When Quan was a year old and could eat mashed pork floss, she decided to use Quan's pork to make sandwiches for Fan. By then Fan had already realized that she had lost her mother's favor and went around dispirited because of it. She would eat the pork-floss sandwiches in big bites and snuggle up close to Tiao, to show the whole family and the whole world: No big deal. No big deal. I have my sister who cares for me.

She exaggerated her loss of favor and fall in status to get attention. What else could she do? She resented Quan, and her resentment was the genuine article, without the least little bit of exaggeration. It was also simple, unlike Tiao's, which was difficult to put into words. Fan hated Quan because Quan was pretty and also knew how to please people. Particularly when she could walk on her own, when she could be taken outside into the complex by an adult, her sweet and beautiful little face and naturally curly brown hair made almost every neighbor fall in love with her. The more people liked Quan, the angrier Fan got. She took every opportunity to pinch Quan with her nails on her chubby arms and legs and small shoulders. She used her thumb and index finger to pinch a little bit of flesh, just a little. It felt like being bitten by an ant, but the pain was enough to make Quan grimace and cry. Fan was not afraid at all. Quan couldn't tell on her, because she couldn't talk.

Wu often took Quan for a walk on the small road in front of their building. When she had things to do, she would ask Tiao or Fan to take her instead. Fan avoided this kind of chore; she didn't like to be with Quan. The passing neighbors would stop to play with Quan and ignore her, as if she were only along to be Quan's foil, giving Fan a sharp pang of jealousy. So Fan would knit her eyebrows and make a great show of having cramps in her legs: "Owww, my legs have cramps, owww . . ." moaning and falling back—butt-first—on the bed. Wu would then ask Tiao to take Quan for a walk, often just as she was going to Youyou's home to study recipes and experiment with cooking. Quan, who loved walking and knew how to entertain people with her expressive gestures, had cost Tiao precious time and interrupted plans for quite a few high-toned banquets with Youyou. But she didn't make up excuses, as Fan did. She obeyed Wu, brought a little stool to the front of the building, and sat down to read. She would read her book for a while and then lift her head to take a look at Quan, who would be strolling aimlessly nearby.

Occasionally her eyes met Quan's and she would coldly study the dark little eyes of this younger sister. Something was wrong about Quan—Tiao felt it from the very beginning, and now the fact that Quan strolled around the whole courtyard in broad daylight made her feel very uneasy. She wasn't jealous of Quan's prettiness and perfection. She had heard from adults that if a child was too good-looking when she was little, she would go downhill and turn out to be ugly later. So she was not resentful of Quan's good looks. Besides, what was the big deal? Why the fuss about her looks? She was almost two years old and still didn't know how to talk. Maybe she was a mute. Tiao felt that something was wrong because she was suspicious about Quan's origin. She believed her birth was a terrible trick Quan had played on their family. She had her reasons for thinking so after Fei came to see Quan.

Fei, abandoned by the dancer and having had the abortion, seemed to be especially observant about babies. She also seemed to talk more bluntly than she used to. One day she suddenly said to Tiao, "Whom do you think Quan looks like?" When Tiao made no response, Fei said, "She reminds me very much of my uncle. Hmm, she might be my cousin."

Fei looked both a little bit angry and sad. Then she gulped, and a kind of miserable look came over her face.

"She reminds me very much of my uncle." Fei's words struck Tiao like a blow to the head, dazing her and sharpening her focus at once. She finally was clear about the question she hadn't dared to ask, and now she had the answer. Wu and Dr. Tang made her sick, and so angry that she wanted to rage and curse at people in the street. The two were unworthy to be the cause of all Tiao's suffering, the anxiety, and then, finally, the relief, that she had gone through because of that letter that never reached Yixun. They weren't worth it. They weren't worth any of it. How frightened she had been that Fei would make her face the secret. But now that it had happened, she realized she had no refuge. She had to take action. So she was determined to act, no matter how vague her idea of what she should do.

As if deliberately conspiring with Tiao, Fan had started to take action of her own. She dug earwax out of Tiao's ear and put the light yellow slivers into Quan's milk bottle. Tiao watched all this and said nothing. Everyone knew the folk wisdom: earwax is poison. People turn into mutes if they eat it.

Quan was probably a mute already, and, if not, she would become a mute for certain after eating earwax. Tiao watched Fan shake the milk bottle and said nothing. Saying nothing was silent approval and encouragement. Fan took the milk bottle that contained earwax and orange juice and walked over to Quan. But the plot failed because, for some reason, her grip loosened and the milk bottle dropped to the floor and broke. Tiao was disappointed, and so was Fan. They didn't discuss their disappointment with each other. Instead, they expressed it by further ignoring Quan. They played the "sofa leisure" game that Tiao had invented, which was more of a way to enjoy themselves than a game. Every time Wu went out, Tiao would drag two fluffy down pillows from Wu's big bed and lay them on two hard-backed chairs. Then she and Fan would sit on them. The warm, soft feeling under their bottoms relaxed them, body and mind. They reclined on their homemade "sofas" and cracked seeds—watermelon, pumpkin, and sunflower. They didn't permit Quan to get near them to take part in their sofa leisure. Or, to put it another way, they invented sofa leisure for the very purpose of upsetting Quan. How they loved to see Quan weep because she couldn't sit on the "sofa." It would be even better if Wu could see the scene, Tiao thought defiantly. Wu didn't dare criticize the way she and Fan treated Quan. And the more Wu was afraid, the more Tiao hated her; the more Wu didn't dare, the more malice Tiao directed at Quan.

Then came that day.

It was a Sunday. After breakfast, Wu sat in front of the sewing machine, planning to make a new outfit for Quan, and told Tiao and Fan to take Quan for a walk. As usual, Tiao carried a stool to sit in front of the building to read a book, and Fan also brought out a little chair. She didn't read. She knitted woolen socks. Every time Wu made clothes for Quan, she would start to make something for herself as if to tell Wu, You don't want to take care of me, but I can take care of myself. She was knitting a pair of woolen socks for herself; she was clever that way.

Quan was on the road in front of the building, strolling along her familiar route. She held a toy metal bucket in one hand and a little metal shovel in the other and squatted under a tree, digging up a few shovelfuls of dirt. She put the dirt into the bucket and carried it to another tree. She shuttled between the two trees aimlessly, and once in a while she banged on the bucket with the shovel, trying to get her sisters' attention. Her big sister buried her face in the book, pretending to hear nothing; her second sister held her finger to her lips and kept saying, "Shh," to her. Why were they so cold and indifferent to her? What had she done to offend and annoy them? It was a mystery she never understood to the end, to the end.

Several old women who had gathered together to sew *The Selected Works of Chairman Mao* beckoned to Quan. They were tired of sewing and needed a break, and Quan was a cute living plaything to amuse them. They clapped at Quan from far away and called her darling and honey. She immediately dropped her bucket and shovel with a clatter and staggered toward the women.

She got on the small road, the one in front of Building Number 6 that people walked on every day. When Tiao noticed that Quan had disappeared from her view, she put down her book and stood up. She didn't want Quan to get too far and was about to call her back, not out of love but out of a sense of duty. Maybe she could have Fan call her back, and if they couldn't get her back with their voices, they could physically drag her back. Fan stood right beside her. Then they saw something that they had never seen before, and events unfolded quickly. A manhole cover lay in the middle of the road, and Quan was walking toward the open manhole. In fact, she had already reached the edge. Fan must have seen the open hole and Quan at the edge, because she seized Tiao's hand. It was unclear whether she wanted to grab her sister's hand and rush to the manhole, or if she was asking her sister for permission to run to the hole.

Tiao and Fan held each other's hands, and their hands were ice-cold; neither of them moved. They stood ten or fifteen meters away from Quan. Both of them were aware that she was still going forward, until she finally went into the hole. When Quan suddenly spread her arms and dove in as if she were flying, Fan's hand felt a gentle pull from Tiao's cold, stiff hand. She would remember this pull of Tiao's on her hand forever; it was a memory she couldn't erase all her life, and would become the evidence, illusory and real, by which she would accuse Tiao in the future.

Tiao would also always remember their holding hands that day, as well as her tug on Fan's hand. The gesture was subtle but definite. Was it to stop Fan, a gesture of control, or a signal that something was coming to an end? Was it satisfaction for a great accomplishment, or a reflex action at the height of fear? Was it a hint at their alliance, or a groan out of the depths of their guilt?

Few things stay in a person's lifelong memory. Major events are often easy to forget, and it's those trivial things that can't be brushed away, as, for example, in such and such a year, in such and such a month, on such and such a day, the tiny tug that someone gave on another's hand.

2

Quan disappeared from the earth forever. For a long time after her death, Wu interrogated Tiao almost every day. "Didn't you see that the cover was off the manhole?

"No, I didn't."

"Did you hear those old women call Quan over?"

"No, I didn't."

"Then when did you notice Quan was not in front you?"

"When I couldn't see her."

"Why didn't you follow her when you saw what was happening?"

"I didn't see anything, and I didn't know she was walking towards the hole."

"You didn't know there was a manhole there?"

"I knew the manhole was always covered."

"You didn't even see it when Quan walked to the edge of the manhole?"

"I didn't see it."

"But you should have, because you were her sister."

"I just didn't. Fan can tell you."

Fan quietly came over and Tiao grabbed her hand. She didn't need to open her mouth. Their hand-holding was the proof of their mutual support, and innocence. The interrogation continued. "Then what did you actually see?"

"I saw a crowd of people surrounding the manhole, and Fan and I ran over."

"Were they those old women who had called her over?"

"Yes, they were there, and two passersby on their bikes. Later . . . there was you."

"Don't talk nonsense. I know I was there."

Wu couldn't go on; tears streamed down and covered her whole face. She then turned from the interrogation of her daughters to people outside the family. She knocked on the neighbors' doors over and over, and went to the homes of those old women who had witnessed what had happened. She stared at them, her hair disheveled and her clothes unkempt, forcing them in a hard voice to talk about what had happened that day. She was much harsher to them than to Tiao, unloading on outsiders all her grief at the loss of her beloved daughter and the anger that she couldn't release at home.

She hated these women, hated them for treating Quan as a plaything because they had no other distractions. If they hadn't gathered there to sew *The Selected Works of Chairman Mao*, they wouldn't have seen Quan. If they hadn't seen Quan, who at the time was shoveling dirt under a tree, they wouldn't have called to her, and Quan wouldn't have walked into the manhole. "Who are you to have called to my daughter like that? Who are you? How irresponsible you are! Do you treat your own grandchildren so recklessly? You didn't even warn her! You . . . you . . ." She was hysterical and even fainted once at one of the old women's houses. The old woman pressed down on the pressure point under her nose and blew cold water onto her face to wake her up. The neighbors didn't like to hear those words from her, words that got harder and harder to listen to, but they understood how she felt and didn't take offense. Besides, those old women did feel guilty about the incident. They hadn't seen the open manhole in the middle of the road; they saw only the angelic little Quan flap her arms, run toward them, and then disappear suddenly. Not until her sudden disappearance from the earth did they notice that the manhole in her path was open and the cover had been moved to the side. So one of the old women told Wu, "The key issue is not the manhole in the road—the manhole has always been there. The question is who opened the manhole and why the cover was not moved back."

The old woman's words echoed Wu's thoughts. She also believed the key issue was who could have been so evil as to remove the manhole cover. No one in the design academy admitted to having opened the manhole. According to the academy's revolutionary committee, none of the plumbers had worked on anything involving the manhole or sewage on that Sunday. Maybe it was some bad kid trying to cause trouble. Every complex had them, like the boy who tried to make Fan lick soap. They were children, not even in middle school yet, bent on imitating older hooligans—bad little kids always wanted to be bad big ones. She resented them the way she resented those old women who sewed *The Selected Works of Chairman Mao*, but where was the proof? If their purpose in lifting the manhole cover was to sell it to the scrap-collecting station for cigarettes, then why hadn't they taken the cover away? The cover had been left beside the manhole. There was no evidence and nobody came forward to supply any.

In the quiet depths of the night, Wu often wept in the wide, empty bed, hugging to her the unfinished outfit of Quan's she'd been working on that day. She would think that perhaps she shouldn't have given birth to Quan. Why would she have given birth to her? Had she done it as a sort of memento of her relationship with Dr. Tang? Before Quan was born, Dr. Tang didn't even know the child was his. Wu didn't tell him, but she was sure the baby was his and she was willing to keep such a child in her life. The child would be a constant reminder of her secrets. She didn't tell Dr. Tang, because she was afraid he would force her to go to the hospital to have an abortion. She knew intuitively that Dr. Tang didn't really love her, and that her longing for him outweighed his need for her. The roots of that longing were mysterious to her. It seemed to be longing that drove her sexual desire, but then again laziness brought about her longing in the first place. Laziness allowed her to avoid many responsibilities but also prevented her from planning for the future in her relationship with others. Maybe even her so-called memento came from her laziness—she was too lazy to use birth control. As a married woman, she had such freedom in these matters, unlike an unmarried girl like Fei. While Fei was miserably gagged with gauze in the operating room late at night, Wu could walk into the ob-gyn in broad daylight to give birth to a child who was not her husband's. How legitimate and righteous marriage was! How secretive and filthy marriage was! She sobbed and thought this might be what people called karma. It was the punishment that God sent her for conducting her life so badly and shirking her responsibilities. She'd decided on her own, and audaciously, to give birth to Quan. She brought Quan into this world recklessly, and did she really think it had been for the child's benefit? Everything was like a dream, starting with the sick leave and ending with Quan's disappearance, which should put an end to her relationship with Dr. Tang. Only now did she truly dare to take a close look at her family, to consider her loved ones. She had been afraid of looking at her family, of thinking about them. And always she had been more afraid of her daughter Tiao than of her husband. She was certain that nothing escaped Tiao's eyes. The child could turn the world upside down when she thought it necessary.

But who could say that Yixun hadn't picked up the scent of her infidelity? In the last two years, he rarely came home except on holidays and during the change of seasons in spring and fall. If Tiao and Fan complained, he would just say the farm was busy and it was difficult to get leave. When Wu sent him a telegram informing him of Quan's birth, he didn't come back until a week later. Wu had spent a lot of time thinking about this telegram. Her original impulse was not to have Yixun around when she was in labor. It would be too difficult for Yixun and too disrespectful to him. Even though he probably did not know anything, she still didn't want to take the risk. She would rather have no one close by and simply welcome the baby on her own. It would seem odd, though, to give birth all by herself, like an admission that there was ambiguity and deception involved in having the child, an admission that she lacked the courage to let the baby face the man whom she called husband. She wouldn't let that happen. Muddling through, if at all possible, was the guiding principle of her life. So she had sent a telegram to the Reed River Farm. She sent the telegram, but he took his time in arriving. His delay was enough to make her wonder, but at the time she didn't even have the courage to wonder. She just kept moving. When he arrived, she leaned back to the head of the bed and pulled up the quilt that covered her body, and then she picked up a glass from the nightstand and swallowed a few gulps of tea. Moving could relieve nervousness sometimes, so she kept moving. Finally, she reached under the covers for Quan and presented the baby to Yixun, who was standing beside the bed.

She never knew how Yixun reacted when he first saw Quan, because she'd kept her eyes cast down the whole time. She'd just lowered her eyes and, steadily, in her outstretched hands, held the baby for Yixun to see—she wanted him to accept her child. If only he had taken the child from her hands, then her heart would have been at peace. But he didn't. On the contrary, he backed off a step. He withdrew his extended hands and slid them into his pockets—he was also fidgeting; he also needed to relieve his nerves by moving. Then he said without looking at her, "I'd better wash my hands. I was on the bus all day and dust got everywhere."

He stayed at home only one night and returned to the farm.

So, who could say that Yixun didn't know anything?

It was time to put an end to things.

This expression very much appealed to her now. One person's death had made her understand that there were things in life that she needed to end. With this thought in mind, she went to People's Hospital to see Dr. Tang. For once, arriving at those two first-floor rooms, she didn't go directly to the inner room but took a seat in the waiting room, and Dr. Tang immediately knew why Wu had come.

They had never discussed Quan's paternity. Dr. Tang hadn't been to Wu's home since Quan's birth. But Quan didn't stop growing and changing because Dr. Tang wasn't around. Soon all those features that obviously belonged to the Tang family started to show in her. She had so quickly grown very different from Tiao and Fan. How little Quan looked like her surprised even Wu. The child's appearance didn't leave any room for doubt in the adults, the families, and the society in which she would have to live. So, when she was a year old, Wu brought her to People's Hospital to meet Dr. Tang. It was a meeting that did not reveal anything new. Between Wu and Dr. Tang no curtain needed to be drawn back: Dr. Tang's heart was as clear as glass when he looked at this baby with the curly brown hair who stared at him with little dark eyes. He seemed somewhat surprised and confused, taking Quan in his arms, slightly embarrassed and a little excited. He must have wanted to kiss her but clearly didn't dare put his lips close to her face. With a lump in his throat, he asked, "What is her name?"

"Her name is Quan."

"Which character for Quan?"

"The character for grass on top, and the one for completion below—Quan, meaning heavenly grass."

He paused, and then asked, "The character for grass above and completion underneath?"

She said, "Yes. Doesn't the character for Fei also have the character for grass?"

It was already too obvious, so they both stopped talking. Besides, she didn't want to discuss anything; she'd just wanted to bring Quan here for him to see.

For this, Dr. Tang was grateful to Wu. He had always been grateful that she let him avoid responsibility toward her and now was even more grateful to be relieved of responsibility toward this child of theirs. Because she'd permitted him this escape, he didn't have to feel nervous and could just relax, which had allowed him to enjoy sex with her. This was the real reason he needed her. In such repressive times, a woman like Wu could provide someone of his family and social background a warm bed in secret to soothe his anxiety and despair. By this stroke of sheer luck, she helped him maintain a relatively healthy balance between body and mind. They both knew the good days wouldn't last, which didn't mean they could have predicted Quan's death. Unlike Wu, Dr. Tang was not shocked that Quan lived for only two years, and he didn't mourn deep or long, either. He had been involved with a shorter life than Quan's—in his niece Fei's abortion. He didn't consider his pessimism about the lives in the Tang family as cruel. In fact, he had predicted long ago that they would live to suffer, just as with his sister Jingjing's miserable death, or his niece Fei's plight, or the awkward life he was living himself. No one had ever understood what was in his heart, and this woman named Wu in particular didn't understand.

Now as he looked at Wu in the chair, her face bloated by grief at Quan's death, the creases at the corners of her mouth, and the strands of gray showing in her dark hair, he couldn't help feeling a surge of compassion. He heard what she said about not seeing each other anymore, and he agreed that they should stop. So filled with compassion was he for her that he felt he had to embrace her and remove all her clothes. Compassion can excite a man sometimes. At that moment it wasn't that he wanted to have her, but rather that he wanted her to have him, to have him one more, final time.

But she didn't cooperate, and it was no show of refusal but genuine rejection. Here was a situation unfamiliar to Dr. Tang; he was accustomed to her eagerness to please, to her taking the initiative, to her undisguised sexual desire, and to her body's consummate ripeness. Her current passive resistance gave Dr. Tang a powerful erection. He held her, trying to pull her into the inner room, and she grabbed hold of the door frame, stubbornly refusing to enter. He then shifted direction, dragging her to the bathroom. He dragged her in and locked the door. She struggled in his arms and begged him with her sad eyes, Don't do this. Please don't. Her sad eyes touched him and also stimulated him. The more he felt compassion for her, the more he wanted to bully her. He couldn't stop. While holding her stiff body, he stood in the bathroom and began to masturbate, jerking himself off so violently that it all ended quickly. His violent motion, his strange, low, husky moaning, and his ejaculation had no effect on Wu at all. She just wanted to go home as soon as she could.

3

One day in fall, late fall, when Quan was only a year old, Yixun came home from the Reed River Farm for the change of season. He got off the bus and ran into Tiao and Fan, just back from grocery shopping, at the entrance of the design academy. He hardly noticed what Tiao carried in her hand but immediately fixed on a string of garlic that hung around Fan's neck. It was fairly long, circling Fan's neck like a boa or a scarf, with two ends dangling over her knees. Her little neck leaned forward, weighed down by the garlic, but she was all happy and smiling. Yixun thought she must have asked to have the garlic on her neck herself because she'd seen the photograph of the former first lady Wang Guangmei being denounced. In the picture, Wang Guangmei is forced to wear a necklace of Ping-Pong balls, so long that it almost drags on the ground. You love to wear necklaces? Then let's put one on you. Fan's garlic necklace instantly reminded Yixun of the photo of Wang Guangmei in the huge necklace, and maybe something else as well. In any case, he was very sad, and felt a sharp pain, as if glass had suddenly shattered into pieces that flew into his heart, violently slicing it apart. He could think of nothing in the world more embarrassing than his daughter having a string of garlic around her neck. Her happy face in the autumn wind just added more to his distress at the embarrassing image, the echo of the humiliation of the former first lady.

Fan caught sight of Yixun first. "Dad," she cried out, and ran right to him, the garlic necklace bouncing on her chest. She ran up to Yixun and dove into his arms, and he immediately took the garlic from her neck. Then Tiao ran over. She said, "Dad, why have you only come back now?"

"Why have you only come back now?" In the sentence Yixun heard complaint and anticipation, and maybe other things. But she had never talked about other things, or Yixun didn't want to hear her talk about them. In a family with dignity, there was no room for "other things," no matter how profoundly someone in this family was shamed, or how deeply the person suffered.

After Quan's birth, Yixun became painfully aware of Wu and Dr. Tang's relationship. He had tried to convince himself, trusting to his luck, that what he sensed and suspected might not be happening, but Quan's birth completely destroyed his illusion. He spent a lot of lonely time thinking hard as he attended the tedious study group meetings, hauled bricks on the big cart, or walked in the solemnity of the boundless reeds outside the farm. The humiliation that was most difficult for a man, he swallowed, tolerating the ugly things that Wu did with extraordinary willpower and without once directly confronting her. Not all of this could be attributed to Yixun's desire to save face, nor was it simply a mark of the low social status of his whole generation. Love for appearances makes someone more intolerant of being shamed, and low status makes it even more likely to have resentful anger flare. Maybe Yixun's upbringing didn't instruct him in beating a woman, and his anthropologist father and his mother, who had studied oil painting with the famous Liu Haili, respected each other all their lives. Maybe there was also his pride, which earned him some reputation in the Beijing Architectural Design Academy. One year, Yixun was nominated for the model worker award, but he turned down the honor because he thought the other two nominees were unqualified. He refused to set foot in the same river with them. Time could dim his pride but not extinguish it. Was it because he was so proud that he refused to lower himself by reasoning with Wu? Things might not be that simple. For now, faced with this troubled family of his, or the troubles in his family, he would bide his time. His avoidance might have had something to do with his pride, but it didn't mean that he would simply let everything go. A shadow had already crept into his heart and things wouldn't be easily remedied. His brain didn't stay idle for a minute, which caused his stubborn insomnia. Still, he insisted on not confronting Wu. As he understood her, he was certain if he asked directly, she would confess everything. Maybe she had prepared long ago to be interrogated by him, and maybe she was looking forward to it day and night. Interrogation would be more acutely painful than the silence between them: Come on, Yixun, scold me all you want or beat me as hard as you can. Why are you such a coward? Dealing with reticence requires strong nerves, which Wu didn't have. She was about to lose her mind because of Yixun's silent treatment. So Yixun refused to ask. As long as he persisted, he would have the upper hand; never asking meant he would have the upper hand forever. He didn't want her to talk, and he was not ready to listen—what husband would want to listen to his wife talk about things like that?

Then Quan died.

Quan's death suddenly freed his tightly bound heart. Sometimes he felt guilty that his heart could be eased at such a moment. If his soul ever had to answer to God, he would rather he had never had this release, but he couldn't fool himself.

This time he came home quickly, rushing back overnight. When he saw Wu, he found her with eyes swollen from weeping, yet she wouldn't risk showing too much grief. Guilt and shame made her hold back her tears in front of him. Right then, he discovered the perfect way to express his feelings. He would exhibit the sadness that Wu was afraid to show, display the sorrow that Wu worked hard to suppress. Why shouldn't he grieve as if he were Quan's real father? So he asked Tiao to describe Quan's death in Wu's presence, over and over again, and asked questions afterward.

"Tiao, you said you had been sitting in front of the building reading the whole time. Was your main responsibility that day to watch Quan or read a book?"

"It was to watch Quan."

"Then why did you only tend to your reading?"

"I didn't expect she would walk so far away."

"Why didn't you expect her to walk so far? She had the use of her legs."

"I meant she usually didn't walk that far."

"How far did she usually walk?"

"She just stayed around the building."

"How far is 'around'?"

"I have never measured. I don't know."

"Who should know these things—does your mother know?" He brought Wu into it.

"My mother wasn't there."

"Where was your mother at the time?"

"She was at home working at the sewing machine."

"Were you at home working at the sewing machine at the time?"
He turned to Wu.

"Yes, I was," Wu said.

"Did you often leave the child in their care and then use the sewing machine at home?"

"Not often. Sometimes I had to make clothes for them."

" 'Them'?"

"Them, the three sisters."

"But I haven't seen them wearing any clothes you made for them. Can you tell me which clothes you made?"

"I didn't say I made all of their clothes. I only said I sometimes made clothes for them."

"But you emphasized the time you spent on making clothes for them."

"I was answering your questions about 'often' or 'not often.' "

"You said you didn't often make clothes, then what did you often do? Could you please tell me what you usually did?"

"What did I usually do? . . . Didn't Tiao tell you everything when she wrote to you?"

"Don't drag the children into this. What do you think she would tell me in her letters? Do you think she was required to report your life to me? Yes, Tiao did write to me often, and she was the only one who did. In her letters, she told me things that happened in her school, and with her friends, Fei and Youyou. Why would she write to me? That's because you never know what she's thinking. This, I truly don't understand—you're . . . you're sick, so you have more time than other people. What did you really do with all the time you had these last few years?"

Dumbfounded, Wu thought the catastrophe had arrived. Yixun's questions were clearly designed to lure her, step by step, deep into a trap. Well, if it's a blessing, it can't be a catastrophe, and if it is a catastrophe, there is no way to escape. She might as well confess. She composed herself for the final trial. Licking her already moist lips, she said, "Can we have the kids leave for a while?"

"That's not necessary." He raised his voice: "There is no need for such a hypocritical request as having them 'leave for a while.' What haven't they seen in this family? From what exactly would they have to turn their faces? There's no need."

"But I need to be alone . . . to talk to you alone."

"In my opinion, being alone is pointless." He interrupted her immediately, as if he were afraid she couldn't hold back her confession any longer, as if he were afraid she would get hysterical and come out with her ugly story. He was pleased at her nervousness, her panic, her trembling lips, and the sudden sagging of her cheeks, which signaled that she was on the verge of collapse. So he had to change direction, or rather say something to steer the dialogue in the direction he intended. He said, "I asked you over and over again what you usually did. I'm sure now you want to say what you usually did was care for Quan. She was a baby and needed care. But it was precisely under your usual care that she died. What kind of mother were you? Do you deserve to be called a mother? You, you didn't need to work . . . didn't even have a job . . . but you couldn't even look after a two-year-old. My daughter, the poor child . . . this poor child . . . she died in the manhole, but she was killed by you. You don't deserve to be a mother."

Yixun smashed a teacup. Then he walked to the sewing machine, pulled out the little drawer that held needles and threads, and dumped it on the floor.

The violence in his voice, his attitude, and his actions actually calmed Wu. To her, Yixun's words didn't sound cruel but, instead, soothed her nerves. She hardly believed what she had heard: he called Quan "my daughter." More than just an announcement and acknowledgment, it might indicate forgiveness, or at least a willingness to disregard all of Wu's murky and sordid past. Could he really have said it? What happened to him? He didn't gloat over her misfortune, and how angry he was at her because his daughter died in her care! If that was what he really had in mind and what he really believed, then why not let him shout at her without mercy? Let him berate her as if she were less than human, hurl dreadful curses at her—that her blood should flow and stink for ten thousand years. What she really wanted was to kneel down before him and submit to a beating. Thinking back to a moment ago, just a moment, just that flash of time—but Wu already used the phrase "think back"—to her it was already thinking back to some "time before," when, cornered and about to confess everything, she had worked out a version of her plea for forgiveness in her mind. After her confession, she'd planned to remind him that God had punished her for him. Making the sinful fruit, Quan, disappear from the earth was the worst punishment that God could send. So Yixun should just let it go. What else did he want from her? Even a murderer pays for the crime by simply having his head roll onto the ground. Not to mention the fact that the one who should die had already died, and the living should just be allowed to continue to live. She'd made up her mind to take this approach, but never had she expected events to take such an abrupt turn: because Yixun claimed Quan as his daughter, and no one else's, Wu would never be forgiven and Yixun would be justified in never forgiving. So just when a clear light rippled through her chaotic heart, a deep guilt sank in.

Guilt is a feeling worthy of study. Yixun had found a method to express his emotions in a way that would position him as a victim all his life, venting what he wanted to without appearing cruel. He would use his "innocence" to maintain the normal operation of a decent family and his own dignity, and at the same time he would also control Wu through guilt.

Guilt is indeed a feeling that needs to be studied. The gift of inducing guilt in another is a very ruthless and a very effective mode of vengeance. Guilt is not dependent on a person being in the right or in the wrong, and it is unpredictable. It enters our hearts unexpectedly. More often than not, it isn't aroused by remorse. Paradoxically, it's at the moment that we have the most combative feelings for our antagonists, when we hate them the most, that we suddenly feel guilty. Maybe Yixun didn't know what he was doing at first. He thought he would control Wu through guilt all their lives, but he didn't expect that in later years it would be Wu's obliviousness to what was going on that would incite his own guilt.

He might accuse her of not washing the cucumber clean enough and she would say she had washed it a number of times. Whenever he heard "a number of times" his head would explode. The stupid, vague exaggeration got to him because "a number of times" does not equate with "clean." Yixun's criterion was "clean" and Wu's criterion was "a number of times." He and she had never reached an accord on this minor standard of measurement. Yixun had no choice but to shout at her that there were chemicals and dirt on the cucumber skin and you needed to use a vegetable brush to clean it. "That's why I washed it a number of times!" Wu said. God knows why she had to avoid the crux of the issue; she had to say "a number of times" to avoid admitting that she had not used the vegetable brush. If Yixun continued to press her, she would lie about the brush. In those moments Yixun couldn't help being tempted to reach out his hands and choke her from behind. He would run to her at the sink and, frightened, she would hurriedly grab the brush. She'd scrub the cucumber with mad ferocity, so fiercely that the bristles scraped the skin and exposed the light green young flesh beneath, which made Yixun desperately want to throttle her again. Guilt arrived right then; just at the moment Wu acted unusually sulky, when she hunched her shoulders and revealed her total lack of virtue, and when he ground his teeth from hatred, guilt suddenly arrived. There was not even a small transition point between the two contradictory emotions, but such a feeling is so real and palpable that it forces us to compromise with life and be less sure of ourselves.

4

When Tiao saw Fei afterward, she could hardly resist the urge to tell her, Do you know, Fei? I was the one who killed your cousin. I killed her! In her heart, she bellowed and shouted the statement again and again, not sure if she wanted to use the confession to make atonement herself, or to accuse Fei. Wasn't it Fei who stirred her to action? Before Quan's accident, Fei went to see Quan frequently, even pointing out the cruel fact of Quan's resemblance to Dr. Tang. If Fei seemed like the director of the play, the lead actor would be

Tiao. Who was more guilty? Tiao couldn't decide. In the end she had to judge Fei innocent because at most she merely provided the idea for Tiao. Just a suggestion to follow or not.

Everything was over now and both Tiao's and Fei's families returned to a state of calm. The extreme awkwardness and secrecy between Tiao and Fei disappeared. When they saw each other again, Tiao clearly sensed Fei's serenity. Tiao might have been able to have the same peace herself, but she had no one with whom to celebrate her successful revenge. She didn't even have the opportunity to feel fear. In order to forget, she buried it deep in her heart. It was the sort of feeling that she couldn't communicate, particularly when faced with Fei's peacefulness. Fei had unconsciously discharged her own heaviness onto Tiao—letting Tiao live to suffer. Tiao harbored a vague resentment toward Fei because of this, but she was not able to end their friendship, nor could she help thinking about Quan because she would suddenly see Quan in Fei's face. If Quan hadn't died, she would have become another Fei. Tiao had an absurd feeling that Quan actually hadn't died; that she instead possessed Fei and became a part of her.

And Quan was a part of Fei, an integral part. In Tiao's presence, she would intermittently shine out of Fei for Fei's entire life, and be forever present in Tiao's life. It was an intermingling. Fei was a version of Quan who could open her mouth and speak, and she brought Quan into adulthood.

By then Fei had moved out of her uncle's place. She had worked in a factory before she finished high school and lived in the single person's dorm; otherwise she would have gone to the countryside to accept the peasants' reeducation, a fate similar to that of Captain Sneakers and her only other option. She feared the countryside. To avoid working there, her classmates with connections all dropped out of school and tried to find jobs. Some worked as salespeople in the stores, some worked as ticket-sellers on the buses, and one girl even hired on at a pickle factory, staying in Fuan by stirring a vat of pickled vegetables all day long. She complained to her classmates about how her hands and arms got soaked in the pickle juice and became so chafed. But she had a job, and could stay far from the countryside. Every day, after finishing her job of stirring pickles, she could go home. No matter how nasty a pickle vat was, the factory was still located in Fuan. Its nastiness didn't rise to the next level; it belonged to a city's nastiness, and therefore could be accepted, if reluctantly. Although not much when compared to situations above it, it was better than the ones below. Sometimes even this kind of nastiness, though, could make a person smug.

Fei observed her classmates with a cold eye. She felt their opportunities were all better than hers. But she also held them in the deepest contempt. Her highest goal was to become a real manufacturing worker, and those few major factories located in the western part of Fuan were the objects of her yearning . . . She believed the "working class" that Chairman Mao referred to in his maxim "The working class leads everything" specifically meant the workers in those factories. Their temperament, their style, simply represented the pinnacle of the spirit and status of the age. Salespeople, ticket-sellers, and workers in a small pickle factory didn't count as working class at all; they were at most in the outer circle, and even saying that had a hint of "passing off paste as pearls." Back then, with Fei's background, that she could have such an exaggerated notion of the range of her abilities made her like the fox that couldn't get the grapes. The sour grapes.

Maybe Fei was that fox, but she wasn't so ready to declare that the grapes were sour. She presumed to eat a bunch of grapes that were simply impossible for her to eat, and she had the guts not to quit until she got them. Her courage probably came from her new view of life, which started from her abortion, from the night when she and her uncle embraced each other, weeping without restraint. Her childhood had ended, and she simply couldn't depend on her uncle blindly, nor did she want to be defeated by the ambiguous stares of her classmates. They all knew her family background, and all expected to see her miserable in the countryside someday. But she insisted on becoming a member of the working class, had to become a part of the working class. Only when she entered the working class would she stand unassailable. She did set a presumptuously high standard for herself because only such a standard could really fire the soul.

When graduation approached, word had it that a manufacturing plant had sent a senior worker to their school who was going to recruit two outstanding students with advanced political consciousness and superior moral character from the boys in the graduating classes. The selection process was based on the combination of a teacher's recommendation and the factory's interview. The news made the boys rub their hands together with eagerness and the girls sigh despondently and then become indifferent. Fei kept mulling over the information, even though there were only two positions and the factory requested boys. She was thinking that maybe she didn't have a chance this time, but she should try to make the acquaintance of that recruiter.

A school campus is like a village sometimes. The arrival of a stranger puts the entire place on alert. Although people might not know everyone in their village, they would immediately spot an outsider. That was how Fei discovered the stranger on campus; she saw a man in his thirties holding a bicycle as he stood in front of the administration building talking to the principal. Her first glance told her he wasn't a teacher. She wondered whether he was the recruiting worker. She dawdled purposefully around the entrance of the administration building, hoping to get close enough to eavesdrop. In the end she didn't hear much of their conversation except for the principal saying, "Master Qi, let's go to my office and talk over the details." Master Qi locked his bike and entered the building with the principal.

Fei walked over to Master Qi's locked bike, which she recognized as a Phoenix Manganese 18, the most fashionable of the day, brand-new and shiny. She squatted down and pretended to tie her shoe. Seeing no one around, she deflated both tires of the Phoenix and pulled out the air valves. With the valves clutched in her hand, she ran out the gate and all the way to the bicycle repair shop on the street corner west of the school. She'd made up her mind to wait for Master Qi there, confident he would come.

Half an hour later, Fei indeed saw someone push a bike out the school gate. As the person drew nearer, she could make out the Master Qi who had been talking with the principal earlier. He knitted his eyebrows together slightly, obviously unhappy about the vandalizing of his new bike. He walked directly toward the shop, and his unhappy expression frightened Fei a little, or rather what she feared was not his expression, but how he would respond to her over her little trick. The closer he got, the faster her heart beat. She felt it almost jump into her throat and she had to swallow hard in order to get it back down. She gulped and watched Master Qi set the kickstand to let the bicycle repairman fit the new valves and fill the tires with air. Unless she could open her mouth and talk, she would have no chance, but she was like a mute and no matter how hard she tried she couldn't speak. It was as if her heart were still bouncing around in her throat and once she opened her mouth it would fly out onto the floor. Master Qi had already raised the kickstand and wheeled his bicycle to the sidewalk. She must open her mouth, and there was no turning back. She addressed the back of Master Qi, who was about to swing his leg up to mount his bicycle. "Master Qi. Aren't you Master Qi?"

He stopped and turned to look at her. He said, "Who are you?"

"Me? I'm a student at the high school." Fei raised her chin toward the school and got closer to Master Qi.

He looked her up and down. "How do you know my name is Qi?"

"I guessed," she said.

"Guessed? What can I do for you?" he asked, still carefully studying the girl in front of him. Clearly, he didn't know what she wanted from him, but he had changed his tone from surprise to calm.

Fei finally gathered herself enough to say, "Well, it's like this—I have to confess my error to you. You came to the bicycle repair shop to replace your air valves, right? You must have been very unhappy to find your bike tires had been deflated at our school. I wanted to tell you that I was the one who deflated your tires, and that the person who took your valves was also me."

"Can you tell me why you did this?" Master Qi asked. He had started to walk with his bicycle, slowly, not trying get rid of Fei, just not wanting to stay anywhere in the vicinity of the school for too long.

Fei kept up with Master Qi's pace. She said, "I wanted to get to meet you and I thought, if I pulled out your air valves, you would have to come here, where I planned to wait and greet you."

She said this in a naïve way, and Master Qi couldn't help smiling. When she opened her fist to show him the two little air valves in her palm, her young, sweaty pink palm, a vague tenderness stirred in him. He didn't dislike this girl who had pulled out his air valves, but he still didn't know what she wanted. An ordinary lathe operator who had just gotten promoted to work in the political department, he had a worker's temperament, simple and straightforward. He was not used to Fei's indirect way of talking, the hint of mystery that made people wonder, but this strangeness clearly attracted him. "There must be an important reason behind all this trouble you took."

"Yes, it's very important. I want to work in your manufacturing plant."

Master Qi became quiet, surprised by Fei's request. He felt he couldn't help her. He had just discussed things with the principal and the two positions had been pretty much assigned. Besides, their factory didn't want to hire women this time. Uncertain of what to say, he kept silent.

By then, though hardly noticing, they had reached the riverbank. It was dusk in early winter. The wind from the river was very harsh and there was no one around. It was not clear that such a quiet and out-of-the-way route had been his unconscious choice or under her conscious direction. She broke the silence. "Actually, I was quite unreasonable to make such a request of you. You don't even know my name. What right do I have to make such a request?"

"What is your name?"

"My name is Tang Fei."

"Maybe you'll have a chance later," he said.

"Later? How much later?" Fei pressed without giving him a break.

"Maybe next year. Maybe—"

"Next year won't do. It'll be too late," Fei interrupted Master Qi.

"As soon as I graduate in spring, I'll definitely have to go to the countryside." Now her tone became impatient, as if she were talking to an old acquaintance.

"Fei." He said her name sharply. "Can't your family—your parents—help you out?"

It was a blunt but sensible question, and Fei didn't mind Master Qi asking. Actually, his question provided her the opportunity to open her heart to him, so she said both of her parents, who had been high-ranking journalists for the central government, had lost their lives in an airplane crash while on a mission abroad. She had no choice but to come to live with her uncle in Fuan, who was a blind man working as a masseur at a hospital for traditional medicine and couldn't even take care of himself. Her aunt took out her anger on her, treating her to curses, if not actual beatings, every day. *Ai*, she, the orphan of the martyrs, couldn't bear such a life under someone else's roof, but she had no other relatives in this city, and to whom could she turn? Then she heard about the recruiting and saw Master Qi, whom she felt was her only hope. How she wanted to be able to make Master Qi family. She really wanted to call him "big brother." Without siblings, orphaned, how she'd hoped to have an older brother. Now it looked like there was no hope for her—she was utterly unwanted in the world, and would rather throw herself into the river and drown than continue living.

Tearfully, she spoke these words into the harsh, chilly northern wind, running down to the riverbank as she spoke. It didn't seem false when she said those false words and shed those false tears; it was self-mockery, delivered in a weary burst. Running down the slope, she heard him pursue her. He was touched by her words, by her tender, pitiful expression. When he dropped his bicycle, ran down the bank after her, and grabbed her waist from behind, she preferred to believe that he had no other thoughts, that he was intent only on saving a girl's life. She knew she was securely in his grasp but still pretended to struggle. Naturally, he pulled her more tightly to his chest, so their bodies swayed and they stumbled, holding each other as they fell to the ground on the dark riverbank.

They lay on their sides on the slope. He felt her turn around to face him and burrow into his chest, melting her body into his. Woodenly, not daring to breathe, he held her, unsure how all this had happened. Never had he experienced anything like it, and never had he been less inclined to take advantage of a situation. But why had she pressed herself so tightly into him? He felt the heat of her breath in the dark, and smelled the faintly sour scent. Thinking about her full soft lips, he closed his eyes; he desperately wanted to kiss her, and that was all he wanted. He turned his head searching for her mouth, but she did all she could to avoid his kiss. This made him think that it wouldn't work, that nothing was going to happen with her. Her melting into him was not seduction but . . . a subconscious desire for protection. As he considered this, he stopped trying for her lips and calmed down a little. What he ought to do now was pull her to her feet, climb up the bank, and send her home. He let go of her and stood, but she pulled him back down by her, so they rolled together again. Eagerly, almost sobbing, she said to him, "Let me take off my clothes for you. I'll take them off now, now . . ."

Blood rushed to his head, and his body felt uncomfortable because of the pressure. The behavior of this teenage high school girl was incomprehensible to him—why she didn't want his kisses but was willing to . . . willing to . . . The vision of her as she stood in front of the bike shop came to him, such a contradiction to what she appeared to be now. Innocence and conspiracy, naïveté and debauchery, seemed to coexist in her. He really couldn't think anymore, or control the overwhelming desire she had forced on him, and he didn't want to lose this opportunity that seemed to arrive from outer space. He took off his coat and spread it on the slope, and then he picked Fei up and set her on the still-warm coat . . .

Two weeks later, Master Qi managed to get Fei a recruiting form. During the political background check, her story about her family turned out to be so much hot air. Master Qi didn't despise her for this, but on the contrary felt more sympathetic toward her. Even though she'd lied to him about some matters, he still felt guilty about her. He often thought if what they had done on the river slope hadn't happened, his helping her would have been innocent and simple, and therefore beautiful. Unfortunately, he hadn't controlled himself. It wasn't something that he regretted; he just felt a little sad when he thought about it. He did his best to help her, getting her, a girl with virtually no hope of staying in the city, a job at the famous state-run factory as a foundry worker. Unfortunately, it wasn't a good job. His influence could only reach so far, and Fei was assigned to the dirtiest, most tiring workshop in the factory.

Foundry apprentice Fei bought Dr. Tang a pair of fashionable nylon gloves with her first paycheck. She also gave Tiao and Youyou a factory tour, and got them some treats at her bachelor's dormitory. She got them fried sugar dough, and two *jin* of them were polished off in a blink of the eye. "No big deal," she bragged, "I'll get some more in a minute. I have money. I'm a person with a salary." She took out a small purse, woven out of light purple glass strands. As she flourished the purse, Tiao saw the tears that stood in her beautiful eyes.

5

It was in Chen Zai's study that Tiao got to know Balthus. When Tiao discovered an album of paintings by Balthus, she and Chen Zai had already been close friends for a long time. She could see that Balthus was an important painter to Chen Zai, but it was just like Chen Zai never to impose his opinions on Tiao. He was usually modest, even shy, when he spoke about the things that meant a lot to him. This was one way he expressed his respect for his beloved.

Tiao happened on the album of Balthus's paintings and opened it. Immediately she was taken by him. His subjects were actually very mundane: several groups of passersby walking an old commercial street in Paris; some children playing cards and strategizing in a living room, and girls reading books or in a sound sleep; a band of hikers with blank expressions and dull eyes, who'd originally come to savor the boundless vista from the mountain peak, but after the ascent became lethargic, swaying and unable to stand, none of them appreciating the scenery, and one even collapsing into sleep. He especially liked to paint young girls. The girls in his paintings—he seemed very particular about their age—are all around fourteen. Balthus rendered their skin with luster and remarkable softness. They are innocent and clean, their bodies blossoming with a mixture of some desire, a bit of fantasy, a little portion of serenity, along with a small measure of unpredictability.

Tiao had never seen work by a painter like him: his characters seemed completely three-dimensional, but the backgrounds—sofa, street, bed, and desk—were often flat. It was through this combination that he created paintings as thick as a wall. In a painting that seemed solid and stable, those images—either flat and straight or slanted, curled, or stretched—created different rhythms and moods, which echoed the painter's internal rhythms. There was risk in the stability, restraint in the flow, closure in the openness, strangeness and the eternal in the dailiness, and a stillness that also harbored anxiety. The viewer felt both at peace and uneasy, a vague tenderness along with panic, even when faced with the girls asleep on the sofa—because Balthus made people feel there was conspiracy lurking around the girls. And there was indeed always the hint of it—a tiny skinny black cat, or a midget twisting his neck and pulling open the window curtain—but viewers were spared panic by Balthus's graceful sense of restraint, which eventually helped the audience find a true balance—a lovely balance—between art and the zeitgeist and a strangeness that was completely convincing.

Balthus used traditionally concrete visual language, and the objects he chose to work with couldn't have been more ordinary. He didn't want to find his materials in the surreal, and he made use of reality in an honest, straightforward, but extraordinary way. His reality seemed superficial but was actually profound, seemed like one thing but was actually another, had the appearance of being ordinary but laid snares everywhere. He had probably long understood that there was no such thing as "right" and "wrong" in art and that an artist should never presume to become an "inventor." In art, "invention" is fairly suspect, a nonsense word. Rodin says, "Originality—in the most positive meaning—is not about making up new words that contradict common sense; it's about using the old words cleverly. Old words are sufficient to express everything; to a genius, the old words are more than enough."

For an artist to add a little something new of his own to the tradition would be a very great achievement. Such deep reflection only comes from those masters who are most deeply immersed in the zeitgeist and artistic expression. They are the true sages, not the "inventors" impelled by the "irresistible urge" to make history by innovation. Art is not about invention; art is honest, quiet labor. Balthus's modesty and his meticulous pursuit of perfection in craft, his sensitivity to the zeitgeist and the perfect form in which he responded to it—his particular inheritance of the excellent tradition of creative rendering—advanced the cause of representational art, constantly under siege in the twentieth century and always endangered, to a level that few others achieved. The intimate distance and familiar strangeness that his paintings communicated were his contribution to art.

She looked at *Cathy Dressing*, a painting inspired by *Wuthering Heights*. It's clear at a glance that the three people in the painting are Balthus's version of the novel's unforgettable characters: Cathy, the blonde, nude and holding a mirror, immediately recalls Catherine; the dark-skinned, melancholy young man who sits in a chair is obviously a re-creation of Heathcliff; the solemn elderly maidservant who stands behind her and combs Cathy's hair seems to work to separate their love from the powerful antagonism between them. Temporarily, she balances the painting as well as their hearts, which alternate between love and hate throughout their lifelong relationship. It's a straightforward painting of three people. The brushstrokes are economical and the use of color is the height of plainness and simplicity, but as you look at it again and again, you sense a poignancy along with a sharpness—it is uninhibited and restrained at once. Cathy's body, nude and facing the viewers, is overpowering at first sight, the brightest, the most dazzling part of the painting; her head tilts to one side slightly, and the gray-brown eyes, directed slightly upward, and compressed lips make her look proud and domineering. Disregarding others' advice, she seems to have made up her mind about her future and thinks herself mature enough to do so, therefore she ignores the young man beside her, who is deeply in love with her and appears on the point of collapse; or else perhaps she despises his miserable look. Her body assists her expression, with the small jutting breasts, the nonchalant stance . . . all brimming with a kind of empty challenge.

But this tall, slender beauty's pubic area is not fully developed— her narrow, thin pelvis, flat belly, and the immature wisps of hair contend with the imperious head and proud breasts, which makes her look demanding and helpless, confident and desperate, indifferent and passionate, cunning and innocent all at the same time. Her inner world is chaotic. She is her own contradiction. She needs to be saved and the young man in the chair beside her is hoping to be saved by her. But she and the gloomy young man can't save each other. He stares at her, her entire body shining, the love of his life, the girl who eventually will belong to another man, but he can't win her back. Through him Tiao is brought to that moment in *Wuthering Heights* when Catherine returns from Linton's home, and Heathcliff questions her desperately, out of his own sense of inferiority. "Why did you have to wear this silk dress? Why did you have to wear this silk dress?" when it's just the stubborn memory of their childhood love that remains, and perhaps only parting forever can free them from that mad and frightening recollection. Tiao felt overwhelmed by an insight into an obsessive fantasy: how people exhaust themselves— or would, if they had the chance—to return to innocent beginnings, to a world of original joy.

A return to joy.

A return to joy.

Tiao continued by examining *Cat in the Mirror.* There were a series of three variations on the same theme, in the same setting, that spanned the sixteen years from 1977 to 1993.

The first is a nude girl, who has just awakened and leans against her bed, combing her hair, comb in one hand and mirror in the other. On finding that the cat squatting at the end of the bed is staring at her, she turns the mirror around to invite the cat to examine itself.

In the moment, the girl's expression and body both appear natural and relaxed, fresh and soft. Her invitation to the cat has an element of playfulness.

The second one: The girl has been leaning against the head of the bed, viewing herself in the mirror, with a little book in her other hand. On finding the cat, hiding at the foot of the bed, staring at her, she turns the mirror around and forces the cat to examine itself. In this painting, the girl has grown older and there is more of both reserve and wantonness in her expression, though she is clothed in a thin blouse and a pair of long pants. Fully dressed, she holds the mirror and makes the cat, who hunches at the end of the bed, see itself, as if saying, Do you want to watch me? You'd better have a look at yourself.

The third: The girl still leans against the bed; judging from her face she is again older. She wears elaborate, conservative clothing and her face reveals a forcefully controlled anger and willfulness. She thrusts the mirror directly at the cat on the end of the bed, whose entire body is visible, as if saying, Why look at me? Why observe me, you seductive, sinister thing! No longer the naked girl, relaxing, briskly combing her hair, she obviously dominates the scene, in the tight clothing she'd prepared in advance—nervous, combative.

How people fear being watched—spied on—particularly by their own kind who hide in the dark. When humans are subject to the cold scrutiny of a cat, who knows all, is ever-present and often pleased with itself, what an unsettling feeling it must be. People love to gaze at themselves in the mirror, but who ever sees the true self in the mirror? All of us expect to see a beautiful face on that self in the mirror. So, to watch others is to shield the self.

To watch is to shield.

When people are annoyed and shove the mirror into the cat's face, they want to watch the cat make a fool of itself—and to shield themselves. The coquettishness of the nervous cat, and the insidious psychology that has it always waiting for the chance to rebel, people fear these things, so they thrust the mirror at the cat. To spy, to embarrass others, is the most basic human instinct.

The cat has no mirror to turn on a person; to a person the cat is a mirror. Squinting its seemingly tired eyes in the dark, it quietly snuggles up to people, in surface harmony, but spiritually distant.

Balthus's work, his relationship with his subjects, which became more chaotic the more he tried to put it in order, his high taste, his emotional but controlled style, all fascinated Tiao. Sometimes she felt she was the cat curling at the end of the bed; sometimes she believed she was the naked, playful young girl, who eventually grew into the fully armed, smoldering young woman: Why do you look at me and why do you observe me? You coquettish, sinister little thing!

All our watching is done to shield ourselves. When will we inspect our own hearts? Almost no one can bear to look closely within. Self-scrutiny leads us into stumbling vertigo, but we must deal with others and have no escape. Others are always our mirrors. The more we fear to look closely at ourselves, the more eager we are to scrutinize them. We comfort our heart's core with this scrutiny of other people's flaws.

Chapter 5

✿ ✿ ✿

The Ring Is Caught in the Tree

1

Like many women in love, Tiao was fearful, bold, and incapable of rational thought. Her emotional entanglement with Fang Jing prevented her from seeing herself—or others—clearly. His surprisingly frank "love letters" not only didn't drive Tiao away but, on the contrary, drew her closer. His repeated tales of dalliances with other women only served to convince her that she was the only woman Fang Jing could trust and that only she had the power to save him. So the mix of Fang Jing's personality, sincerity plus hooliganism, drove Tiao to distraction. After hearing his story of the tenth woman, she became reckless and crazy, demanding that he have her, as if that would help him cleanse his previous impurity. She was no longer the Tiao of before, who couldn't even find his lips, whose heart was excited and whose eyes were opened by his love letters. Not wanting things to have the least suggestion of barter, she didn't even think about marriage. Marriage. That would be his request of her later.

After knowing her for two years, he finally had her.

Her body felt no pleasure but her heart was content, some part of which was vanity, as well as a young woman's primitive instinct for love, simple and unaffected to the point of silliness.

He finally had her. He was, in every way, satisfied, happy, even delightfully surprised, the biggest surprise of all being something he wouldn't confide to anyone—he had never told Tiao, either—that she had restored his manhood.

For years Fang Jing had been impotent, which he attributed to the enormous mental and physical suffering he'd endured in the decade of the Cultural Revolution. When he regained freedom and his talents began to be recognized, the most important thing in his life was to find a cure. Big hospitals and small hospitals, folk remedies and secret family potions—he stooped to anything, even visiting those shady little clinics with ambiguous names and clear theme located in backstreets and tucked away in alleys. But none of the treatments worked on Fang Jing. He didn't understand why life would play such an ironic joke on him, which filled him with hostility and made him curse the overwhelming temptation that came his way.

So he made a point of exaggerating his various relationships with women, intending embellishments and fabrications to carry juicy news of his debaucheries to the world. How he wished he were a real hooligan, or at least a man with hooligan potential.

It was difficult to tell whether his initial approach to Tiao had any clear intent or not, and therefore difficult to say that he had seduced her gradually with his letters. Those letters represented, in part, a test of his own charm as well as his response to the inexplicable impulse of his attraction to this young woman. Later, on the night they said farewell, when she gave him that irrelevant half kiss, his missing her became real hunger and thirst. Hunger and thirst. Yet expressed through avoidance; suddenly he was afraid to see her. He was afraid to smell her breath, to embrace her, to touch her soft hand, or to look into the depths of her large, dark eyes. He was afraid he couldn't take her, or give himself to her, as a lover; he was afraid to humiliate himself on her body—he didn't care about other women's bodies, whom he had experimented on dozens of times already, each more of a failure than the last. He made a fool of himself while feeling superior to those women, an arrogant pretense of superiority he used to cover up his embarrassment and helplessness, which he would rather die than do with Tiao. For a while, he'd put her off stiffly in rough language, even when she took it on herself to come to Beijing and called him. Afterward he wrote her a passionate letter. He intensified his secret quest for folk cures and "miracle" doctors, and any quack could raise his hopes. Once, late at night, after a visit to an old folk healer, he covered his face and wept in a quiet alley, a grown man crying like a baby, his sobbing enormous and defenseless, like that of a wronged, homeless orphan.

He avoided Tiao and at the same time desperately longed for her. Not until the New Year's party hosted by the Beijing film circle would he encounter her. Certain he would be there, she showed up without warning; she just wanted to see him. Her appearing unexpectedly made him happy as well as nervous. They saw each other but didn't greet or invite each other to dance. They pretended to concentrate on dancing with others, changing partners frequently until the music died and people began to leave. Tiao went down the street without looking back. She told herself proudly but with anticipation: I won't look back. I would never look back; never turn my head. But please follow me. Please follow me. I believe you will follow me.

He followed her, and he'd decided to follow her before the party ended. Quietly, he followed her all the way to her hotel, and up to her room. The door gently closed behind them. He locked it firmly and pulled her into an embrace. They both knew what was going to happen. Holding her as she trembled, no longer able to control his desire, he was determined to make love to her, like a gambler desperately betting everything on one last throw of the dice.

It was on this night he discovered she knew nothing about sex. Her ignorance made her doubly precious to him, and also made him want to laugh. He was thinking that it was impossible for him to be embarrassed in front of her because she didn't even have the most basic means of judgment. Her ignorance and complete obedience touched and pleased him. He had never thought, never imagined, she would be like this; it was impossible for her to look down on him. He suddenly felt relaxed and filled with a strength he didn't recall—empowered by calm, long absent, appearing in a flash with his happiness and ease. Despite the pressure in his head and with temples throbbing, he went forward, not caring, or else daring to enjoy the happiness, though still afraid that happiness might lead to a carelessness that would ruin his long-awaited recovery, the priceless and joyful recovery.

He finally succeeded. His eyes brimmed with tears and his heart overflowed with a gratitude to Tiao that words couldn't describe; he had never loved Tiao as he did right now. Also, he also loved and valued himself more than ever. Afraid the recovery might disappear, he insisted unreasonably that Tiao concoct all kinds of excuses to stay in Beijing day after day, wanting to be with her every minute, day and night. He wouldn't have admitted to experimenting with himself, but their bodies together over and over finally convinced him that his success wasn't the one-night bloom of a moonflower, but that he would be a real man forever, feet firmly on the ground, able to shoulder the world.

Tiao woke up one morning to find Fang Jing kneeling beside her bed and gazing at her, and then she heard him say, "I want to ask you something: Marry me. I want you to marry me."

These were the longed-for words that she never expected to hear. Overjoyed as she was, a voice from her heart had already begun warning her: maybe this wasn't right. Later, from deep in her, that warning voice would continue, but she ignored it—and when her actions conflicted with the warnings of her inner voice, she trusted her actions. Even when Fang Jing in ecstasy forgot himself and shouted out wildly, "I want to fuck every woman in the world," she still failed to grasp the insult to her in the words. She preferred to credit Fang Jing's truthfulness: this must be the secret desire of many men. Who else would blurt out the truth the way Fang Jing did?

Once they took the bus to the zoo. Tiao casually tossed away their used bus tickets when they got off, but Fang Jing immediately picked them up. "From now on, don't throw away these tickets. I want to take them back and get reimbursed. Hmm, I'd even claim reimbursement for a five-cent ticket—not that I need money, but because of how much they owe me." He cast his gaze into the distance, and the expression in his eyes was cold and faintly indignant. His eyes and words chilled and surprised Tiao, and she felt there was hatred inside him, but to whom did "they" refer? Unable or unwilling to make the connection between Fang Jing's "getting reimbursement" and his "I want to fuck all the women in the world," she was just a confused girl in love who rejected logic. Only many years later, in retrospect, would she recognize the common thread in his two desires. He was a middle-aged man who had suffered greatly. Once free of suffering, he couldn't help demanding compensation—urgently, madly—from the entire society, the human component, all the men and women. Time flows on like water and he knew more and more clearly that he was no rival for time.

Tiao had no concept of that kind of demand for compensation. Was it because she was still young? Youth is capital. It was because of that perishable capital that Fang Jing was jealous of her even when he loved her the most. Her dewy fullness, her lack of romantic experience, and even her ignorance of her own value made him groan with jealousy. Ah, all this proved that she still had plenty of time to gallop through the broad world as she pleased, but for him a faint, strange voice resonated constantly in his ear, telling him he was getting old.

This alone provided him ample reason to make demands on the world, and it formed the psychological basis of his misuse of his status, talent, and gender to manipulate society and people. It made him treat Tiao capriciously, sometimes even harshly. Once he said to her suddenly, "I don't think I can marry you. Our age difference is too great, and sooner or later you'll get tired of me. I would always worry about someone taking you away from me. Do you know worrying will make me age faster?"

Tiao swore to him, "I'm not afraid of your getting old. I want to get old with you. No matter how old you are, I'll be with you to take care of you. I want to take care of you." Not only didn't her words move Fang Jing, but they made him fly into a rage. "I don't want you to take care of me. I don't want you to see a mouthful of my dentures and the fungal nails on my feet. You've seen them, right? Tell me you've seen them, and they disgust you, don't they?"

Even when preparing to divorce his wife and marry Tiao, he was still chasing women indiscriminately or being chased by those women who pursue celebrities. He couldn't explain himself: it seemed as though the more he loved Tiao, the more he felt compelled to be with other women, as if by continually abusing others and himself he'd prove his youthfulness, charm, and value. Then he would be worthy of Tiao, for how could a man who proved so attractive not be worthy of Tiao? This was Fang Jing's logic. He couldn't extricate himself from it because he was so obsessed with the years of his youth that were gone forever.

It was indeed an era when celebrities were idolized and talent revered, so much so that all Fang Jing's capricious and extravagant behavior was blindly rationalized by Tiao. It truly was blindness, of a new sort, derived from the pursuit of civilization, progress, and openness, that allowed the public to accept martyred celebrities with such enthusiasm. When Tiao, a victim of this blindness, told Fei everything about Fang Jing, Fei just sneered at Tiao's affair. "Never get involved with a married man!" she warned Tiao from the very beginning.

Never get involved with a married man.

"But he's no ordinary married man!" Tiao defended herself.

"What's so unusual about him? Does he have three legs? Who gives him the right to divorce his wife and beg to marry you while he keeps chasing other women nonstop? Who gives him the right?" Fei said in disgust.

Tiao said, "I'm willing to forgive him everything. You don't know how much he suffered!"

Fei snorted and said, "Don't give me that crap over the little bit of suffering he's had to bear. Academically, I'm not as good as you two—I didn't go to any fucking university—but I despise Fang Jing's kind, who hold up a high-powered telescope to their suffering. They magnify it infinitely, until society has no room for any other but theirs. Their suffering is everywhere, and everyone owes them, left and right. Don't others suffer? Are we not supposed to because we're young? What is suffering? Real suffering can't be told, unlike in the movies and novels . . . Don't you know that if suffering can be put into words, then it's no deep thing?"

Tiao's face turned red and she said, "I don't know, and I don't want to know, either."

"Didn't I just tell you? Why do you still not know? Do you pretend you don't know, or do you really not know?"

Tiao said, "I know you suffered a lot and you haven't found love. But I've found love, and love can heal suffering. I've been trying hard to love—"

Fei interrupted Tiao and said, "What the fuck is love? The most fragile thing in the world. I noticed long ago how you lost your head over 'love.' I really hoped you and Fang Jing could eventually marry, but I'm sure that Fang Jing won't marry you. And if he doesn't, it'll be the biggest blessing of your life."

"Fei, don't talk to me like that. Don't say such unlucky things."

"My God," Fei said. "My words might be a little unlucky, but think about it, what about Fang Jing was lucky for you? Which of the things he said to you and did to you was lucky? How many men have you known so far? What the fuck do you know about men?"

Fei's rough talk brought the past back to Tiao. She remembered when Captain Sneakers took Fei away from Youyou's house, when he slapped Fei, and Tiao questioned him in a shrill voice about why he would hit her, and he said to Tiao in contempt, "You know fucking nothing."

Their words might be rough, not educated or elegant enough, but only years later did Tiao understand the truth in Fei's rough words.

2

Generally speaking, truth is hard to take in; at least it's not pleasing to the ears. But Fei's true words sank into Tiao's heart and were hard to dislodge. The harder she tried, the more they would move through her, circulating through the cracks in her soul. Reluctantly, she pretended she was waiting with all her heart for Fang Jing to divorce his wife and marry her, but in the end she had to admit to herself that her hopes for marriage had become increasingly faint.

Fang Jing told her about a recent, unconsummated "amorous encounter" of his with a painter in Guangzhou—he made the confession to get some credit for what he had done, and he really expected Tiao to be proud of him.

He said, "I stayed in the same hotel with the painter. We made each other's acquaintance at dinner. She recognized me first and immediately introduced herself, adeptly spotting the key that I'd put on the table. She looked at my room number on it and said, 'We're actually neighbors!' She was a big, strong woman with broad shoulders and back, who walked in strides—a bit slovenly and careless in her appearance. After dinner, she came to my room, asked me if I was working on anything new, and also brought me an album of her paintings published in Hong Kong—she'd just had a one-woman show in a gallery there. After a while, she asked me whether I was lonely or not. Before I said anything she said she was lonely. She recently had gotten divorced because her husband couldn't stand her using male models, making it a rule that if she had to paint a male nude, he had to be over seventy or under fourteen. For that reason, he often showed up at her studio unannounced to check on her. But the checking hurt no one but himself. He found his wife didn't really care about his rule; in her studio there were young men in immoral poses. When she got home, he grabbed her by the hair and beat her—he really couldn't take the fact that there were so many male organs on display in front of his wife. The painter laughed at this point. She smoked, and cigarettes made her voice hoarse.

"She said to me, 'So, my husband and I just broke up. I feel lonely, but it's a free sort of loneliness. What about you? The newspapers say you have a happy family. Actually you're also lonely. And your loneliness is worse than mine, because yours is not free.'

"I responded, 'How do you know I'm lonely?' She said that my question was naïve. All highly intelligent people are inherently lonely. She looked at me meaningfully, with either the eyes of a painter studying a model, or those of a woman looking at a man. I wasn't sure which—maybe both. Whichever it was, her eyes were confident, confident about her charms and my inability to resist them. I didn't feel nervous with her; this type of woman doesn't make me nervous. But to be honest with you, I didn't want to make love to her, not that I looked down on her, but—Tiao—I really thought about you at that moment. I felt I should save myself for you. This I'd told myself thousands of times, although I was often unable to do it—but I did this time. I swear to you I did it for you. Seeing that I didn't respond to her, she simply stood up, took the pipe from my hand, and put it on the table. Then she took me by the hand and said, 'Come.' I didn't want to, so I picked up my pipe and continued to smoke, puffing jets and billows, as if to use the smoke to shield myself from her attack. Indeed, she did stop, and said with a sigh, 'I guess you must have someone you love very much.'

"I said, 'Yes, I do have someone that I love very much.'

"She said, 'Can you tell me what kind of woman she is?'

"I said, 'Sorry. I can't.'

"She said, 'Why do you make simple things complicated? I don't want to replace anyone.'

"I just kept saying, 'I'm sorry, but I can't.' Tiao, do you know, when she came near me and took the pipe from my hand, I smelled something in her hair that I simply couldn't stand? You know how important smell is between men and women. For me, if it isn't right, there's no way I can get aroused. I just couldn't get used to hers, and I couldn't even exactly describe what it was. In short, something that put off a man like me. The closer she came to me, the more unexcited—even limp—I got, until she left my room. What do you think, Tiao? Don't I deserve praise? I beg you to congratulate me."

Fang Jing thought Tiao would be moved by his story and proud of the loyalty shown on that occasion: his rare rejection of another woman, hard for him to believe it himself. He didn't expect Tiao to fix on the "smell" aspect of his story.

"You claim you saved yourself for me, and then you said when she got near you smelled something in her hair that you couldn't stand. A woman with the wrong scent simply couldn't arouse you. So, what if her smell hadn't put you off but, instead, aroused you when she approached? Would you still have saved yourself for me?"

He said, "You really surprise me. With a devoted heart, I tell you everything about the well-behaved me in Guangzhou, and I expect your encouragement and praise, but listen to you."

"What do you want me to say, then? You make the basic moral code that a man should follow into a special case, an achievement to brag about, an unusual event that a woman should be thankful for, but even you admit that it was the woman's smell that turned you off, right?"

"What I did wrong was that I was too truthful with you. I wanted to tell you everything, but instead you have to split hairs with me."

"It's not hair-splitting; it's a fact! I'm never your priority. Your need—your need for the right smell is your priority. You thought I would be grateful to you? If I have to thank someone I should thank that painter with the wrong smell. It's her smell that propelled you back to me. Isn't that a fact?"

He said, "Can you just shut up and stop talking about 'smell'?"

She said, "I'm very sorry, but I'm not the one who brought up 'smell.'"

He said, "Okay, okay, okay. I mentioned it first, but why can't you see the side of me that values and loves you? Why have you become so cutting and bitter?"

"Maybe I have gotten bitter—" Tiao said. Right then Fei's warnings came to mind, which annoyed her and increased her anger. She was no longer the generous, forgiving Tiao who dreamed of saving Fang Jing. Her sense of her role had changed; she was judging his behavior as Fang Jing's would-be wife, and it made her cutting. She'd suddenly woken up to certain aspects of their relationship. The more she wanted to establish her everyday, number-one status in Fang Jing's heart, the less she could accept his "truthfulness" as if she were a stranger to him. His "truthfulness" seemed like domination, a way to demean her rather than a demonstration of respect and trust for a partner. She told Fang Jing, "Maybe I have become bitter, but it's hard for me to imagine anyone else accepting your truthfulness without getting bitter. Try and find such a person. Go find her . . ."

He said, "Why talk this way? Where do you want me to find her? How did you get so fussy?"

She despised the word "fussy," especially the way Fang Jing labeled her with it. She reacted strongly—with panic—to their mutual criticism. To cover the panic, she tried to show her toughness to Fang Jing. She hated the toughness on her side but felt she had to keep going. She said, "Save your 'fussy' for someone else. I'm not the housewife in your family."

Right then, he stopped talking. She had no choice but to ask him again and again, "What's wrong? Why don't you say something? Won't you tell me what you're thinking?"

He suddenly gazed at her as coldly as if she were a stranger. "I'm thinking of my daughter. I'm thinking that I've paid too little attention to her since meeting you. I'm thinking that maybe it's time for me to go and see my daughter. I'm not a good father."

It had the sound of self-criticism, but every word struck Tiao's head and heart because what Fang Jing said about missing his daughter was merely a way to show Tiao her diminished importance and to express his regret about their relationship. She wanted to save their relationship, but, inexperienced as she was, she didn't know how. Actually, it was a relationship that was headed nowhere, and Fang Jing had just signaled his withdrawal by accusing Tiao of being bitter and fussy. He was tired. She was also tired. He was tired and wanted to withdraw into his unfree sort of loneliness; she was tired but was still frantically willing to dive into the trap.

He was determined to distance himself from her. He had seen the way she'd matured; no longer the clay that he could mold any way he wanted, she didn't appreciate his truthfulness and argued with him. She was no longer a kitten or puppy that could only nip, and even when it was very angry, the tiny pain it could cause would only remind you to pet it. She was no longer a kitten or a puppy, but a full-grown animal with fur and claws, everything necessary to cause a big stir. Animals of that size wouldn't be easily controlled and might even turn on you.

He backed away.

Avoiding her, he didn't take her phone calls or answer her letters. Because of this, Tiao wasted away day after day. She didn't dare to look at the photographs of herself at the time, where what was left of her seemed to be two large sunken eyes. She suffered from insomnia, lack of appetite, and her hair withered and dried. She went to work reluctantly, and handled her duties at the publishing house, but the plan for publishing a series of celebrities' childhoods had disappeared long ago—without her connection with Fang Jing, how could she have any chance of doing it? When she was with Fang Jing, she turned love into her main concern and her profession into a sideline, and now he'd broken up with her as soon as the thought crossed his mind. She had to come up with a topic to work on while waiting for his reply. She considered doing a series called We Reap What We Sow. When the title occurred to her, she was pleased. But then she immediately associated it with her relationship with Fang Jing, which was certainly a we-reap-what-we-sow relationship. And she felt the name was deadly boring. She rejected it but had no other ideas. As she sat in her office, her brain often went blank for long periods.

Ashamed of herself, she stayed away from Fei. After a while, Fei came to the publishing house to see her. Nothing escaped Fei; Tiao's haggard, weakened look told her everything had turned out as she'd predicted; only she hadn't expected it to happen so fast.

She sat across from Tiao, who pulled open a drawer and lowered her head, searching through it. Finally, she took out a bag of dried fish and tossed it to across the desk to Fei. She smiled at Fei, but the tears streamed down her face. They had already been welling up when she lowered her head to rummage around in the drawer. She'd kept her head down for a long time in order to control her tears, which Fei clearly saw dropping into the drawer. Many years before, in the alley in Fuan after the movie, when Fei told Tiao, "I don't have a mother," Fei had smiled this way, tears streaming. It was awkward to face dear friends, wanting to let emotions out and also wanting to keep them in. Fei had to move away. She stood up, walked to the window, and looked out for a while. Then she plopped her bottom down on the sill. Back against the window, she faced Tiao, her legs dangling, took out a cigarette, and lit it.

For a moment Tiao felt she was about to scream. Astonishment held back her tears. The office was on the fifteenth floor. Even though the window was closed and the sill was wide, the way Fei sat touched off an intense feeling of disquiet. Tiao couldn't tell what was off-kilter: The scene outside was stable, the window frame was upright, then was it Fei? Tiao couldn't say, but she was in the grip of nightmarish anxiety, unreal and real at the same time, just like the dream she kept having. In her recurrent dream, she had a full bladder and had to go to the bathroom. When she finally found one, and opened her legs to squat down, the pit suddenly collapsed and she was stained with shit all over . . . She suppressed her scream and waved to Fei to come down.

Fei didn't. She sat on the window ledge and asked Tiao, "What are you planning to do?"

"I love him. I don't know how I'm going to live without him."

Fei said, "Do you still think that way?"

"Yes, I still do. Go ahead and yell at me."

"You'll die if you continue like this."

"It's better to die than live this way."

Fei said, "You must be crazy."

Tiao said, "Yes, I'm crazy. Let me go crazy once. What else can I do?"

Fei turned around and pushed the window open with a scraping sound. Wind blew in and lifted some paper on the desk. When Fei turned around, the tears welling in her own eyes were flung out. She didn't want to cry in front of Tiao, even though Tiao's emaciation moved her deeply. She jumped down from the windowsill at Tiao's repeated pleas and said, "I don't understand why you're so afraid of me sitting on the windowsill. Do you think a grown person like me would fall out?"

"You won't fall. You'll never fall, but—I'm still afraid."

"Tiao, tell me what I can do for you. Tell me."

Tiao shook her head.

"I know what you want me to do. You want me to go to Beijing to talk to Fang Jing."

"No, I don't."

"Let's not waste time. Give me his phone number and address. I'll go see him for you."

"No, no, please don't."

"Why, what's the problem?" Fei asked.

"It's not that, there's . . . I think you shouldn't act rudely," Tiao told her.

"That's the kind of thing only someone like you would think of," Fei said. "Even now you're still protecting him!"

Tiao began asking how Fei was going to meet him, and it was clear Fei's fierce sisterhood buoyed up the dispirited Tiao.

3

Feeling the unfairness of what had happened to Tiao, Fei set out for Beijing, intent on standing up for Tiao with Fang Jing. However, on her way to Beijing she thought constantly about her uncle, Dr. Tang. The two were completely unrelated: Dr. Tang and Fang Jing didn't know each other, and would never have a chance to meet.

In the spring of 1976, two years after Fei started at the factory, Dr. Tang became acquainted with a nurse in the surgical clinic. He'd hurt his hand in a bike accident and had gone there to have it dressed. The nurse cleaned his wound, put on some ointment, and then bandaged it efficiently and carefully. They were colleagues. Although one worked in internal medicine and the other in surgery, they greeted each other with a nod every time they passed. Around the hospital, there was talk about the nurse. Her husband worked in another city and couldn't get transferred to Fuan, so she'd had affairs with some men in the hospital. She wasn't too choosy about the men, nor did she mind much what other people thought. At a time when "lifestyle problems" were second in seriousness only to political ones, she wasn't shy about her "lifestyle problem." In her department, she was the butt of the jokes of the middle-aged men and women. When they teased her with double entendres, her thick-skinned, blunt comebacks would startle them. She often said, "What can I do if a man wants me? Can I forbid him to want me? I can't stop him, so I have to let him come to call." In this way, she turned the unmentionable into the stuff of everyday life, like shopping, cooking, and eating. Likewise, her whole being radiated earthiness. Whether they were electricians in the hospital or cooks from the canteen, it was all the same to her. She never looked down on the cooks, so she always got served heaping portions of food—and who doesn't live to earn a mouthful of food in this world? The servings on her lunch tray, supposedly for one person, were enough to feed her and her two children. Her carefree lovemaking also seemed to make her complexion glow with health. She loved to laugh, often giggling while she lay on men's bodies, and had never felt that she was less than they were or that she was being taken advantage of; she always believed it was the other way around. This was not the rationalizing Ah Q spirit helping her to deceive herself; it was simply because she was ordinary, practical, simple, and emotionally detached that made her a spiritual victor. She was the vampire, and Dr. Tang's wounded hand gave her a chance to suck his blood.

Dr. Tang would sit, while she stood to change the bandages, and she would take longer and longer each time. Changing bandages gave him a reason to sit in front of her, and her a reason to stand in front of him. Whether by accident or on purpose, her knee brushed his. He didn't react or try to avoid it. She got closer, and her knee pressed against his knee. Next, she used both of her knees to sandwich his, tightly. There were others in the room; not far from them, the unit director was checking a man whose face was twisted into a grimace by the corns on his feet. The nurse's brazen seduction made Dr. Tang nervous, even though her knees were somewhat hidden by her white smock. But the public seduction also gave him a special thrill; his knee was wedged, his wound, which was not too serious, was being bandaged in routine fashion. He quickly glanced over at the clinic's beds, but no one was paying attention. It was a moment of extreme boredom, and people often need to do something to relieve their boredom. By the time she let go of him, he was thinking, what the heck, why not have a relationship with her? They lived in the same hospital compound, only two or three dormitories away, so there wouldn't even be any travel involved.

Both appeared willing, and hit it off very well, with no expectations between them, just sex and stolen pleasures. Dr. Tang and the nurse mostly did their business during the day, when her kids had gone to school and the residential area was quiet, often disappearing from their offices suddenly for a while, half an hour or forty minutes. The hospital was chaotic all day long, and who would notice? Maybe they'd gone to the bathroom, or maybe they went off to meet the acquaintances whom every doctor and nurse would have. Usually Dr. Tang went to the nurse's apartment. They'd enter, close the curtains, and then rush to their purpose without any extra words. The nurse had many tricks, and she allowed Dr. Tang to experience many vulgar pleasures—and vulgar pleasures are still pleasures, after all. He often thought about what she said the first time he came home with her: "Now I only leave the door open for you." Expressions like this were strange to Dr. Tang, but they conveyed a feeling intimate beyond words, which seemed to suit a country woman like her well. The door that would be reserved for him alone also called up a concrete image for Dr. Tang. It was a door that a house in the northern countryside would have, like those he had seen when he served his short internship in the countryside after graduation: double doors made of locust and poplar wood and studded with rusty iron rings. This reminded him of those filthy words those women would howl at each other: "Come out, you slut with a kept *han*. You shameless stinky dog cunt . . ." He played with the word *"han,"* always feeling the word *"han"* was a more masculine-sounding word for man than other words. When he pronounced the word *"han"* he had an expansive feeling, vast and carefree. *"Han"*—man—plain and vigorous as crops. Sturdy and responsible. Was he a *"han"*? In what way did he seem that sort of man?

He and his nurse thought they had managed to keep things secret and that no one knew of their affair, but they failed to escape the eyes of the security department after all, though they didn't have a clue that the security department was on their trail. As they skillfully slipped out and went home to do their business, two security men were planning a raid on them. The security department was very well aware of the nurse and had caught her in flagrante more than once. It was exciting to expose adultery: the plotting beforehand, the stakeout—and then the actual scene of exposure—all gave people a joyful feeling. It serves as the cruelest and most thorough punishment of the adulterer and adulteress; it's the most open and aboveboard channel for all the participants to gratify their sexual desire. Exposing adultery contributed to the cultural life of a boring era by providing entertainment. However, to bring about the exposure requires a fresh story, and only new characters and a new story could get people interested. The nurse had lost the interest of the security men; she was no longer a new person in adultery who could offer a new story. She was beyond being even "an old bottle filled with new wine," just those shameless things with the electricians and cooks happening over and over. Someone has to be completely shameless to make people lose interest entirely.

Dr. Tang was a different matter altogether, and the one that the security department valued. His dubious family background, his position as a doctor, along with that quiet, standoffish manner, were all an irritant to people. If the goal was to humiliate someone in public, he would be the right person; it would be more fun to watch the humiliation of his sort—much more interesting to watch him than a piece of damaged goods of whom so many people were already aware, wouldn't it?

One afternoon, someone from the security department came to the residential area, opened the nurse's door with a duplicate key, entered the apartment, and hid underneath the bed. Another man outside locked the door and lay in wait nearby.

They patiently waited for the nurse and Dr. Tang. When the man and the woman were enjoying themselves fully, the man hidden under the bed took all of Dr. Tang's clothes, including his shoes and socks, and dragged them underneath the bed. At the same time, suddenly there was knocking on the door, or, rather, pounding. The people pounding on the door were not waiting for the people inside to open the door; they'd intended to break down the door and enter the house from the moment they started pounding on it. They believed they had the right to break into other people's houses.

They broke in.

Naked, Dr. Tang jumped out of the bed and automatically looked for his clothes—he had at least to cover himself first, but he found nothing. The man under the bed hadn't even left him underwear. Dr. Tang was really scared, but no matter what, he wasn't going to let himself be taken by them. When the security men broke into the room, Dr. Tang leaped to the windowsill, and, without a stitch on, jumped out of the room and down into the courtyard. Maybe he wanted to run back home to find clothes to cover himself, or maybe he was just desperate to escape from those men closing in on him. It would have been a lopsided encounter, a group of men in clothes surrounding a naked man. Intent on fleeing from people, he completely forgot there would be even more people outside. Those who rushed there after word spread got a chance to see this once-in-a-blue-moon scene, so satisfying to their souls: a lively nude man who'd leaped out of the nurse's apartment in broad daylight.

He was trapped in the crowd, like a cornered animal. The way back home was blocked, and he couldn't remain here on public display. He could only run, but where to? He first ran in circles in the residential compound and then out of the compound and across the hospital. He passed the laundry room, the canteen, the humming boiler room, and then went up the black craggy coal pile. More and more people gathered behind him, even residential patients with crutches and head bandages staggered along, with the security men at the very front.

He stood at the top of the coal pile and looked at the surging crowd. He stooped over, his skinny bleeding feet clinging tightly to the coal pile. His male organ, startled at first and then bobbing along all the way, lay shrunken at his groin like a crumpled, soiled dishrag. The crowd was approaching closer and closer. Where else could he go? Then he caught sight of the tall chimney—maybe the coal beneath him linked him to it. Without thinking, he clambered off the coal pile and ran to the chimney. He reached the chimney, glanced down at his feet, which were stained with coal dust and blood, and then started to climb. By the time he was halfway up, he had slowly composed himself. Far away from the crowd now, he clung to the sky-scraping, warm chimney and looked down at the cluster of people on the ground, who had become very small, and were getting smaller and smaller. No one would come from the crowd to try to catch him; none of them had the right kind of psychological preparation, a preparation for dealing with someone saying farewell to life, embracing death.

He continued to climb. When he reached the top he felt a total serenity. The sun was setting, and the light was very soft. His view had never been so broad and he had never breathed so easily as now. He scanned the city and the hospital where he had worked and lived, and then his eye paused at the window of the ob-gyn operating room, a window he'd once covered with a blanket. He had performed an operation on Fei that neither could forget. Pressing against the rough chimney with his naked body, he quickly reflected on his life, which hadn't been very long. The only regrets he had were toward Fei; in many respects he still had debts he owed this poor child. Maybe he should tell her what she had always wanted to know, who her father was.

Who was her father? Actually, Dr. Tang's sister had never told him the whole story, either; he didn't even know the man's name, only that he was an outstanding person who worked for the military at a secret scientific institute. Their own grandfather had held the position of minister for education during the Japanese occupation. To fall in love with a woman of such a family would be a mistake, not to mention the fact that the man was already married. He probably considered divorcing his wife and marrying Jingjing, but when he learned of Jingjing's background, he realized that couldn't happen. Just then Tang Jingjing found herself pregnant and, not wanting to sabotage his great future, she left him and gave birth to Fei on her own. Her reticence and pride prevented her from complaining to anyone, including her younger brother. She swore she would never see the man again, and she kept her vow. Her hope was that Fei's father might try to find out about her and her daughter, even without their knowledge, which would at least prove that he thought about them. All her life she anticipated this search, even if it were to happen only once, but she and Fei had never been looked for. She didn't expect to die, but she died. Other than asking Dr. Tang to help her raise Fei, she didn't leave a will. She had nothing to say to this world. Now Dr. Tang also stood at the edge of death; he also had no time to say anything to his niece. Perhaps that was a regret in his life; perhaps it was another kind of perfection. All perfection is relative. Did Fei have to know who her father was? Her father had never been around when she needed a father most. Ah, perfection. Sometimes not knowing is even more of a perfection.

It would be hard to imagine what else Dr. Tang had thought about on the chimney. Perhaps he thought about the two-year-old girl named Quan, his own child, and about how he was about to follow in her footsteps. Perhaps he thought about the word *"han,"* his favorite word for man. When he ran down the coal pile and climbed up the chimney, maybe he had the word *"han"* on his mind. No matter how mediocre and tedious his life was, he still respected his naked body. He drove himself down a blind alley because he didn't want to surrender his naked body to several clothed men.

In that clamorous and quiet dusk in the spring of 1976, many people in People's Hospital witnessed Dr. Tang's naked body fly down from the tall chimney. He stopped breathing the moment his body touched the ground.

So many years later, all the way to Beijing, Fei thought about Dr. Tang's death, his quite undeserving flight down. His body hadn't hit anyone there, nor had he merely hit the ground—it struck Fei, body and soul, because she was his only family member and only a real family member would have the feeling of being struck, even if Fei had never really liked her uncle. She felt a strong and suffocating sadness. Fei couldn't figure out why, in an era so far removed from the days of eating raw meat and drinking blood, such a man wasn't allowed to wear his own clothes in public.

If something similar had happened to Fang Jing, then it definitely wouldn't have been a reality. It would have been fiction—a movie, a TV drama, or a tall tale—capital for attracting women, with the clear premise that Fang Jing would never jump from the chimney in reality. A thousand times over, he would be just about to jump, or would feel that he "wanted to jump." But Dr. Tang was simply an ordinary doctor, with a reckless lifestyle. The suffering of an ordinary person can't be taken seriously; it had no influence or public appeal, thus it was not worth mentioning. Suffering is only true when it happens to other kinds of people; it almost has to play the clown among the celebrities. Suffering leaps at us in a variety of somersaults, wearing a clown hat and painting his nose white. You have to prepare to cheer while shedding tears. Obsessed with her uncle's death, Fei couldn't help thinking how different Dr. Tang's and Fang Jing's fates turned out, though they both were intellectuals living during the same period. She couldn't have guaranteed that Dr. Tang's situation would have improved or that he would have established a peaceful family if he'd lived, but she could guarantee that Dr. Tang wouldn't have taken advantage of his suffering by selling it because he was at best an ordinary doctor.

The real reason for her disgust with Fang Jing was about to emerge, and her disgust was a much stronger and more solid feeling than her sympathy for Tiao or her desire to stand up for her.

4

Beijing was where Fei was born. She hadn't been back there since Dr. Tang had taken her away from Denger Alley Elementary School. Beijing stirred all sorts of mixed feelings in her. She could smell shit in every alley, the shit long ago kept in a teacup. But she didn't hate Beijing. She might be a little crude, but was never muddleheaded at important moments. She understood she couldn't accuse Beijing of eating shit just because Beijing forced her mother to. Maybe she could say Beijing itself had eaten shit before. It was the era that made a city eat shit. The era had turned many cities into shit-eaters.

She didn't hate Beijing. Beijing always made her feel stable and expansive. Beijing was different from Fuan, where she was too involved and too occupied; there was no room left in her heart to cultivate Fuan. She left Beijing at a fairly innocent age, so she was able to retain a misty impression of the city, a view that wasn't too specific, yet not too vague. Her father must live there. She felt strange that she didn't much miss her mother and uncle, with whom she'd lived. Her longing for her mysterious father remained endless, an unchanged background color. It became persistent and strong when she was in Beijing. Fei was thankful to Tang Jingjing for never having criticized Fei's father, but she also never told her who he was and whether he died or was still alive. So Fei chose to believe her father was alive and lived right in Beijing. Sometimes she would bring to mind various images of men and pretend one of them was her father; sometimes she felt her father was Beijing. The city of Beijing was her father, a little aloof and elegant, a little kind and peaceful. She was willing to believe her father hadn't abandoned her mother and her, but rather that he hadn't known her mother was pregnant. She absolved her father even when her heart felt most desolate, which brought some warmth into the barrenness. There probably wasn't going to be any love in her life; only a very small amount was left. She would like to preserve it for the man who gave her life.

She called Fang Jing from a public telephone booth, and he happened to pick up. She identified herself, and Fang Jing went silent for a moment. Then he adjusted himself and talked in a resonant voice. "Oh, it's you, Comrade Old Tang. Long time, no see. Did you come to Beijing for a conference? Screen script?"

"I must see you today. I came to Beijing just to see you, on behalf of Tiao," Fei said.

"I should go to your hotel to call on you, but unfortunately there happen to be a few foreigners at the international club—"

Fei interrupted him. "In that case, I can go to your house and wait for you there. I have your address."

Fang Jing immediately changed his tone. "That's okay, too. I can come and see you this afternoon. At which hotel are you staying?"

"I'm not staying at any hotel. I'll be taking the night train back to Fuan."

Maybe Fei's words about leaving Beijing the same night reassured Fang Jing. Why would he feel threatened by a woman who was not going to settle in Beijing? All of a sudden he became animated and said, "Comrade Old Tang, do you mean the National Political Consultative Conference's Hall? Good, good. Let's meet there. I'll treat you to dinner at Da Sanyuan."

After putting down the phone, Fei realized that Fang Jing wanted her to meet him at the National Political Consultative Conference's Hall. Those words he meant for his family to hear made her sympathize with him, and also look down on him.

They met in front of the National Political Consultative Conference's Hall as agreed. To prevent being recognized, he wore sunglasses, but Fei still singled him out at a glance. She had to admit he was a charming and attractive man, in another class entirely from the men she had known. She had met many men, but never felt nervous and inferior as she did this time. Then Tiao's little emaciated face came to mind, and she stopped her assessment of Fang Jing.

Fang Jing took off his sunglasses and shook hands with Fei with his usual courtesy to women. He smiled and said, "Miss Tang, I apologize for calling you 'Comrade Old Tang' over the phone. I'm sure you'll forgive me. Tiao often spoke about you, and another girl, Youyou, the Beijing girls. No matter where they go, Beijing girls are always Beijing girls, like you. I've never even seen a picture of you, but I still picked you out right away."

Fang Jing's friendly—but rambling—chitchat distracted her from her plan to condemn him as soon as she saw him, but she wanted to get the conversation on the right track. She said without looking at him directly, "It's probably inconvenient for you to stand on the street talking."

Fang Jing said, "You're very considerate. But it's too early to go to Da Sanyuan. How about we go to Jing Mountain Park? The park is very close to Da Sanyuan and we can go there for dinner after we talk."

They found a place to sit down in Jing Mountain Park and started to talk. Fang Jing asked about Tiao, and Fei said, "Not good. Very bad."

Fang Jing sighed and said, "She's still so young."

"According to you, you're not responsible for anything. It's all because she's so young. Now, suppose you tell me something: Didn't you know her age when you asked her to marry you? Why didn't you complain she was too young then? You're right. She is young compared to you, so young that she gave herself completely to you, leaving herself nothing. You're older than she is, so much older, but you robbed her of everything and now you turn around and get sarcastic."

"I wasn't being sarcastic. I love her. I can tell you sincerely, I have never loved anybody the way I love Tiao, and I won't in the future. You mark my words."

"So you are still prepared to marry her, right?" Fei asked. "Then why did you try to go back on your word? Why did you stop writing her?"

"I can't," Fang Jing said.

"Which can't you do? Marry her or write her back?"

"I did promise to marry her, but now . . . I'm afraid I can't do it. When I can't do it, not replying and not meeting are the only ways to cool down a relationship."

"Why can't you marry her? Have you thought about what it means to Tiao?"

Fang Jing grinned self-deprecatingly and said, "Getting divorced is like getting married—both require passion. I feel right now that I've completely lost the passion for a divorce. As for Tiao, I think she is a person with great inner force. I have a hunch that I wouldn't be able to keep up with her. She appears to be pleading with me now, and you have also come to plead on her behalf—if I'm correct. However, as far as the relationship goes, she'll be the winner in the long run. The one destined to be dumped is not her, but me, me! You'll see. The sooner I marry her, the quicker I'll get dumped. What I told you is all true. Believe me. Time will tell all."

Fei carefully observed Fang Jing, trying to decide whether this piece of convoluted eloquence was his way of evading responsibility, or evidence of an inferiority complex hidden deep in his heart. Finally, she started to think he might be telling the truth. But why hadn't he thought about these things earlier? Why didn't he think about this before he had Tiao? she questioned. He said, "Reason prevents us from making mistakes, but it also causes us to lose possibilities for joy."

"So what you're trying to say is that your falling in love with Tiao is not reasonable? You really don't have the right to say things like that. You don't have the right to treat Tiao the way you treat other women."

"I always treated Tiao differently from other women. I told you, Tiao is the only woman I've truly loved."

This was what Fang Jing said, word for word. He seemed emotional when he said this. As much as Fei was willing to believe him, she also felt the sharp sting of jealousy. It was almost an instinctive reaction that any woman would have when hearing a man express strong feelings for another woman, even though the other woman was her best friend, even when the woman herself was meeting with this man on her best friend's behalf. The jealousy normally wouldn't lead to anything unpleasant; it would only produce a momentary uneasiness in a woman, as if, when a man expresses his love for another woman, he unwittingly belittles the woman he is with.

Fei would definitely pass along Fang Jing's words to Tiao exactly as he said them, although she already felt reluctant to do so.

Reluctance. This sudden mood surprised Fei herself. Had any man loved Fei in this way? Compared to her, Tiao might be considered lucky, even though she sat in the office all day long, head lowered and dropping tears into a drawer.

"So, you don't plan to marry Tiao?" she asked.

"I think that's right." Fang Jing then added, "Maybe when we age so much that we can't get any older, we'll finally be together—if she still wants me."

"It sounds like a waste."

"It is a waste," Fang Jing agreed.

Fei took out a cigarette from her purse, and Fang Jing began to smoke his pipe as well. Smoking made them relax, particularly Fei. She simply didn't understand herself. She had intended to persuade Fang Jing to go back to Tiao and fulfill his promise of marriage, and she indeed had been blaming him and questioning him. Why, then, did she feel relieved when Fang Jing told her that he wasn't going to marry Tiao? Perhaps only she could know what she felt relieved about. And other than feeling relief for her friend, were there things in her own psychology that couldn't be explained?

She sensed Fang Jing observing her, her smoking, maybe, though it wasn't at all unusual for a city girl to smoke in the mid-eighties. She said, "Are you watching me smoke? This is a very ordinary cigarette, our Fuan local brand called Bridge."

"No, I'm observing your mouth—you have a mouth like Vivien Leigh's. Have you noticed that?"

She curled her lips and said, "No, I haven't. Do you have a habit of observing other people's mouths?"

"Maybe I've been doing some research about mouths lately."

"Is it a professional habit?" she asked. "A director has to consider the body and features when selecting an actress. The mouth is included, I suppose."

"The research is not solely related to casting," he said. "Of course, the mouth is extremely important to an actress's face, sometimes more than her eyes. Why else, when we shout at someone, would we use the expression, 'Look at your face and mouth'? Face and mouth—the two are closely related."

Fei smiled at his repetition of "face and mouth." She looked at Fang Jing through narrowed eyes and said, "Don't you cultured folks often say that the eyes are the window to the heart?"

"If the eyes are the window to the heart, then the mouth is the path to the heart. Without the mouth's talk, how can we reach each other's hearts?"

Fei said, "Did you say that the mouth could help us reach each other's hearts and that the mouth was the path to the heart? I think it's the opposite; the mouth is the barrier to the heart. Otherwise why do people say, 'Your mouth says yes and your heart means no'? To be honest with you, I myself often don't say what I mean. The path from mouth to heart is often blocked. It's nearer the truth to say that the mouth is the path to the stomach. Notice what most people around us are doing with their mouths?"

"What are they doing with their mouths?"

"They are using their mouths either to eat or to lie."

"But the mouth has another important function," Fang Jing said. "Mouths should express love. I read some research that might be anecdotal, but says that in China more than half of couples middle-aged and older don't use their mouths when they make love. They never kiss; they unwrap their sexual organs but shut the mouths that would lead to their hearts. This is not Asian reserve but might well be caused by their disgust with each other. The continual deterioration of modern people's mouths is caused by an excess of disgust and a shortage of love. Our ancestors were more sincere and generous than people today when it comes to expressing love. Just take a look at those marvelous stone carvings from the Qin and Wei dynasties, and you'll know what I mean."

"You're probably playing a harp for a cow," Fei said.

"You're no cow listening to a harp," Fang Jing said. "You're a woman with a beautiful mouth. Only the right corner of your mouth might give a nervous twitch once in a while. You must do that unconsciously, but you should try to correct it consciously. Please forgive my straightforward suggestion to a woman with such a beautiful mouth as yours."

Fei licked her lips unconsciously. This was a mouth she herself truly loved, but she had never been aware of this flaw until Fang Jing pointed it out. She had to admire the accuracy of his observation, although his opinions about mouths could hardly be considered profound. She didn't want to pursue the topic any further because she'd already started to feel a bit uncomfortable about her mouth. This mouth of hers, which had never kissed or been kissed, was at once full and empty, moist and dry, rich and desolate. It seemed as if it were her last piece of territory, her last piece of virgin land. Fang Jing made her self-conscious about it, and she almost told him this sad secret of hers. Not that his opinions about mouths moved her, but the sophisticated conversation of a mature man confused her. Never in her life had someone like Fang Jing made her the subject of so unique a form of flattery. She thought of what he said about her Vivien Leigh mouth. No matter how sure a woman is that a man has something up his sleeve, she'd have a hard time resisting such flattery. But Fei kept quiet to avoid having the mouth say yes when the heart means no, as the expression goes. No one—not even a celebrity—could broach this subject with her, no more than he could touch the mouth.

If the mouth says yes when the heart means no, who could know exactly what was on Fang Jing's mind when he talked to Fei about the uses of the mouth? The mouth is truly the mysterious abyss of the human body. Fang Jing's research on mouths probably needed to stop right there.

So, with Fei falling silent, Fang Jing realized he should change the subject. He stood up and led the way out of the park; he was going to treat Fei to a meal at Da Sanyuan.

Restaurants in Beijing in the mid-eighties had few customers and little variety. Da Sanyuan, a venerable Cantonese restaurant, stood out like a crane in a crowd of chickens. They didn't spend much time eating. Fei seemed to be the one who governed the rhythm of dinner. She'd said that she needed to get back to Fuan on that night's train.

During dinner, Fang Jing found a little fault with Fei's table manners, commenting on the fact that she hadn't learned to chew with her mouth closed. It was a sharp but warranted bit of fussiness, although almost crass, for what risked injuring a woman's vanity more than finding fault with her chewing? Fortunately, Fei wasn't sensitive about this because she hadn't been aware that chewing without closing the mouth was considered impolite; she didn't quite understand Fang Jing. Still busily chewing her sizzling beef and working her lips, she said, "You mean I make a smacking sound when I eat?"

"No, no. You're not making a smacking sound," Fang Jing said, feeling sorry for her. After all, most Chinese people didn't know how to eat with their mouths closed, so what? He retreated from his efforts to correct her, saying, "I didn't mean to offend you. I have a habit: when I'm faced with something or someone beautiful, I want everything about her to be beautiful."

"You mean chewing only with the mouth closed is considered beautiful?" Fei asked.

"Not beautiful, maybe more . . . more refined."

Fei tried to eat with her mouth closed but felt a little awkward, as if the food lost its flavor this way. She watched Fang Jing and saw that he did chew food differently than she did. Maybe his was the correct way. Their eyes met and they laughed.

After dinner, he took out a deep blue jewelry box from the inside pocket of his suit and said it was a ruby ring that he had bought in Paris. He asked Fei to pass the ring on to Tiao.

He opened the jewelry box and suggested that Fei try it on. He said, "I thought a size six would fit Tiao, so that's what I got." Fei put the ring on her ring finger and it felt a little tight. Then it would fit Tiao perfectly, she thought, because Tiao's fingers were a little thinner than hers. She removed the ring and carefully put it back in the jewelry box.

"What should I say to Tiao?" Fei asked.

"Just tell her it's a keepsake," Fang Jing said.

They left Da Sanyuan and the night outside seemed drowned in darkness. They walked to the trolley station and Fang Jing suddenly stopped, standing on the sidewalk and saying, "Fei, can we part in an unusual way?"

"What way?" Fei asked.

"I think I would consent if you wanted to kiss me."

"What did you say?" Fei pretended she hadn't heard properly.

Fang Jing repeated himself. The right corner of Fei's mouth twitched again unconsciously. Her lips felt swollen, like they were stung by a bee or she had eaten something too spicy. The impression that Fang Jing had made on her from their initial meeting through the dinner was much better than she had expected—his talk in Jing Mountain Park had brought about a strange, and not very respectable, flash of emotion. Even his advice about her chewing had given her the feeling that he was concerned about her. But the way he proposed a farewell kiss brought her back to herself. How conceited and hypocritical! Later, she would wonder what would have happened if he hadn't said, "I think I would consent if you wanted to kiss me," but "Can I kiss you?" What would she have done? Maybe she would have broken her rule and let him kiss her—she was no saint. The chance to meet someone like Fang Jing didn't come along every day. Only once. In her heart, she would have first asked forgiveness of Tiao.

But that was not how Fang Jing had put it.

The cool evening breeze sobered Fei. She suddenly swept aside her nervousness and the sense of inferiority she had experienced in Fang Jing's company all afternoon; she felt now that she was no less a person than this celebrity in front of her. She stood facing him with her arms crossed and said, "You mean you are willing to grant me a kiss? A kiss, right here on this main street?"

Fang Jing stared at her mouth and said, "I've already agreed."

"But I haven't agreed," Fei said. "You think every woman can't wait to kiss you? Do you want me to thank you for taking advantage of me? You've got the wrong person. Isn't the mouth the path to the heart? Now this mouth of mine is telling you what my heart most wants to say: 'In your dreams.'" That said, she ran across the street in quick steps, leaving Fang Jing alone in the shadows of the trees on the opposite side.

She sat in the dimly lit, smoke-filled train and felt lucky that Fang Jing's final proposition had given her a chance, a satisfying chance, to reject and embarrass him. He'd asked for it. In retrospect, she also felt a little panic, she'd come so close—just an inch more and she would have crossed the line and let Tiao down. What kind of person was she? She looked at the dark mass outside and caught sight of her reflection on the window glass, her eye sockets deeply sunken, her face sallow. She suddenly wanted to cry.

5

A well-dressed woman with an elegant gait crossed the main street in downtown Fuan and turned into a quiet alley. She had just been treated to lunch by an author who had published a book with her publishing house. She finished her meal and said goodbye to everyone in her party. Passersby wouldn't have seen anything unusual about the woman, who strolled at a leisurely pace but who was actually fighting an ongoing battle in her mouth, with the tip of her tongue against her teeth. During lunch, a piece of donkey meat had gotten stuck in her teeth. Covering her mouth with one hand, she'd wielded a toothpick in the other, but she hadn't succeeded in dislodging it. There is a saying that goes, "The eyes can't take a grain of sand." Actually, a mouth can't take a grain of sand, either, or a speck of food, or a bit of meat. The foreign thing in the woman's teeth distracted her, but she managed to appear calm, which was the only way she could behave on the busy street. Tightly, she closed her mouth; fiercely, she used all her strength to lick the crevice with her tongue. Her tongue had already located it but was unable to drag the meat out. Fingerless as the tongue is, all it can do is lick. Her annoyance grew as she licked. It must have been an old donkey, otherwise why was the meat so tough? But why did she have to eat it? Donkey meat is a delicacy of Fuan. Although it's hardly considered elegant, most Fuaners love it. She loved the meat but not the word "donkey." Many people avoid saying certain words, and without necessarily having a good reason—she herself didn't like to say "donkey" because it felt as if she were saying a bad word. Now here she was, troubled by "donkey." Finally, she turned down a very quiet alley. Looking around and seeing no one, she opened her mouth and inelegantly inserted her hand. Her fingers reached the meat that had been bothering her. With head cocked, and mouth grotesquely gaping, she finally extracted the meat. She felt triumphant. Because her mouth had stayed open for so long, she'd drooled and her jaw felt sore. She wiped away the saliva with a tissue, and to exercise her jaw she loudly smacked her lips. With the help of publicly unacceptable behavior, she'd finally gotten rid of the "foreign element" in her mouth. Her manners had been truly unrefined, but when she looked around and found the alley still empty, she seemed pleased with herself.

The woman was Tiao.

Who made Tiao a person so generous with life, dutiful to her employer, the publishers, and full of kindness toward her colleagues, and even the unfriendly ones? Who made it possible for her to smile even at people who hurt her? What made her forgiving of Fan's meanness and tolerant of Fang Jing's wanton behavior? Who had such power? Who? Tiao often asked herself these questions. Her heart told her that love and kindness alone wouldn't have such power. It was Quan.

Quan, who had rushed into the manhole with her little hands waving many, many years ago, had always been the most intimate shadow in Tiao's heart, her closest companion, who would come at her beckoning but not leave at her dismissal. This little two-year-old beauty turned Tiao into someone furtive, a perennial debtor. Poor and vulnerable. Vulnerable and poor, burdened with a lifelong debt she could never repay, she feared Quan, on whose account she had lost her innocence forever, and she was also grateful to Quan. This dead child terrified and fulfilled her at the same time. She couldn't possibly have imagined how a dead child would shape a living personality. When people praised her she would lose herself in the momentary intoxication. She almost believed that she was born with such kindness and honesty. How absurd that was! In her heart, she laughed at herself, and speculated maliciously that many excellent people like her, or those who were considered excellent, hid secrets that couldn't stand the light—were more secretive than ordinary people, she perversely believed. Their values came not from inborn excellence but from their lifelong efforts to annihilate the darkness in their hearts.

Once Chen Zai had told her a story about a worker in the factory in which he used to work. The man lost his father at a young age and his family was very poor. He had to support his mother and two sisters on one salary. But he especially enjoyed helping people, volunteering to fix watches, radios, and bikes for his colleagues, in addition to buying the parts with his own money. Slowly, he became the first person of whom people in need would think. He went to the hospital to take care of the sick for his colleagues and to the train station to pick up people. Later he committed a crime; he strangled his roommate. He committed the murder because the roommate caught him stealing sixty *jin* of rice coupons from him. It was a period of rationing in China, and almost everything had to be bought with coupons. Rice was precious, so rice coupons seemed more precious than rice. At the time they were not twenty years old yet, an age when their bodies were growing and hunger was a constant sensation for them. His roommate had just brought the sixty-*jin* coupon, which his parents had saved and given to him, and he happened to come on the worker when he was stealing his rice coupons. Chen Zai said the roommate must have been shocked—not that someone was stealing his rice coupons, but that the thief was someone of whom no one would ever think this, a person known for his good heart and for having done all he could to help people, never turning down any request for assistance. He was shocked, and his shock must have been hard for the worker to take, so he had to destroy the shock in the form of the person. He strangled his roommate. When the news broke, the entire factory was dumbfounded—no one could believe the worker was a killer. When people learned of the motive, they were even more dumbfounded. So he was a thief; a person who helped people all the time could be a thief. Chen Zai said the worker was soon sentenced to death. On the day of the execution, many from the factory went into the street to see him. Back then, convicts condemned to death would be put on display before the execution; they generally didn't know that they had the right to refuse to participate in the demonstration. Hog-tied, the worker was escorted on a truck that drove around the city, so every passerby could observe him. Chen Zai also saw him on the truck. He said there was no fear in his eyes. Hatred was there instead. At that moment, Chen Zai felt he couldn't comprehend him. It was unclear whether the man on the truck hated humankind or merely himself. Those who saw him in the street wouldn't have known what had happened to him, what he was like before, and it would be impossible for them to know later.

Tiao felt a familiarity and an unease when Chen Zai told her this story, particularly when he said the word "killer." "Killer"—she'd thought about the word hundreds of times, and sensed some connection between herself and the executed worker. Then she desperately tried to absolve herself: the worker killed to eradicate his own dishonor; she "killed" to eradicate the dishonor of her family. The adults in her family created the dishonor and it should have been those adults who eradicated it, but she took on the responsibility. She played the role. When Quan rushed into the manhole with her little arms waving, Tiao pulled on Fan's hand. The pull was an attempt to stop Fan and therefore an effort to kill Quan. Who was Fang Jing? Wasn't Fang Jing the first person who emerged to punish her?

Perhaps she had wished to be punished long ago. Let Fang Jing be unfaithful to her, let Fang Jing make no commitment to her, and let Fang Jing tell her about his amorous encounters as much as he wished. She seemed to welcome, to endure all, with the psyche of a masochist. The ax was raised, and she couldn't wait for it to fall. So, when she suffered the most, she actually felt most at peace. She was receiving her punishment, the long-deserved retribution.

Kindness and forgiveness without a reason don't exist; that's for fairy tales. Only a heart hoping for redemption can produce great tolerance of humankind and of the self. When Fang Jing abandoned her, she sat in her office and dropped her tears into the drawer. But on this saddest of occasions, she felt extremely relieved. She didn't dare admit to her lightness of spirit, or wasn't aware of it. It was her secret of secrets, in her heart of hearts. Of course, she had to feel sad because sadness was her most reasonable feeling at the time.

A small transition in her life started with the end of the love affair. Fei called her on the day following her return from Beijing. It was a Sunday, so Tiao asked Fei to come to her place. Tiao still lived with her parents in the compound of the Architectural Design Academy. Fei came and the two, feeling how difficult it was to talk in the apartment, went out to walk in the small garden in front of the building.

It was already early winter, and the leaves had all fallen from the trees. But the scene didn't look desolate. On the contrary, it had a sense of brightness and openness.

Fei said, "I think he really still loves you very much." Abruptly, she decided not to pass along to Tiao Fang Jing's exact words about how much he loved Tiao.

Tiao looked into Fei's eyes and said, "Actually, when you went to Beijing, I already knew there was no chance of saving the relationship."

Fei avoided Tiao's stare and said, "Then why did you still let me go and talk to him?"

"I didn't let you go. You wanted to go yourself."

"Whatever. Say that I chose to go all on my own, but I wanted to do it for you."

"Not for yourself, at all?"

"If we continue along these lines, things will end up getting ugly," Fei said.

Tiao said in a very calm tone, "Fei, don't worry. I don't want to talk about it at all. Do you know why?"

"Why?"

"Because I know I've already freed myself," Tiao said. "Just a moment ago, when I met your eyes, that all suddenly receded into the past. Do you remember how miserable I looked before you went to Beijing? I wasn't all right back then. I was still very depressed and fragile, but I tried to put up a tough front, as if I could handle everything on my own. Now I want to tell you that I'm really free. It happened only a moment ago, everything just became the past in an instant. It was really a strange phenomenon, as if there had been a visible, actual gap that lay between those two completely different emotional states of mine, a clear and distinct boundary, cleanly cut with not a strand left to connect the two. Once I passed from that bleak mood and flew across that line—a visible, physically real boundary—I felt grounded and calm. Believe me. Truly, I mean it. Feel my heart." Tiao took Fei's hand and placed it on her chest, and Fei felt the pounding of her heart, regular and strong. "Therefore,"

Tiao said, "whatever Fang Jing did and wants to do has nothing to do with me anymore. Do you understand, Fei?"

"You don't hate him at all?"

"That's the strangest part of it. I don't hate him at all. Then where did the love come from? It's even made me doubt my love for him. If I don't hate him at all, it just proves I never loved him. It's terrible. What kind of love did I have?" Tiao asked, and then went on to answer herself. She seemed to be opening her heart to Fei, but she would never tell Fei that her calm and freedom might have come precisely out of Fang Jing's tormenting of her. Were she to be tortured, brutally and thoroughly, then she would no longer owe anyone anything.

Fei handed Tiao the ring that Fang Jing had asked her to bring to Tiao. She said, "Fang Jing guessed you wore size six and I think he was right." Tiao opened the jewelry box and took out the ring, but didn't put it on her finger. She played with it for a moment and said, "This toy called a ring sometimes resembles a period, and sometimes a bottomless hole. I think it'd better be a period." After saying that, she raised her arm and cast it backward over her head.

Fei grabbed Tiao's shoulder and said, "What are you doing? It's platinum and ruby and it must have cost him quite a few francs."

Tiao turned to look in the direction in which the ring flew and said, "I know it's platinum and ruby. But don't you know that, in this world, things that can be bought with money are all cheap?"

While they spoke, neither's eyes left the ring in the air—arcing through the blue, spattering a trail like drops of dazzling blood and falling into the tree, it trembled there.

The ring was caught in the tree.

They'd clearly seen its flight and fall; the way it descended, dropping toward a young London plane tree to dangle finally on one of the branches. From now on, the tree would wear a ring. What else could a tree with a ring be if not a woman? A ring belongs on a tree. Maybe none of us observe the trees in the garden or on the streets carefully enough. Their simple, aloof presence hides many secrets of their own. Serenely, trees wave their arms above, and for them to wear platinum and ruby is completely alien to them. We don't know how many such rings are caught on the branches of trees, and maybe trees are hands. If the earth is a woman, then all the trees of mountain and plain are her arms and hands. Let the ring remain on the branch, much better there than chafing flesh.

From where they stood on the ground, it seemed that the ring's flying into the branches of the tree could only have been an accident; to the ring in the air, it had been an invitation, an invitation extended to it in midflight, when it was alone, abandoned, and without a destination.

They looked at the branch from which a tiny light shone. Still holding Tiao's shoulder, Fei said, "What did you just say?"

"I said in this world, anything that can be bought with money is cheap."

Fei said, "That's me. Don't you know that I'm cheap? If someone pays, I give myself to him. That's why I felt sorry about that ring, the ruby ring in the tree."

"But you won't climb up the tree to get the ring," Tiao said.

"It would be lousy if someone else got it—you see how calculating I am."

"It's unlikely that someone else will find it," Tiao said. "Nowadays, no one stares at a tree for long."

"I would," Fei said. "And when I need money, I'll definitely come to this tree."

6

London plane trees seem to grow very well in the city of Fuan. The water and soil here don't particularly favor them, but as long as the tree takes root, it will grow vigorously, with single-mindedness, and ask for no attention. The young London plane tree with the ring in the design academy's garden soon grew into an adult tree, with a palm-sized leaf covering the ring. The ring must be there still.

Fei did come to the tree, by herself, on several occasions. She thought, a little obsessed with money, that, although she wouldn't climb up to get the ring, if the branch happened to break and the ring dropped to the ground, she wouldn't hesitate to pick it up. Often she thought of the tree as having a piece of matter stuck in it called ruby. The oddness of her refusal to consider a tree itself as matter—even the trees growing in the city, lining the sidewalks and rustling in the wind—struck her. Matter would be those buildings hidden behind the trees, and the electricity poles, vehicles, neon lights, and stainless steel trash cans. But trees aren't matter. She recognized that architecture was matter because of the way all the buildings in the world appeared to resist loneliness, saturated with human will and molded by human hands, according to artificial design—altogether entangled with the human. Trees, on the other hand, are natural and independent, and grow while quietly connected to the land, inhaling the sunshine. Trees are spirits that are hard to approach; they have compassion for human beings but don't want to get too involved. Trees are thoughts that are beyond the power of human comprehension.

Fei looked helplessly at the London plane tree in front of her and told herself, You'd better give up on the ring. Do you have nothing to cook in your wok or are you at the point of selling all your possessions to pay for your debts? You're no longer the old you, the one who tried to bribe the vice director of the foundry with a Shanghai Coral Jewel watch to get a better job.

Master Qi had helped Fei fulfill her dream of working in a state-run factory, but her job was unsatisfactory. Given her background, she was grateful at first for just being able to become a worker. But never had she imagined that the foundry work would be so dirty and exhausting! Naturally, she worried about her face, hands, and skin, which were the only capital she possessed and which she would have to use over and over again. She must tend the meager advantage she had, which was why she especially dreaded the dirty, heavy work. So she went to see Master Qi again.

On several occasions she'd asked to meet with Master Qi at the riverbank after dinner, but was turned down every time. He was avoiding her, trying to play down what had happened that evening at the riverbank. He had never displayed any signs of that subtle complacency that some men have after possessing women in need, nor did he try to make further advances. He genuinely felt guilty about what had happened. Once he even told Fei seriously, "You can't behave this way anymore. You should work hard. You'll have to grow up and live a good life." Master Qi's words didn't seem to strike a chord with Fei. Maybe she wasn't aware there were decent men like Master Qi in the world. She could only interpret it as Master Qi's reluctance to help her further, which just strengthened her resolve. She went to the political department to talk to him.

It was in the afternoon, when people were about to leave work. Fei rose from a long nap after her night shift, washed her hair, intentionally leaving it wet, and came to the political department. Her wet hair gave her an excuse not to braid it, and she looked particularly charming with her hair falling down about her shoulders, useful in piquing the male imagination. She entered the political department with her wet hair down, but Master Qi was not there. The only person in the room whom Fei knew was the vice director of the plant, Yu Dasheng. Sometimes he gave speeches when the factory held an all-employee meeting.

Yu Dasheng didn't recognize Fei. In a state-run factory with more than a thousand employees, it was impossible for a director to know everyone. But Fei certainly caught his eye. She looked like a worker, and she must be one, as she wore the factory uniform, the canvas shirt with the stand-up collar, a clean blue. It wasn't the uniform that attracted his attention, but probably because she was a female worker arriving at the office during working hours with her hair down. He glanced particularly at her hair, shoulder-length, with water still dripping, and two wet spots on her shoulders like epaulets. He addressed her as if he were the host of the room. "Whom are you looking for?"

She tossed her hair as if in an unconscious gesture and a faint scent of lemon wafted out. She said, "I . . . I want to talk to you, Director Yu. Is this your office?"

Perhaps she decided to say this the very moment she pushed open the door and saw Yu Dasheng. She had a gift for weighing a situation in an instant and seizing an opportunity. She acted as if the office she was entering were Yu Dasheng's and introduced herself. "I'm a worker in the foundry department. I would like to report a situation to you."

Yu Dasheng said, "This is not my office. I came here to look for someone. You—why don't you talk to your department director, if you have something to report?"

"You're the one in whom I have the most confidence. In the whole factory, or even the entire city of Fuan, the person in whom I have the most confidence is you," Fei said smoothly.

It was flattery, and Yu Dasheng was well aware of it. Still, he couldn't have been prepared to have a strange, pretty female of such a young age come and flatter him so obviously for no apparent reason. Compared to the women in the factory with whom he usually dealt, Fei was much prettier, and also more educated. She used the word "confidence," which the workers here seldom used. It was a good word, even though it implied familiarity. But to be trusted by people was a pleasant feeling, so Yu Dasheng told Fei, "In that case, you can come to my office with me. I can listen to your report."

They went to Yu Dasheng's office. Yu Dasheng sat behind his desk and Fei chose a seat near the door. Yu Dasheng said, "Okay, what would you like to talk about?"

Fei cleared her throat and said, "It's like this . . . Oh, right. I forgot to tell you my name, which is Tang Fei. I always pay very close attention when you give a speech, because you speak Beijing dialect. You're a Beijinger, right? So am I. I'm pretty sure we're fellow Beijingers."

"Yes, I'm a Beijinger," Yu Dasheng said. "You just said your name was Tang Fei, so your family name is Tang?"

"Yes, my family name is Tang, a very common family name."

"Can you tell me what you want to report?" Yu Dasheng calmly put the conversation back on track.

Fei said with determination, "It's actually about my own situation. I want to change jobs. I work in the foundry department . . . I'm sure you know how dirty and exhausting the job is. The working class shouldn't be afraid of dirty, hard work, but my skin is allergic. I get an allergic reaction as soon as I walk into the workshop."

Yu Dasheng gazed at the smooth-skinned girl, with her healthy complexion, and said, "I understand your situation, but I'm afraid I can't change jobs for you as you ask. There are so many workers in the factory. What would other people say if I go and assign you another job?"

"You probably don't believe my skin is allergic. Let me show you my arm . . ." She stood up from her chair and walked quickly to the desk, moving close to Yu Dasheng and rolling up her sleeve for him. On her forearm, along with the visible traces of light purple blood vessels, there were indeed two penny-sized, slightly swollen red ulcers, caused by aspirin. When she'd gone to the factory clinic for these ulcers, the doctor had already told her to stop taking the painkillers because she might be allergic to aspirin. Now she was trying to blame her allergies on the foundry department with the evidence of these few small spots. Shouldn't she be given a transfer to some other place, when her arm was so badly affected? The foundry department might get her whole arm rotted off if she stayed there. Emboldened, and with the help of the ulcers on her forearm, she moved even closer to Yu Dasheng. Almost leaning her body against him, and at the same time bending over slightly, she put her afflicted arm on the desk in front of him, her damp hair brushing tantalizingly against his ears. For a few seconds of stillness, she felt the way both she and Yu Dasheng stared at the arm she'd laid on the desk. Concluding that Director Yu had no intention of avoiding her, Fei grew daring now, thinking it was possible for her to seize the chance and sit on his lap, just by pretending to stagger and plunging forward. She put her little trick into practice and sat smoothly onto his lap, only to be picked up immediately. His actions with her could be best described by the phrase "picked up." Although she was above and he was below, she still had a feeling of being picked up—always embarrassing and undignified to have that done by someone. She didn't remember how she got picked up, only the result. With one hand gently pushing her elbow, he sent her back to her chair by the door and then returned to his behind the desk. "You are still a child," he said, deliberately, one word after another.

She was so ashamed that she couldn't say a word. She hadn't felt shame for a long time—Director Yu forced her to be reacquainted with it, but deep down she refused to admit defeat. However, the courage to continue to sit there left her.

A strong sense of failure settled in her after she returned to her dorm. "You are still a child"—these words of Director Yu's went around and around in her mind. He was probably forty-something, old enough to be her father. Of course he could say, "You are still a child." It was more like subtle urging than a reprimand or a shaming. But at the time Fei was unable to understand the implication. She believed she was no longer a child; she had long ago stopped being a child. She was an adult, the head of her own family; she was mother to herself and father to herself, her own master. "You are still a child." Such words were not offensive to her; they were just too light, too easily said, and could no longer move Fei. Director Yu could embarrass her but he couldn't repress her desire to leave the foundry. He didn't fall for her ploy, but she was determined not to lose this one-in-a-million chance.

She remembered that Shanghai Coral Jewel watch, the keepsake that the dancer had left, which she had been keeping as property she might use as a last resort. She thought it over and over and asked herself numerous times: Is this my last resort? Yes, she answered herself every time. Only leaving the foundry as soon as possible would enable her to keep her looks, her beauty, and her youth, to which she was so attached. Because she loved her looks so much, she must offer the watch. She was indeed still a child, believing that just because she thought the watch was valuable property, everyone else thought so. She took out the watch, carefully cleaned it with a handkerchief, and wound it. Then she walked into Director Yu's office again with the quietly ticking watch, intending to give him the precious watch in exchange for the favor of getting her transferred.

When she first pushed open the door, there were a few people talking to Director Yu in loud voices, so she closed the door and wandered around outside for a while. When she returned, he was alone. She entered the office, walked directly to his desk, took out the watch, and put it down. Director Yu said, "Whose watch is this?"

Fei said, "Oh, it's mine . . . no, it's yours."

"What are you talking about?"

"It's yours—I'm giving it to you. Can't you see this is a man's watch? I'm a woman. It doesn't suit me."

Director Yu asked, "Who put you up to this?"

"No one."

"What do you mean by 'no one'?"

"I mean no one. Nobody."

Director Yu took the watch, looked at it, and then put it back on the desk. He stood up and turned his back to Fei and said, "Now please take this watch and leave my office."

So he didn't go for this, either.

It made her angry and suspicious. She was thinking that he couldn't possibly be a man who didn't go for anything. He'd probably rejected her because he'd heard a lot of gossip about her, things she had done in high school, which had long ago circulated around the whole factory. She even heard two workers betting on her. One said, "If you can fuck that girl Fei from the foundry, I'll buy you a pack of cigarettes." The other said, "Oh, her. I've fucked her plenty. All I have to do is wave and she comes running . . ." Anytime they felt like it, they would make those bets; she became a plaything for them, a verbal outlet for the relief of their sexual tensions. She was sure that Director Yu had heard the gossip and was afraid to be associated with her. It would be his loss. Still, after all, he was the vice director of the factory, not Master Qi. Her dream of leaving the foundry had been thwarted, and in such an embarrassing way, being humiliated by a decent man at the same time. Her face turned cold. If her opponent was so decent, she had to show some indecency, meeting decency with indecency, as if they could at least reach a standoff and she could avoid such a thorough defeat. She raised her voice at the back of Director Yu and said, "You think I admire you for refusing the watch, right? Hmm, actually I think you're a chicken. Your guts couldn't fill a thimble. It's not like you don't want . . . a good-looking girl like me . . . you're afraid I'll get you dirty and spoil your reputation. You actually misjudge me. If you slept with me, I'd absolutely not tell a soul. I—"

Director Yu walked to the door, opening it with a crash, and, pointing out the door, he said, "Let me repeat it one more time: take your watch and get out of this office."

She went out, returned to her dorm, and cried her heart out. But a week later, the department director informed her that she was being transferred to the factory's office to work as a typist.

It was clear to her who had helped her. She was pleasantly surprised and puzzled at the same time, but she could no longer bring herself to go to his office, not even to thank him.

7

Perhaps it's better for a woman like Fei not to get married, but she still did—she couldn't take Little Cui's constant pestering.

Little Cui was a worker in the foundry department. Fei knew in her heart that out of the many men who were interested in her, Little Cui was the one who truly liked her. Little Cui was a man with a sluggish spirit and a stubborn temperament, and his big eyes were always bloodshot for no reason. He didn't listen to advice, and if anyone tried to give him some, an obstinate expression would come over his face—the look of a man prepared to march down a road to the very end. After Fei got transferred to the factory's office, there was even more gossip about her. Little Cui got into knife fights with people over it. Later, knife in hand, he went to Fei and said, "I want to marry you."

Fei said, "This is not something to joke about, Little Cui. You've heard the stories about me."

Little Cui said, "I don't care what you did before; I just like you as a person."

"You better not lose your head. A man looks for a decent girl to be his wife. Your family would never approve of your marrying me."

"If I marry you, you'll be my family."

Fei felt a lump in her throat on hearing his words. She said, "You can take that back for now. We'll talk about it in a few days, when you cool down."

Little Cui cut his index finger with the knife and said, with his finger dripping blood, "I made up my mind long ago. I swear you are the woman I want to marry. Let's get married. We'll settle down and live a good life."

"Live a good life." Fei remembered that Master Qi had said that to her. Who doesn't want to live a good life? Who can deny that living a good life is the highest goal for most people? Fei was moved—didn't she want to live a good life with a man who cared about her?

They were married.

Their marriage made many of the men in the factory unhappy, as if a woman who was originally public property had been taken from them to become Little Cui's sole possession. Also, his courage in daring to marry a woman no one else would made them feel small. Their annoyance with Little Cui was especially sharp, as if he were a traitor to all men, had betrayed the brotherhood. Several hooligan types among the workers went out of their way to pick fights with him; they publicly insulted him as well as slandering Fei. They'd say brazenly, "Little Cui, guess where I went when you were on night shift? I was in your bed all night long. Your wife wouldn't let me go until daybreak . . ."

Little Cui hadn't expected things to turn out this way; nothing was as simple as he'd thought. But he couldn't leave Fei. Her body had provided him with countless pleasures. He started to drink, staying drunk twenty days out of a month. When he was sober, he would tie Fei up and beat the hell out of her, sometimes using a leather belt and sometimes a shoe. One day, he interrogated her while beating her: "How did you get to be a typist? Tell me, how did you get to be a typist . . . ?"

Fei dodged his belt and said, "Little Cui, I really don't know. I didn't do anything."

Little Cui said in a hoarse voice, "Everyone knows but me! Everyone knows but me."

"What? What does everyone know?"

Little Cui said painfully, "You . . . you and Director Yu . . . Yu Dasheng." He said the three words "Director Yu Dasheng" with great difficulty, but he also felt happy to get them out. The long-repressed thought finally saw the light of day, and now he wanted to know all the details of the imagined situation. He got close to Fei's ear and asked, as he pinched the flesh of her arm, "Tell me, where did he fuck you and how did he fuck you? Tell me."

The pain brought tears to Fei's eyes and she said, "He didn't. Really . . . he didn't . . . I'm telling you the truth."

Little Cui pinched Fei harder and said, "In his office, right? It must have been in his office . . ."

Fei almost fainted at the pain. If telling the truth was so painful, then why do it? So she told Little Cui that she had indeed seduced Director Yu and that it had happened right in his office. She let him see the ulcers on her arm as he sat in his chair and he grabbed her arm, forcing her onto his lap . . .

Little Cui began to untie Fei during her "confession." The confession stopped his pinching and he suddenly had a strong desire to fuck her. He grabbed one of her arms and pulled her to the bed, anxiously asking as he removed his pants, "What happened next? What happened next?" Her clothes were all stripped off and, naked, she continued to make up her story. She said Director Yu had trapped her in his arms, groping her, and then pushed her down onto the desk . . . Little Cui had already started to thrust himself into her violently, and meanwhile continued to press Fei for what Director Yu did and when and how. Listening to Fei's narration so filled him with excitement, it even led him into the novelty of role-play: as if the woman he entered now were not his wife but a dissolute whore that any man could have. And he was not her husband, either; he was Director Yu and could do anything that Director Yu had done. He was doing it, right along with Fei's detailed account, and experiencing an unparalleled intensity of stimulation and pleasure. Unsure of whether he was in a struggle with Director Yu or merely having an affair with a shameless woman, he discovered he simply needed this, needed it desperately. In his savage and insulting language Fei also found sexual sensations of a strength and variety that he had never before given to her. So good, she was thinking. To die for—she felt. It was under these peculiar circumstances that her first real sexual pleasure was awakened by her husband. To be beaten painfully, and then ravaged, made her feel a pleasure to die for, such as she had never experienced. For this kind of pleasure she would have been willing to be beaten a thousand times over.

From then on, that became the prologue to their lovemaking: Fei had to tell Little Cui of her sexual encounters with other men. She went back to middle school—from Captain Sneakers, then the dancer, until the time she started to work for the factory. Most of the time she just made things up, normally arranging the accounts of what happened from far to near, eventually reaching the bed in their own home. She told Little Cui that she often brought men home when he was blind drunk, and those men would fuck her in their bed, right next to him. She would say, "Little Cui, what do you think? Don't you think Fei is too tempting?" Little Cui would throw himself on her body with eyes flaring, as if he wanted to compete with those men, as if a drunk weakling of a husband, who was absolutely not Little Cui, were right then sleeping next to this woman, who was about to be fucked to pieces. Little Cui was not Fei's husband. It was too hard to be Fei's husband. He felt cornered.

A marriage like this was doomed to be short-lived. The more these two howled their way through sex and entangled themselves in this sort of love of theirs, the more they knew in their hearts that the end was coming. Finally, one day, they stopped the screaming and storming. Instead, unusually bright mild days began to arise between them. Little Cui eventually found someone else, his apprentice, a girl named Er Ling.

After having Er Ling, Little Cui stopped forcing Fei to tell him stories—he had become like those characters in Fei's stories, seeing another woman outside of his marriage, which brought some peaceful life back to his long-withered heart. He didn't feel sorry for Fei; he merely felt that he could begin to forgive her.

It was Fei who asked for a divorce first. That day, she bought him a bottle of One-Acre Spring, two rabbit ears, and a small piece of donkey sausage, and they sat drinking together, face-to-face. She came straight to the point: "Er Ling is an innocent girl from a decent family. Little Cui, you shouldn't fool around with her."

Seeing that Fei knew everything, Little Cui blushed and said, "What do you want? What right do you have to criticize me?"

"Don't worry. It's true that I don't have the right to criticize you, but I have the right to tell you one thing."

"What is it?"

"We should get a divorce. Er Ling is the girl you should marry."

Little Cui hadn't expected Fei to say this, which was exactly what he wanted to say but found it was too hard. She allowed him to preserve his dignity, to keep intact that old image of himself as the man who had cut his index finger and, dripping blood, sworn to marry her. Embarrassed, he gulped a mouthful of alcohol as if to wash out the hidden underside of his heart. He said, "Fei, I actually wasn't thinking about this, but—"

Fei raised her glass and interrupted him. "There are actually a lot of 'actuallys' in our life, but let's not talk about it. Let's drink." She drained her glass, licked her lower lip, and then clasped her hands. "Let's go and take care of that tomorrow." She said this very calmly, and, while Little Cui heard every word, he was much more focused on Fei's habit of reaching out with her tongue to lick her lower lip. He would have been unable to describe the feeling that this small gesture gave him, but it moved him greatly—how she extended the pink tip of her tongue, just a little, and then quickly, almost more quickly than the eye could follow, licked her slightly trembling lip, like a cat, like a small wounded animal licking its wound out of sight. In the background was their empty home, which had nothing in it except for a bed and a quilt. All the money had disappeared into Little Cui's bottles of alcohol. Even Fei's salary had been readily taken by Little Cui as convenient for his use. Fei had never argued with Little Cui about money; she just let him spend it any way he wanted. She herself preferred to wear old clothes, or just uniforms all year long. He looked at

Fei in her old uniform, at the sudden flicking of her pink tongue. For a moment his resolution to get a divorce almost wavered. He recalled how her attraction for him began with her mouth, how words were unable to describe the beauty of the corner of her mouth; her mouth made him dizzy. Years of drinking had damaged his memory and he had forgotten many things, but now some of them came back. He remembered Fei had never let him touch her mouth, even after she became his wife. So now he wanted to kiss her. When they'd decided to get a divorce, the beautiful, mysterious Fei from before their marriage started to return to him little by little. He wanted to kiss her, but she pushed his face away with her hand. "Don't," she said.

"And this alone I will never figure out," Little Cui said.

Fei stood up and turned her soft young neck slightly, proudly, and sternly, with an expression that seemed to radiate rejection for a thousand miles, as if she were suddenly transformed from a cheap, discardable woman to some unapproachably beautiful creature. She turned her head and looked away. "I'll move back to the singles' dorm tomorrow."

Little Cui looked at this distant Fei and couldn't help coming to the conclusion that she was a woman whom he had never known. A woman like her was not someone that a man like him could afford. He was afraid of her, and felt that he should, indeed, marry Er Ling. He felt some inferiority as well as some relief. Inferior and relieved, relieved and inferior, that was the way Little Cui divorced Fei.

Fei started to live the single life again. In those days, she missed the friends of her childhood and teenage years. Tiao and Youyou, who used to envy her working-class life, had both grown up. The time she gave them a tour of the factory, and bought them treats, was long ago. Everything happened so quickly. College-girl Tiao and the would-be tourist guide Youyou both tried to persuade Fei to go to college, but she said with a sneer, "Me? Someone like me?"

Things were changing and Fei, of course, hadn't resigned herself to loneliness. One of Tiao's relatives was the principal at an art academy, so Tiao planned to introduce Fei to him, in order to get her some work as a model for the oil-painting students. Fei asked about the pay and Tiao said, "The money you'll make in two half days, which is six hours, would equal the salary you earn in a month now."

Fei said excitedly, "Damn! Why would I hesitate?"

"But it's in the nude. You have to take all your clothes off."

"I like to be nude. Someone should have painted me nude long ago, don't you think?"

It was an era during which China had just opened its door to the West. For many people, unfamiliar with the idea of models and alarmed by it, nude modeling fell into the category of the shady and unrespectable. The first generation of models in this new era, even when they lived in big cities and worked for art schools, still modeled without their families' knowledge. The high salaries they commanded were a happy surprise to them and made them the first group of women in China who could afford furs and luxurious clothes, long before the women who made money in business. Models didn't risk wearing those clothes at home, concealing their despised profession from parents or boyfriends, along with the considerable money they earned. They often left home in ordinary clothes, changing to expensive fashions to promenade the streets glamorously, smugly enjoying their secret.

But Fei had nothing to fear back then; she was her own family. When she mounted the stage nude in the studio, she knew what to expect from the teachers and students. Not evil looks but appreciation showed in their eyes, along with some repressed excitement. So she simply stopped going to work at the factory. What was so special about being a typist? How much money did a factory director make? Director Yu? No, Bureau Director Yu—he had been promoted to the directorship of the province's Bureau of Manufacturing. How much could a bureau director make? she thought with contempt. Busy and popular, she was on sick leave all the time. By then she had gained some fame in the art world, and besides universities and colleges, individual painters were also willing to hire her to model at their homes. Young artists often fought over her, which she handled in a simple and straightforward manner by going with whoever gave her the most money. A young painter fresh from some training at the

Central Academy of Fine Arts (one of the sort who likes to toss his long hair) paid five times the going rate, and she, of course, immediately went with him. He lived with his parents in their spacious house, and had his own studio. Later, Fei learned that the young painter's father was the vice mayor of Fuan. The painter told her what pose to take and started to paint, but after just a sketch, he threw away the brush and held his head with his hands. Fei said, "Hey, why have you stopped painting?"

The painter said, "You distract me."

"I have an idea."

"What is it?"

"Sleep with me," Fei said calmly. So the painter slept with Fei and then was able to focus on painting. He even fell in love with Fei.

He was an innocent young man, quite a few years younger than Fei. She told Tiao that when he buried his head in her breasts, she felt he was like a baby. He told her it was his first time, but Fei remained unmoved, and only by remaining unmoved could she conquer all. Later, he fell out with his vice mayor father over Fei because the vice mayor himself expressed a particular interest in her. He insisted on taking her out to dinner after seeing Fei a couple times at his home; he also asked to stay in his son's studio to watch him paint.

Fei didn't like the painter's father: his worldly laugh, his shifty looks, along with that oily face of his, all disgusted Fei. She believed the attractiveness of this sort of person came solely from his power; he was a symbol of power. Once his power disappeared, what would be left for him as an individual? Her opinion of the father didn't mean she loved the son more than the father. No, she didn't love anyone. She told Tiao that she was eager for father and son to get into a fight, so she could get away from the pair. She didn't want to waste any more time on them.

Fei thought Tiao was an innocent listener, but she was not. Having graduated from college that year, Tiao was assigned a teaching job at a high school in Fuan. She had never liked the teaching profession, and wanted to work for a publishing house. Based on what she read, she believed that publishing would become a big industry at the beginning of the new century. She was worried about her career; she had no powerful connections to get her out of the high school and into publishing. And then she heard Fei talk about the vice mayor, which turned her into a not-so-innocent listener. A little despicably, she told Fei what she wanted, begging Fei to talk to the vice mayor for her.

Maybe it was a mutual and tacit understanding that Fei owed Tiao something. The debt was long-standing but never forgotten. For so many years they hadn't asked anything of each other, but now that Tiao brought it up, Fei knew it was time to pay her debt. She didn't hate Tiao for it, and even felt happy that Tiao had given her the opportunity.

Fei went to the vice mayor and took care of the business. It wasn't that hard for her, only a little disgusting. Trying to ignore the shudder that went through her when he rubbed his fat, oily belly against hers, she just kept thinking about Tiao: How I want to do this for you.

So Tiao preserved her own innocence by sacrificing Fei's dignity and got into the children's publishing house as she wished. Ten years later she was the vice director.

Once, she confided in Fan about it, wishing with all her heart that Fan would side with her as Fan had when she was little. She wanted Fan to say, That's nothing. That's nothing at all. Fei is that kind of person to begin with. What's the difference between selling yourself once or ten times? How Tiao longed for someone to say something like this for her. Then she could feel free of guilt, and not so despicable. But Fan didn't say that. Instead she said, "Shame on you. You're so shameless!"

Chapter 6

❈ ❈ ❈

Fan

1

Some people are fated to leave their own land and live with people from other races, like Fan. When she was in high school and Tiao asked her about her future plans, she said without hesitation, "To go abroad."

She had a gift for learning languages and an excellent memory. In elementary school she already could recite the famous "Little Match Girl" from the middle school's English textbook. She also carried on English conversations with her mother, Wu, on weather, food, hygiene, etc. She got excited whenever she saw foreigners in the park, volunteering herself to be their tourist guide, even with her limited English. Later she went to the Beijing Foreign Language Academy to major in English, and her foreign classmates often asked her, "What year did you return to China?"

Her English made people think she'd grown up among native speakers. She would tell them clearly, "I have never been anywhere. I learned my English in China." Later, she made the acquaintance of an American fellow named David, and she followed David to America. Tiao asked her, "Do you plan to come back?"

She said, "No, I don't. My life will be much better than yours, plus I have David." She was very conceited, perhaps because she had the capital for conceit: her American husband, David, and her fluent, slightly British-accented English—she even corrected David's grammar from time to time. She had passed level B for typing in English while in high school, and TOEFL was a breeze for her. Unlike those Chinese who seemed daunted and uneasy, unable to open their mouths as soon as they left China, Fan was comfortable speaking to foreigners.

A traveler who can communicate with people anywhere on earth is guaranteed success in life. Fan thought about this sort of success constantly; she had to go abroad just to be worthy of this beautiful English she spoke. In America many, many wonderful things seemed to await her, more than China could offer, much, much more. What could China offer? China had her family, but at her age then, she didn't much value family ties. She had valued her older sister when she was little. She had loved her, worshipped her, and her older sister had been the first person to whom she would run when she was in trouble. They shared happiness and sufferings and . . . and also the evil little secret that nobody else in the world knew. Fan never doubted her memory; what she remembered was what had happened—the open manhole on the small road at the design academy, the waving little hands of Quan when she fell into it, and the unusual clasp of hands between her sister and her, icy-cold, moist, and cramped . . . it was not that she'd pulled Tiao's hand, but the other way around. Over and over, she'd repeat to herself that she hadn't pulled Tiao's hand but Tiao had pulled hers, that she had been passive, and had been pulled, had been stopped. Twenty years had passed, but the force that Tiao had applied was left frozen into her hand. That wasn't the reason she had left China, was it? She didn't want to analyze all this too closely. Although she'd only been seven that year, even then she had a strong desire to be a very good child. The manhole, Quan, the clasping of hands between the sisters . . . their gesture of vengeance and the elimination of the alien element . . . all this made her desperate to be an excellent child, the best child, as if it were the only way for her to be worthy of the death of that other child who, ever since her birth, had made Fan unhappy and jealous.

As great as her desire to be that good child were her expectations of Tiao. Under a shadow that couldn't be lifted, Fan no longer loved and worshipped her sister single-mindedly, and Tiao couldn't have her unconditional obedience anymore. Yet Fan longed intensely for Tiao to love and spoil her so she could show in every way that she was the most important person in the family. Their first disagreement started with a windbreaker. She was studying at the Beijing Foreign Language Academy then, and Tiao, back from a business trip to Beijing to solicit manuscripts, called her to go out. They could hardly wait to go to an ice-cream shop for yogurt, for which they both had a passion. Back then, Kraft's and Wall's dairy products hadn't made their way to China yet, and yogurt in Beijing was sold in thick, clunky white porcelain bottles, sealed with waxed paper tied in rubber bands. People used a straw to poke through the seal and then made hissing noises as they sucked up the yogurt—it was delicious. Tiao treated Fan to yogurt and also took out a short woolen knit skirt that she had bought for Fan when she attended a conference in Shanghai. She liked to buy clothes for Fan, always remembering to do it wherever she went. But what Fan noticed that day was not the skirt but the windbreaker Tiao was wearing. She said, "Tiao, the windbreaker is very nice. I like it."

"Yeah, I like it, too."

"Get one for me."

"It was imported from abroad."

"Who bought it for you?" Fan asked.

"Fang Jing."

"You mean you can't find one in China?"

"Probably not."

"Then what am I going to do?"

"Just wait. When I find something similar, I'll buy it for you."

Fan said, "Actually, you can give this one to me now and buy yourself something similar later on."

Tiao hadn't expected Fan to say something like this. It embarrassed Tiao that her sister had asked her so directly to take off her windbreaker and give it to her. She would have given Fan many things, but not the windbreaker, and not just because it was imported and a gift from Fang Jing, but because the way Fan demanded things from her seemed strange and troubled her. She didn't know what to say and they paused awkwardly. Then Fan asked, "Older sister, do you like me?"

"I like you. You know I like you."

"If you like me, you should give me the things I like."

"Is that how you see 'like'?"

"Yes."

"But I don't see it that way."

"So you're not going to give me the windbreaker?"

"I don't think I can."

It was pretty much the first time that Tiao had said no to Fan. She said it very quickly but unambiguously. Feeling uncomfortable, Tiao didn't know exactly what the trouble was. Maybe she had been wrong. Why couldn't she give Fan whatever she liked? But she couldn't.

Fan's mood obviously darkened—she never tried to disguise her moods. The two of them sat there facing several empty yogurt bottles, not knowing what else to talk about. Changing the subject would have been a way to cheer things up, but they were even unable to do that. They were sisters and knew each other too well. Changing the subject is for people who are not related, but for sisters it would have been too artificial. They avoided each other's gaze, sitting silently for a while, and then Fan glanced at her watch and said, "I should go."

Tiao said, "Don't forget your skirt." Fan reluctantly picked up the new woolen skirt and stuffed it into her backpack carelessly, as if saying, A skirt isn't enough, isn't the equivalent of the windbreaker . . .

Some events out of the past are taboo subjects—and there can be many of these in families—like the incident of the windbreaker. Other things get brought up all the time, to hearty laughter. When the family spoke about Fan's unusual gift for mimicry, they would always recall the way she imitated a relative with a stiff neck: she tensed up her neck but twisted it before she got to open her mouth, ending up with a stiff neck herself, and missing two days of school. When Tiao had to use a hot rolling pin to massage her neck, Fan said, in a Fuan accent, "Give me the rolling pin"—except the word for "pin" sounds the same as the word for "cabinet," so it became "rolling cabinet." It was Fan's discovery that Fuaners pronounced "pin" like "cabinet." These are the sorts of things that can be brought up anytime; they were part of her, a source of both her liveliness and her down-to-earth quality. Even after Fan became an American citizen, and was constantly in conflict with Tiao, her cold heart, which was also so fragile, would suddenly warm when these things from her teenage years came up.

However, it was just momentary warmth. To have lasting warmth didn't seem like American behavior to Fan, who had learned to be a perfect American citizen—drinking cold water, gulping down large quantities of coffee at work, using mint floss after meals, adding a lot of ice to Coca-Cola, taking a hot shower in the morning, washing shirts after wearing them only once, eating pork only occasionally, avoiding stir-frying food in the kitchen, driving skillfully (particularly when backing up the car), visiting a dentist regularly, taking vitamins—absolutely no quilt nest for the bed, and the fewer covers, the better . . . She was the kind of person who could quickly adapt to her environment, or, to put it another way, she was eager to adapt to David quickly.

David had never said he didn't love Fan; he continued to call her "my little sweet pea." But not too long after they got married, he began an affair with a German woman, an old friend who was ten years older than he was. His getting married didn't stop them from having a relationship. If he loved Fan, what was this affair with the German woman all about? It was something that Fan couldn't tolerate, particularly since she lived in America. If it were in China, instead of fighting with her husband she could go back to her parents' home and complain, or turn to her friends for help. But she lived in America, where her parents didn't, and she had no really close friends. Her fluent English removed the obstacles to communication with anyone in this land, but language couldn't do anything about the obstacles in the heart. And the obstacle was in her heart. When David was seeing the German woman, she realized for the first time that she didn't belong in this country. She was a foreigner and would never be able to understand all the mysteries of what happened in the United States of America between David and his German girlfriend.

She had had heated arguments with David, and called him "son of a bitch" without any difficulty, but her screaming only drove David to see his girlfriend more frequently. He didn't want to divorce Fan, because his girlfriend already had a husband.

Fan never told any of this to her family in China; the hurt of having nowhere to complain was something she brought on herself. Like someone who had a disease, Fan suffered from aftereffects. David's unfaithfulness made her emphasize particularly in her letters how deeply they loved each other, despite the fact that she felt very confused about David. No one knew better than Fan that it was almost impossible for an Asian and a Westerner to understand each other completely, even if they had been a happy couple all their lives. Sixty percent's worth of a mutual understanding was good enough. Fan was unwilling to admit this, but her life led her inexorably to this conclusion, a conclusion that she couldn't share with others, because she wanted to seem a winner. She wanted her family to recognize that she, indeed, lived a better life than they did.

But what about the aftereffects of her disease? They controlled her, making her fear for no reason. She instinctively sensed David's attraction to older women, so she had to be vigilant against all older women, including Tiao, who was six years older than both she and David. She was sure not to put Tiao's pictures on display, just a childhood picture of them, in which Tiao knitted her brows and seemed very unhappy while Fan laughed foolishly. David asked her, "Why don't you have a recent picture of your sister? I'd like to see her pictures now. Didn't she send us some?" Fan explained that she liked to reminisce about the past, that only childhood pictures could bring her back to the past, her past in China.

Ah, her past in China.

When Fan's confidence reached its lowest point, she even refused to go back to China with David. To have David screw the German woman in their house would have been preferable to returning to China with him. She was so afraid that she couldn't bear to hear Tiao invite David enthusiastically in English, "You would be so welcome to come home!" She held on to the extension and interrupted Tiao's conversation with David, "Older sister, your accent is horrible. Where did you learn your English?" She ended the conversation between Tiao and David by criticizing Tiao's accent; she'd almost shouted for Tiao to shut up. Fan's rude interruption annoyed David. They quarreled after they put down the phone. David said, "I have the right to talk to anyone I want to. You shouldn't interrupt our conversation."

Fan said, "I didn't interrupt you and her. I was just encouraging my sister to speak more English. She'd made some progress."

David sneered. "You were not encouraging her; you were ridiculing her."

"You don't even know Chinese. How can you talk such crap?"

"I can understand your tone—it was unfriendly—besides, your voice was so loud. You Chinese people talk loudly."

"What's wrong with being loud? Since you know we Chinese talk loudly anyway, then you can't draw the conclusion that a loud voice means an unfriendly tone."

"I stand by what I said about your tone a moment ago. I know you."

"You know me? You could never know me if you tried the rest of your life."

"Don't say that. Don't say the rest of your life."

"The rest of your life . . . the rest of your life . . . the rest of your life."

David suddenly laughed and said, "Let's make up." Maybe he did love Fan; there were simply a lot of things that he didn't understand about his Chinese wife. For instance, he had no idea why Fan wouldn't allow him to return to China with her. He hadn't been back to China for five years. Back then he was an intern in his father's agency in Beijing and learned a few simple Chinese sentences, of which he could remember only one, "Have some cola." He genuinely wanted to revisit China and see his wife's parents and his sister-in-law.

2

Tiao waited for Fan at Beijing International Airport. Not yet the vice director of the Children's Publishing House, she was the managing editor at the main editorial office. The story of her and Fang Jing had become entirely a thing of the past, which meant a genuine release for her from the misery of that love. She'd needed to rest and to heal, to "recover," and only complete release could have brought recovery. Maybe all women capable of love have the ability to "recover," like the range grass, full of exuberant life: "Even the fires that sweep the prairie cannot kill the long grass, / which rises once again in the light winds of spring."

Tiao recovered.

For those few years of her recovery, she channeled all her energy and intelligence into her work. Focused and clear-thinking, with an inner calm, she succeeded in making substantial profits for the publishing house. Her tears no longer dropped into the desk drawer and her appearance slowly began to improve. Was there still some opportunity lying ahead of her? She seemed to be waiting, with the composure of the experienced and the anticipation of the persistent. Except now, with her understanding that real happiness couldn't be won by struggle, she no longer had the heart to compete. Sometimes she would think about a girl she had seen in the post office. It was during the National Day break, when she went to the post office bank to withdraw some money. There were a lot of people waiting in line, and she was standing near the end and overheard a girl's telephone conversation. She didn't want to admit she was eavesdropping; in fact, at first she was just looking absently at the girl's back. Judging from her back, the girl on the pay phone seemed to come from the countryside—the way she braided her hair and stood, the strength in her stance, and the hand that held the phone—all evidence of her country background. She was healthy and a little ungainly, not all that comfortable in her skin. The content of her phone conversation established that she was a student, at college or technical school, which meant she must have gotten into a school in Fuan through her exam results. Apparently the person she was talking to was male, and Tiao heard the girl ask in country-accented Mandarin, "How many days off does your school give?" The other person answered, and the girl said, "We get three days off, too. I don't plan to go home, do you?" The other person apparently said no, and the girl said happily, "That's great. Come to our school and have some fun." The other person refused, and the girl started to work on him. It was then that Tiao started to pay attention, eavesdropping on the conversation.

To Tiao the girl now seemed more nervous than earlier, with her right arm clenched closer to her body, as if something under her armpit urgently needed to be held in place. She kept feeding coins into the slot to get more minutes, and her back looked quite uncomfortable. She said, "Come on, everyone in our dorm is gone and it'll be a fun time. What? You need to prepare for the exam? No, no, I want you to come . . ." While saying this, the girl started to wriggle slightly, which made Tiao a little uneasy but also supported her impression that the person on the other end of the phone was a man. The girl obviously was using an unfamiliar strategy to entice the man, repeating, "No, no, no, just come. There won't be anyone else in our dorm, no, no . . ." Now persuasion turned to earnest invitation, to begging, to mumbling, to . . . to what? In the end she composed herself with some difficulty, trying to adopt a casual tone. "No problem. You don't have to apologize. I know exams are more important than having fun. Then, let's plan to meet later. Okay, 'bye . . ." But at the same time, Tiao noticed the hand that held the phone trembled, the knuckles pale. When she hung up the phone and rushed out, she was in tears. Tiao's heart was full of sympathy for this strange girl with her pretense of unconcern. It was a moment that people hardly noticed, the noise and bustle of the post office covering the girl's embarrassment. Tiao noticed but was unable to show the girl her sympathy, to tell her that she was not the only unhappy person in the world. Her phone call was undoubtedly aggressive, an effort to take over a man's holidays. As long as the girl assumed an aggressive posture she was doomed to fail. In the past, Tiao had attempted to take over things; all young, energetic people had tried to conquer life, one way or another—it was naïve but not ridiculous.

Fan's plane arrived. From far away, Tiao immediately singled out her younger sister, whom she hadn't seen in five years, in the crowd waiting for luggage. Fan was much thinner than before, and with the scarlet wool coat she had on, which almost touched the floor, she appeared taller. She pushed a luggage cart over and they hugged. She didn't look that well. Tiao had noted long ago that many Chinese from America didn't look very healthy; their faces seemed to have turned browner among the hordes of white people. Even someone like Fan—who had a nice family and career, an MBA and a job at an international investment company—her privileged life still didn't nurture her complexion. When she smiled, Tiao noticed the wrinkles around her eyes. She wasn't quite thirty years old that year.

Compared to her, Tiao, this Chinese woman still a resident of her native land, shone. Fan couldn't help saying with a sigh, "Older sister, I didn't expect you to have grown even more . . . more attractive than before."

"Do you really think so?" Tiao asked.

"I really think so," Fan said. They left the terminal, came to the parking lot, and got into the Peugeot that Tiao had gotten from the publishing house. Fan said, "I thought we were going to take the train home, like when I was in college."

Tiao said, "We don't have to do that anymore. See, I drove the car here."

"Is this yours?"

"No, it belongs to the publishing house."

"Is the use of the publishing house's car part of your perks?"

"Not yet, but for special occasions it's not a problem."

"There is nothing like this in America," Fan said. Tiao couldn't tell whether Fan was envious or disapproving.

It was a ninety-seven kilometer trip, and they arrived home very quickly. Though it was already late at night, Yixun and Wu were up waiting for them, wide awake. They still lived in the compound of the Architectural Design Academy, but had recently moved to a new apartment—four bedrooms with two living rooms, three times bigger than the one they'd had during the Reed River Farm period, twice as big as the one they'd had before Fan went to America. The difference was obvious, and Fan sensed various changes as soon as she got off the airplane. The only thing so far that remained unchanged was the airport itself, dark and crowded, with the customs officials as indifferent as ever. But everything seemed transformed once she was out of the airport and arrived at the house. Her parents and her older sister surrounded her at their brightly lit, warm home, and a familiar aroma of spare-rib soup immediately greeted her. That was the base for the wonton soup that Yixun had prepared especially for her—they all knew wonton soup was her favorite.

The steaming soup was brought out; tiny light yellow shrimp, emerald scallions, minced mustard greens flavored with garlic, drizzles of seaweed and sesame oil, all set off the delicate soup. Fan finished two bowls in a breath, put down the chopsticks, and said several times over, "That was really delicious." She had been prepared to arrive with a condescending attitude, to return as some kind of conquering hero. But after two bowls of wonton soup she surrendered, finding her old homeland not that different from her new one—the way Tiao had driven the publishing house's car to Beijing to pick her up, and how she also had her own apartment. So she couldn't hold on to her American attitude anymore and lost control of her emotions. She started to cry, not sobbing but wailing. She raised up her face and opened her mouth, without a thought to how she looked, and out came the weeping. This was the kind of crying that Tiao couldn't help admiring and that she herself couldn't do. Only when Fan wept did Tiao start to feel that her younger sister had truly returned and that this person truly was her younger sister.

Fan's crying made everyone sad. When she stopped, Yixun asked, "How are things going?" Fan then started to talk about her life in America, about things they had learned from her phone calls and letters. They all knew that "David and I love each other deeply," but had no idea that Fan had worked in a restaurant. Smiling, she told them that she had decided to get her master's degree several years ago, but that David didn't like the idea. Out of pique, she refused his money and worked in an insurance company while she studied. A French classmate, Virginia, encouraged her to work in a restaurant to earn her tuition. Fan said she had never expected to wait tables, or maybe wash dishes, in America, things only someone with neither English skills nor a green card would do. She had American citizenship and a home, so why would she work in a restaurant? Virginia told her that the cash came fast. When you counted out handfuls of tips from your apron pocket after work, you'd feel differently. A person became addicted. Virginia already was. She arranged for Fan to come to the restaurant in the wealthy neighborhood where she worked, and the boss asked Fan what she was good at, whether she had any special talents. Fan said, "Hmm, I do have a special talent—I can speed up a song."

The boss asked, "What do you mean, 'speed up'?" Tiao said she could change the speed of a 33 rpm record into a 78. She then opened her mouth and sang a song. The boss laughed. How could he let a clever girl like Fan wash dishes? Her quick wit and fluent English impressed him, so Fan became the hostess for the restaurant. Fan said she did become addicted and almost quit her job at the insurance company. How could you not get addicted when you watched those actual dollars become your own? There were unpleasant moments, of course. The restaurant was located in a wealthy neighborhood and the clientele were all dressed to the nines. One day David's parents, her in-laws, came to the restaurant. Desperate not to have them find out she was doing restaurant work, she panicked and hid in the back. Taking advantage of her absence, a fancy couple left without paying their bill. Fan discovered this and ran after them, determined to collect no matter what. If she couldn't get the money back, the boss would dock her pay. She said it was apparently no oversight, judging by how fast they were walking. She hurried in pursuit and, reluctant to shout on the street, ran tenaciously until she caught up, finally, two blocks later. On the inside, she had been shouting to encourage herself, saying, Stinky dog shit. Stinky American dog shit! Coming up to them, she tried her best to keep calm. "Sir, you forgot to pay the bill." That tall blond man and woman put on a surprised look, both almost at the same time, which Fan only saw as revolting evidence of nervousness and hypocrisy. The phony looks of surprise were meant to persuade Fan that she'd made a mistake, but Fan repeated, calmly and politely, "I'm sorry, sir, you forgot to pay. This is your bill." Compared to them, Fan seemed small, but her stern face and formal English forced them to take her seriously. When the man tried to protest, Fan added, "If you don't pay the bill, I can call the police." Without further argument, they paid up, and even gave Fan a tip.

"What happened with the job later on?" Tiao asked, tears starting to well up in her eyes. Fan told her that later David discovered that she was working in a restaurant and went to find her. He took her home and told her that she shouldn't be doing that sort of work. He agreed to her continuing to study for her master's degree and said he would pay for her, for his "little sweet pea."

Though Fan was a little tired, neither of the sisters felt sleepy, and they didn't go to bed until the next morning. Tiao had a bad dream then. She dreamed that she was passing above a dirt embankment and heard a tiny voice from below calling her: "Older sister, save me! Older sister, save me . . ." Tiao squatted down and saw Fan trying to climb up from the bottom of the embankment. She looked the way she had in elementary school, hair cropped, wearing a pink corduroy jacket with small black polka dots, her chubby face smeared with dirt. Tiao hurried to pull Fan to her bosom. There was no river down the slope, yet Fan was thoroughly soaked. With wide-open eyes and mouth, she kept panting, her mouth reeking of fish, and slowly disgorged seaweed. Tiao was very sad; the seaweed in Fan's mouth meant that she had been living underwater for a long time. Tiao didn't want to see the seaweed in Fan's mouth, so she reached her hand in to scoop it out while holding Fan tightly with her other hand. Or she might be described as pulling weeds, the weeds growing in Fan's mouth. The strands seemed endlessly long, and she had to reach her finger down into Fan's mouth to scoop and probe . . . until Fan was probed to the point of vomiting, and Tiao woke up.

She woke up to find herself still sobbing, and Fan on the bed across from hers was sleeping soundly. Fan slept for a whole day, turning to one side and another, flat under the quilt like a frog, as if she were making up for all the sleep she had missed in America, the way Wu had slept after she came back from the Reed River Farm. It also seemed that the five years of sleep in America were not real sleep. Only sleeping in China is a real sleep, and a Chinese person has to have Chinese sleep—the carefree, relaxed sleep where your family waits beside your bed when you wake from a nightmare.

When Fan finally yawned and stretched, she saw Tiao gazing at her with red, swollen eyes. She blinked and said, "What's wrong?" Tiao told her the dream she'd had. A little superstitiously, she believed the power of a bad dream would be dispelled once she told it. Fan seemed unmoved. She rested her head on her hands and stared at the ceiling, saying, "Actually, none of you need to worry about me. I'm not as miserable as you have me in your dream. I'm fine."

Tiao explained, "I'm not trying to say you're miserable. It's just concern, and I can't help the concern in the dream. After all, you're out there by yourself."

"How am I by myself? Isn't my husband, David, family? Speaking of being by yourself, you're the one. You're by yourself but you're always ready to pity me."

Tiao started to feel once again that she didn't know Fan. Her moodiness suggested that her life in America was probably not as good as she portrayed it, but Tiao could say nothing.

3

There were some happy moments during Fan's visit. One day, Tiao's high school classmate Youyou, the friend of her teenage years, treated Fan to dinner.

Youyou had eventually fulfilled her dream of becoming a chef. She opened a small restaurant in downtown Fuan called Youyou's Small Stir-Fry across from Big Dishes from South and North, the Freshest Seafood. Youyou's stomach turned every time she saw the other restaurant's sign, thinking that the words amounted to crude bragging. So, you claim to be big? I want simply to be small, small stir-fry, small but not insignificant, with the sort of intimate, trustworthy family atmosphere that never goes out of style. The name was not her idea. On Yabao Road in Beijing's Ambassador District, there was a restaurant called Auntie Feng's Small Stir-Fry, which had overflow business. Tiao had been to that restaurant and had told Youyou about it. Youyou said, "I can open a restaurant called Auntie Meng's Small Stir-Fry."

Tiao said, "Stir-Fry sounds fine, but the Auntie Meng part isn't a good idea. For some reason, whenever I see the word 'auntie,' I think about that spooky aunt in that old movie *Secret Mission to the City of the Ram*. Why don't you call it Youyou's Small Stir-Fry? Yeah, you should call it Youyou's Small Stir-Fry." With specialties like Shanghai eel, honey-plum spare ribs, beer corn chicken, tilapia with preserved vegetables, and crispy turnip pancake, Youyou's Small Stir-Fry did excellent business. The cuisine, which no one could classify precisely and Youyou didn't care to, included a little bit of everything, from Cantonese to Shandongnese. Youyou was very open-minded and would cook whatever was delicious. For instance, tilapia with pre-served vegetables was merely a local Fuan dish, but it was delicious and Youyou prepared it with great care.

Tiao asked Fan, "You still remember Youyou, right?"

"Of course I remember her, and also that great beauty, Fei," Fan said. She remembered how she had offered to contribute her milk and followed Tiao to Youyou's home when she was little, waiting eagerly for them to make the mysterious grilled miniature snowballs.

They were eating and drinking at the cozy, elegant private room at Youyou's Small Stir-Fry. Fei soon joined them, bringing Fan a red-lacquered antique bracelet as a gift. Not until that moment did it occur to Fan that she never thought about bringing gifts for her sister's friends. Americans aren't as much concerned with etiquette as Chinese are, and don't give gifts as often. But was Fan really an American? Deep down, she had never thought of herself as one, but unfortunately she was no longer Chinese, either. Chinese affection and friendship, feigned or sincere, all felt foreign to her.

While she was thankful to Fei, she was also upset by the idea she didn't belong anywhere. She offered Fei a cigarette, More 100 Slims. They looked each other over as they smoked. Fei had on a black leather coat and a matching miniskirt, soft and smooth as silk. The leather would be considered of the highest quality in America. Her dress and her wavy, waist-length hair made Fan think about some of Fei's life experiences, which she had heard about from Tiao. She didn't feel comfortable asking about Fei's current job; someone like Fei would probably always be involved in something suspect. Again, she had to admit that life in China now was much better than when she lived here. From what her sister and her friends wore, it seemed like the clothes made in China compared well with those made in America. She listened to their conversation and gathered that Tiao and Fei regularly brought customers to Youyou's Small Stir-Fry, particularly guests of the publishing house. Tiao told them about a Canadian couple, special guests invited by the publishing house to write and edit a series of Fun with English books for children. Youyou's crispy turnip puffs were their favorites. When they were about to leave Fuan, they came to Youyou's Small Stir-Fry three days in a row, ordering nothing but a pot of chrysanthemum tea and a dozen delicious and inexpensive turnip puffs. Youyou said, "Tiao, guess what I do to the customers Fei brings here?"

"What customers can Fei bring in?" Tiao asked. "The people she knows are all super-rich, and why would they come to your place?"

Fei chuckled and said, "I've brought quite a few sets of customers here. I would call Youyou before I came and have her show them the second menu, the one with the prices changed, where thirty becomes three hundred. Those new-rich types never ask, What's good here? Instead it's, What's the most expensive dish here? They like to order expensive dishes, so even carp with preserved vegetables gets to be a hundred and eighty."

Tiao laughed and said, "They deserve it. If I were you, I would have added another zero and made it eighteen hundred." Their conversation left Fan cold; the minor Chinese trickery annoyed and offended her, not because she was above it, but because she couldn't be a part of it. She envied the ordinary chatter her sister could have with her two girlfriends, which no longer seemed possible for her.

When the dinner ended, Tiao called Chen Zai and then told Fan that Chen Zai would drive here to pick them up. He was going to take them to see the villa on Mei Mountain that he designed.

Chen Zai had returned from England to become a noted architect in Fuan. He had successfully designed Fuan City Museum, the Publishing Hall, and the Mei Mountain Villa, commissioned by a Singapore businessman. This year he was building his own studio. He was married, but even marriage didn't prevent him from thinking of Tiao. He couldn't do enough for her; anything she wanted. They saw each other often, and their meetings were innocent and furtive at the same time. They talked about everything. He wasn't family, but why would he be the first person Tiao thought of when she was in trouble? This man and woman, maybe they didn't want to think about the possibilities. He only knew she lived in the city where he lived, and she knew he lived in the city where she lived; they lived in the same place, and that seemed enough.

Chen Zai drove them to Mei Mountain Villa, which was truly a beautiful place in the suburbs of Fuan, very close to the city. The sudden change of coming upon a quiet, spotless village from a noisy city was captivating. After passing a scattering of houses on the hillside, they came to Villa Number One. Everything inside was new, as yet unused. As the designer, Chen Zai had the privilege of enjoying everything in the villa. Fan admired the design of Villa Number One very much—Spanish style, simple, rough-hewn, and practical. They took a sauna, and then had a candlelit dinner. The sweltering sauna made their faces shine. Fan suddenly asked for a drink, so they drank Five Grain Liquor. Tiao drank very fast, and Chen Zai asked her to slow down, with sincere concern. He said the words simply enough, but Fan could discern the tenderness that came out of their long regard for each another. In fact, Chen Zai had been talking to Fan most of the time. When they spoke in English, he complimented her excellent pronunciation. Tiao looked at them with a smile; she liked to see Chen Zai treat Fan so well and for Fan to be so pleased about it. Even so, Fan still had a deep sense of loss. The hospitality and care that they showered on her didn't cheer her up; on the contrary, it served to emphasize Tiao and Chen Zai's deep attachment to each other. Under the guise of playing a prank, Fan urged Tiao to empty each of her glasses, with the hope that Tiao would make a fool out of herself by getting drunk, and Tiao really did start to drink recklessly.

Chen Zai had to take her glass from her, saying to Fan, "I'll empty this glass for your sister. She . . . she can't do it." Fan's eyes misted over. Everything she didn't have was here, and the greatest luxury was the mysterious unspoken understanding between this Asian man and woman. She envied this and felt a longing to be with an Asian man. She remembered a college classmate of hers when she was studying in Beijing. They had a crush on each other. A native of the Shandong countryside, he once told Fan about his childhood; his family was poor and he was adopted by his uncle after his parents died. He always remembered how, at his father's funeral, a family elder patted his head and sighed: "Poor child, you won't have a good life from now on." He kept the words in his heart and used them as motivation to study hard and to fight for a good life. Other children often bullied him, and he would be sure to get back at them. His mode of vengeance was unique; he would take a small knife and bring along some Sichuan hot peppercorns to the courtyard of his enemy's house. If there was no one around, he would use the knife to cut into a poplar tree and bury the hot peppercorns. The next day the poplar tree would begin to die. Those who had bullied him all paid by having their poplar trees killed in this way. Too young to take revenge on people, he got back at their trees instead. Fan thought him unusual but wasn't altogether sure if embedded Sichuan peppercorns would really kill trees. She asked him where he got the idea, and he said it was from a beggar passing through from the neighboring town. Fan stared at the poplar trees on campus, sorely tempted to bury some Sichuan peppercorns in one. In the end, she didn't, hoping to let the story stay a story. The truth of a story is more fascinating than reality, and lends charm to the teller. Fan simply believed that a man should be like her classmate, who had great ideas, ideas out of the ordinary. Only after she met David did the poplar killer fade from her memory. Now she thought about him again. On this quiet night, a night drinking Five Grain Liquor and with Chen Zai and Tiao's hearts resonating with each other, the man she was thinking about was not David, but her college classmate, maybe because he was Chinese. Fan had never dated a Chinese man.

The three of them spent the night in Villa Number One, with Tiao and Fan sharing a bedroom. Both a little bit drunk, they lay, each in her own bed, carrying on an intermittent conversation. Fan said, "Are you attracted to Chen Zai?"

Tiao said, "Chen Zai is married."

Fan said, "His being married and your being attracted or not are two completely different matters. Why don't you answer my question directly?"

"I'm not attracted to him. I'm not attracted to any man right now."

"You're lying."

"No, I'm not."

Fan asked, "What if I were attracted to Chen Zai?" Tiao said nothing. Fan continued, "Look how scared you are, so scared that you can't say a word."

"That's enough. Stop being foolish."

Fan sighed. "You're right not to let yourself be attracted to him. Don't expect a married man to have any true feelings for you." Her feelings of superiority surfaced as she said this, and she was about to use herself and David as an example. David had been unattached when they got together. But Tiao didn't reply. She fell asleep, or pretended to.

They ate, drank, and slept late, and didn't go back to Fuan until the next afternoon. As soon as they arrived, Wu announced cheerfully that the whole family was going to eat Japanese food that night. Wasn't Japanese food very expensive in America? She had already called the restaurant and made the reservation. Fan knitted her eyebrows slightly and said, "Does Fuan have a Japanese restaurant?"

Wu said, "Yes, it just opened." Yixun said its raw ingredients, steak, and fish were all shipped from Kobe to Tianjing first, and then came from Tianjing to Fuan by air. Still feeling troubled, Fan said she had to wait for a while to decide about going out because she thought her stomach hurt a little, after which she went back to her own room and lay in bed. She seemed unhappy, and the fact that Fuan had a Japanese restaurant seemed to make her unhappy.

Wu and Yixun both felt a little disappointed, but still went to her and asked her patiently, "Why would you have an upset stomach? Did you eat anything spoiled at Mei Mountain Villa?"

Fan said, "I don't know. Maybe."

Tiao immediately said, "It can't be. Why is my stomach fine?"

Fan said, "I'm different from you. Don't you know that I'm not used to the environment here? I had diarrhea the second day after I came back. "

"If you'd been having stomach problems, then you shouldn't blame the food in the villa."

"I wasn't blaming. I just said maybe."

"But you implied it."

Suddenly Fan sat up in the bed and said, "I know what you mean better than you know what's going on with me. Just because your friends treated me to food, entertainment, a sauna, and a driving tour, should I be spouting thank-yous every minute? Do I have to compliment everything? Why do you need people's gratitude so much? Why should I thank you? What have you done to make me thank you?"

Disgusted by Fan's sulky and difficult attitude, Tiao also got angry and said, "Haven't you just come back from civilized America? How come you haven't learned the basic civilized act of appreciation for other people's kindness?"

Fan was now completely enraged by Tiao's sarcasm, and maybe she welcomed the provocation so that she could let out her irrational anger all at once. Even if Tiao hadn't supplied a provocation, she would have picked a fight with her. Otherwise, the indignation pent up in her chest would find no outlet and she would have no peace with herself. Now the chance to get her own back had come. She looked at Tiao coldly and said, "Appreciate other people's kindness? It's your kindness you want me to appreciate, right? But I'm sorry. I don't plan to. Because every time we've gone out to eat, other people have paid. Taking the sauna and staying in the villa were Chen Zai's gift. Why would I thank you?"

Yixun broke in, "How unkind of you to say that. To welcome you home, your older sister took several days off work and drove to Beijing herself to pick you up—"

Fan interrupted Yixun. "I was going to mention the car. That's the publishing house's car. What does it show when she drives a government car to take care of personal business? Yes, you all live a pretty comfortable life here, but it's at the cost of corruption and darkness. You thought I would envy you? And those friends of yours! That shabby restaurant that changes its prices for different customers is simply vulgar. Only in China can that sort of thing happen! And still you people blab about it with such enthusiasm and you . . ." On and on she poured out the vicious words, in a way that reminded Tiao of street people who stop ranting only long enough to pick up their bowls to eat and then put them down to shout again. Remembering how Fan loved the crispy turnip puffs at Youyou's Small Stir-Fry and how she asked Tiao to bring some home after the dinner, Tiao was completely baffled by Fan, not knowing where her towering rage came from. Wu also tried to calm Fan. "Stop, now. Get a hot-water bottle to warm your stomach. We'll still try to go to the Japanese restaurant in the evening."

Fan immediately directed her anger at Wu. "I really don't understand why you constantly ask me to go out and eat. Especially you, Mom. Since I was a little girl, how many meals have you cooked? What can you cook? Why don't I have any idea? Now that I've come back from so far away, why can't I just stay home for a while? Why do I have to sit in restaurants all the time? I'm not going. I'm not going to eat Japanese food tonight. I don't want to talk about eating every three sentences. I hate it that you Chinese can't ever forget about eating. Eat, eat, eat. Why do you get so happy about just eating a bit of good food . . . ?"

Having remained silent for a while, Tiao suddenly said with an air of pride, "Let me tell you: I'm exactly that kind of Chinese—I get very happy as soon as I eat something good."

Fan knew Tiao was trying to make her angry. She couldn't help wanting to slap her at this display of phony pride.

She hated Tiao.

4

They fought. Fan stayed in China for only a month, and they fought almost from the moment when Fan got off the plane to the moment she got on the plane. Strangely, Fan's complexion was getting better and better day by day. She also put on weight and got some color in her face. All this seemed to be the result of the arguments: she felt at ease in her homeland, both physically and mentally. She argued in Chinese and when she was tired or hungry afterward, she lapped up Chinese porridge and ate Chinese food. At the end of the day, she could sleep without worrying about appearances—she could sleep late in a Chinese way.

In the aftermath of every argument with Tiao, she'd feel refreshed and relieved, which frightened her a little, and made her wonder if she had come back to China to fight with people. No, it wasn't something she'd intended, but somehow she couldn't help it.

In between the fights, when she consumed with relish the plain rice porridge, the porridge with red beans or pork, and the preserved eggs that Americans would never touch, when she found her sister Tiao didn't hate her at all but even tried to please her, she felt a little guilty. Guilt brought temporary peace to their home, as if nothing had happened—as if Fan had never gone abroad and still wore that expression of hers when she'd come home from high school and toss the swollen bulk of her fake-leather backpack onto the desk, sending out a burst of overripe classroom smells. Once, rushing back from a mediocre performance on a college entrance exam, she was like that, lips parched, face pale and dripping hot sweat, saying, "Bad, bad, bad," in a trembling voice as soon as she entered . . . Tiao missed that Fan with a helpless face; her nervousness and helplessness were more genuine and convincing than her arrogance and toughness.

When they were calm, they managed some small talk. Fan praised

David's talents and complained about his naïveté. She said once David saw an old baby bottle—and insisted on spending fifteen dollars on it just because it looked like the one he had used when he was little. The old milk bottle could bring him back to the good days of childhood. Fan said, how could an old milk bottle be worth fifteen dollars? But he insisted on buying it anyway. Tiao said, "That makes sense. It's human nature to want to look back on the past. You two don't share the same past and he can't reminisce with you, so he wants to indulge in a little nostalgia through an old milk bottle." Fan immediately got touchy again. She said, "It's true that I don't have that past with David. When he talks about his childhood with his cousins I always shut up. I only have the present. The present. So what?"

Tiao said, "You have a past. Your past is in China. I don't understand why you have to banish your past, our common past. Those high school classmates of yours—why don't you have any desire to see them?"

"It's not that I don't want to see them now. I never had anything to say to them."

Tiao said, "One of my high school classmates went to Australia. Every time he came back, he would have a reunion with his classmates. I went to the reunions quite a few times, not what you'd call intellectual but very touching. He'd been in my class since the sixth grade and liked literature—although there was no real literature back then. Once our teacher assigned us to write a composition titled 'Our Classroom,' and this classmate wrote, 'Many of the windowpanes in our room are broken, as if our classroom's face were smiling.' His composition was severely criticized by our teacher, who believed he'd insulted our classroom by making the pattern of broken windows into the personification of a smiling face. This classmate explained that that was what he sincerely imagined, and that he didn't think broken windows would necessarily make a place look desolate and embarrassing; they truly gave him feelings of happiness and freedom because then he could look outside during class without anything to block his view." Tiao said many years later his classmates still remembered what he'd written. At the reunion, when someone recited from this old composition—"Many windowpanes in our room are broken, as if our classroom's face were smiling . . ."—people smiled, as if they had traveled back in time to become their younger selves.

Fan said, "Are you comparing me to your classmate in Australia? You know how I hate that. I hate it that you always compare me to others. If you go on, you'll probably give me a series of examples—so and so bought a house for his family when he came back, or so and so got ten of his relatives out of the country after he went abroad . . . just the sort of thing Mom has been nagging about. This is exactly what I can't stand—this sick attitude that Chinese people have about going abroad. They believe people go abroad to get rich, that everyone who went abroad should get rich. Why do you put so much pressure on people who have gone abroad? Why do I have to listen to you even about whether or not I should see my high school classmates?"

Tiao said, "You're being unfair. No one in our family wants you to get rich abroad. We just want you to have a peaceful and happy life. And if you talk nonsense, ignoring the simple truth, then there is a problem with your character."

Tiao's stern words overpowered Fan's bluster a little bit, but then she used Yixun as an example. "And Dad pressured me in other ways. He kept asking me why I didn't get a PhD degree. It's my business whether I want to get a PhD or not. I'd like someone to tell me why Dad doesn't push you to get a PhD. You don't even have a master's but you seem successful. How did I become the one who didn't try hard enough? What kind of person do I have to be to satisfy you all?"

There was an interval of awkward silence.

Tiao said, "You're too sensitive. Since when have you become so sensitive? Why do you hate life in China so much?"

"I'm disgusted by your fraud and tax evasion—you told me yourself that you never pay taxes for most of your extra income. This is your so-called good life. Do you know that in America you'd go to prison for evading taxes?"

"Yes, I've evaded tax, but I think you're not angry about my tax evasion, but about the fact that you can't do it yourself."

"You're projecting your own corrupt psychology on me. Americans' sense of responsibility about taxes is much stronger than you people's."

"Don't make living in America sound like wearing the seamless garments of heaven. Didn't you go through the back door to become an American citizen three months after you got there? You told me yourself that your father-in-law got you a false birth certificate to prove you were born in America. Were you born in America? Were you? You're a Chinese who was born in Beijing and grew up in Fuan, and your Chinese name is Yin Xiaofan!"

"I would rather I hadn't grown up in Fuan and I wish I didn't have that history."

"What history? What part of that history makes you so bitter?"

"Do you really want me to say it?"

"Yes, I really do," Tiao said.

"Seven years old," Fan began. "One day when I was seven years old, I was knitting a pair of woolen socks and you were reading in front of the building. She . . . she was shoveling dirt under a tree, holding a toy metal bucket. After a while some old ladies called her from a short distance away—they were gathered there to sew the bindings of *The Selected Works of Chairman Mao*. She couldn't hear them calling her, but I did. But then she saw them waving at her and clapping, so she . . . No, I won't say the rest and I don't want to talk about it."

Tiao's heart started to sink as Fan was telling the story. She thought Fan would never mention this long-suppressed history; she thought perhaps Fan didn't have such a clear memory, but she did remember, and now was bringing it up at last. Tiao had no right to stop her, nor could she, either. Maybe her day of judgment had come at last. Let Fan tell their parents and announce it to society and let Tiao be free from that moment on. Now, into her sinking heart came a desperate sweetness, like that of an abandoned lover assaulted by an overwhelming surge of hopeless love for the one lost. So she urged Fan to go on; she couldn't stand to have her drop the subject right in the middle. Fan should have the courage to finish if she had the courage to start.

She urged Fan to continue, but Fan refused. She said, "I don't want to talk about it anymore. Sorry, I won't talk about it."

"You have to finish," Tiao said.

"Then she saw them; they were waving and clapping their hands at her," Fan said. "So she . . . she dropped her little metal bucket and went toward them. She ran down the small road, and there was the manhole in front of her, which was uncovered. At that moment both you and I saw the open manhole and her running toward it. The two of us were standing there, behind her—twenty meters away, thirty? I remember I wanted to call out to her to avoid the hole, but I knew it wouldn't work because she wouldn't hear. I wanted to run over, and then . . . then you pulled on my hand; you didn't just pull, you stopped me, not just pulling but stopping."

"Yes, you're right, I stopped you. Everything you said is true," Tiao said. "The pull was to stop you." She added that one last sentence.

There was another brief interval of awkward silence.

Tiao's frank admission of the way she stopped Fan came more or less as a surprise to Fan. The blame finally belonged to Tiao, and Quan's death had nothing to do with Fan. Fan finally emerged from the shadow of twenty years before, the sickening history that so disgusted her. But she didn't feel relieved, because she was unable to bring herself to face the question that Tiao raised then: "Did you like Quan?"

The adult Fan presented her seven-year-old self as a hero who was about to save someone; but who could prove she really meant to perform the rescue when she stepped forward back then? If she had truly dashed forward, Tiao would not have been able to restrain her. She had taken Tiao's hand herself, and maybe she had done that out of fear—they stood, hands clasped, almost shoulder to shoulder that day—though all her life she refused to remember it that way. It was a fact that Fan couldn't digest, either through her conscience or her intellect. Only a pragmatist would attempt to make such matters appear reasonable, which was Fan's unconscious strategy now. Maybe she didn't feel too guilty about long-dead Quan; what she wanted more than anything was to keep Tiao down—the pull on her hand twenty years ago was originally Tiao's shame, and Fan wanted her sister to know that there was no chance that she had forgotten. Only when the discussion returned to the basic "Did you like Quan?" did Fan's evasiveness begin to emerge, and she said nothing about it. But Tiao told her frankly, "I didn't like Quan." She almost told her the real reason behind her dislike, which certainly didn't resemble Fan's instinctive jealousy. She couldn't tell her what it was, though. Other than Fei, she couldn't tell anyone the real reason.

Fan envied Tiao's complete frankness. She suddenly realized that freedom did not lie in transferring responsibility onto others; in fact, freedom meant facing one's own responsibility directly. When Tiao felt the overwhelming approach of the dark cloud, she had actually started to free herself, but Fan had lost this opportunity forever. That was why she had no sense of victory, although Tiao had been so defeated by this subject. Tiao sat there staring off somewhere with her large, dispirited eyes, and her body seemed to have shrunken in on itself. How was it possible for Tiao to judge Fan's life in America with calm and detachment? How could Tiao enjoy her easy, secure life? That was the crux of the matter—Fan's annoyance with those who could live that easy, natural way in their native place.

As the separation approached, they tried to be polite with each other, but it was futile; the pretense was suffocating. Tiao flattered Fan. "Fan, your figure seems to be getting nicer and nicer. Does that have something to do with scuba diving?"

Fan said condescendingly, "Older sister, all your clothes are so much prettier than mine." No sooner was it said than each attacked the other's hypocrisy. Later, to ease the tension between them, Tiao bought for Fan from the Friendship Store a boy rag doll in a red flower-patterned cotton jacket and infants' split pants with a tradi-tional watermelon cap. The doll's manufacturer was obviously pan-dering to foreigners' taste. Clearly, it was especially designed for them. Tiao remembered Fan saying that she wanted to buy a gift for David's little niece. What was more suitable than this Chinese doll who wore split pants? Fan immediately named the doll Wang Dagui and was particularly amused that Wang Dagui could even have his little tool exposed, which was two inches of cotton thread.

Fan's China trip ended with Wang Dagui. When she brought the doll with her to Beijing International Airport and said goodbye to Tiao, she abruptly grimaced and burst into tears. When she finished checking her bags, confirmed her ticket, and was about to go through customs, she suddenly turned, waved at Tiao, and called out to her, "Older sister, I always miss you."

Tiao would probably remain the person she'd miss most in the world.

Tears welled up in Tiao's eyes and her feelings were as tangled as a bunch of twine. Looking at Fan, who was disappearing from her view, she suddenly felt she had abandoned her. Fan had come home especially to tell her this long-past incident, to denounce her, with a victim's deep compulsions. She had abandoned her sister on that long-ago Sunday, when they stood behind Quan and she pulled Fan's hand, providing this American citizen in her red wool coat a chilling excuse to torment her anytime she wanted.

5

From then on, it seemed to Tiao that every time Fan came home, her purpose was to make her family suffer—and she had made many trips back since then. The international company she was working for did business with China, and as a departmental manager, she had to travel every year—Beijing, Paris, Toronto, and Tokyo. She always set aside some time to visit her family on these business trips. Having accused Tiao of corruption, she could hardly ask her to drive the publishing house's car to Beijing to collect her. Forced into a corner, she turned to Chen Zai for help. He had his own car and Fan was willing to ask him to pick her up in Beijing. A hundred times more calculating than Tiao, Fan was determined not to spend any money on car rental.

Or maybe there were other reasons. In America, every time she talked to Tiao on the phone, she would call Chen Zai afterward. Not that she was checking up on Tiao and Chen Zai or trying to find out how intimate they were. Nothing in particular, she just wanted to chat and hoped that, during her stay in China, she could spend a few hours with Chen Zai, on the drive from Beijing to Fuan, say.

Twice, Chen Zai drove to pick up Fan. On the highway, Fan even asked to try his car for a while. Here in China, she said, she hadn't dared to drive. When she was in high school, she'd bicycled very well but was now even afraid to ride a bicycle. She just couldn't get used to so many people anymore; it made her nervous. She drove beautifully, and her long, elegant hands, with their fingernails polished in glossy red, rested confidently on the wheel, looking very stylish. Constantly she'd bring her hand up to tuck back the hair that fell in front of her ears—she wore her hair long. Every move, and every gesture of hers, the rhythm of her speech, the control in her voice, and the expression on her face when she tilted her head to observe Chen Zai, all displayed the manner of a worldly American. She asked Chen Zai casually, "What do you think of me?"

"I think you're very smart and capable," Chen Zai said.

Then, again in a casual tone, "And compared to my sister?" Smiling, Chen Zai turned his head to look out the window and said nothing. Perhaps he felt the way Fan asked the question was naïve, and because of the naïveté, she seemed pushy. His smile and avoidance of talk about Tiao gave Fan another sign of the important place Tiao had in Chen Zai's heart. She was not for casual mention; he didn't intend to allow her to be a topic of conversation. Here was an intriguing man, Fan thought. She couldn't see through him. He was not as easygoing as he appeared. To be fair to Fan, she wasn't really attracted to Chen Zai, but she vaguely wanted Chen Zai to be attracted to her. She wanted to make the men who liked Tiao like her better. Whether it was because she wanted to compete with Tiao or just out of a sense of mischief, she didn't know.

Once she stayed for a few days in an apartment Tiao had recently gotten. She liked her sister's new place, particularly the furniture. She asked about the price and manufacturers, and all of it had been made in China. China now really had everything, and things were very inexpensive. She clearly remembered in the early eighties how people even prized plastic bags and the way many families would save and reuse them. In a few short years, the bags had become white pollution. Paper bags replaced plastic as a status symbol; only, unlike America, China still couldn't replace all the plastic bags with paper. Once, Fan was watching TV at Tiao's place, the news on Fuan's local station, when the mayor called on the residents of Fuan to make a little bit more effort when disposing of the plastic bags, to tie them in a knot before discarding, to protect the environment, to prevent thousands of these little bags from flying all over, falling into tree-tops and dropping into the food containers of the animals at the zoo, many of which died from accidental ingestion of the bags. Fan was not much interested in politics or current events, but it was from such details that she gauged the progress China had made, even though the mayor didn't even speak good Mandarin and had stained teeth. He probably didn't know to clean them; many well-dressed officials in China had stained teeth.

Progress in China and change in Fuan made Fan almost lose her appetite for describing how advanced America was. Recently, David's parents had invited their children to go to Ecuador to celebrate their golden wedding anniversary. They chartered a big cabin cruiser and more than twenty of them stayed on the boat for a week. Fan talked about Ecuador to Tiao, and Tiao talked about Jerusalem to her. In the last few years, Tiao had traveled abroad frequently, which surprised Fan and made her envious. She couldn't call Tiao's trips corruption, because all of them had something to do with publishing, either collaborating with foreign publishers or attending international conferences. She always remembered to buy some little gift for Fan even though she knew that Fan didn't want for anything. It was just a long-established habit; she had an unbreakable attachment to this sister who had become more and more difficult. She saved the gifts and waited for Fan to come back to show her. Tiao was especially pleased with an Italian Trinity gold bracelet that she'd bought in Tel Aviv, and a British St. Michael linen sun hat purchased from Marks & Spencer, Hong Kong. Indeed, Fan liked these things very much, but felt some disappointment. She'd thought it would be the other way around, that she would be the one to bring her family exclusive items, and that only she would be able to bring back from abroad fine things to which her family would have no access. But now it was the opposite. Then what was the significance of her going to America? Why did she have to live among Americans?

She seldom allowed herself this sort of thinking, resisting any hint of self-doubt. Then she discovered that the water pressure in the showerhead in Tiao's bathroom was too weak, suspecting a showerhead with such small volume simply couldn't clean her hair, and there was also the water quality. She complained that the water in Fuan was too hard, which was particularly damaging to long hair. Moving close to Tiao, shaking that precious long hair of hers in front of Tiao, she said, "Feel it. You feel it. My hair doesn't feel like this when I'm in America. That's right. The water in America is very good. In my house, we have a wood-lined room especially used for saunas, and there's always enough water pressure." At last she'd found a reason to put down China. Reluctantly, Tiao touched Fan's hair, and said, "I think your hair feels fine. I can't feel any difference."

"How could you tell the difference? You've always lived in the same place."

"Yes, I have lived in the same place. This is my home. Where else would I live if not here? You just happen to live somewhere else."

So, once again, an argument started, and emotions ran high in both of them. Perhaps Tiao should have been conciliatory; after all, Fan was her guest. But, feeling Fan's nitpicking was simply ungrateful, she got a little stubborn. Fan said, "I noticed long ago you're the kind of person that can't stand to be criticized. The problem is, how did I criticize you? I was talking about the water."

Tiao said, "The water has always been like that. Why didn't you bring some water softener with you when you came back? Or just bring your own water, like Queen Elizabeth does—too bad you're not a queen yet. Spare me the big performance."

"You think this is a performance? It's your vanity that can't take it, right? Now that you're the vice director of the publishing house, you want me to act the brown-nose around you, like your colleagues and subordinates? Don't forget how you got into the publishing house. If Fei hadn't sold herself for you, you would still be eating chalk dust and teaching high school. What messy relationships you have. That filled me with disgust whenever I thought about it."

"You can leave if you're so disgusted," Tiao said.

"All right." Fan packed up her stuff and actually left. "Fine . . ."

They didn't talk to each other at all the next year. Yixun and Wu blamed Tiao for trading darts back and forth with Fan; when the sisters argued, they always sided with Fan. "Let her have her way" was their unalterable principle. They never thought of Tiao and Fan as two adults, who therefore needed to control their emotions and deal respectfully with each other. Instead they would always say, "Let her have her way. Let her have her way." What did they know? Tiao looked at her parents quietly, her heart filled with an undefined sadness.

So Yixun made an international phone call to Fan. Pretending nothing had happened, he said, "Fan, why haven't you called us? We all miss you very much."

Fan said, "Why do I always have to call you? You can also call me. Is that so difficult?"

"Didn't you tell us that phone calls in America were much cheaper than here?" Yixun said.

"It still costs something even though it's cheap. Besides, you have money yourself. If you don't even want to pay for phone calls, how can you claim to miss me . . . ?"

Tiao was present during Yixun's conversation with Fan, and it made her sad and angry the way Fan talked back to Yixun like that. Let the facts speak for themselves. Let facts change her parents' principle of "let her have her way."

What else did she need to do to "let her have her way"? She was angry. But, as with Yixun's treatment of Wu, the deepest guilt came in the moment Tiao most resented Fan. Really it was a guilt beyond words, with no causality or logic involved. In short, she felt guilty and finally called Fan. She told her sister that she would be going to America to attend a conference. Would Fan be in America then? If so, she wanted to see her very much.

She flew to Chicago from Minneapolis after the conference and they met in America. It was in early winter, and Chicago was windy, but what a refreshing wind, chilling people to the bone, but waking them up completely. The dazzling gold of the fallen leaves all around Lake Michigan also left a deep impression on Tiao—they were not withered or crunching underfoot, either, because every one of them was soft, shining, supple, with a delicate sheen, like silk, gathered there like a silent carnival.

Fan showed her hospitality beyond expectations; maybe she wanted to make up for her spiteful departure the previous year. When she was far from China and reflecting on those hurtful words she'd hurled at Tiao, she must have had some bad moments. She hugged her sister enthusiastically, and when they got home and Tiao took out the Italian Trinity gold bracelet and the St. Michael linen sun hat that Fan had purposely left behind, she cried, and Tiao also cried. Their tears were genuine at that moment, and washed away the ice in their hearts, both the old and the new. Fan gave her a house tour and showed Tiao to her room. Her cat, a large white animal called White Goat, appeared then and clumsily rolled over in front of Tiao, welcoming her. Although she didn't really like cats, not to mention the fact that he was shedding, Tiao felt obliged to please Fan, and, pretending to be charmed, reached out to scratch his chin. She knew Fan didn't like cats, either, but David did. His preference dictated hers, so she liked the cat unconditionally.

Tiao could stay in Chicago for only two days, and after that she had to go to Austin, Texas, for a few days. A friend had invited her, she told Fan. "Two days isn't enough," Fan said. But at least they would have those two days to spend together. Fan requested two days off from her company and told everyone that she needed the time because her sister was coming to visit. Her childhood attachment to her sister seemed to come back; she still missed Tiao in a way she didn't even understand herself.

She took Tiao to the mall, and they bought things for each other at Macy's. Tiao got her a long windbreaker, she got Tiao a leather handbag, and then they bought things for Yixun and Wu. Unlike

Tiao, Fan wasn't very interested in shopping, and she had to summon tremendous patience to accompany Tiao. When they got tired, they would go to a coffee shop to sit and get something to drink or eat. They went to the store's bathroom together while an American woman, who had apparently been holding herself in with some difficulty, rushed in and farted loudly. They couldn't help exchanging a glance and smiling. Fan said, "There are a lot of these vulgar types in the States."

"She'll hear us," Tiao said.

"I guarantee you that she doesn't understand Chinese. The language barrier can come in handy—she might think you're complimenting her even though you're actually cursing her." They laughed.

She and Tiao took a walk down the elegant Goethe Street near the lake. She went into a flower shop on their way and insisted on buying a white lily for Tiao to hold. Although she felt that it was a little affected, Tiao's heart was warmed by Fan's thoughtfulness. As she held the fragrant lily and walked along Goethe Street, a fluffy puppy ran past them. The owner was a well-dressed thin old lady, but the strange thing was the puppy kept turning back toward them while it ran forward, which made Tiao and Fan keep looking at the puppy, too. Fan said, "Tiao, I think the dog looks like Maxim Gorky." The comparison surprised Tiao, who just couldn't imagine a puppy resembling a person, but they did look alike. Then, as if to confirm their conclusion, the puppy turned around to them again. Tiao couldn't help cracking up, and she laughed so hard that she doubled over. The lily in her hand almost got crumpled and Fan pulled her into a restaurant called Big Shot. Both would remember the walk for a long time, and how they ran into "Gorky" on Goethe Street.

David came home in the evening and the three of them went to eat Japanese food. Time flowed like water with the arrangements, and everything seemed to go very well. Fan stayed in Tiao's room until late at night, chatting. They hadn't indulged in any girl-talk in ages, and now Fan started first—with confidences about a couple of brief affairs she'd had. Tiao then mentioned the friend named Mike who had invited her to Texas. "So the friend is a man," Fan said.

"Yes, it's a man," Tiao said. "We met at a conference. His Chinese is very good, and he worked as an interpreter for my paper at the conference. Now he's studying Chinese at Beijing University."

"Are you interested in him?" Fan asked. Tiao said nothing. "Then he must be interested in you," Fan said.

"He's too young, seven years younger than I am. What does he know about love?" Tiao said.

Fan said, "Here people admire you if you have a lover who is seven years younger than you are. Older sister, I really envy you. I never expected you to be so . . . daring."

"Me, daring? But nothing's happened."

"He . . . What color are Mike's hair and eyes? Do you have his picture?"

"No, I don't, but you can talk to him and try his Chinese. I also need to give him my flight information. He said he would come to the airport to pick me up."

They went ahead and called Mike. Both felt the need to avoid David, so they chose to make the phone call in the kitchen. Tiao and Mike exchanged greetings and talked a little, and then she introduced Fan to Mike. A Chinese who speaks English so well, and an American so fluent in Chinese, wouldn't it be fun for them to have a conversation? So Fan took the phone and started to talk to Mike.

She insisted on talking to Mike in English instead of Chinese. Mike must have been complimenting her English on the other end of the phone, because Tiao saw her smile proudly. She was smiling, and speaking English at length, ignoring Tiao, who was standing next to her—maybe it was exactly because Tiao was next to her that she insisted on isolating her from them with English. Isolation was certainly what it was, with some condescension and insensitivity. The message seemed to be directed at Tiao, with this graceful and melodious English, that this was America, and no matter what kind of relationship Tiao was going to have with Mike, she was still a person who couldn't speak. Tiao and Mike couldn't talk like Fan and Mike could. She rattled on in English, making happy gestures and laughing heartily, as if she had known Mike forever. Her sense of humor and cleverness were enough to make their conversation lively and interesting. "Oh, Mike, why do you have to speak Chinese? Forget Chinese. Don't try to tell Tiao you love her in Chinese." She went on and on, maybe starting to feel nervous about the fact that Mike could speak to Tiao in Chinese. What right did Tiao have to be friends with an American? How could she have an American friend, considering her survival-English skills, her bare ability to ask for food on the airplane, directions in the street, or to buy simple things at the store? Unfortunately, it so happened that the American fellow spoke good Chinese. Her luck just confirmed the Chinese proverb: "The gods send good fortune to fools." So she couldn't have tolerated Mike speaking Chinese to Tiao. If she didn't hear it, her heart could be at peace. For her not to hear meant it didn't exist. Once heard, it would have become a reality: an American's vocal cords could produce the sounds of Chinese, and those sweet words were not spoken to Fan but to this strange Tiao beside her. She couldn't bear it, and hated her own vulnerability.

This English phone conversation had been going on for too long, long enough to make Tiao suspicious. Finally Fan brought the phone away from her ear and held it out to Tiao. "Mike is asking if you have anything else to say to him."

For some reason Tiao grew apprehensive about taking the phone. The way Fan had seized control of the phone conversation and that tone of hers, assuming the role of the host—"Mike is asking if you have anything else to say to him"—only brought a single word to mind: cruelty. She lost interest in talking to Mike, and whether out of a sense of inferiority or low spirits, she hung up.

They halfheartedly said good night to each other and returned to their own rooms; both seemed to be trying to maintain a semblance of good relations.

If Tiao hadn't made a small mistake the next morning, her stay in Chicago might have ended as well as it began. Unfortunately, she had a little accident; she had been having her period and accidentally got blood on the bedsheet, a very small spot, the size of a nickel. Immediately she got up, pulled off the sheet, and went to the bathroom to wash it, where she ran right into Fan, who was brushing her teeth.

Fan's mood had changed overnight. For some reason Tiao holding the bloodstained bedsheet set her off. "Older sister, what are you doing?"

"I have to wash this spot."

"You don't have to wash it. I'll take care of it when I do the laundry."

"Let me take care of it."

"Put it down. Put it down. Can't you just put it down?"

"Why are you getting so worked up?"

"I don't understand why you don't use the tampons. I always do, and it never stains the sheet."

"Didn't I tell you that I wasn't used to tampons?"

"Why can't you get used to them? Why can't you get used to the things that Americans are used to?"

"I don't like stuffing things into my vagina."

"But your thingies with the little . . ." In her exasperation, she momentarily forgot how to say winged pads. "They leaked on the sheets."

"I'm sorry about the sheets, but it's my choice to use the kind of pads I want to. Why do I have to use what you order me to?"

"I'm not ordering you, but I do have the tampons at home. Only you refuse to use them. Didn't I drive to the store to accommodate your habits—the fussiness you brought with you from China to America? What more do you want me to do?"

"You're right that I'm fussy in some ways. I've always known that you didn't like that about me. My clothes, my luggage, my friends, my job, all of it annoys you, makes you unhappy. You want me to say that only what you do is best, right? Your cat, and your tampons. I have to throw my arms open and embrace everything you recommend, right?"

David came over and asked them what they were talking about. Fan lied and said they were gossiping about a mutual acquaintance in China. David noticed their strange mood, but couldn't understand a word they said. That was the convenience of the language barrier; they could talk about vaginas and tampons right in front of David.

Fan lied to David and then turned back to Tiao. "You're right that I'm not happy. It was you who brought me all the unhappiness. You! When I was seven years old . . ."

Tiao knew very well where they were headed yet again; the unfortunate "before," the "before" that was embedded in her heart, tormenting her constantly. Strangely, though, she was not as panicky as when Fan first mentioned it in China, as if the change of venue had performed some magic. Even the most shameful thing, when mentioned in a strange place, far from its original setting, didn't seem that terrible. Strange places are ideal for recalling past horrors. So Tiao wasn't frightened by Fan's reference to the event. She even felt that she had the courage to stand here, in Chicago, Illinois, right in front of Fan, to retell the whole story from beginning to end, and simply to declare again, I was the murderer. Her candor, no matter how detailed and complete, would be overwhelmed by the vastness of America, because America doesn't care—has no interest in denouncing the secret crime committed by a strange foreigner. It made her feel as if she were about to tell someone else's story—half truth and half fiction—with calm and detachment. This was a new discovery for her, which disconnected her from the incident. Maybe she was not all that detached, but she was at least granted calm by the foreignness of the place. Calmly, she interrupted Fan. "I want to say something that I have held in for a long time, and today I'm going to let it out: don't you try to terrify me with 'before.' Even if everything I did before was wrong, it doesn't mean what you did was right."

Even if everything I did before was wrong, it doesn't mean what you did was right.

Fan must surely have heard, and taken it in—there are words that can force a person to remember.

Tiao left Fan's home ahead of schedule. She called a taxi and went to the airport seven hours before her flight. It was a day of rain and snow, and Fan drove to the airport after her. She wanted very much to run to her sister and to hug her, as she had done when she'd picked her up two days earlier, and then to tell her, I was wrong. But she didn't have the courage. A man named Mike went in and out of her mind. Yes, Mike. Didn't Tiao have too much? She was going to fly to Mike's city. She was abandoning Fan again. A sharp sadness struck her, and Fan felt a moment of dizziness. She was a victim; she had always been a victim, lonely, with no one on whom to depend. The deepest suffering in her heart was not the loneliness, but the fact that all her life she had no one to turn to, no one to tell.

Chapter 7

❦ ❦ ❦

Peeking Through the Keyhole

1

Tiao was preoccupied on the airplane to Austin; Fan's bitter face was flashing in front of her eyes all the way. She knew she had upset Fan, and this time she'd used Mike. Why would she mention Mike when Fan was talking about the several brief affairs she'd had? Using Mike as counterpart to Fan's short-term lovers made it seem like Mike had become Tiao's lover, or at least implied that Mike was going to. This wasn't Tiao's style; it sounded a little like bragging, it was immodest, and seemed like a conscious provocation of Fan. But maybe that was what she had intended; gradually realizing Fan's weaknesses, she'd provoked her on purpose, although she was reluctant to admit it to herself. Perhaps, though, she hadn't said it to provoke her but, instead, only wanted to indulge herself. Breathing foreign air seemed particularly conducive to self-indulgent thoughts, even if they merely remained thoughts. In another country no one pays attention to you or bothers to talk to you, unlike those above or below her in the publishing house, pleasant or unpleasant, and those incompetent little plots they liked to spin and believed to be clever. There were also one or two men in particular who were corrupt. If you went along with them, you would win their cheap approval; if you looked down on their contemptible behavior, they would get back at you with ten times the contemptible behavior. You don't have to notice, but it's hard to ignore because it's such a part of the reality of your life. In another country no one pays attention to you or bothers to talk to you, so you pay attention to yourself, which means indulging yourself, caring for yourself and not caring too much about what others think. Yes, not caring too much. In her own country she cared too much, every word she said and every action she took, every time she made a move, her job in the publishing house, the chance to advance her position, the chasing after national book awards every year, and the profit the publishing house made . . . every slipup might result in a huge loss. Caring too much should be the opposite of being cruel, right? She needed compensation, and she had the right to it, any compensation, good or bad. She needed to escape from her own demons and carve out a space for herself, her own space in which she could care for herself. Where was it? Was it here, in other people's country? Wasn't the conclusion a little absurd? She could find her own space only in someone else's country.

She cast a glance from the corner of her eye at the neighbor on her right, an American man with blond hair and conservative dress, who had the look of a senior corporate executive. He let down the tray table soon after the airplane took off and started to write something on a stack of paper. He was left-handed, as many Americans seemed to be. That was how Tiao noticed the fancy oval cuff link on his expensive-looking shirt. It must have been silver, with a kind of black luster like titanium's. Even senior executives wouldn't wear cuff links every day, so the appearance of the left-handed man beside her suggested that an important occasion awaited him as soon as he got off the airplane. Of all the accessories for men, Tiao was fondest of cuff links, and found them elegant. The impression might have come from a pair of cuff links that Wu had, which were eighteen-karat gold and diamond and had belonged to Wu's father, Tiao's grandfather. The story went that the grandfather's lover had sent the cuff links to him as a gift when he returned from studying in England. The gift from the lover eventually came into the hands of his daughter, Wu, which must have made her feel uncomfortable. She had saved them probably because her love for the cuff links surpassed her disgust for her mother's rival. It was the pair of old diamond-studded cuff links that wakened Tiao's initial secret yearning for men. She asked

Wu hundreds of times about the lover, with appreciation, sympathy, and envy that crossed generations. Only at a distance of generations could someone respond to a family's complicated suffering with those emotions. Unfortunately, Tiao had never seen pictures of her grandfather's lover, which, according to Wu, had all been burned by Tiao's grandmother. Later, when Tiao's relationship with Fang Jing was at its unsteadiest, she'd even thought about stealing her grandfather's cuff links and giving them to him. She was really crazy, so crazy that she got the roles thoroughly confused. Obsessed with becoming Fang Jing's wife, she decided to follow the example of her grandfather's distant lover, who was so tenacious with her love. Did she understand this as the dream of all women—to be the best wife for a man and at the same time to be his best mistress? No, Tiao wasn't aware of it; she was far from reaching this kind of self-realization.

She had become acquainted with Mike at a conference in Beijing, sponsored by an American research institute for women and children. Tiao was invited to attend the conference and to present her paper, "A Lecture to Mothers." The paper explored the mother-child relationship, and Mike was the interpreter the sponsor had hired. He was studying Chinese at Beijing University then, and dreamed of becoming a translator and helping cultural communication between China and America. His fluent and accent-free Chinese made him something of a star at the conference. It was hard to believe he was an American if you listened to him with eyes closed. He was six feet tall, had curly auburn hair, a pair of clear green eyes, and his voice was soft and gentle. During the break Tiao was waiting behind him to get water from the water dispenser. Mike got himself a cup of water, and filled another for Tiao. He turned around and handed it to her.

Holding their cups, they moved aside and chatted. Mike said attentively, "I know you don't like to drink cold water. What you prefer is colder than hot water, but hotter than lukewarm, am I right?"

Tiao savored the temperature of the water in her cup and said, "You managed the temperature perfectly. How did you know what I wanted?"

Mike put on an air of mystery. "If I want to get to know someone,

I can find out everything about her." Tiao smiled without saying anything. Mike asked, "Why are you smiling?"

Tiao said, "I smiled because you used the word 'lukewarm.' I thought you wouldn't know the Chinese for that."

Mike said, "I can also recite some Chinese nursery rhymes. I'm sure you learned them when you were young."

"Really? Say them for me."

"Do you really want to hear?"

"Yes, I really do."

Mike drained the water in his cup, stepped forward to throw it into the nearby trash can, and then returned to Tiao and started to chant solemnly, "'Eat the milk. Drink the bread. Beneath your arm, carry the train. Ride on a briefcase, instead. Afterward, get off the case. Eastward, then, turn your face. There you'll see a man bite a dog. Pick up the dog. Give a stone a whack, but then the stone will bite the dog back . . .'"

Tiao couldn't help bursting into laughter. Mike said, "Listen to this one: 'Riding on a bike, arriving at the bank. Meeting the head banker and giving a salute. The banker said, that's all right, that's okay, we all work in the bank anyway.'"

Tiao asked, "What else?"

Mike said, "'A little car is honking, beep, beep, beep. Chairman Mao sits in the backseat.'"

"What about the one that goes, 'The car is coming but I don't care. I'll give the car a phone call over there. The car turned around and ran my little feet down'?" Those old wordplays and nursery rhymes gave Tiao a familiar, warm feeling, especially "The car is coming but I don't care. I'll give the car a phone call over there." It was a nursery rhyme that came out of her childhood, a period when both the car and the telephone were rarities. For children, the proof that they were not afraid of a car was that they were bold enough to call it on the phone. Ah, the car is coming but I don't care. I'll give the car a phone call over there.

Over the next few days, Mike and Tiao were pretty much together all the time during the breaks. He would pour her a cup of water at the right temperature, she'd take the water with a thank-you, and then they would start to talk about things related to their studying and work. One day Tiao took half a day off from the conference because her publishing house needed her to preside over a book release in the Great Hall of the People. During the break the next day, before Tiao walked up to the water dispenser, Mike, who could hardly contain himself, ran to her and said, "Finally I see you. You weren't here yesterday and I thought you wouldn't show up again. I was terrified."

"Why would my disappearance frighten you so much?"

"I don't know, but I meant what I said. How are you?"

"I'm fine. You sounded like we hadn't seen each other in years." Tiao was just joking, but Mike got serious and said, "I did have the feeling that we hadn't seen each other in years."

All of a sudden Tiao felt a bit awkward about Mike's serious turn, or maybe she didn't want anything else to come out of it, so she said to him calmly, "Mike, can you satisfy a small wish of mine?"

"Of course, what is it?"

Tiao pretended to be nervous and lowered her voice. "Please, get me a cup of water, cooler than hot water but hotter than warm water."

Mike tapped himself on the forehead and said, "Of course! I forgot about the water." He quickly disappeared from Tiao's view and then cheerfully returned with a cup of water. He handed Tiao the water with two hands and said, "Please, cooler than hot water but hotter than warm." He watched Tiao finish the water, and then the bell rang to resume the conference. When Tiao was going to throw away the paper cup, he took it from her and said, "Allow me. Let me throw it away for you." Tiao never noticed that the cup remained in Mike's hand all the way back to their seats.

On the night the conference ended, Mike invited Tiao to a readers' salon, a discussion group, at a bookstore called Distance near Xidan, saying he was very friendly with the couple who owned it, and they often recommended good Chinese books to him. Mike said, "I've noticed that the Distance Bookstore almost never sells children's books, which is unfortunate because China has so many children and they get so much more attention and love than those of any other countries because of the birth control policy. Why don't you recommend some good books published by your publishing house? Your publishing house will be better known, and the Distance Bookstore will also gain customers." Tiao listened politely to Mike's suggestion, although she didn't take it too seriously. Mike didn't know much about publishing. Tiao was much more familiar with the business, the distribution networks and connections than he was, but she didn't want to spoil Mike's generous gesture; his consideration for her work touched her. Together they went to the Distance Bookstore, and the owners were very friendly, asking Mike and Tiao to stay after the salon to chat and have an evening snack. They prepared poached eggs in rice wine for Tiao and Mike, saying that Mike was especially fond of their poached eggs. Tiao also liked poached eggs, but her great concern at that moment was to find a toilet. She'd planned to head for the bathroom right after the salon, and hadn't expected the couple to invite them so enthusiastically to stay. She held her bladder and pretended to eat the poached eggs calmly. After a bowl, her need only grew stronger. She looked around and saw no bathroom. She was reluctant to ask the woman, because she didn't know her well, nor was Mike an old acquaintance, either. It would have been a little embarrassing for her to ask people she had just met where the bathroom was, and what was more irritating was that Mike still sat there talking to them endlessly. Tiao had held herself for too long and her face apparently showed concentration. If Mike continued to talk she would simply stand up and run out. Fortunately, Mike stopped. When the woman asked him another question, he glanced at his watch and said, "I'm sorry, but we have to go. It's getting very late."

They took their leave. As soon as they walked out of the bookstore Tiao blurted out, "Mike, I'm sorry, but I'm desperate to get to a bathroom." She didn't expect Mike also to grimace and say, "I'm sorry, Tiao. I have to go right away myself." Single-file, they ran to look for a restroom on the street. Tiao complained, "Why did you talk nonstop if you also had to go to the bathroom?"

Mike said, "Isn't that good manners in China? They were so courteous, how could I interrupt them? Besides, you seemed to be listening so attentively."

"That wasn't attentiveness. My eyes were fixed because I was holding in the pee so hard."

Mike said, "Me, too. I squeezed so hard, tears almost came out." They spotted a restroom by the side of the road, stopped talking immediately, and rushed in. When they came out, they looked relieved, and their walk turned to a leisurely stroll, ease written all over them. Their shared trial and embarrassment brought them closer to each other and they laughed with tacit understanding.

It was late at night, and they were walking on the quiet Changan Avenue. Stepping on the rectangular concrete bricks with sharp edges, Tiao asked, "Mike, do you know what's underneath these bricks?"

"No, I don't know."

"Let me tell you. There were toilets here. Years ago—you were probably not born yet, or just born—when Chairman Mao received the Red Guards during a parade for National Day, because of the crowd, they had to build temporary facilities at these spots underneath our feet." Mike lowered his head to observe the ground. "I can appreciate latrines, because now I understand how painful it can be if you can't get to them."

"They were restrooms, not just latrines," Tiao corrected him. Mike looked into Tiao's eyes and said, "Do you know you're very lovely?"

Tiao said, "I'll accept the flattery."

"It wasn't flattery. It was what I had on my mind, particularly when you became serious and had to correct me. You were just like a schoolteacher."

Tiao interrupted him. "Let's talk about something else." She suddenly ran off the sidewalk and onto the empty street. Mike caught up with her from behind and took her hand.

She didn't try to avoid his hand. They stood on the street holding hands. Looking at the occasionally passing cars, both started to recite the rhyme about the car at the same time. "'The car is coming but I don't care. I'll give the car a phone call over there. The car turned around, and ran my little feet down . . .'" This children's rhyme made their hand-holding intimate and innocent, with no ambiguity or awkwardness. It was a perfect connection, Tiao thought.

She already sensed Mike's love clearly, and she liked this young man who was holding her hand. But love was not easy for her. The inoculation from the plague of that other love still had its impact on her. Love would never again come easily for her.

But she told Mike that she was going to America to attend a conference. Mike said that coincidentally he would be in the States during that time and hoped that, no matter what, she would accept his invitation to visit Texas.

The left-handed man on her right side lifted up his tray and Tiao realized the airplane was landing. She'd arrived at Austin.

Mike welcomed Tiao at the Austin airport. While rain and snow took its toll on Chicago, Austin in the south was still very warm. Tiao saw Mike, who had on an eye-catching red T-shirt and was waving at her. Tiao felt a little nervous; the closer she was to Mike, the more she wanted to run away from him. She resented this urge, which she often had when she decided to take action. It made her seem neurotic, like an actor with stage fright. She finally got close to Mike. She reached out her hand, and he opened both his arms to her.

He hugged her, and naturally she hugged back. The urge to run away disappeared, and her heart calmed down. It was the first time she was close enough to breathe in his scent, a healthy light smell of mutton mixed with the lingering fragrance of Tide detergent. For many years after, she'd persist in using Tide for the comfort of its distinctive smell, which always reminded her of the Austin airport, Mike's hug, her racing heart, and the fleeting confusion caused by it.

When they left the airport, it was already dark. Mike drove Tiao home, and his parents gave Tiao a friendly welcome. His father, a graceful man with a scholarly bearing, who was a professor at the University of Texas, told Tiao, "We all saw your picture. Now I want to tell you that you're even more beautiful than the picture." Puzzled, Tiao looked at Mike, and he explained that it was a group picture from that conference. Mike's mom took Tiao to her room and told her it was Mike's sister's room before she got married, and her clothes were still hanging in the closet. She said that as long as the clothes were there, she could feel as though her daughter were still living at home, so she liked having them, but, really, a daughter can never manage to take all her stuff out of her parents' house. Then she led Tiao out of the room and showed her the guest bathroom.

Mike's parents made a very good impression on Tiao; their sincerity and effortless hospitality put her at ease. They said to her, "It's the weekend, and maybe Mike has made plans for you, so we'll say good night right now." After his parents said their good-nights, Mike took Tiao to his father's study. He showed her an exquisite folding fan, explaining that it had been brought back from China by an ancestor and passed down to his father. Carefully he opened it to its full length of over a foot, a mass of brilliance immediately appearing before Tiao's eyes. A group of lively, colorfully dressed girls were embroidered on the fan, and their bean-sized faces of inlaid ivory shone with a soft and delicate luster. Tiao had never seen a fan like it—the fine embroidered clothing and the ivory-inlaid faces made those festively dressed girls look like they were about to walk off the fan. Tiao felt pride at her countryman's superb craftsmanship, particularly in front of Mike. Mike said his interest in China started with this fan, and also with food. In his childhood, whenever he and his sister were reluctant to finish what was on their plates, his father would say, "Do you know there is a country called China in the Far East? Many people there still don't have enough to eat." Mike said it was very hard for him to associate these two things with China, a country that could make such an exquisite fan but couldn't afford food. A little bit uncomfortable, Tiao didn't respond to Mike's comment. Although not having enough food was a thing of the past, and Mike's father meant well by teaching his children to value food, Tiao still felt herself the object of pity. Maybe she thought too much with the deep-rooted insecurity of a third world citizen. Her uneasiness came precisely out of her sense of being pitied; she didn't like to be pitied. Noticing Tiao's quietness, Mike said, "What's wrong, Tiao? I didn't mean to make you sad."

Tiao said, "I wasn't sad."

"Then why were you so quiet?"

"I was listening to you."

"No, you weren't listening to me; you were spacing out," Mike said. Tiao had to admire his careful observation. She said, "Okay, I'll stop spacing out and listen."

"Do you want to see my room?" Mike asked.

"Yes, I do."

They came to his room, which had a few pieces of simple furniture, and a bed only partly made. The top drawer of his dresser was half open, revealing the neatly folded underwear, leaving the impression that Mike had forgotten to close it after looking for clothes. The neatly arranged undergarments and well-organized dresser gave Tiao a comfortable and warm feeling because she had similar habits. Even Mike's messy bed seemed natural, because it was a clean disorderliness. Then she saw a paper cup on top of the bureau. Mike took it down and asked, "Remember this cup? It's the one you used in Beijing." Tiao looked at the cup without remembering at all and saw the light red outline in the shape of a new moon, the imprint of her lipstick. She hadn't expected Mike to keep the paper cup and bring it back to the States, which she hoped was just his exaggerated way of demonstrating that he missed her. Already she had the sense she would not be able to return his feelings for her. She allowed for his age, twenty-seven, when she was already thirty-four. To keep the cup a woman used might seem normal to a twenty-seven-year-old, but a thirty-four-year-old woman wouldn't necessarily be excited by the gesture. She cautioned herself and suggested to Mike that they go back to the living room.

As they returned to the living room, Mike asked with some excitement, "Are you tired?"

Tiao said, "No, I'm not tired."

"Let's go out, then," Mike said. Tiao glanced at her watch, and it was eleven.

They left the house and went to Austin's famous Sixth Street for a wild night. On weekends Sixth Street never slept. It was a streetful of bars and nightclubs and people, with all sorts of activity—late-night pizza stands, rock and roll bands, portrait artists, Mexican-American gangs driving low-riders, those special cars popular in the seventies in Los Angeles, which bounced as they went, and also formal dance night, when high school students could wear adults' tuxedos or gowns and rent hotel rooms. Mike pulled Tiao by the hand and snaked through the crowds in the bars, each place bubbling with enthusiasm and playing music loud enough to strike someone deaf. He dragged Tiao to the famous Amy's Ice Creams shop to taste the exotic cinnamon ice cream. The employees in the shop kneaded all kinds of ingredients into the ice cream and tossed it onto stainless steel counters the way country people in northern China kneaded and tossed floured dough. Tiao found it both exhilarating and satisfying to watch. They stood on the street eating sausage pizza, Mike's favorite, each of them holding one palm-sized slice. Tiao liked that, too. For a moment she thought about Youyou, those sweet times they cooked crazily to make up for the delicacies they couldn't have. Back then she never would have predicted that someday she would be standing on a street in a foreign country with a stranger at midnight, heartily chewing delicious pizza. Yes, Mike was a stranger to her, a strange American man, but she liked him more and more. His energy, his youth, even the concentration he had when he was eating, all broke down her reserve and her nagging awareness of her age, with an irresistible force. The experience was utterly new to her, to be with a man eating and wandering the streets late at night, out simply for pleasure. On this night alone, it was exactly what she longed for. Her heartbeat seemed especially strong and her legs full of energy. With great appetite, she polished off two slices of pizza in a row, and chose to go into the bars with so much noise that conversation was impossible. Mike tried to shout above the din, but she couldn't hear a word, just watched his mouth and face busily moving around. Finally they fled the bars and set out for home holding hands. They walked onto a bridge with the deep, dark Colorado River flowing underneath. Mike said, "What is happiness? Happiness is to be in your hometown, holding your sweetheart's hand, and eating your favorite food! That's me right now. I'm very happy."

In your hometown, holding your sweetheart's hand, and eating your favorite food . . . sounds good.

Tiao looked at Mike on the bridge and his happy face moved her, but she was also reminded of her own hometown. She wasn't sure whether she was happy, because, of the three ingredients included in Mike's recipe for happiness, she had only the delicious food. She couldn't say she was happy, but she enjoyed going around a little drunk. When they finally admitted to each other that it was time to go home and sleep, the sky had already started to light up.

They slept in their own rooms for two hours, got up, and showered. Then they ate breakfast quickly and took off again.

They drove to San Antonio, near Austin. On the American highway, they sang Chinese children's rhymes. "'Eat the milk. Drink the bread. Beneath your arm, carry the train. Ride on a briefcase, instead. Afterward, get off the case. Eastward, then, turn your face. There you'll see a man bite a dog. Pick up the dog. Give a stone a whack, but then the stone will bite the dog back . . .'"

"'A little car is honking, beep, beep, beep, Chairman Mao sits in the backseat.'"

"'The car is coming but I don't care. I'll give the car a phone call over there. The car turned around and ran my little feet down.'"

Mike demonstrated for Tiao how he could drive with his knees, showing off, and his efforts to please Tiao made her feel tenderly toward him.

San Antonio, full of tropical flavor, lay before them. Gigantic plants, sweet-scented flowers, and a green river leisurely meandering through the town and then circling around it, all made San Antonio romantic and sentimental. Walking on the riverbank, they waved casually at the passengers on a river cruise, who looked so relaxed and peaceful surrounded by the flowers that decorated the boats. Just then Mike suddenly embraced Tiao, kissed her tentatively but passionately, and Tiao couldn't help kissing back. Everything happened so quickly but seemed entirely natural to Tiao. Their lips pressed together, and for a moment Tiao's mind went blank. Suddenly applause rose from the river. It was the passengers on the cruise, who cheered, "Go! Go!" for them. Tiao heard the applause from the cruise, which made Mike hold her even tighter. Her legs felt limp—it was as if she were floating, and a serenity and joy that she had never felt before filled her whole body. The river, flower fragrance, and applause from the cruise . . . all of it allowed her and Mike to kiss each other openly and without self-consciousness, passionate and innocent, full of fervor and grace. She felt on the point of being smothered by him, but even the threat of death couldn't stop her. She forgot shyness, unashamed of kissing Mike in public to the sound of applause. It was such a pure thing, and she'd so longed for such essential purity. Maybe this is my compensation, she thought.

He finally loosened his hold on her. Trying to catch her breath, she smiled at him, and he, also gasping, returned her smile. He said, "You blushed. I love to see you blush." He took her in his arms again and whispered in her ear, "You have no idea how lovely you are. You have no idea how young you are!" He kissed her again and she kissed back.

At the site of the Alamo Mission, he told her when he saw a policeman, "I'm going to kiss you and make this policeman jealous." Then he gave her a long kiss.

In a Mexican restaurant, he told Tiao as he saw a waiter pass, "I'm going to kiss you and make this *muchacho* jealous." He kissed her for a long time.

In the famous Double D Ranch House Grill & Bar—where the waitresses were known for their big breasts—when he saw the waitress he said, "I'm going to kiss you and make Ms. Big Breasts jealous." He gave her a long kiss.

He chattered nonstop with excitement—truly nonstop. He cupped her face with both hands and then stroked the nape of her neck with its covering of fine hair. He said, "How delicate and soft your skin is! You're my *xiruan*, my exquisite one. You're just my *xiruan*!" Tiao couldn't help being touched by the word "*xiruan*." She told him that in Chinese, in addition to meaning soft and delicate, *xiruan* also was used to indicate things that were easy to carry with you, valuables or jewelry. Mike said, "Then I was right. You're my little *xiruan*. Little *xiruan*."

They didn't drive back to Austin until very late.

They said good night to each other, took a shower, and then went back to their own rooms. They said their good-nights a little bit stiffly, with some nervousness—as if they didn't know how to go back to before, the time before they went to San Antonio.

They hadn't slept much already for a day and night, but Tiao didn't feel tired. She didn't want to lie down; she stood in front of the mirror looking at herself.

Mike opened the door quietly. He opened the sides of his big, loose-fitting bathrobe, like a pair of white wings, and enfolded Tiao against his chest.

2

They kissed again, as if it were the continuation of their kisses on the bank of the San Antonio River. They kissed very deeply, so deeply that both could hardly contain themselves. With his height and strength, Mike took control and steered Tiao toward the bed, and Tiao felt dizzy and staggered, which aroused Mike more. They stumbled onto the bed and he kept whispering in her ear, "My little *xiruan*, my little *xiruan* . . ."

All of a sudden, Tiao strangely became not so *xiruan*. She stiffened, rose from the bed, and stood up resolutely. Surprising herself with her own strength, she grabbed Mike and shoved him in the direction of the door. She kissed him passionately but also forced him to leave with equal determination. She got him to the door, reached out a hand to open it, and gently pushed him out. Then she locked the door.

Feeling a bit confused, she leaned against the door and listened. She knew that Mike was still there, and she had a moment of regret. She had only a vague understanding of why she'd rejected him. She heard Mike knocking on the door gently, apparently not wanting to wake his parents but persisting. Trying to ignore him, she held her breath and pretended she'd gone to bed. Then a note slipped through the space under the door. She picked up the note and, holding it against the door, read the big Chinese characters: "I love you. Please let me tell you in person!"

This was something she was afraid to hear because she didn't know what to say. When she read these words, so clearly set down, she suddenly understood that the one she loved was not Mike. She loved Chen Zai. It was the kind of love that ran deep and long in her and couldn't be torn out. Maybe when she'd been discarded by Fang Jing, left on the bench at the waiting room, when she was crying her heart out in front of Chen Zai, she had already fallen in love with him; when Chen Zai was about to get married later and asked her opinion, she was in love with him. But never had her love and yearning been like it was now, so certain and turbulent, so tender and strong. She felt happy and sad at once because of this abrupt realization of love, which happened when she was in someone else's country and room, when someone else was revealing his love to her. She felt sorry for Mike because it was Mike who had so forcefully awoken her deep love for Chen Zai. She wasn't that saintly and noble. What had she really wanted to achieve by being with Mike? Self-indulgence and pleasure led her to him. Self-indulgence and pleasure, which made her feel ashamed. She got up, took a pen and a piece of paper, and wrote, "It's gotten too late. Please go back and sleep."

She sent the note through the space under the door and got another from him: "I love you. Please let me in." She wrote back, "Don't talk nonsense. Please leave."

Through the gap under the door they played a note-passing game. "My little *xiruan*, I can't stand it anymore. Please open the door for me."

"I can't. I can't. I can't."

"You can. I know you want me, too."

"It's not real."

"It is real. I'm going to break in."

"Don't be silly. I'm tired."

"You're not tired. I'm coming in unless you tell me you don't love me."

"All right. I don't love you. I'm very sorry."

"I want you to open the door and tell me in person." After slipping this last note in, he started to pound the door loudly. Finally she opened the door for him. He held her and kissed her desperately. She also kissed him but started to cry. Then he let her go and said, "I'm sorry. Please forgive my rudeness."

She shook her head and said, "I don't want your apology. It's just— you don't understand. You don't understand." Holding his hand, she sat at the edge of the bed. She looked into his clear green eyes, in which she imagined she must appear like those women on that antique fan that his family treasured, mysterious and exotic. What did he know about her? Nothing—and she knew nothing about him. Sooner or later, he would find out that it was not love, as she already knew right now.

When they kissed again, she was even more certain. Kissing him, she cried, imagining him as Chen Zai, whom she had never kissed. She loved him and missed home very much, missed all the memories she and Chen Zai had shared—the pitch-black windy night long, long ago, when she stood on the street and pounded the mailbox helplessly, how Chen Zai asked her, "Child, what's the matter?"

Mike, you don't understand. How can you understand? You'll never be able to understand anything about me.

She held Mike's hand and her heart had completely quieted down. Then, out of nowhere, she made a random suggestion. "Let each of us eat an apple."

She picked up two apples from the fruit tray and handed Mike one. With a crunch, she bit into hers first.

Mike stared at Tiao, who was crunching on the apple, and said, "I believe now that you don't love me, but I still love you—I'll keep it to myself from now on, though. I'm not as naïve as you imagine. I don't just see you as someone like the beautiful girl on the fan. You're an ageless woman, someone who can be young and old at once. Sometimes you're like a person who has gone through it all, with that knowing expression in your eyes that seems to see life and the world through a hundred years of history; sometimes you're like a baby, with such clear eyes, and that pure down on your face. Your face drew me to you. You never knew how much your face and your expression attracted me. I lied to be with you, saying that I would happen to be at home on vacation when you were in the States. The fact is I didn't have any vacation. I asked for leave from the school and came back especially for you. Please believe that my attitude, my . . . my . . ." He started to lose control of the tones—when he spoke too much Chinese, his accent began to drift. With a bit of Shandong mixed with a little Shanxi, he continued in these strange tones: "My . . . my . . ."

After a while his talk trailed off, and with the apple in his hand, he fell asleep. Overcome by exhaustion, drowsiness, and a deep sense of defeat, he slumped down midsentence, his head falling onto Tiao's legs. She liked pillowing his head on her legs. As she looked down at this young head fast asleep on her legs—the pink ear which looked especially innocent because of his age—her heart filled with deep gratitude. It was Mike who had offered her, so freely, the untainted love she'd never had; it was Mike who inspired her to feel confident about her life and youth, and Mike who spurred her to take action. It was his love that awakened her strong love for Chen Zai.

Oh, Mike—so sound asleep—I'll be grateful to you all my life for everything you have done and for my not loving you.

3

Beijing Airport was always so crowded, and the expressions on the custom officials' faces so cold. The coffee was always lukewarm, the bathroom tissues dark, and the pay phone receivers smelly. Tiao couldn't wait to call Chen Zai before she got out of the airport. She couldn't wait to tell him that she had returned from the States and would see him soon. When she heard his calm, deep voice on the phone, she knew that she had truly come home. The only thing she'd been thinking about all the way was that as soon as she got off the airplane, she could hear his voice. Now that she heard it, even the smell of the phone seemed less distasteful.

She left the airport. The air in Beijing was not very good; the sky was gray, and the cars had a light coating of dust. Everything was somewhat grimy and messy, but still it felt dirty and dear.

Dirty and dear.

She returned to Fuan, and Chen Zai phoned and asked to come to see her at her house. She didn't let him. Usually he would go to her place, and when he was there she would complain to him about those bad patches she hit, how she was unhappy, how she failed to get elected CEO of the publishing house, how Fan gave her a hard time, how someone who didn't even remotely know how to write fiction got a book published through the use of powerful connections . . . She never treated him like a guest; he could sit wherever he liked. When he was thirsty, he'd pour himself some water, and when he was hungry, he took food out of the refrigerator himself. Once, she remembered discussing a haircut with him; she wanted to cut her shoulder-length hair short. He said, "I think you'd better not. You look pretty good this way."

Tiao said, "All my colleagues say I would definitely look good in short hair. Why do you have to say I wouldn't?"

Chen Zai said, "You don't have thick hair, and cutting it short would make it look even thinner."

"What makes you think my hair is thin? It's your hair that's thin."

Chen Zai said, "Okay, okay. My hair is thin. Happy? But you still shouldn't cut your hair."

Tiao said, "I'm going to cut it anyway. What can you do?" She didn't know why she had to be so unreasonable with Chen Zai, as if it were her birthright. After she got her hair cut, everyone said she looked good, but the compliment she most wanted to hear was Chen Zai's. She'd cared about him so much and for so long, it had become a part of her consciousness.

Now he wanted to come to her place to see her, but she forbade him. She had a hunch that she was going to say something very important to him, and this very important thing made her jumpy about their meeting. She'd never felt that way about seeing him, but now she did, and it made her more nervous to think about seeing him at her home, so nervous that she felt cornered, so that she had to go out somewhere, to go out with him. In the evening, he drove to her place to pick her up, and they drove around and around Fuan in the middle of winter. Tiao said, "When I was in America this time, other than attending the conference, I also visited Texas for a few days."

Chen Zai said, "Yes, you stayed in Mike's home."

Tiao said, "How did you know?"

"Fan called me."

"She called you? Just to talk about this?"

Chen Zai said, "What's wrong with that? Can't she call me?"

Tiao swallowed her anger and said, "Of course she can. Anyone can call you. Anyone can report my whereabouts to you, particularly Fan. I left Chicago after a big fight with her. She made me feel cold. I needed warmth, and Austin is warm."

Chen Zai said, "Yes, Austin is in the south, and the temperature is higher than Chicago's."

"I didn't mean temperature, though."

"You meant people?"

"Yes, people."

Chen Zai went quiet. Tiao asked, "Why aren't you saying anything? Don't you know whom I meant?"

"I don't know."

"You're lying. You know. You know I meant Mike."

"Oh, it's Mike."

"Yes, it's Mike. Didn't Fan mention him to you? She must have told you that it was Mike who invited me to Austin and that I was happy to go, that Mike is seven years younger than I am and that we had a chance to become lovers. Well, Mike is certainly seven years younger than I am, but he's not as naïve as I imagined, and much more mature and sincere, too. Our meeting in Austin wasn't a coincidence. He didn't just happen to be home on vacation during my trip. He arranged to take a leave from his school to wait for me there.

His parents were extremely nice to me, and I felt very comfortable with them. We took a trip downtown and went out at night—to Sixth Street for a wild night. I'd never wandered around the streets late at night. I remember you telling me how hard you worked when you studied in England and that you didn't have much entertainment. What a boring and serious life our generation has lived! Why could I stay up all night when I was with Mike? The next day we drove to San Antonio. Let me tell you, Mike is very clever. He can drive with his knees, which allowed him to put his arm around my shoulder—all the way to San Antonio. We ate the famous Mexican food there, and how particular he was. There were a lot of customers, and we had to wait in line to get a seat. It was a restaurant on the river, with half of the seats indoors and half of them outdoors. On a nice day with bright sunshine and a warm breeze, people prefer to sit outside. A long wait makes people less choosy, but Mike gave up many chances to be seated, insisting on getting one of the small tables facing the water until we finally did. He ordered Lone Star beer, Mexican mashed potatoes, corn cake, and a kind of barbecue meat that was extremely tasty but also extremely spicy, spicy enough to administer a jolt. He even taught me a Spanish word: Thanks—*gracias!*"

Thanks—*gracias!*

"I learned. He told me, 'When the *muchacho* brings you the wine, you just say thanks in Spanish. Spanish is the official language in San Antonio.' The *muchacho* brought the wine to us. When he was pouring me the wine, I, who had been quiet while Mike ordered, suddenly smiled at him and said, '*Gracias!*' The *muchacho* was very surprised, so surprised that he actually knocked over my wineglass. It seemed normal to him that I, the Asian, couldn't speak, and when I suddenly came out with Spanish, it was like a mute found her voice. I repeated '*Gracias*' to him, he kept saying, '*De nada, de nada,*' and then rushed to replace the wine. Mike said, 'Do you know why he was so surprised? It's because your pronunciation was perfect. He must think you speak Spanish. I really want to teach you. You definitely could learn it.' I told Mike, 'It's impossible. I'm too old to learn Spanish.' Mike said, 'Don't say it's impossible. Never say impossible to life.' Mike seemed to have made me see the path back to happiness, and Mike seemed to have given me the courage to return to it. I almost forgot I had been happy before. That was when I was three, climbing tentatively with my butt out onto the sofa with broken springs. That was my happiness—innocent, flawless happiness—happiness without history, happiness without any events. We didn't go back to Austin until dark. That was the night Mike told me that he loved me. Did you hear me, Chen Zai? Mike told me he loved me."

Chen Zai said, "Yes, I heard you. Mike said he loved you. Do you love him?"

Tiao said, "I want to love him. I really want to love him. I really want to tell him that I love him. I . . . I . . . I simply love him and I must love him. The problem is . . . the problem is, I've said so much to you and I want to know what you think of it all. Before . . . I told you everything about me before, so I want to hear what you think of it."

Tiao rambled on, but this speech of hers wasn't sincere. It was not the "most important thing" that she wanted to tell Chen Zai, but she couldn't lead the conversation to the most important thing no matter how hard she tried. She didn't know why she would babble about Austin or why the more she loved Chen Zai, the more she praised Mike. It was probably also a kind of timidity, hypocrisy and timidity. Again she repeated what she'd just said—timidly and hypocritically—"I want to tell him I love him. I must love him . . ." Her heart felt such pain that she was at the point of tears.

Chen Zai slowed down and parked his car on the side of the road. He rolled down the window as if to get some fresh air. He said, "Tiao, if you really love him, other things, like age, are all secondary."

Tiao said, "Is that your opinion? Is that what you want to say to me?"

Chen Zai got quiet for a while and then said, "Yes, that's what I think." Tiao's face suddenly changed toward him—Chen Zai knew it even in the dark. Her expression was grim, resenting herself as well as Chen Zai. "Tell me again what it is you think." Chen Zai turned his face to the darkness outside the window. "If you really love him, other things aren't important."

Tiao questioned him sharply, "Do you really think like that?"

"Yes, I really do."

Tiao said, "You're talking nonsense. You always talk nonsense. Deep down, that's not really what you think. You said it because you think that is what you should say. You're hypocritical through and through. You've always been hypocritical through and through. Why do I bother to talk to you? Why am I talking crap to you? I hate you. I've never hated you as much as I do now . . . You . . . you! Now I should go. Goodbye!"

Tiao stepped out of the car in one stride, slammed the door, and walked into the dark. She walked quickly, whether it was because she was determined or simply desperate, it would have been hard to say—people in either situation might walk as she did. Desperate people might have the more hurried manner. So, then, she was desperate. She walked desperately, ignoring Chen Zai's following after her and calling out. He said, "Can you stop your aimless walking? Come back to the car." She walked even faster and shouted back, "You're the one who's walking aimlessly. Leave me alone."

She kept walking ahead this way, and he trailed at a slow speed. She thought about the late night on Sixth Street in Austin, and finally understood that when she and Mike held hands and looked at the dark Colorado River flowing under the bridge, she wanted to have a night like that with Chen Zai. Now here they were late at night, but what an unfortunate muddle of a night it was. She walked desperately and her heart was entirely gloomy. She was angry at herself because she had ruined everything. What had passed seemed to have passed forever, and Chen Zai had long ago become another woman's husband. The other woman, what was her name? Oh, Wan Meicheng. Wan Meicheng, Wan Meicheng, what a beautiful name, much nicer than Tiao's. What right did Tiao have to demand that Chen Zai give an opinion about her relationship with Mike? What obligation did Chen Zai have to give it? Wan Meicheng, Wan Meicheng, Wan Meicheng . . . he was Wan Meicheng's husband, and they had been husband and wife for ten years. He was nobody to Tiao—not before, and wouldn't be in the future. If she tried to force him to be someone to her, then she was fooling herself. But that was exactly what she'd been doing, and, ashamed of it, she felt she had to escape from Chen Zai, from his car, immediately. She rushed from the sidewalk into the middle of the road, intending to stop a taxi.

She waved at an approaching taxi just as Chen Zai got out of his car and grabbed her arm. The taxi stopped in front of them, and they were almost wrestling as Tiao tried to free her arm from Chen Zai's grasp, screaming, "Let me go! Let me go!" But Chen Zai held her even more tightly. When she pulled open the taxi door to get in, Chen Zai swept her up in one motion and strode over to his own car. He hurled the door open, threw Tiao into the backseat, and then drove the car off as fast as possible.

The car sped off, leaving Tiao's taxi far behind. When they passed a movie theater, Chen Zai turned into the small parking lot in front of it, stopped the car, and turned off the engine. He got out of the car and then got in through the back door, sitting on the seat with Tiao. He breathed heavily in the dark, and his breath struck Tiao's face as if it were a solid shape. His face was right beside hers, so close that he gave her the feeling that he was going to bite her. She moved away from him a little and said, "Why are you bullying me like this?"

He embraced her tightly and, breathing heavily, said, "Yes, I just want to bully you. I should have bullied you long ago." Then he kissed her on her lips, firmly and tenderly.

The situation was one that neither had predicted but both seemed to have anticipated. They had known each other for over twenty years, but had never been so intimate. They had kept missing the chance to connect with each other, as if it were a test of their long affection and friendship. Now neither could take it anymore. As they finally kissed, the damage to their long-standing feelings began. But they didn't care too much about the damage. It wasn't enough just to have affection and friendship. They needed the marvelous damage. At this moment, as their kisses turned deep and mellow, they even sighed at how long the damage had taken to happen.

Frantically, they inhaled each other, as if they could inhale each other into their hearts.

4

They didn't realize how much time had passed until they started to feel out of breath. Such a narrow space couldn't contain their expansive kisses. It occurred to them now to drive back home to Tiao's place.

Once there, she managed only to get out her key and open the door and lock it behind them before he had to take her in his arms again. He held her and pushed her back, step by step, all the way to that gray-blue three-seater sofa in the living room. He finally made her stretch out on the sofa, hungry to lay his body on hers, to press into her. Leaning over her, he whispered, "Tiao, let me lie on you. Let me lie on you."

His whispers made her heart race, but she didn't really want him to lie on her on that sofa. She never even sat on it, and when Chen Zai pressed down on her to the point of suffocation, she seemed to hear fits of screaming from underneath them. It must be Quan's voice. Quan had always been sitting here. Now Tiao and Chen Zai had disturbed her and pressed down on her—yes, she screamed because Tiao and Chen Zai combined to bear down on her, for their pleasure and out of their desire. She screamed to interrupt Tiao and to warn her, forcing Tiao to push insistently on Chen Zai's shoulder, saying, "Let's go to bed. Let's go to bed."

Let's go to bed.

He heard her invitation, so quick and straightforward, which actually minimized its erotic element. Let's go to bed—as if they were playing house. They got up from the sofa, and she led him by the hand to the bedroom and onto her bed.

On the bed they sat talking, face-to-face and cross-legged. Holding hands and knee to knee, they stared into each other's eyes, understanding that everything had just begun. So there was no desire in their eyes, and their bodies were freed from the night's agitation.

Chen Zai kissed Tiao's hands and said, "Ten years ago, when I was planning to get married, I asked you the same thing I'm asking you now. Why didn't you tell me that you loved me?"

Tiao kissed Chen Zai's hands and said, "Because you never said you loved me."

Chen Zai said, "But you knew I loved you. I've loved you since you were twelve years old. I was only seventeen at the time and didn't really know what love was. Still, I just loved you. When you jumped the rubber-band rope in front of the building one afternoon, I even spied on you. Later, you fell and loosened your little braids, and you got up embarrassed and ran off. I loved your embarrassment, all your indignities, your tears and disappointments. No other woman ever revealed so much of herself to me; no other woman ever gave me so much trust. I have known you so long, and I often swore to myself that even had you traveled to the ends of the earth, you would still be a treasure in my heart, embedded in me, blood and bone. You're my family, and you have to be my family. I didn't know how to tell you all of this, and it seems I've never been given a chance like this. I always believed that the right to 'tell' wasn't up to me. It was you who controlled how close we could be from the very beginning. Every-thing that happened tonight surprised me very much. I was surprised at myself and at you. I hope this isn't something you're doing on impulse. When the sun rises, things that happen at night often seem ridiculous."

Tiao shook her head at Chen Zai and then nodded. The words of love he'd held on to for so long stirred a lot of different feelings in her. She said, "I can tell you, Chen Zai, I'm not acting on impulse. I love you now, not when I was twelve or twenty-two, those years I treated you as my older brother. Hundreds of times I tried to figure out when I fell in love with you, and I suppose it started the day Fang Jing left me in the waiting room of the train station. He threw me down from the heights of a dream and you caught me before I hit the ground and held me up, with all my tears and hurts, my humili-ation and bitterness. If you were not the dearest person in the world to me, how could I have cried in front of you that way without any self-consciousness? But I didn't know at the time; I had no ability to analyze myself. My soul fell in love with you, but this soul of mine didn't inform me. Later on, I finally figured all of this out, but by then I felt I had no right to your love. I didn't deserve it. Behind my apparent pride, I hid a deep sense of unworthiness. You had seen all my misery and embarrassment and I couldn't offer that shameful confused mess of myself to you. I couldn't. How could I grab on to your love while still grieving the loss of Fang Jing's? How could I be so shallow and careless? Maybe I was too concerned with your impression of me. Maybe I was desperate to have you think I wasn't so silly. When I loved you the most, I also resisted you the most. When you told me that you were going to get married, I tried my best to keep myself composed. Looking back now, I thoroughly hate myself—for putting on an act, exaggerating my happiness for you, and pretending to be calm. I said you should have gotten married long ago. Wan Meicheng, such a beautiful name . . . my heart felt like it was being cut by a knife, but in my mind I kept thinking about how sensible I was! How moral! And how wise I was! Let me hide at a corner and love secretly. Let me treat your happiness as my own—"

Chen Zai reached out and covered Tiao's mouth with his hand. He said, "But you know I'm not happy."

Tiao removed his hand and said, "But Wan Meicheng is happy. She has what she wants."

Chen Zai said, "I haven't given her what she most wants, though."

"What is that?"

"A child."

"So . . . you can't?"

"No, I don't want to. I don't want to because I always had a vague hope for a different future. I didn't want to reconcile myself with the life I had, although it wasn't fair to her. She is about to go crazy because she wants a child so much. But I won't do it. We had an arrangement before we got married. She agreed not to have a child as long as she could marry me."

The day was breaking and they couldn't remain sitting this way and continue talking. Chen Zai would never have been able to leave if they kept talking like that. He got off the bed, splashed cold water on his face, and then left Tiao's place without saying anything more.

Tiao also needed to go to work. She took a hot shower, washing her breasts carefully, letting the clear water and her hand massage them. She held the showerhead and swept her whole body with it, letting the strong flow spout onto her vagina, which had been so long unstirred.

She set off for the publishing house energetically. As soon as she entered her office, she got Chen Zai's phone call. He said, "Tiao, are you listening?"

"Yes, I'm listening."

"I can't live without you in my life. I want to marry you."

5

"Are you ready?" she softly asked from a distance as he lay naked in the dark. She came out of the bathroom, pushing open the door, letting the light stream into the bedroom. Following the path of the light, she moved to the bed. "Are you ready?" she asked softly again when she was next to him, boldly and joyously gazing at his unfamiliar naked body.

He got up suddenly and lifted her trembling body and laid her down on the bed, and in the dim light cradled her face in his hands. He started to kiss her, kissing her hair, kissing her ears, kissing her eyebrows and eyes, kissing her burning cheeks. He kissed her chin, kissed her collarbone, kissed her small, firm breasts. What else did he kiss? He kissed the beautiful curve where her lower back met her pelvis, he kissed her knee—the knee that she had hurt when she fell down jumping rope when she was twelve—kissed her leg, kissed her foot, and bit each one of her toes; he licked the small cold soles of her feet. His kisses stopped her trembling. His kisses made her relax her body and stretch out passionately, and at the same time he slid his head between her legs and put the tip of his tongue for a moment in that most tender and smooth of places. Unable to hold back, she let out a brief, sharp moan, a very particular sort, not human, but the moan of an animal always utterly candid in expressing its pleasure. At that instant, her face had the fierce grimace of someone with ecstasy in reach. It was beauty, beauty of a kind people are unwilling to acknowledge. As she continued moaning, he bore down and force-fully entered her.

She made him ecstatic; he couldn't have imagined that they would be so much in harmony, that it could be so good. The more he felt in love with her, the deeper he wanted to be inside her; the more he felt the pain of love, the more he attacked her; the crazier he was for her, the more he tormented her; the more he treasured her, the more he wanted to ravage her, to break her apart.

There was no way he could make himself stop, and she didn't let him stop, matching his motion with her own, entirely in rhythm. They moved together perfectly in unison.

He made her feel ecstatic; she couldn't have imagined that they would be so much in harmony, that it could be so good. She was joy-ful at how deep he was in her, how he attacked her, tormented her, ravaged her. When he clutched her firm round buttocks and pressed down against her chest, she couldn't help crying out again. She made him drip with sweat; he made her drip with sweat. Sweat soaked their hair. Still, he couldn't stop. He lifted the hair from her face, and with a muffled voice muttered hoarsely, "Oh, sweetheart, sweetheart, darling cunt, I want to fuck you to pieces, fuck you to death." Drops of sweat ran down her face and stung her eyes; sweat ran into his eyes and stung them, too. They couldn't stop. They rolled from the bed to the floor, as if no space in the world could hold them in their feverish gallop, really it was a kind of gallop, as he grasped her, steered her, heaved her, and she lay under him melded to him as if she had no bones.

They savored each other and ravaged each other, ravaged each other and savored each other.

Always they would remember the last moment of their first time, when his movements quickened, doubly fierce, and suddenly, with a leopard's low growl, he said, "Tiao, Tiao, I can't hold back any longer," and then she felt a hot current flow through her whole body and then an awakening of bliss as if she'd been roused from a long deep sleep. She was in bliss. A short while later she lost consciousness. When she awoke, still in her ear was the echo of his low growl, "I can't hold back any longer." To the end of her life she would love the sound of his growl, so innocent, so passionate, so intimate. They now were truly lovers, lovers for two lifetimes, three lifetimes.

She awoke, her entire body limp, to a shining light, the lamp that he'd turned on. He was staring at her in the lamplight. He stretched his arms out to her; she rolled her head onto his arm and was wrapped in his embrace, resting her head on his broad shoulder. He said to her that his shoulder and chest had grown just right to cradle her head, a perfect fit, perfectly matched.

The two sweaty bodies stuck to each other. He said, "You are my dear."

She said, "You are my little dear."

He said, "You are my dear little sister."

She said, "You are my dear big brother."

He said, "You are my little mother."

She said, "You are my little father."

He said, "You are my little one."

She said, "You are my good little child."

He said, "You are my young wife."

She said, "You are my older husband."

He said, "I want to do it again. I want to do it again." So they started over. He was even more carefully attentive to her. She was even more playful in catering to his needs. So sweetly intimate and close, they were like glue—like paint—on each other, forgetting everything around them, completely in love.

Tiao sighed sadly, wondering why this day had taken so long to arrive. She also sighed that finally it had arrived. All the pleasure and happiness that he gave to her made her cry tears of joy and gratitude. He leaned over to lick the tears, to kiss her moist eyelashes, to say, "My little one, what's the matter?" In reply, she hugged him tightly around his sturdy waist, as if to embed her arms in his flesh, to be absorbed into his body and never to be stripped away.

One day in late spring, he drove with her to the outskirts of Fuan, a place near the mountains where he'd bought a small plot of land. He told her, "I want to build a house here and furnish it with everything you want."

"What would that be?"

"A big kitchen," he said.

"That's right. Naturally I would like a big kitchen."

"A large kitchen should be the second thing, though."

"What should be the first thing, then?"

"The first thing should be a bed with me in it."

She lowered her head and smiled, and he led her by the hand toward the small plot of land. There was a bare slope, with no crops yet planted, and a half-grown walnut tree stood at the crest of the hill, full of oval green leaves like the huge eyes of Buddha, serene and transcendent, as if keeping vigil. By the roadside they passed some cassia trees and wheat fields and headed up the hill toward the walnut tree, where bunches of snow-white cassia flowers gave off a pure, sweet scent. She wanted him to pick her a strand of the blooms and he picked many for her. Laughing, he watched her cram her mouth, wolfing them down. Chewing on the cassia blooms, she asked him what he was laughing at.

"You must be laughing at how I can't do anything else—I can hardly breathe—when I eat."

He said that she looked a little bit like she couldn't breathe but that wasn't why he was laughing. "I was laughing at that look of concentration you get on your face. Have you ever eaten green wheat grain?" As he spoke, he bent over and pulled up a handful of the heads of wheat, ground them between his hands, then blew away the chaff, pinched a few seeds, and put them in her mouth. He gathered up what remained in his hand and put them into his own mouth. He chewed and asked, "What flavor do you taste in this wheat?"

She was chewing and had already made a paste of the wheat seeds; a warm, pure, and dark green flavor filled her mouth and slowly passed into her. "It doesn't have the fragrant sweetness of cassia. It's more pungent, with much more power—it's the flavor of sex, the flavor of reproduction, freely vigorous and exuberant, that magnificent instinct that propels life." She pulled him toward her and quietly said that she wanted wheat, wheat, right now . . .

They made love beneath that serene walnut tree. She turned

toward the sun and he parted her legs. She let the sunlight and his caresses make her sex shine, shocking his eyes and astonishing his heart, so that he would always remember that radiant color in the sun's translucent rays.

While he faced the confrontation over the divorce from Wan Meicheng, he continued to see Tiao. Nothing could stop them from meeting. Even a short time without making love was unbearable to them. It would have been a sort of truancy as they earnestly attempted to make up for the emptiness of more than ten years that yawned like a gulf between them . . . She'd often act a bit spoiled, and badgered him, insisting that he "tell me again when you first fell in love with me."

"When you were twelve."

"You loved a twelve-year-old child?"

"I loved you when you were twelve."

"Why?"

"Because you were ugly."

"No, I wasn't ugly."

"You were ugly, when you were twelve you were a little ugly strange ball."

"You shouldn't describe me like that. I wasn't nearly as ugly as you say."

"Bystanders have the clearest view. You were ugly. But I was able to see the potential; a twelve-year-old girl who is a flawless beauty will surely grow up to be an ugly woman. She's reached the heights and it's all downhill from there." She said, "I understand what you mean. You loved me because you thought I would develop into a beautiful woman."

"Don't be so conceited, you are not a beautiful woman."

A little unhappily, she said, "Well, then, what am I? What am I?"

He thought for a moment and then said, "You are an eternal woman." As he said this he came up behind her and wrapped his arms around her waist, kissing her smooth neck. "You are my little woman, my little sweetie!"

In his arms, she beat his chest and said, "You speak absolute fool-ishness, and how could you tell that as a twelve-year-old girl I would be eternal? You must tell me why you loved me!" She pushed him away as she spoke.

"I loved you because I was a hooligan, okay?"

"I want you to talk nicely to me."

He said with a sigh, "Because, when you were twelve, your eyes had a strange look of agony, suffering that no one could understand. I didn't understand why your eyes showed such pain, but I saw it, and it became a long compulsion because it was a challenge to me. I imagined that I would be able to understand your pain. Tiao, this is one of the dreams of my life, to make you happy. I only want you to be happy."

"I am happy, and only you can make me so happy. When I was twelve years old I was unhappy. There was a letter I wrote, a letter I wrote and mailed to my father, dropping it into the mailbox by the entrance to our compound. I regretted that later. I wanted to smash the mailbox to get it out." At the beginning of their conversations, she just kept telling him to say why he loved her, a little arrogant, a little flirtatious. After a while, she had to talk about the distant past, about Dr. Tang and Quan, long gone, vanished forever. All of it she willingly poured out to him, even the parts about Fan. Finally, she told of the death of Quan. She spoke about her falling into the manhole. "You know that manhole, the one for wastewater in the road by the entrance to our building."

He stroked her back, as if soothing a frightened cat. He said, "I know that manhole. All the children in the compound knew how Quan fell into it. But all of that is in the past, in the past. Now we have our new life." She said that Quan herself walked into the manhole. He said, "That's right, everyone knows that she walked into it by herself." She said, "Chen Zai, can you hold me? Hold me!" He held her tightly, and with infinite tenderness kissed his distraught woman. She also kissed him, nervously kissing his brow and biting his ears. She was unable to hold back her agony, showing every sign of desperation. In the end, though she struggled, she was not able to reveal her guilt to Chen Zai and felt deeply ashamed. She seemed to be hearing the three of them, the sisters, scrambling under the sofa in the living room with spirited shrieks. It was at this point, and only then, that she also remembered the night in Austin and the day in San Antonio, the flowers, the river, Mike's green eyes—galaxies! Galaxies in them! What past does not have some joy in it, what relationships did not have their pleasures? But her love was Chen Zai. She'd run away, fled all the way until she finally found his embrace. Only this great friend could help her clear away what had choked her heart for so long. Why didn't she speak? Only a short distance to go, and then she could have been completely free.

He was so willing to give her everything, to give her his "wheat," and more and more eagerly she looked forward to it.

One autumn night, they drove back from Beijing, and as soon as they got into the city, it began to rain heavily. They parked on the street. While the storm washed over the car, they nestled together, quietly watching the lightning out the window, listening to the thunder outside the car. There were no other cars on the street and no people around, as if they were the only ones left in heaven and earth. They had to make love—so joyful to do it in the flashes of lightning and the sounds of thunder. Wildly, he threw her on the seat, and she cried to him, "I want your wheat . . . I want your wheat." Sky and ground teetered, and in the midst of her dizziness she felt him grasp her, swing her over on top of him, and she arched herself above him. Then she rode him, as if she were riding a powerfully agile leopard, as if she were riding a handsome white horse. She rode him as if she were flying away from the world of rain, riding high and far.

She trembled with him; she also made the car and the ground tremble together. She never knew she had such passion and strength. She rode him as if she were riding him for all of the days of her life, ecstasy and pain rushing out of her body, purging her of all fear.

Chapter 8

✿ ✿ ✿

Disgusted

1

Fei didn't feel well that winter. One day, she came to visit Tiao. As soon as she walked in she rushed directly to the living room and staggered onto the three-seater sofa. She took out a pack of cigarettes and said, "Tiao, bring me an ashtray. I want to smoke."

Her voice was hoarse, her face dull, and her body seemed especially frail, all of which gave Tiao an ominous feeling. It was the first time that Fei demanded to smoke at Tiao's place as if by right; she knew that Tiao didn't allow her guests to smoke in the apartment. But still she insisted rudely, "Did you hear me? Bring me an ashtray."

Tiao said, "You know I don't have an ashtray here. Besides, you'd better take a look at yourself before you smoke."

Fei sneered. "What's wrong with how I look? But, of course, how can I look better than you? I know you feel wonderful in every way, top to bottom, inside and out. Look at your face, and the shine of your eyes; they're so dewy that even your eyelashes are wet. Only women who are loved, adored, and cherished by men would look so healthy. Look at your lips, so much thicker and fuller than before. It must be Chen Zai's kisses that do that? They must feel puffed, swollen, and great, right? . . . Oh, and your hands. Come over and let me feel your palms—they must be warm. Those who are loved have warm palms. Come here, come here and let me feel them. Why don't you come over? What are you afraid of? Are you afraid that I'm unclean? Are you afraid that I'm contagious? Why weren't you afraid of me before? Why weren't you afraid of me when you wanted to get into the publishing house and asked me to sell my body to that bastard vice mayor for you? Look at what a nice life you're living now. And me? I can be summed up like this: no schooling and no skills and living in a drunkard's haze. What do you think, Tiao? Think I fit the description? The way I used to trade on my beauty before, I take advantage of my illness now. I don't blame you for being afraid of me. I have had many illnesses. Now let me tell you which ones I like the best, my favorite diseases. What makes me happiest is venereal disease. Look at the latest newspapers, big or small, every ad in every inch of them is filled with lists of venereal diseases, and I've had them all. It scared me at first, but not after a while. With so many drugs for treatment—and so many clinics—it seemed like all the clinics in China were kept in business because of it. Also, I wasn't afraid because I didn't need to see the doctors secretly; I strutted in to see them. Twice someone phoned while I was getting a nitro drip. I called him back and told him, right in front of the doctors and the patients who were getting nitro drip like me, 'I can't do anything right now; I'm getting treatment for my venereal disease.' I knew both the doctors and patients were pricking up their ears listening to me. Even at a place like this where people couldn't care less about shame, they were still shocked, exchanging glances about me. I stood out even at that sort of place. I stood out because I wasn't like them, those people who changed their expressions as soon as they talked about the disease. At the time I had the idea that, because disease had such power over people, I should live like a disease, let me live like a disease . . . no, maybe that's not accurate. I should say, I am disease, I am disease!"

Apparently not having the energy to talk at length, Fei had sweat on her forehead. She curled up, holding her thin knees to her stomach, but still tried to continue. Tiao sat on her armchair and gazed at her, recalling scenes of their teenage years . . . She remembered how, after the three of them—she, Fei, and Youyou—tasted the gourmet food they'd cooked themselves, discussed the Soviet story about jealousy, and appreciated Fei's "Cairo Night" fashion show, when Youyou sighed that she longed to live as if life were a movie, Fei declared proudly, "I am a movie."

I am a movie.

Now she was sick. What was all that about being a movie? Now she was a disease; a disease, exactly. Fei's announcement saddened her. Puzzled, she stared at Fei on the sofa and couldn't understand why Fei had to say it. Why must she say such things? Tiao didn't want to hear words like that, which made her uncomfortable, both physically and psychologically. She interrupted Fei and said, "Let me pour you a cup of tea. You close your eyes and take a rest."

Fei said angrily, "Why do you interrupt me? You think I would use your cup to drink your water? I want to smoke. I asked you to bring me an ashtray, and why didn't you do that? Do you want to suffocate me? You!"

Tiao took a plate from the kitchen, placed it in front of Fei as a makeshift ashtray, and said, "I'll light the cigarette for you." She picked up Fei's lighter and flicked it on awkwardly. The flame shone on Fei's face, a face full of manic excitement. Fei pulled a cigarette from the pack, moved closer to the flame, and greedily inhaled a few puffs. Then she leaned back on the sofa and swung a leg over the top of it, in a loose and indecent gesture. She breathed the smoke in and out and said, "I am disease. After a while, I became less anxious when I got a venereal disease; I wanted to give the disease to them first, to those stinking men who had status and were so fond of their reputations, and to have them pass it on to their wives. My pastime was to lie in a big dark bed with curtains drawn tightly and imagine their miserable looks after catching the disease from me. I knew the disease wouldn't defeat them; they have their own discreet channels for treatment—imported shots, expensive medicine—none of that would be in short supply for them. People would be eager to volunteer to supply them treatment, and maybe they would get to stay home and be cured with ease. Do you believe it? I simply liked to imagine the way they looked, miserable and embarrassed, miserable and embarrassed but still with their high-and-mighty expressions . . . that was truly satisfying—such a pitiful satisfaction was probably all

I deserved. Only at moments like these I wouldn't think myself lower than they were. I live with a clearer conscience than they do. Tell me, don't I live with a clearer conscience than they do? Don't stare at me like that. Will you, please? Hey, hey, why don't you say something?"

Tiao heaved a sigh and said, "Fei, don't torture yourself like this. Something big must have happened, as big as the sky. Which man have you been staying with recently? Can you tell me?"

Fei said, "I . . . my beauty is gone. Beauty is gone. Do you understand? I've been with nobody recently. I just stay by myself, home alone, at that place of mine in Shenzhen, the apartment that Boss Wang bought me when he was leaving. But something big did happen to me; I became more and more suspicious of one person. I spoke to you about Yu Dasheng, right? Yu Dasheng, the current vice governor of our province, used to be the director of my factory twenty years ago. I told you that I'd tried to use my body and my Coral Jewel watch to seduce him in order to get another job. I sat down on his lap and he lifted me off. He threw me out but transferred me to the office to work as a typist, which didn't make sense. I'd never met anyone like him in my life, a man who intimidated me but also made me very much want to get close to him. But I didn't even dare thank him. I felt he was the kind of man who didn't like to express his personal feelings. He wasn't cold, just very strong, and you would never know what he was thinking. After I left the factory, I gradually forgot about him. Later, it was Little Cui who reminded me. Last year, Little Cui and Er Ling came to see me out of the blue. His niece—Little Cui's niece was already so grown up—fell two points short of the college entrance exam and they wanted me to find some connection to smooth things out. I couldn't think of any, and Little Cui said I could ask the big leader to give a word from above. I said I didn't know any big leader, and Little Cui said, 'Don't you know the vice governor, Yu Dasheng? He used to work in our factory.' He exchanged a look with Er Ling after saying this, the kind that's not very straightforward. Apparently they still firmly believed that Yu Dasheng and I had some kind of relationship, just as Little Cui had imagined when he was beating me or bent over my body. These looks and little gestures didn't bother me anymore. What interested me was that Yu Dasheng was the vice governor of our province. You know I never paid attention to politics, never watched news on TV or read newspapers. It was ridiculous that I didn't know Yu Dasheng was our vice governor until so late. I felt strangely excited and readily agreed to try to talk to him. I phoned the number that Little Cui provided and reached Governor Yu's secretary, introducing myself as a worker who had worked in the factory where Governor Yu used to work, an ordinary worker, whom Governor Yu had helped and who just wanted a few minutes of Governor Yu's time on behalf of a child.

"Two days later, I saw Yu Dasheng at his office. I'd never tried so hard to tidy myself up as I did then, putting on makeup, choosing clothes so carefully, and still I was so dissatisfied with my face. I knew this was because I was getting old, and I had lost confidence in my looks. I had dark circles under my lower eyelids, and my index and middle fingers had been stained brown by smoking. When I looked at myself in the mirror, I saw that the skin on my cheeks was already a little sunken. I took turns slapping myself with both hands, to speed up the circulation, to make my cheeks full and rosy again. Wasn't I crazy? I was simply a crazy woman. I walked into Yu Dasheng's office in fancy clothes and heavy makeup and immediately felt unsteady on my feet. It seemed to me later that it was because the office was so big. Such a big room was intended to make people feel small—and I felt much smaller than usual. I walked to the office desk he sat behind. Hardly moving, he pointed at a cushioned chair in front of the desk and had me sit down. He said, 'Fei, we haven't seen each other for many years. My secretary said you came to me on behalf of your child? How old is your child?'

"I said, 'It's like this: She's not my child. She's my ex-husband's niece.' I tried to explain the situation as briefly as possible because I knew that, as always, he preferred things straight to the point with no small talk. After that, I handed that child's information to him. I noticed he was particularly interested in my hands. So I got a crazy idea, the habit of many years emerging boldly again. I extended the hand with brown, smoke-stained fingers toward his face, almost touching the tip of his nose. I said, 'Look at my hand as much as you want. You can even . . . touch.' As I said this, I was prepared to be thrown out of his office, as I had been years before, and I wouldn't have regretted it, even had that happened. But, surprisingly, he reached out to hold it, actually taking up my hand and beginning to study it attentively. For a moment I was moved, because the way he held my hand was not like the flirting between a man and woman. He held my hand in his as if it were scalding hot and fragile. There was nothing sexual in his eyes. On the contrary, the expression in them was distant. He seemed to focus on my hand, but also not to. I can't explain my feelings at the time: I studied his hand while he studied mine. I noticed something very strange; my hand looked very much like his. I must have lost myself at that moment, because something in the depths of my heart made me want to throw myself into his arms and cry and cry, but not the kind of crying a woman does with a man, but like a child with an adult. Do you understand? Not that he could have known what I had in mind, but he immediately let go of my hand and said, 'I didn't know a girl could smoke that much.'

"Everything went back to normal. He kept at an appropriate distance and I didn't have the nerve to reach out toward the tip of his nose again. Soon he indicated that I should be going, saying, 'I'll try my best to help the child. I have a meeting in a moment and you can leave now.' Apparently he was as good as his word, because Little Cui's niece was admitted by a university of science and technology. Only, after the meeting, I didn't get to see Yu Dasheng again. Every time I phoned, his secretary would say that he wasn't in. I had the sense this vice governor knew everything about me, even my indecency. What right did I have to waste his time? Even though he might be my . . . he might be my father. Tiao, you will never understand when he took my hand how strong, how irresistible the feeling was."

"Is this the big thing that you wanted to tell me?" Tiao asked Fei.

"No." Fei coughed violently. She said to Tiao with an enraged face, "I wanted to tell you that I hate you and I'm disgusted by you, because you're too healthy and I can't stand your health."

Tiao knelt in front of the sofa and wanted to hold Fei's hands.

She said, "You'd get well again, if only you wouldn't allow yourself to drink and smoke so much."

Fei threw Tiao's hand off. "Don't touch me. Don't you know I'm contagious? I don't have venereal disease. Not this time. Venereal disease is nothing! It's my liver that's the problem. Liver, liver, liver. It's liver cancer, late term! Ah, let me live like a disease, let me live like a disease. I am disease. I am disease . . ."

Tiao's eyes blurred. It seemed to her that here was a grown version of Quan thrashing her arms and legs. She knelt there, afraid to provoke her further, but she couldn't stop her, either.

2

"Now you know why I'm talking so much to you. I'm going to die, but I haven't lived enough," Fei said bitterly from the sofa.

Tiao took out a blanket and covered Fei. She said, "I'm going to call Chen Zai and ask him to drive over. Let's go to the hospital now."

Fei waved her hand and said with a bitter smile, "I just got out of the hospital. I have my diagnosis and I don't want to go back. Hmm, the doctor didn't want to tell me in the beginning, asking me to send a family member to him. A family member. Tiao, that's when I feel the most miserable. What family do I have? Where is my family? I really need one, don't you think? Even if it's just to hear a diagnosis of late-term liver cancer."

Tiao bit her lower lip and almost cried. She said, "It's my fault, Fei. I haven't called you for so long. Let's go to the hospital. Let's go to the hospital now."

Fei said, "Don't cry like a baby. I understand you and am also jealous of you. What woman in love isn't selfish? Doesn't everything become secondary compared to Chen Zai? I was really afraid to bother you, which was why I didn't call. To be honest with you, I even thought about killing myself, jumping from a high building, suffocating myself with gas, or cutting my wrist with a blade . . . All of it seemed too painful. I just couldn't do it to myself. Only taking sleeping pills seemed okay, to get sent to another world peacefully, without knowing. I went to two drugstores and bought two bottles of sleeping pills, two hundred pills, which would be enough. I went home, gave myself an herbal bath, put on festive clothes, changed the sheets and pillowcases, and then cleaned the rooms. While I was doing all these chores, I kept thinking about the scenes after my death, thinking about all those men I had been with. Who would feel the saddest after hearing? Who would regret that he hadn't married me? Who would be sorry for how cruelly he had treated me? How they treated me like I was less than human, like an animal? To put it simply, I hoped my death would send a shock to their hearts for a moment—that it could make some of them feel regret and guilt. For some suicides, the whole purpose is to make the living feel regret and guilt. I was lying on the bed and dumping the two hundred pills onto a piece of white paper and telling myself, 'I'm going to take the pills. I'm going to take them.' Then I got obsessed with imagining all kinds of expressions on the faces of those men, as if I were watching a movie. I realized later that a person who cares too much what other people would think about her death wouldn't actually kill herself. The more I looked forward to making others feel guilty, the less I wanted to kill myself. In the end I simply dumped all the sleeping pills in the toilet. My death wouldn't shake anyone's soul, so I'm not going to kill myself. I want to live to the last moment of my life. There is only one wish left in my heart: I want to ask you to help me conduct an investigation . . . help me find out about Yu Dasheng's past. I know he spent his youth in Beijing. Do you think it's possible that he's my father? *Ai,* besides our hands really looking alike, I have no other evidence. My mother and uncle didn't leave me any clues."

Despite deep reservations, Tiao nodded and said, "I'll try every way I can to help you find out. You can trust me." Her heart was telling her it was too absurd. Fei missed her father so much that she was already out of her mind. But in a situation like this, she didn't want to dash Fei's hopes.

She didn't expect Fei suddenly to laugh at herself. "Tiao, I'm fine with just having you say that. Do you think I would really expect you to investigate? Who am I? How can I dream of working my way up to attach myself to a governor? Not to mention the fact that he's not my father. Even if he is, would he admit it to someone like me? Take me home. Call Chen Zai to take me home."

Next day, Tiao and Youyou, at Fei's suggestion, went to Fei's apartment for dinner. She asked Tiao and Youyou to cook, and decided on the menu herself: puffed rice noodles, crystal pork, pork skin aspic, muxi pork, and also, for dessert, grilled miniature snowballs. Tiao and Youyou remembered that this had been the menu for their first dinner so many years ago, a banquet that Youyou had spent a large sum of money, fifty-two cents, to put on. Youyou still knew how to make these special dishes. While she and Tiao bustled in the kitchen, Fei also made a request for marinated rabbit head. Tiao remembered that it was the snack that Fei had bought for them on their way back from the movie: three cents for a marinated rabbit head, the price of a popsicle, so crunchy and delicious. Tiao asked Chen Zai to go out to buy it. Unfortunately, present-day Fuan didn't sell that kind of thing anymore, and even Youyou didn't know how to prepare it.

They sat down to eat, and, of course, to drink wine. They drank red wine. Fei, tormented by pain and sweating profusely, got up from her bed, walked over gracefully, and seated herself, her look of misery gone. Her gaze went around to everyone, charming them all; her manner was elegant and appealing. They couldn't help feeling that the great beauty Fei had returned. She would use red paper to dye their lips and make them look very seductive, and then she would put on a raincoat to perform "Cairo Nights." Look, she picked up the glass of red wine and drained it in one gulp. Wasn't it the drunkenness that made her eyes cloudy? This intoxicating dream life of Fei's! This determined great beauty!

None of them could taste anything out of these special dishes, but they all exaggeratedly nodded their heads to show how they had found their past; from the pork skin aspic, from the crystal pork, they had rediscovered their innocent joy. Except their tears didn't cooperate but fell into their glasses and made the wine salty. They were laughing.

They were laughing.

* * *

Two weeks later, Fei died in the hospital. Tiao and Youyou had taken turns staying beside her bed. No one else came to the hospital to visit her, even though she kept glancing toward the door. Where were those men, those men who'd enjoyed her and used her and were also used by her? Toward the end, Fei stopped glancing at the door; she didn't have the strength anymore—she slipped in and out of a coma.

She had woken up on a sunny afternoon and recognized Tiao by her bedside. She raised her arm and said, "Come close, come close." She pointed at her lips and said, "Maybe you won't believe me, Tiao. I've had many men but none of them touched my lips. None of them. I didn't allow them to. Once, a local rich guy, who got rich by dealing cars, treated me to dinner. He suddenly reached his hand over the table, grabbed my neck, and attempted to kiss me. I turned my face away and said, 'What are you doing?' He said, 'What do you think I want to do?' I said, 'If you want something, you don't have to try so hard. We can do it now.' He gave me a cocky grin and said, 'I never thought I'd hear you say anything like that so soon. I didn't expect you to be so straightforward. There are two types of women in my experience—the lowbrow kind and the highbrow kind. The lowbrow let you touch the lower parts of their bodies as soon as you start; and the highbrow only permit you to touch the upper parts. See, I had you in the highbrow category . . .' Tiao, come closer, come closer, listen to me. My lips are clean. They're the only thing on my body that's respectable. Let me kiss you. Let me kiss you."

Fei propped herself up stubbornly and held Tiao in her arms, and then with her pale and icy lips kissed Tiao's left cheek.

Tiao gradually felt a burning sensation on the left side of her face, and believed there must be a clear outline of lips on her cheek. When she went to the funeral home for Fei's service a few days later, she could feel the lip mark still imprinted on her left cheek. A strange man with gray hair stood in front of the funeral home and stared at Tiao's face, which embarrassed her. She supposed that he must have seen the imprint on her face, a material presence that had a shape and life and didn't disappear with the disappearance of Fei. A living thing that Fei had planted on Tiao's face, it remained and frequently made the left side of Tiao's face feel swollen. The gray-haired man stared at Tiao's face and said, "The person you had the funeral for is Fei, right?"

Tiao said, "Who are you?"

The man said, "I'm an old coworker of hers from the factory." Tiao looked at his clothing carefully; he had on a dark blue khaki cotton jacket with a brown plush collar, out of date but very clean. Tiao said, "Are you Master Qi?"

"My last name is Qi. How did you know?"

"From . . . before . . . Fei told me."

"Are you her family—?"

"No, I'm not her family. I'm her friend."

"I haven't seen her for years. What about her family?"

Tiao got a distant look in her eye. "She has no family."

He said, "Oh."

He turned to push his bicycle, an old Phoenix Manganese 18 bicycle with rust-stained rims, the former symbol of a family's prosperity. As she looked at this classic, nicely designed old Phoenix, Tiao's heart quivered with tenderness, as if she were seeing an old acquaintance who had been out of touch for years, as if she were seeing the living witness to Fei's story. The stories that Fei told her became so real and definite. She imagined the time Master Qi rode that bike into their campus, locked it in front of the administration building, and how Fei, seeing no one around, pulled the air valves out. Tiao gazed at that phoenix symbol, with its delicate and beautiful design—three tails, gracefully lifted, bright red, golden, and emerald green, all of which would call up good associations for Tiao forever.

Master Qi got on his bicycle and left the funeral home. The back of his figure on the bicycle looked lonely and disciplined, and Tiao had the thought that this old worker with his gray hair might be the only one who had truly loved Fei. She was convinced that he had seen Fei's lips on her face, and maybe he even imagined that Fei's lips would open and talk from her left cheek. But this was probably just her fantasy. Tiao thought too much.

3

The sofa was still the same, gray-blue satin brocade, in the same place, soft and clean.

She pricked up her ears to listen while she led him by the hand and walked toward the sofa. It wasn't important that she was pulling with her hand; the important thing was listening. What she valued at that moment was her ears. The light wasn't on, so the room was dark. Until, after a while, as they started to get used to it, the darkness didn't appear so solid; light from the building across shone in through the open curtains of the windows. Stillness was everywhere, and she heard nothing, from either Fei or Quan. The sofa made no sound; the screaming had vanished. In her heart was a deep emptiness, but also a relief that she didn't want to admit. She missed Fei, but she also felt relieved by her death, as if because of it, from now on, Quan would completely disappear from the sofa; only Fei's death could guarantee that. The sofa now made no sound; the screaming was gone.

All of a sudden tears poured down her face. She felt a sense of complete relief—as when enormous tension is lifted, as though a free and deep sleep had arrived at last, as deep as could be wished after a hundred years of being deprived of it. Her tears unhurriedly washed away the obstacles of all kinds in the depth of her soul, unhurriedly welled into her eyes. Immediately he saw that she was crying—by the sparkle of reflected light from outside—and he kissed her wet face.

He must have thought her crying was caused by great sadness. Sadness would linger for many people after a funeral. He tried to comfort her with his kisses and wanted to turn on the light in the living room, but she didn't let him. She didn't allow him to turn on the light, and she didn't want him to kiss her. She was annoyed now, because when he kissed her face, she felt the pressure on the left side again, which was Fei's lips. It changed the kissing, making it as if he were kissing Fei, not her—kissing Fei's lips on her face. So Tiao became the intermediary between Chen Zai and Fei, as though she were intimate with both of them, while they took no notice of her, busy only with their own communication. She was like a bed is to a couple who are engrossed in making love; they can't do it without the bed, but the bed means nothing to them. The thought upset Tiao very much; she evaded Chen Zai's lips and made him feel awkward. Then he held her by the waist and told her to lie down in bed. He thought she should rest.

In bed, she held on to his hands. As though prompted, he started to remove her clothes. He took off almost everything, and her arms and legs obeyed and seemed happy to cooperate. She was left wearing only a small pair of underpants, white, the kind with embroidery on the front and lace on the sides. The tiny underwear excited him, aroused him even more than her naked body. His hand touched the crotch of her underwear. The small soft and moist spot there gave him chills. He began to take off her underwear, but she seemed desperate to stop him. She insisted on guiding him into her, partly moving aside her underwear. He felt uncomfortable but it also gave him a new, exciting sensation. He didn't understand her insistence, as if she were purposely setting up obstacles for both of them. Too smooth is not smooth, just as too much freedom is no freedom at all. But soon he was tired of the novel feeling, because it hurt. He tore off the little thing with a couple of tugs and rammed into her without any interference. She seemed to escape the awkwardness she felt from the left side of her face, and his concentration and devoted energy moved her, also. She was willing to cooperate with his rhythms; she was willing to bring about their happy climax at the same time; she was willing to believe he truly loved her and not something else; she was willing to believe that the past had truly become the past.

But more and more she felt distracted. She was very thirsty, and her face began to feel burning pain again, which distracted her. She knew someone shouldn't be distracted while making love, and that even a grain-sized pimple could affect one's mood sometimes. Now the left side of her face hurt, but he didn't notice anything and just kept banging away. She forgot it was she who had grabbed his hands tightly; she forgot it was she who wanted him to sweep away her uneasiness with his actions. Withdrawing into herself then, she was thinking unreasonably, Why does he have to do this to me right now? When she was thinking like that, she couldn't go on. She said rudely, "Can we just stop? I want to stop." She said this and started to push him off. She pushed him off her body, grabbed a bathrobe, and went into the bathroom.

She took a hurried shower and stood in front of the mirror to look at her face. Very clearly, she could see a lipstick print on her left cheek, a pink one with a distinct outline. Anyone who knew Fei would recognize it as her lips. She dipped a towel into the water and rubbed her face, and also used disinfectant soap that she had brought back from abroad to wash her face clean of it, but she failed. She looked at her face in the mirror and thought that she still hadn't escaped from her past. She needed to talk, and she must talk, no matter what Chen Zai thought of her.

She put her bathrobe back on and came to the doorway, as if she had just come in from outside. She started from the doorway, and skillfully turned on all the lights one by one in order: wall light, ceiling light, mirror light, floor light, big desk light, and small desk light . . . she left the entire place brightly lit. Then she led Chen Zai to the armchair and sat across from him. She said, "I'm going to tell you something."

Looking across at her, she seemed uncomfortable, and he said, "Do you have to talk about it tonight?"

"Yes, I have to."

"Maybe you should go to bed. I know you're very tired."

"I don't want to sleep, and I'm not tired, either. Don't interrupt me."

"But your mood is very unstable."

She smiled gently and said, "I'm very stable. My mood has never been as stable as today. Do you still remember Quan's death? In our compound, there was a manhole on the small road in front of our building. She was playing, shoveling dirt under a tree that day, and a few old ladies who were sewing *The Selected Works of Chairman Mao* called her from a distance, so she walked towards them. She walked over, walked into the manhole, and died. She was two years old."

"You've spoken about this before. Everyone knows the incident."

"No, no one knows. You don't know, either. When she was walking to those old ladies, I was right behind her, ten meters away, or maybe fifteen meters. I saw the manhole, saw the lid was not on for some reason. Both Fan and I saw it. We also saw the old ladies wave at her, and their waving made Quan more eager to get there. I didn't stop her, didn't run forward and carry her back. I knew I had enough time, but I didn't do it. Fan and I just held each other's hands tightly and watched her throw open her arms and fall into the manhole, as if she were flying. Chen Zai, this is me, this is the true picture of me. Not only didn't I save her myself, but also I pulled Fan back. I can never forget our holding hands and the pull I gave on Fan's hand. I had tried to explain that it was because I was paralyzed by fear—people can't take action when they're paralyzed by fear—but I knew that I wasn't. My mind at that moment was as clear as it is now. I didn't like Quan, and neither did Fan. I understand her dislike for Quan, but I can never reveal to her the reason for mine. I'm a murderer, a criminal who has escaped punishment. I planned never to tell anyone, but I was really tempted to tell you after I fell in love with you, not because I wanted to prove my honesty, but because the more the time passes, the clearer the scene of Quan's death becomes. I really don't have a heart so big and powerful that I can hold the painful past secret and secure. It kept disturbing my heart. I need someone to help me, to share it with me, and this person is you. I trust you a thousand times more than I trust myself, but I'm also afraid to lose you. Now that I'm finally confessing, Chen Zai, I'm experiencing the kind of relief a person feels once in a thousand years, no matter what you think of me. Do you understand?"

"Tiao, I also need to tell you something: Fan told me all these things a long time ago. When I listened to her, I didn't hate her or you. I just pitied her; I was even ashamed to tell you. She was not a murderer, but she's more pathetic than you are."

"Why do you say that?"

"Because she was trying to prove her own innocence by exposing others. You definitely couldn't hate her."

"No, I don't hate her."

"Then why did you hate Quan?"

Suddenly she felt ashamed, more ashamed than she was at admitting to murder. But she had already made up her mind to bring everything out into the open, so she said, "Because Quan was the child of Wu and Fei's uncle."

"So that's why Fei also got involved in the incident, right?"

Tiao didn't understand Chen Zai. "No, Fei just told me of her suspicion."

Chen Zai said, "I also remember something from long ago. It was in the same year, the night before Quan's death, my mother had a heart attack and I took her to the hospital and then came back to fetch a basin and thermos. When I entered the front gate on my bicycle, I saw someone riding a bicycle in front of me who looked very much like Fei. It was pretty late by then, almost twelve. I wondered why Fei had come at that hour. She could only be there to see you, but why so late? Had anything happened to your family? My concern for you made me curious, so I followed her in secret and, sure enough, she stopped in front of your building. I didn't want her to see me, so I pushed my bicycle to the side of the road, in behind a row of hollies. She didn't lock her bicycle and go upstairs. Hesitating for a while, she held her bicycle and then turned back to the small road. Next, she stopped at a particular spot. Now she had me really curious, so I left my bicycle leaning against the hollies and worked my way closer to her. Finally, I saw what she was doing: she stood by the manhole and looked at it blankly. She stared for a while and then looked around. When she saw no one, she pulled out an iron hook from her bicycle, the kind we used to pick up the lid of the stove. She grabbed the iron hook and started to pry up the manhole cover. She panted and huffed quite a bit and finally opened the cover. Then she strained to push it aside and revealed the dark hole. I was hoping that she was not trying to jump into the hole to kill herself, but I dismissed the idea immediately. Manholes are very shallow and that fall couldn't kill her. Maybe she was looking for something, something she had lost in the hole. Before I could give it any more thought, she had already gotten on her bicycle and ridden away. It looked as though she were just leaving temporarily to get some tools or find a helper. After she was completely out of sight, I walked over to the manhole. The hole was a bit smelly, and the cover was moved aside, only touching the edge of the manhole. The iron hook was gone, too. I didn't understand what was going on, but I had no time to figure it out. My mother was still in the hospital. So I went home, got money, basin, and thermos, and rode back to the hospital. I stayed at the hospital to keep my mother company for the night. When I went home the next day at noon, I heard that a child had fallen into the manhole. I immediately thought about Fei, who hadn't opened the manhole to search for anything. Her purpose was to open the manhole. At the time, I didn't know her name was Fei, only that she was your best friend; you see how I was back then. I remembered all your girlfriends just because I liked you. Many, many years later, when we grew up and you introduced Fei to me, I still believed without a doubt that she was the one who opened the manhole. It was always a mystery to me. I didn't understand why your good friend would open the manhole and let your sister fall into it. Now that I know why, I feel guilty beyond words: because I was the only one who saw the cover was off, but I didn't put it back . . ."

Tiao seemed to understand everything. She was willing to trust Chen Zai's memory, even though Fei had already died and nothing could be confirmed. Maybe it was because there was no proof that everything could appear so clear. Maybe Fei wanted to tell her this in the last moments of her life, but the cancer took away her courage. So she could only leave her confessing lips on Tiao's face.

"I feel lucky that I can tell everything to you," Tiao said.

"I also feel lucky that I could tell everything to you."

"You want to say that it's not only my responsibility."

"Yes, it's three people's business."

"But you're innocent."

"No, one can't be innocent if he feels guilty."

"My courage came too late."

"But you have more courage than I do. There seems to be a disagreement between you and me. If you hadn't opened your mouth, I wouldn't have had the courage to talk about that night."

She arose from the sofa and walked to Chen Zai. She knelt and buried her head in his lap and said, "I love you, Chen Zai."

He picked her up and sat her on his lap. "I love you, Tiao."

"I love you. Nothing can stop me from loving you."

"I love you. Nothing can stop me from loving you, either."

They held each other and fell asleep. Next morning, when she went to take a shower in the bathroom and looked at her face in the mirror, to her surprise she found the pink lipstick print was gone. Her cheek was smooth and clean.

The shower last night was as unreal as a dream, and was also so real that it didn't feel like a dream.

4

It wasn't too difficult for Tiao to get to know Vice Governor Yu Dasheng, but she didn't want to do it artificially, as most people did when they needed to ask a favor from a governor, through connections or networking. Most of the time people would get stuck with the secretary, sometimes not even with the main secretary, but some secretary on duty who would get rid of them easily. Tiao didn't have any favor to ask, so she didn't have to use that approach. She wanted just to talk with Yu Dasheng about Fei. It was Fei's final wish and she'd made a promise to her, even though she thought it was absurd.

So she felt it was even more urgent to get to know him naturally.

She was looking for an opportunity, and then the opportunity came to her. One day the publishing house received a notice informing them that Vice Governor Yu Dasheng was going to accompany a visiting group from Seoul on a tour of Fuan Children's Publishing House. In addition to making arrangements for the reception at the publishing house, Tiao also rearranged her office in a special way. She found a picture of her and Fei at home, taken a few years earlier by Chen Zai. In the picture, Fei had on a loose black pullover sweater, with her hair cascading like a waterfall. Her expression was a bit flirtatious, but charming. Tiao sat with her, shoulder to shoulder, and looked very serious. She framed the picture and deliberately placed it on the most visible spot of her desk. She was thinking she would definitely try to get Governor Yu and his guests to her office.

The visitors came, and after a brief colloquium and a book-giving ceremony from the publishing house, Tiao proposed that they could take a look at the editors' working environment. The director's office was the closest to the conference room, and next was the vice director's office.

With things arranged this way, Yu Dasheng finally walked into Tiao's office. He caught sight of the framed picture as soon as he stepped in. Tiao felt that Yu Dasheng was paying attention to the framed picture, and she must seize the moment while he was staring at it to strike up a conversation. She said, "Governor Yu, you must know the person in this picture."

Yu Dasheng hesitated for a moment, a very small moment of hesitation that normally would have gone unnoticed, and then said, "Yes, yes, I know her. She looks like a worker in a factory where I used to work. Her name is . . ." He looked like he was trying very hard to recall her name.

"Fei."

"Yes, Fei," he said, no longer looking at the framed picture. He commented on how modern and pretty the office equipment looked and then left. Tiao followed him into the hallway and then took her chance to say, "Governor Yu, Fei is my friend. I need to talk about her with you."

Yu Dasheng seemed alarmed and asked, "Talk to me?"

Tiao said, "Yes, you're her old leader anyway."

Yu Dasheng hesitated again, another small hesitation, and said, "Okay."

He made an appointment with her.

He sat behind his huge office desk and looked at her, and she sat in the soft guest chair looking at him. He was probably about sixty years old, his hair turned gray, but his back was still straight. She liked men and women who didn't dye their hair, feeling they always looked younger than those who had fake black hair. A few minutes ago, on her way to the provincial government's office building, she suddenly had an urge to turn back, like the time she was to meet Mike at the Austin airport. She had these urges when a decision had been made but not put into action yet. Suddenly she doubted that the meeting made any sense. Did she want to force him to admit that he was Fei's father? That was too ridiculous. How could she take Fei's sickbed ravings seriously? She was still thinking about turning back after she entered the elevator of the governor's office building. She stared at the second button of the shirt of a male employee, who entered the elevator at the same time as she did. She was thinking that if this fellow got off the elevator before she did, then she would leave with him and not see Yu Dasheng; if he got off the elevator after her, then she had no choice but to see Yu Dasheng. As it turned out, he pressed the button for seven and she needed to go to level three, so she got off at the third floor.

There was an awkward silence between them at first, then Tiao glanced at the brown paper bag by her feet and remembered she had brought books for the governor. She took out a set of Children's English, finely printed with a fragrant smell, and said, "This is a series of fun English-learning books that our publishing house brought out in cooperation with a Canadian publisher. Governor, maybe your grandchildren will like them—you must have a grandson or granddaughter, right?"

The atmosphere was softened—words like "grandson" and "granddaughter" could ease all kinds of tension. Yu Dasheng said, "I have a granddaughter. I'll give this set of books to her."

Tiao said, "When Fei and I were little, we were not lucky enough to have so many pretty books. Back then there were a few old back issues of *Soviet Woman* in our house, which Fei and I read over and over. We read all the fashion articles, recipes, and stories in them."

Yu Dasheng became attentive. He said, "Oh? How old were you?"

Tiao said, "I was thirteen, and Fei was sixteen. We also passed around some Soviet spy stories to read then, such as *Red Safe, Amber Necklace*—"

Yu Dasheng interrupted Tiao. "These stories were around even when I was young."

Tiao said, "Oh, then you'll recognize this story if I tell you the details. It's about a man and a woman who live in the same courtyard but are never seen talking to each other. They appear to be strangers even though they have been neighbors for many years. The ending is something quite unusual. The police solve a spy case, and the spy is the man in the courtyard. And his assistant is the woman who lives next door but apparently has never talked to him. How did they manage to work together? It turns out the woman's wardrobe against the wall is a secret door to her male neighbor. Every night, as long as she gets into the wardrobe she can go to the male spy's place. Do you remember this detail, Governor Yu? Both Fei and I got really frightened. It was exciting and scary at the same time. Ever since I read those stories, I got suspicious even about our wardrobe, always thinking there was a secret door in it. I was afraid to leave these sorts of books by my pillow at night. I had to toss them far away because I was so afraid the spies in the book would jump out and choke me to death. One day, Fei borrowed my *Red Safe*. Next day she told me that she had thrown my book away. She said it was too dark when she was on her way home. She mumbled to herself as she was walking. The book in her backpack seemed like a spy who was trailing her, and the leaves underneath crunched as she went along. Finally she couldn't take it anymore. So she took out the book, threw it into the darkness, and then started to run. After that she asked me, 'Hey, Tiao, do you have other books like it? Lend me another.' You see how we were back then, scared but still wanting to read—the more scared we were, the more we wanted to read. Later we read much less. After Fei became a worker, she probably didn't read those kinds of books anymore."

"Has your friendship lasted to this day?"

"You can say that. We all admired her when we were little. She was a beauty. She had been a beauty since she was little. Don't you think so?"

Yu Dasheng made no comment about this. Tiao started to relax and decided to lead the conversation to Tang Jingjing. She said, "Fei was a beauty because her mother, Teacher Tang, was also very beautiful."

Yu Dasheng took a careful look at Tiao. His body, which had been leaning back in his leather swivel chair, almost imperceptibly leaned forward. He said, "Her mother, Tang Jingjing, do you also know her?"

Tiao said, "I was still living in Beijing when I was in the first grade. Teacher Tang was a math teacher for the higher grades. I saw her stand on a stage being denounced by people, with a sign hanging in front of her chest. The sign read 'I'm . . . I'm . . .'"

"I'm what?"

"The sign read 'I'm a female hooligan.' They asked her to lower her head and she refused, so they made her eat shit and she did."

"You mean she ate . . . ate shit?"

"Yes, she ate shit, because if she hadn't they would have brought her daughter, Fei, to the stage to be put on display. I knew only after I grew up that Fei was her illegitimate daughter. Fei is a child without a father."

Yu Dasheng held his interlocked hands in front of his chest. Tiao looked at his hands and tried to judge with as little emotion as possible: the pair of hands did look like Fei's. Maybe it was just a coincidence. But because she had a strong desire to probe Yu Dasheng, she would rather everything was true. She stared at that pair of hands that seemed to be suffering and said, "Later, Teacher Tang died."

"Yes, she died in a very miserable way."

"Did you know her?"

Yu Dasheng said, "No, I didn't know her—Teacher Tang. I had left Beijing by that time."

Tiao said, "You mean if you hadn't left Beijing, you might have known Teacher Tang?"

Yu Dasheng said, "No, maybe I misspoke, because one Beijinger doesn't necessarily know another Beijinger."

Tiao said, "I agree. For instance, a Beijinger like you and a Beijinger like me have been living in Fuan for so many years, but haven't we only just gotten to know each other?"

Yu Dasheng laughed quietly.

"But Fei didn't think so. She believed that in the ocean of people, the ones that are meant to meet will meet eventually, such as family members, or a father, for example. For a while, she was convinced that her father lived right in Beijing—"

Yu Dasheng glanced at his watch and interrupted Tiao. "I'm afraid I can't give you too much time—I have a meeting that I need to attend. Your friend Fei was indeed the worker in my old factory. Not too long ago, maybe last year, she came to me with a university admission issue concerning her relative's child, and the problem was solved. Is there anything else that she wants you to ask me to do for her? Or is there anything I can do for you?"

Tiao stood up from the chair and said, "No. Both Fei and I don't need you to do anything for us. Especially Fei. She won't be coming to see you anymore."

"Why?" Yu Dasheng asked. He also arose from his leather chair, ready to see his guest out.

Tiao said, "Because she has passed away."

Yu Dasheng sat back in his chair and signaled Tiao also to sit down. After a short silence, he said, "I didn't know. This is very unfortunate—I mean, it was unfortunate for her. What was the illness—it must have been an illness?"

"Liver cancer."

Tiao said, "I was with her when she was dying. I'm her family. Family, do you understand? She was a wounded beauty with hundreds of scars. And she told me that only her mouth was clean; her mouth had never been touched by a man. Many times she told me about the feelings she had for her father in her heart, saying she didn't hate him at all. I assume she probably saved her lips for her father; she must have longed to kiss him with a mouth as innocent as a baby's, grateful that he'd given her life. No one can maintain such discipline without turning discipline into faith. Fei had faith in her heart. Don't you want to know what that was? It was her love and her quest for her father. Are you crying, Governor Yu? Can you tell me why? Just for a female worker's death? Are you crying just for a female worker's death?"

Yu Dasheng vaguely nodded his head and said, "I think you should leave now."

"Don't you have anything to say to me? I'm Fei's friend."

He said, "I know you're Fei's friend and your name is Tiao, the vice director of the Children's Publishing House. You can come to me if there is anything for the publishing house that I can do for you. After all, Fei used to work in my factory. Let's stay in touch."

His tone calmed suddenly as he was saying this, and his body, which was leaning against the back of the chair, straightened up. There were no traces of tears on his face at all. Maybe Tiao was mistaken in what she had thought she'd seen. She still couldn't make him out. This man, if he didn't have enormous self-control or excellent acting skills, then he must be . . . what must he be? Unless he really was not Fei's father.

She came out of the provincial government office certain that it was impossible for her to manage a conversation with a man like him, not to mention that he had already defined their relationship. She remembered the words he'd said that made her feel awkward: "After all, Fei used to work in my factory."

That was all.

She felt pangs of dull pain in her heart.

Just then the pager in her purse went off. Wu was beeping her.

5

Wu lived a retired life now, a complete idler. As she'd gotten older, her dizziness had actually disappeared little by little. She no longer felt dizzy, since she didn't have to use it to avoid the revolution in Reed River Farm. Maybe some degree of avoidance persisted in her life, though; she hid from her husband. There was some helplessness in her avoidance; it wasn't that she was compelled to avoid him, but Yixun expressed his disgust for her more and more bluntly than ever.

He couldn't bear to sit across from her during their meals together, nor could he tolerate the sound of her chewing. And the loud sounds she made when brushing her teeth and rinsing her mouth in the morning, along with her constant coughing, all tormented him. He hadn't remembered her like this when she was young, or maybe she had been this way, only he didn't notice. When you were young, you were young. He had worked in an army song-and-dance troupe before he went to college. He simply despised those comrades of his who thought they were funny. For instance, Comrade Zhang purposely said "beer water" instead of "beer": "Let's drink beer water, let's drink beer water!" Comrade Li said "neat" instead of "meat" on purpose: "The canteen will serve neat today. Serve neat!" Everyone laughed except for Yixun, who thought it was vulgar. Another example was that when the soldiers wrote letters, they liked to use sentences like this: "One day apart seems three autumns . . ." Many felt it was touching, but Yixun thought this sort of exaggerated rhetoric made people squirm. One comrade of his liked to collect famous quotes and epigrams in a notebook he titled *Bits of Gold and Jade.* Everyone thought the name was wonderfully witty, but Yixun felt it was tacky. He never said what was on his mind, but always believed his taste better than his comrades'. However, he tried to ignore Wu's habits in the bathroom. He would rather pretend that she didn't have these habits, which emerged in middle age, a result of self-abuse and neurosis. She had a lot more time to spend with Yixun at home, so those habits of hers crashed into him like massive waves.

They quarreled. He accused her of purposely making those hair-raising rasping noises while brushing her teeth, of watching TV until two a.m. and in the process managing to eat an entire grilled chicken, of using scalding water to make tea for a guest but not warming the rice porridge hot enough before serving him—also of sleeping late, of serving dirty cucumbers . . . She listened to his accusations, sometimes saying nothing and sometimes protesting mildly. When she answered back, he accused her of trying to make sense out of nonsense; when she kept quiet, he would say she was using silence to express her hatred.

In fact, Wu never hated Yixun. She had grown quiet because she knew her crime against Yixun was unpardonable, that it disqualified her from any forgiveness. She began to enjoy going out more; only when Yixun saw her less could she escape his accusations. It was actually Youyou's mom who first gave her the idea. One day Youyou's mom wore her wig to market when she was buying food and ran into Wu, who was also shopping there. Youyou's mom asked, "What do you think of my wig?"

"Not bad at all. It looks real," Wu said.

Youyou's mom said, "People who didn't know me thought it was real. But I also embarrassed myself twice. Once, our senior fashion show team had an open-air performance at the square of the Workers' Cultural Center. All of a sudden a big wind rose up and blew off my wig. The audience roared with laughter. You could see how embarrassed I was! From then on, whenever I encounter a windy day, I always remember to keep my hand on my head."

Soon Youyou's mom brought Wu to join the senior fashion performing team. Wu didn't covet the wig Youyou's mother wore, because Wu had taken good care of her real hair. Wearing different fashions and giving public performances made Wu more conscious of her own appearance. She'd always been embarrassed by her nose, which she felt was not high and straight enough. The urge to have plastic surgery, starting with a nose job, took hold of her. Her youth had been spent during a time when women were encouraged to love guns more than makeup. So hadn't she the right to make herself prettier nowadays? She went home and discussed it with Tiao, who immediately expressed her disapproval. Tiao's opposition made Wu unhappy, but the troubled expression on Tiao's face only strengthened her desire. She took the position that "I'm responsible for my own face" and "I make the important decisions about my own life." Wu went to the hospital and had her surgery.

She was very satisfied with the surgery that the doctor performed. When she viewed the elevated bridge of her nose and how the distance between her eyes seemed less because of it, she experienced the thrill of the brand-new, despite the slight discomfort. She didn't expect it to cause Yixun to sleep in a separate room from then on, and Tiao not only to refuse to go shopping with her but even to visit home much less often. Month after month, Tiao made the excuse that her job at the publishing house kept her too busy and she had to stay at her own place. Even when she did come home, she tried to avoid looking at Wu's face, and also refused to let Wu look at hers. Even when Wu stood at the far end of the living room, even when Tiao closed her eyes, she could still feel Wu's gaze on her face. This made her very angry; she would lose her temper all of a sudden and say, "Mom, why do you always stare at me? Would you not stare at me like that?"

Wu said, "You don't come home very often. What's wrong with me looking at you? Don't you know what I'm most concerned about is you?"

"What you're most concerned about is that face of yours."

"Tiao, how can you talk to me like that? How?"

"How do you want me to talk to you? If you want me to respect you, you have to respect yourself first."

"How have I not respected myself? Having nose-correction surgery is my own business. I didn't interfere with other people or force anyone else to do it with me. What does this have to do with self-respect?"

"But you force your family to look at your face, to accept a stranger with a strange face. Before, your face was real and natural, and it was at least my mother's face. I'm sorry, I can't accept your current face; at the very least I have to have some time to get used to it."

After saying that, Tiao left home without eating.

Now she went back because Wu had beeped her. Knowing her status in her daughter's heart, Wu seldom beeped her. But she had today, which made Tiao wonder whether something unusual had happened at home.

As soon as she entered the house, she noticed Wu sitting on the sofa with a pair of sunglasses on. The melodrama of wearing sunglasses in her own living room, ominous and silly—Tiao couldn't describe the complicated feeling she had, but her instinct told her that Wu's sunglasses had nothing to do with any illness but with her plastic surgery. She sat down across from Wu, quickly scanning her face and the sunglasses, which looked steady on the bridge of her nose because of the surgery. Tiao wondered whether this time perhaps she'd fixed her eyes. She got straight to the point. "Mom, is there some kind of emergency you need to talk to me about?"

"Yes, it's an emergency. It's about you and Chen Zai."

"What is it about Chen Zai and me?"

"I heard from Youyou's mom that Chen Zai was making a big scene about divorce, over you."

"Me?"

"Yes, over you."

"Yes, he's trying to get a divorce, but he didn't make a scene out of it. As far as I know, his wife, Wan Meicheng, didn't make one, either. They're discussing it. Can you not use the phrase 'make a scene'? It's so vulgar."

"It's not whether they make a scene or not. What's important is that he's doing this because of you, right?"

Tiao went quiet for a while and said, "Yes."

"Tiao, I just want to tell you to stop right here. It's not something to be proud of. Word has spread all over the compound, and your father and I are colleagues of Chen Zai's parents. We live in the same compound and have to see each other on a daily basis. It's embarrassing; besides—"

Tiao said impatiently, "Besides, what?"

"Are you urging me on, or interrupting me? Besides, divorce is something that can get very complicated. Chen Zai has been married for ten years and might not be able to get a divorce."

"How do you know that he can't get a divorce? Why can't you say something positive about my business?"

"Because I need to be responsible for you. Both your father and I would like to see you end up well. But that won't happen with Chen Zai. Neither of you are young anymore, so don't do things on an impulse."

"I appreciate your sense of responsibility, but what bothers me is why you talk about things so important to me with sunglasses on. It looks like you're an actress. Can you take off your sunglasses to talk to me?"

"I put on sunglasses precisely because of you. I just had surgery on my eyelids and it will take a while to recover. I'm afraid you won't want to see me. You didn't want to see me when I had the surgery on my nose, did you?"

"I hate to see you wear sunglasses even more."

Wu took off her sunglasses and said, "Then I'll take them off."

When she took off her sunglasses, her red, swollen eyes were hard for Tiao to bear. The thought occurred to Tiao that Wu was truly carrying out her plastic surgery plan, step by step. She had said her eyelids were too loose and droopy, and that after the nose she would have eyelid surgery, and then fix her double chin, tighten her facial skin, and extract the fat from her belly, etc. That she would risk her life in these operations on her face and pour money into the plastic surgery department made no sense. She was also stupid not to consider, what with her lifted nose, stitched eyelids, and sunglasses, how Tiao could take her seriously on an important personal matter. It would be more accurate to say Tiao's personal life didn't enter her mind, rather than that she was concerned with Tiao. Maybe her instinct as a mother was alerted by her daughter's dangerous relationship with a married man, but she wasn't able to express her worry and concern in a prudent and solemn way. Her strange appearance only added to Tiao's distrust.

Tiao said with loathing, "Given the way you look now, do you think you can make me listen to your advice?"

"What's wrong with the way I look now? I'm your mother anyway."

"That's not necessarily true. My mother doesn't look like that. I probably wouldn't recognize you if we met on the street. Don't you want to sew your double chin and tighten your skin? That would make it more difficult for me to recognize you. Why do it? You're not an actress or a television emcee. Why do you have to ruin your own appearance and embarrass and frighten us?"

"Don't exaggerate. Do I really frighten you? If I do, how can you manage to stay here and argue with me?"

"I'm arguing with you because even when you ask me to come home and talk about an important matter like Chen Zai's divorce, you're still distracted. You're only interested in your own face and body. You make it impossible for me to talk to you about all the things that a daughter would like to talk over with her mother, love or marriage. You've never given me the chance. You just call me here according to your own whim."

"I'm not doing anything according to my own whim. I'm truly concerned with you and Chen Zai. No matter how many plastic surgeries I have, I'm still your mother."

Tiao stood up from the sofa and said, "You're a . . . a . . ."

"A what? A what?"

"You're a monster."

Yixun walked out of his study to reprimand Tiao for talking so disrespectfully to her mother, and added, "Tiao, don't leave yet. I need to talk to you."

6

Tiao reluctantly followed Yixun into his study and chose to sit on a chair far away from him.

Yixun's attitude today took her by surprise, and she was not happy about his taking Wu's side and criticizing her. Yes, she had spoken disrespectfully to Wu, with whom she used the formal address but whom she called a monster. But that was a fact that Yixun knew better than anyone else. Compared to Tiao's disrespectful language, Wu's new look was far more upsetting to him. Could he really tolerate living in the same house with a woman who fixed her nose and eyelids, walked around in sunglasses, and gargled loudly right in front of him? Had he really become so big-hearted and tolerant? Or was the change because he had made common cause with Wu, overlooking her disagreeableness in turning their sights on Tiao? Tiao had a hunch that on the issue of Chen Zai, Yixun would take the same stand as Wu did.

She was right.

And Yixun was even firmer than Wu was.

He simply told Tiao, "I object to your continuing to carry on a relationship with Chen Zai."

"We're serious about each other. He's getting a divorce."

"What do you mean, 'getting a divorce'? You're not young any-more. Why are you still so naïve?"

"Dad, you sound like Chen Zai is deceiving me. He and I have known each other for many years, and you've known him for many years, too. Clearly you know him very well. Why would you still say things that are so unfair to him?"

"Yes, I do know him well, but I'm not bewitched by him like you."

"He didn't bewitch me; I'm no longer a child."

"That's why you're pathetic: because you don't know you're bewitched by him. Of course you are, and he has the accomplishments to bewitch you: a successful career and reputation, the design of some buildings on both provincial and national levels, money and family, extra time and energy to devote to you. But in my opinion, there's nothing special about people like him; he just showed up during good times. His smooth sailing was paid for by the sacrifices the previous generation made in the political movements that came, one after another. Has he been to a place like Reed River Farm? No. I was pulling loads of bricks on the farm at his age. Where were my designs and my work at the time? I was only worthy of driving a horse cart and pulling loads of bricks over and over again. There were always pits and hollows lying before us, and we jumped in to fill them, to smooth the roads with our labor for these Chen Zais. In my opinion, his designs are not always successful. For instance, he designed Fuan Publishing House, which I don't think is that good."

Tiao immediately interrupted Yixun and said, "I think it's very good. The Publishing House is one of my favorites among Chen Zai's designs. A place like Fuan needs architecture like this, simple from materials to design but with its own character."

Yixun said emotionally, "Never mind its own character. It's okay to use the gray fire-clay bricks for the lower part of the building, but why did he have to strain after novelty by using Brazilian hardwood for the upper part? Did he take into consideration that using wood to decorate buildings wasn't suitable for Fuan's dry climate? The Publishing House accepted the design because they got money. Is this what you think is 'its own character'?"

"I'm very surprised at how upset you get as soon as we talk about Chen Zai's designs."

"Am I upset? I'm just expressing my opinion. Just because Chen Zai designed the Publishing House, can I not even give my opinion of it?"

"Of course you can. You can simply say his designs are worthless, seeing as you take so much pleasure in putting down Chen Zai's works."

"Who's upset now? Honestly, I can't bear to see how crazy you are about Chen Zai. He's far from becoming a master. Even if I weren't coming from an expert's perspective, even if I were just a casual observer of architecture, I would still have the right to express myself."

Tiao stared at her agitated father as though she had never known him. His almost out-of-control look, and the caustic comments he had made about Chen Zai's work, made him seem pathetic, a member of a pathetic generation. This was something she hadn't felt until a moment ago. She suddenly wanted to ease the tension, to comfort her pathetic father. She said, "Dad, I wasn't right a moment ago. Some of Chen Zai's work has left people with regrets—"

Yixun raised his voice to interrupt Tiao. "It's more than regrets. Some of his work is intolerable. Take Yunxiang Square in the downtown area, for instance; it looks exactly like a cannonball with half of it sliced away. The incline looks like a flat face. A flat face on a cannonball is ugliness beyond words, unrivaled ugliness."

Tiao held back her temper and said, "When I said there was some 'regret,' I didn't mean Yunxiang Square. Yunxiang Square is his prize-winning work."

"I knew you would defend him, and your admission that you were not right was completely insincere. What's the big deal about prize-winning designs? The work that wins a prize isn't necessarily excellent work; excellent work often doesn't win a prize."

Tiao felt there was no way to ease the tension between them and that it was impossible to calm her father down, so she just allowed herself to get angry again. She said, "Dad, you're right. Is what you are trying to say that while your designs didn't win any prizes, they're excellent? And also that even though you can't compete with people like Chen Zai, that doesn't mean you're not as good as they are? I think I know what you mean. I get it."

Yixun said, "You're ridiculing me. You're ridiculing your father for the sake of a man whom you're not even sure will marry you."

"I know he'll marry me."

"I know he won't marry you."

"Why?"

"Because I'm also a man, and do you know how often I think about divorce?"

"Then why don't you do it? Maybe because there is not another person in your life that you love."

"Maybe yes. Maybe no."

"Then you can't prevent others from pursuing their happiness just because of this maybe yes or no."

Yixun suddenly raised his voice, stood up, and paced back and forth in his study. "What do you mean by that? What do you mean by that?"

Tiao said, "I hadn't planned to say it, but you force me. I mean you are jealous, anxious, and unbalanced. You don't want to be faced with young people's achievements, nor do you want to face up to the trouble in your own life. You . . . you're even afraid to admit you've been deceived and injured. You think you can maintain your image as a strong man this way? Did you think you could forget everything in the past? No, you haven't forgotten anything, and you're not strong, either. A strong man wouldn't get so emotional or angry as easily as you. You can't even channel your emotion and your anger into your career. You claim that the times have caused you to waste the most productive years of your life and that you no longer have the chance to study in England or other countries. Well, time is merciless, but then you should have the courage to admit the cruelty of time instead of dumping all your bitterness on the innocent Chen Zai. Do you know how I felt when you tried so hard to diminish Chen Zai a moment ago? I wasn't angry; I just felt sad. I felt sad for you. As I said, I'm no longer a child. I'm an adult. I feel I understand your suffering. For many, many years I've understood. I was often tempted to say it out loud for you, but your expression and attitude stopped me, which made it clear to me that you were well aware that I knew. You were terrified by my knowing and dreaded that I would speak out of my knowledge, as if you would lose your dignity as a man and a father that way. Why couldn't you have tried to think of things differently—because your suffering is also my suffering? As your daughter, I did a terrible and stupid thing to eliminate my family's suffering. You can't possibly know what it is and I will never tell you."

Yixun stepped in front of Tiao and said, "Are you finished?"

"Yes, I'm finished."

"Get out of my room."

Chapter 9

⁂ ⁂ ⁂

Crowned with Persian
Chrysanthemums

1

Three years later.

It was the night Chen Zai went on a business trip to the south that Tiao read Fang Jing's sixty-eight love letters. The night deepened, and she felt tired. The love letters were scattered all over the bed and the floor and she felt she couldn't put them back in order at the moment, so she let them stay a mess and slipped into her quilt nest to sleep.

In the dream, she senses someone opening the door with a key and then entering her bedroom. It is Chen Zai. Only Chen Zai has the key to her place. She doesn't need to open her eyes—with Chen Zai walking into her house she never needs to open her eyes. Half asleep, she listens to the sounds he makes in her room, very softly, careful not to wake her. Next she hears the water from the bathroom, the clean smell of his body and the fresh fragrance of bath lotion slowly assailing her. He steps on the scattered love letters and lifts her quilt. He leans over her and kisses the tip of her nose gently, and then he slips into the quilt nest and holds her warm body tightly. He tries to awaken her. "My little sweet gum candy, I'm back. My little sweet gum candy, I'm back." The endearment is a favorite of his. Still asleep, she pillows her head on his shoulder, thinking, why hadn't she tidied up those love letters before he came back? Will he find them at daybreak? She feels reluctant to let him see the love letters on the bed and floor, but, at the same time, she wants him to read them. She doesn't know what is wrong with her. Perhaps her vanity has come to pay her a visit again? It isn't good timing, and it is also wrong. She longs for Chen Zai, the man who is going to marry her, to read another man's love letters to her, so he will know how she deserves his love just because she had been loved so deeply by another man. How insecure she is! About to get married, she turns to old love letters for help. She feels tickling at her ears. Chen Zai is licking them. He finally wakens her and turns her over to lie on her body. Their movements shake the letters from the bed to the floor with a rustling sound, but Chen Zai sees and hears nothing. He is always so passionate and intent when making love to Tiao; his single-minded devotion to please and satisfy her is precious to her. It is truly devotion, the richest form of nurture a man can provide a woman. He nurtures her with his devotion and strength, such strength that she feels he is going to melt her. And there is a wild, uncontrollable spasm deep in her body, which carries on into her waking. She sighs, and feels embarrassed about this sensation that she'd never had before in sleep.

Everything in the dream made her miss Chen Zai more. Gazing at the translucent curtain lit by the morning rays of sunlight, she decided to burn all the love letters scattered on the bed and the floor. Even though, with Chen Zai's temperament, he wouldn't have been troubled if she'd kept them, she just wanted to burn them and concentrate on the life of love she would have with Chen Zai. She got up, brushed her teeth, ate breakfast, and then started the burning. She gathered all the love letters in a stainless steel washbasin, took it to the kitchen, and struck a match to light them, using chopsticks to turn the flaming pages over so they could burn more completely. It felt like a method of cooking, something related to food. Her meticulous and thorough hand movements didn't seem like destruction but creation. Maybe she was even aware herself that she was indeed making something with the burning. Otherwise, why would she have chosen to use kitchen utensils? Finally only a thin pile of ashes remained in the basin, very light, almost weightless. She collected the ashes into a juice glass and then poured water into it, which turned black. This glass of black water contained all the words that Fang Jing had written to her. Those pages of small, elegant characters he had written with black ink, his frenzied love for her, were all dissolved in this glass of black water. She had the desire to drink it, to give those black words a chance to survive or die in her body. So she drank, first a small sip, and then a big swallow. In the end, she drank it all, this glass of black water.

She left the kitchen and came to the living room, sitting where she usually did, in the armchair she liked. She didn't feel any discomfort in her stomach or intestine, and she was confident that her mood was stable. She wanted to call home and tell Yixun and Wu that Chen Zai was divorced. Hadn't they said three years ago that it would be impossible for him to get a divorce? Hadn't they called Tiao naïve, and didn't Yixun tell her to "get out"? Now he was divorced, actually divorced. She wanted to call her parents to gloat, with a victor's smugness, but also intending to relieve their worries. Ever since Yixun told Tiao to "get out," she went home only on holidays. But just then the phone rang. She answered, and it was Fan.

Lately, the main topic of their phone conversations was Wu's plastic surgeries. When Tiao described over the phone, with indignation, how Wu had nose and eyelid surgeries, she thought Fan would be more annoyed than she was. But quite surprisingly, Fan just paused for a second and then laughed until she gasped for breath. "That's hilarious. That's so hilarious. Well, won't I have a new mother this way?" And she laughed again. Her laughter contained neither anger nor approval; in it, there was an observer's detachment that allowed for watching others make fools of themselves, and Tiao's indignation made her laugh even harder. She truly looked forward to seeing people in China make fools of themselves, and was also curious to see Wu's new face. When Tiao refused to send her Wu's post-surgery photographs, she simply called Wu for them. Her request for pictures encouraged Wu to plan more surgeries. No longer shy about it, Wu openly talked with Fan over the phone about her vision of face-lifts and liposuction. Wu and Fan, the mother and daughter, had grown close because of Wu's plastic surgeries, which made Tiao remark acidly during one of their phone conversations, "Fan, you've given Mom plenty of spiritual support. But when she went to do her abdominal liposuction, I was the one who took her to the hospital and then picked her up afterward. Are you aware that this kind of surgery is dangerous? Why don't you come home and visit her?"

Fan said, "Next time. When she does her breast augmentation, I'll come back." Tiao just wanted to slam down the phone when she was listening to her sister.

But Fan's phone call this time was not to discuss Wu's plastic surgery. She said, "Older sister, guess who came to Chicago. Fang Jing."

"Really? Do you want me to get you an introduction to him?"

"No need. I've met him. When he was giving a lecture at the University of Chicago, I was his interpreter."

"Really?"

"I told him that I was your sister. He said he would have guessed even if I hadn't told him."

"Is that so?"

"Then he invited me to dinner. When I was with him, he didn't mention you at all. He kept praising my English."

"Really?"

"Later, I drove him to the art museum. He likes Marc Chagall's paintings. He likes this Jewish guy."

"Really?"

"Why do you keep saying 'really'? Don't you want to know what I think of him?"

"No, I don't want to know."

"But I want to tell you. He called me every day, so one time I spent the night at his place."

"Really?"

"I'd say he's a nice-enough guy, but unfortunately I don't love him. He's naïve, and after he told me that two of his teeth were rotting, I lost interest in him entirely. But just a few moments ago, right before I called you, he phoned."

"Really?"

"So, what do you think about it?"

Tiao took a deep breath and said with great deliberateness, "Fan, I wanted to tell you that Chen Zai is divorced."

"Really?"

"I think you should be happy for me."

"Of course, I . . . am happy for you."

Tiao put down the telephone and stood up to stretch. The black water was circulating through her body, and the words that Fang Jing had written filled her insides. Her body was filled with a long-vanished true love. There was no hatred in her heart, only her hope for the future.

On the same day, at the publishing house, a woman she'd never met arrived at her office to see her. The woman introduced herself. "My name is Wan Meicheng. I'm Chen Zai's ex-wife."

2

Tiao was rattled at Wan Meicheng's unexpected appearance at her office. She wasn't afraid that Wan Meicheng had come to attack her, though; it was not the first time that Tiao had come between a married couple. She was determined to marry Chen Zai openly. No, she wasn't afraid of Wan Meicheng; she was simply a little nervous, with mixed feelings of guilt and sympathy.

She led Wan Meicheng to the sofa near the door and sat across from her. She didn't stare at Wan Meicheng but carefully took her in. Chen Zai had mentioned that Wan Meicheng was ten years younger than he was, which meant she was five years younger than Tiao, so about thirty-three years old, but she looked even younger than that. She was gentle and delicate, but her forehead was full, with shiny hair all combed back and secured with a red-wood hairpin. She had light eyebrows, and her large eyes with their frank gaze seemed to conceal no ill intentions. Her makeup and clothing were tasteful. Tiao remembered that Chen Zai had said she was an art teacher in a high school, and she looked exactly like an art teacher: honest, responsible, but also with an underlying romanticism that she restrained. She took out a pack of cigarettes and asked Tiao, "Can I smoke here?"

"Technically speaking, no. I don't even have an ashtray."

Suddenly she seemed disoriented and said, "Well, I mean, I never smoke at school or in front of the students. It's just I'm here with you . . . and we're meeting for the first time and I'm very nervous. I'm thinking that smoking might help a little. But still I shouldn't smoke, I know."

Wan Meicheng's admitting to Tiao that she was nervous made Tiao feel she was more honest than she was herself. Tiao picked up a paper cup, half filled it with water, and placed it in front of Wan Meicheng. She said, "You can flick the ash into the water. It's informal, but practical."

Wan Meicheng said "Okay," lit a cigarette, and started to smoke. The way she lit the cigarette, smoked, and flicked the ash was hesitant and ungraceful. Apparently she was a novice smoker, and her technique suggested that she hadn't learned it long ago at all, very likely after her divorce from Chen Zai. Smoking makes a woman look sophisticated and worldly, but Wan Meicheng's awkward smoking was reminiscent of a teenager learning to be bad behind her parents' backs. Tiao had no reason to dislike Chen Zai's ex-wife, but what exactly had brought her here?

Wan Meicheng said, "Tiao, you must be wondering why I came to see you. I want to tell you that there's nothing I want from my visit. If I'd wanted anything, I would have come to you before the divorce, and I would have begged you to let go of Chen Zai and return him to me, which I did think about doing from time to time these past years. Now, with everything over, Chen Zai and I already divorced, and you two about to get married, why would I want to come to see you now? What's my purpose in coming? You might not believe me if I told you that I was desperately asking myself that same question on my way here. And it occurred to me that it was because I still love Chen Zai so much. I so yearn to get near him that I even yearn to get close to the one dearest to him. That you're his dearest is a fact that I learned long ago. Your breath has his breath in it, your eyes have his gaze, and your skin has the warmth of his body. When I pushed open the door and entered your office, when I first caught sight of you and came closer, I saw and smelled him, his body. That's exactly why I came. I want to sit with you for a moment, just a moment. I didn't come here to fight with you, or to accuse you. I've thought thousands of times that our marriage was wrong from the beginning. He married me because he was pursued by me so much that he had no way out. Today I want to tell you honestly that he should have been yours to begin with. But none of it can stop me from loving him. He left the house to me after the divorce, and I haven't seen him for a while. I know he's away in the south, so I especially wanted to take the chance to see you. Only when I'm with you do I feel close to him, and safe. Safe, you understand? You make me feel safe."

Tiao hadn't expected anything like that out of Wan Meicheng, and the special feeling she described was something that Tiao had never heard of, either. She stared at this woman who was smoking clumsily, and couldn't help thinking of how she had ruined Wan Meicheng and Chen Zai's marriage; as a result, Tiao should, by rights, have been the least safe element in Wan's life. So she remained suspicious. Maybe Wan Meicheng was using mockery to attack her. Tiao would have preferred something more direct.

But Wan Meicheng didn't appear to be mocking. She smoked awkwardly but her expression was sincere. She threw the cigarette butt into the water in the paper cup, leaned forward slightly, and said, "One day after an afternoon nap, I sat in front of the window in a daze—I'm very good at that. Particularly in the last few years when Chen Zai tried to discuss divorce with me, I could sit for hours in a daze. That particular day I sat dazed and thought about my first meeting with Chen Zai. It was during a summer break, before I graduated from college. I returned to Fuan to work as a tutor for a factory director's child. That same day Chen Zai was involved in a car accident with me, which was actually my fault; I went through a red light—I was rushing to get to the factory director's home. I ran into Chen Zai's car and my body was thrown from the car. My knees and hands were scraped. Chen Zai was very worried and immediately drove me to the hospital. He took me to have the cuts and scrapes treated and then accompanied me to get a complete examination. He asked me whether my head had struck the ground and I said it was nothing, but he insisted that I go for an X-ray. After I finished the checkup, he drove me home, explained the situation to my parents, and left his phone number, beeper number, and cell phone number—back then, few people had cell phones. He left me all these numbers without any hesitation and told me that I should call him if something happened. He was a gentleman, a true gentleman, which was the only word I could think of when I was lying in bed. I didn't doubt that there were excellent men in the world, but I hadn't met one like him.

"The next day I called him and he picked up the phone, which proved he hadn't deceived me with a fake number. I felt a deep joy, and not only because he'd given me the real number. Over the phone, he asked me how I felt and offered to take me back to the hospital if I needed a ride. I told him that I did have the need, but it was really the need to see him that I had. Then he drove to my parents' home. We went to the hospital four times within a month and chatted in the car. When he learned that I'd majored in painting, he asked me if I liked the French painter Balthus, and I had no idea who he was. At the time, I hadn't seen Balthus's paintings yet, not even reproductions. Chen Zai didn't laugh at my ignorance, he was so considerate; to avoid embarrassing me, he quickly changed the subject. I was grateful for his sensitivity and kindness. By the time I recovered, I found myself in love with him. I returned to the school, as the summer break was over, and started to write him—I guess you could call them love letters. I also drew some cartoons, like you see in those girls' comics. They all had plots that showed how much I loved and missed him. I sent all these to him but never received any replies. Tiao, please note that he never wrote me back. Then winter break came and I couldn't wait to get back to Fuan. And the first thing that I wanted to do was to see him.

"We met. I told him very directly that I loved him. He smiled his apology at me and said I was still a student and he was much older than I was. He hoped I could consider my life and future seriously.

I said, 'I'm very serious. I don't mind the ten years' difference in age as long as you're not in love with someone else.' Given his age then, he should have married a long time ago. He didn't reply even though I kept pressing him. I said, 'If you don't respond, it must mean there is another woman in your heart, right? Am I right?'

"'Yes, I've loved her for many years.'

"'Then why don't you get married?' I asked. He became quiet again. I was pretty emotional and again insisted he tell me why. Finally he told me that he wasn't sure whether the one he loved was in love with him or not. His words made me feel hopeful and I said something very silly: 'But you know I'm in love with you.' He looked at me helplessly, such a deep helplessness. I realized how unreasonable I was being and at the same time became bolder. I told him I must have him, and that I could compete with the woman he loved. Then I asked him what he thought of that, and he said it was pointless. Love shouldn't be a competition. I said I would compete because I wanted to win love, and he said, 'You'll only win suffering that way.' I knew he had already turned me down. His way of expressing it might have been indirect, but he left no room for doubt.

"That night I ran a high fever, nearly forty degrees, which made me talk deliriously. The fever stayed high for two days and I had to be sent to the hospital. There was no inflammation in my body and the doctor couldn't find what was wrong with me. I couldn't eat anything. I couldn't even keep water down. My body temperature kept rising to more than forty degrees, and half the time I was raving his name. My parents called him, and he came to the hospital to see me. He sat by the bed and held my burning-hot hand, and the strange flush on my cheeks touched him. He told me to listen to the doctor and get myself well first. We could talk after I got better. His words revived my despairing heart, the best fever reducer for me. My illness miraculously disappeared, which to this day I still can't explain, just as I don't know why I got sick without any apparent reason. I knew I had been really sick, but I think I'd been lovesick, love-crazed. With all my heart, I leaped into that fire. After I left the hospital I didn't get to see him. He went abroad, and I had to go back to school.

"There was one semester left before my graduation and I could hardly wait for him to come back from abroad. When he returned a month later, in desperation I asked for a leave from school and went to Fuan to see him. I came to his place, his apartment. It was evening, a spring evening. I completely lost control of my emotions and cried my heart out in his room. The intrusion must have made him very uncomfortable, and I can see now how I made his life unbearable. He wiped my face with a hot towel and kept offering to take me home. What an awkward situation it was for a decent man. What did I hope to achieve? I said I was willing to do anything for him. I cried and said, 'I love you, Chen Zai. I love only you. Marry me. You're the only one in the world I would want to be with.'

"He kept saying, 'Let me think it over. Let me think it over carefully. But it's too late tonight. You should go home.' He helped me on with my coat and drove me home. As soon as his car left I ran back to his place. I stood downstairs and gazed at the light in his window, and then I leaned against his door. I wanted to get close to him this way, to express my loyalty to him. I was like the old cat my family had years ago. He was so old that he could hardly walk anymore. And we didn't want to see him die at home. One day my father took him on his bicycle and rode a long way, leaving him on a tractor parked on the side of the road. But two days later, when my father opened the door to go to work, he saw the old cat curled up there waiting for us to open the door. He'd found his way home by himself. I sat at Chen Zai's doorway like that cat, hoping I would move him the way the old cat moved our whole family. I sat in front of Chen Zai's apartment for an entire night until he found me next morning when he was leaving. I'd fallen asleep by then. He carried me into his apartment and put me on his bed. He held my cold hands in his hands and said, 'Why do you have to be like this?'

"I couldn't take it anymore and kissed him desperately. He began to kiss me back. That day he didn't go to work. He stayed home all day to keep me company. He was so gentle to me, and he cried on the wedding night. He howled. Do you know, Tiao, I'd never seen a man weep like that. I was awestruck by it, caught midway between joy and panic. I knew he was crying for you, and his crying made me feel at the very moment I had him, I'd also lost him forever.

"At the very moment I had him, I also lost him forever."

Wan Meicheng was finished talking, or maybe she just stopped temporarily. "Would you like some water?" Tiao asked.

Wan Meicheng shook her head and said, "You're crying, but I don't want your tears. I don't know why I would say these things—this isn't what I wanted most to say today."

"I think I could listen to you all day."

"I wouldn't want to disrupt your work in the office. If you like, we can make an appointment to meet. I'll get your phone number and you can take mine."

"Yes, you get my number and give me yours, too."

3

They began meeting when Chen Zai was not in Fuan. The first time it was Wan Meicheng who called, and Tiao played a passive role. She felt she should, that she couldn't initiate anything with Wan Meicheng, who was the "victim," although Tiao already felt so curious about her.

They met at Yunxiang Square. First they talked about the square that Yixun had described as representing unrivaled ugliness, and both actually liked Chen Zai's "flat-face" building very much. Then they went to the café in the "flat face." Tiao ordered a cup of La Taza coffee and Wan Meicheng a cup of Irish coffee. Wan Meicheng sipped the coffee and said, "I'd never drunk coffee before I married Chen Zai. My stomach would hurt as soon as I drank it. But because Chen Zai liked it, I felt obliged to drink it as well. Sometimes he worked very late, and I would stay up and keep him company by drinking coffee with him. He didn't notice at all that I didn't like coffee. I forced myself to put up with the pain so he wouldn't find out. I was so afraid that he didn't like me and I wanted to mold myself to him in everything. Strangely, I actually got used to coffee and my stomach stopped hurting, which gave me some confidence. I came to believe that as long as I was determined to learn something, I would succeed, just as I learned from you."

"Learned from me?"

"Yes, learned from you. Imitated you."

"Imitated me?"

"Chen Zai never told me who the woman he loved was, but I instinctively knew it was you. The first time I saw you was when you went to Chen Zai's parents' place. I remember clearly it was a Sunday. We originally planned to go together, but something came up and Chen Zai couldn't travel along with me, so I went ahead by myself first. Whenever I went to Chen Zai's parents' home, I liked to stand on their balcony for a while, from where I could see the small garden in the Architectural Design Academy. My deep secret was that I hoped to see you from there. I knew you and Chen Zai had lived in the same compound and your parents still lived in the Architectural Design Academy. Did you go home to visit your parents? I so looked forward to seeing you—the one I most feared. I imagined what you looked like thousands of times, sometimes as very ugly, and other times as very beautiful. Then that Sunday I stood on the balcony to look into the small garden, wondering if there were any stories of you and Chen Zai that took place there. It was a very simple garden with a London plane tree, a green fence, grass, and some hardy rosebushes. Unlike the flowers and grass in a park, these weren't purposely set there to try to attract the attention of visitors. I stood on the balcony and imagined that you would walk out of there. Then I saw Chen Zai's car. He parked in front of the building, got out, and ran around to open the door. In the blink of an eye, I hid myself behind the large, wide cinnamon tree on the balcony. Just in that split second I had a feeling that he was opening the door for you. Sure enough, you got out of the car. The two of you stood by the car and talked for a while, and then you walked farther into the compound along the small road. Chen Zai's mother heard the car and also came to the balcony. I asked her who the person was that had just been talking to Chen Zai. She said, 'That is Tiao, Yin Xiaotiao. Her family lives in the same compound as we do.'

"Sure enough, that woman was you, Tiao. For a long time the name 'Tiao' had frightened me, made me feel uncomfortable and tense. When you first appeared that Sunday, I felt a pang of emptiness and unease. From my momentary glimpse of you, as I hid behind the cinnamon tree, I remember your hairstyle, clothes, and shoes. I had imagined you as someone very avant-garde, with short hair like a boy's. But you wore your hair gathered up and used a hairpin to fix it into a tidy ponytail, casual and unusual. Your smooth forehead and graceful walk also left a deep impression on me, making me both envious and ill at ease. I even remembered you held a light, soft straw hat in your hand, decorated with a linen ribbon that had Persian chrysanthemum patterns. Ah, crowned with Persian chrysanthemums, I thought. I had no idea why such a poetic description would pop into my mind just when I was at my lowest: crowned with Persian chrysanthemums.

"Anyway, you were crowned with Persian chrysanthemums. Do you remember having that straw hat?" Wan Meicheng said, and scooted the chair under her bottom so she could be closer to Tiao. Tiao could see her nostrils flaring, which made her seem like some harmless small creature with a keen sense of smell. She was sniffing Tiao, or maybe she wasn't sniffing Tiao but trying to sniff out Chen Zai through Tiao. She was driven to get close to Tiao, and the closer she was to her, the closer she was to Chen Zai. Maybe her nostrils were not flaring, and it was just Tiao's imagination. Still, she believed Wan Meicheng's eagerness to be around her was because of her yearning to be around Chen Zai, exactly as she'd said at their first meeting. It made Tiao feel a little insecure, and yet she was also drawn to Wan Meicheng. Wan Meicheng hadn't come to condemn her and provoke her; their meeting felt more like a heart-to-heart talk, with frankness and compliments enhancing each other. Wan Meicheng was either very sincere or very crafty, but one thing Tiao was sure of was that she wasn't threatening. What had she asked her? Oh, she'd asked if Tiao remembered that she used to have a straw hat.

Tiao said, "I did have a straw hat like that. Linen ribbon printed with Persian chrysanthemums. I don't know if you like Persian chrysanthemums, but I do. The first time I saw some was at the Martyrs' Cemetery at Fuan when I was still in elementary school. On Tomb-Sweeping Day each year, our school would organize us to sweep the Martyrs' Cemetery. We carried homemade wreaths, walked a long way, breathing the dust all the way to the Martyrs' Cemetery located in the outskirts of the city, and dedicated the wreaths to the martyrs. Then we would listen to the guide talk about the heroic deeds of those martyrs in the tombs.

"I remember once a young woman guide took us to a white marble tomb where a heroine of the war against Japan was buried. Betrayed by a collaborator, she was captured by the Japanese. They scooped out her breasts, and, to stop her angry curses, cut out her tongue as well. The guide was very young and looked almost like a middle school student. To this day I still remember how round her face was, and that round face didn't match the somber atmosphere there. She started her introduction. 'Students . . .' she said. 'Students . . .' she said again, and then she began to laugh. It was shocking that she could laugh on such a solemn occasion. She laughed very hard, the kind of laughter that sounded almost like crying, her voice getting higher and higher and her shoulders shaking. She couldn't control herself. Neither my classmates nor I laughed, and our teachers didn't, either. We had been taught long before that laughter was forbidden in the Martyrs' Cemetery. We were all very disciplined in this regard, and some in the class would even arrange their sad expressions in advance. Everyone was frightened by her laughter, seized by a feeling of impending disaster. Our teacher found the director of the cemetery, who took the guide, still in the grip of hysterical laughter, away.

"Later, we heard from our teacher that the guide had been charged with antirevolutionary activity and sentenced to prison. How dare she laugh in front of the martyr's tomb? When I thought back on the incident as an adult, I supposed her mind must have been in a highly nervous state. She must have taken her job so seriously and wanted to do it so well that she began to laugh right at the most inappropriate moment. Just as in school: The more we told ourselves not to make mistakes in our presentations, the more likely it was that we would say something wrong. We were afraid we might even shout out anti-revolutionary slogans at critical moments. Another guide, an old man, took over. Standing at the heroine's tomb, we listened to the touching story of the martyr. It was at that moment I noticed several Persian chrysanthemums in front of the tomb, but they were not real, since they don't bloom in April. Who dedicated these flowers to the war heroine, and why choose Persian chrysanthemums? Was it because the martyr had liked the flower when she was alive? I liked them, too, with their long stems and simple petals. Later, when I saw real Persian chrysanthemums on some old obscure graves in the west mountain area of Fuan, I also liked their frail but independent posture. I thought about the heroine in the Martyrs' Cemetery, whom I always confused with the girl guide with the round face. Because the two were mixed up in my mind, sometimes I would imagine that the round-faced guide was the war heroine who had leaped out of the tomb, leaped out and laughed, with slender Persian chrysanthemums growing on her head. I liked the straw hat I used to have. Do you know what it felt like when you wore it? I felt I was gliding over the ground like someone from the tomb, soundless, invisible to people except for the fully blooming Persian chrysanthemums. You said it so well, crowned with Persian chrysanthemums. Tell me, doesn't every one of us have a day when we are crowned with Persian chrysanthemums? When we are crowned with Persian chrysanthemums, do we still merely walk? What do you think?"

Wan Meicheng listened to Tiao talk about Persian chrysanthemums with fascination. It was the first time that Tiao had spoken about herself and her childhood, which Wan Meicheng took as a friendly gesture. She didn't mean to express hostility to Tiao in any way. When crowned with Persian chrysanthemums, did we still merely walk? Wan Meicheng didn't know and had never thought about it. She said, "I don't know, but on that Sunday, when I saw you were crowned with Persian chrysanthemums, I was determined to buy the same straw hat.

"Chen Zai came upstairs and I returned to the room from the balcony. I said nothing about you, and neither did he. We drove home in the evening and I sat in the place where you had sat. Your breath and scent still seemed to linger in the air. I simply closed my eyes and said nothing. Chen Zai asked me if I was ill and I said no. We got home, took a shower, went to bed, and made love. He was very aggressive, unusually aggressive. Everything seemed different from before, and I even started to imagine he was about to give me a child. Please give me a child. Oh, please let me conceive a child! I tried especially hard to please him to get him to do what I wanted. Both of us said embarrassing things that we normally wouldn't say. When I got very excited and was about to come, he suddenly called, 'Tiao, Tiao—'"

Tiao interrupted Wan Meicheng and said, "Please don't go on."

Wan Meicheng said, "Don't interrupt me. I have to get this out. He called out 'Tiao, Tiao,' which saddened me to the point of desperation. But do you know what? I murmured back to him anyway. It wasn't that I was utterly without pride; I still had the delusion that if he really thought I was you at that moment, maybe he would let me have his child . . . But I failed again. He realized his slip of the tongue and was embarrassed about it. My biggest achievement that night was that I confirmed you were the lover in his heart, you, crowned with Persian chrysanthemums.

"I sat in front of the mirror and looked at my face; I pulled the bangs off my forehead and to the back. I wanted to change my hairstyle. I wanted to cut my shoulder-length hair and expose the nape of my neck. Tiao, you were my archenemy, but how I wanted to become you. One day I put on the same kind of straw hat, the exact same skirt you had worn on that Sunday, and sat in the room waiting for Chen Zai to come home. He was truly stunned when he came back, and then said, 'What is this all about?' That's what I wanted to tell you, Tiao. I'm a complete failure. How is it possible for me to really become you? You ruined my life, after all. But I want you to know that I don't hate you now, because I love Chen Zai, and if I love him,

I should love whom he loves—which is a very difficult task. But if I can do it, then I'm a winner. I am trying to get close to you. Please let me."

Chen Zai's return interrupted their meetings. Excitedly, he told Tiao that he had ordered a set of Swedish kitchen appliances, very practical, the dishwasher came with a garbage disposal, and Tiao was going to love it. He kissed her and asked how things were at home and was there any news? Tiao said everything was fine and nothing had happened. She twined her arms around Chen Zai's neck and draped herself against his body, listening, mesmerized, to his quickening breath, and she concealed her meetings with Wan Meicheng.

She found indescribable excitement in her secret. She was not sure what to do yet, but Wan Meicheng's unexpected frankness and sincerity attracted her.

That summer, Tiao called Wan Meicheng behind Chen Zai's back. This time she initiated the appointment. She invited Wan Meicheng to meet at Youyou's Small Stir-Fry so that she could treat her to a meal there. She didn't know whether she wanted to use the occasion to seduce Wan Meicheng into more talk about her past with Chen Zai, to show her sincere gratitude to Wan Meicheng for her openness, or to hope that everything would stop right there. Even though neither had any ill intentions, there seemed to be the threat of turmoil beneath the surface.

Wan Meicheng came to Youyou's Small Stir-Fry as they agreed, and Tiao watched her as she crossed the street. She wore the straw hat with Persian chrysanthemums and had on a white skirt like the one Tiao used to have. All this made Tiao feel as if she had another self. Didn't Wan Meicheng and she look a little like each other? She remembered reading somewhere that if a man had been married twice, his two wives, no matter how different from each other they looked, must have some similarities that ordinary people couldn't discern.

In what way did they resemble each other? Could it have something to do with the silent, scentless Persian chrysanthemums?

4

"How are you going to drink the liquor, cups or glasses?" Tiao asked Wan Meicheng.

"How do you want to drink it?" Wan Meicheng asked.

Youyou brought them a bottle of Five Grain Liquor and Wan Meicheng said, "Good, Five Grain Liquor is perfect. Out of all the kinds of liquor, Chen Zai drinks only Five Grain, right, Tiao?" She looked at Tiao, and her nostrils started to flare again.

Tiao said nothing, but she agreed silently. Chen Zai just loved to drink Five Grain Liquor and had almost succeeded in teaching her to like it, too. But she didn't want to start their discussion with this subject. Two women talking about the habits of the man who had been intimate with both embarrassed Tiao, and she worried that it might be painful to Wan Meicheng.

Wan Meicheng said, "We can drink out of a teacup, or the rice bowls. I remember, in a movie that had a farewell scene for a hero, they all used rice bowls for liquor. No one used those little wineglasses."

Youyou said, "Teacher Wan, we aren't heroes and none of us can hold our liquor very well. Let's not use rice bowls." Youyou's daughter was a student at Wan Meicheng's school, so Youyou addressed her as Teacher Wan.

Wan Meicheng said, "No, we're not heroes, we're . . . heroines, not to mention the fact that I'm really leaving, off to the wars. Youyou, bring out your bowls, pour us the liquor."

Youyou took out three rice bowls and poured the bottle into the three bowls, and the odor immediately assailed their noses.

Wan Meicheng raised her bowl first, playing the hostess, and said, "Cheers."

But Tiao and Youyou didn't move; they had both heard Wan Meicheng say that she was leaving. Tiao asked, "Where do you plan to go, Wan Meicheng?"

"I plan to quit my teaching job and go to Gabon. My uncle sells clothes in the capital, Libreville, and needs a helping hand. He wants me to come and I want to go, too."

Tiao said, "You mean you're going to leave China? I thought you were going off to another city on some personal errand."

"I didn't intend to mention it today. Why should I talk about myself? Tiao, what's your relationship with me? Unlike you and Youyou—you're friends—we have none. And Youyou, neither do we—I'm just your daughter's art teacher. It's nobody's business that I'm going to Gabon. I could just slip away quietly, but human beings all have their weaknesses. I want to be generous but I can't quite manage it. Tiao, the closer I've gotten to you, the more pain I've felt, but the more the pain, the more I've wanted to see you. You're the only bridge between Chen Zai and me. Are you afraid? Don't be, I'm going away, aren't I? I know I can't go on like this anymore. One day I read a book that asked what the most intact thing in the world was, and the answer was that nothing is more intact than a broken heart. Everyone says books lie, but I don't think so. When you're most desperate, one line in a book could be a straw to clutch when you're drowning, and even though it's just a straw, it's made me understand that I'm not that bad, but that I can't keep pestering you like this, Tiao. Come on, let's drink!"

Wan Meicheng picked up the bowl with both her hands and took a swig of Five Grain Liquor. Then she put down the bowl and asked, "None of you want to drink? I'll drink by myself." She took another gulp.

Tiao and Youyou picked up their bowls and drank. Neither of them could say anything to Wan Meicheng's announcement. They could neither encourage her to leave nor convince her to stay. Tiao, particularly, felt that whatever she said to Wan Meicheng would seem cruel. No matter what she said, she'd just look like someone who was simply standing back to enjoy the commotion. As she kept drinking, she could only tell Wan Meicheng, "I never thought you were pestering me. Please don't say that."

Wan Meicheng sneered. "Tiao, this is where you're a hypocrite. Do you really like for me to be so close to you? When you heard that I was going to go as far as Gabon, you must have felt great relief deep in your soul. Only, the you on the surface still can't face your soul, so you feel guilty about me. You're not really sorry. It's just how you were brought up. Do you think my words make . . . any sense . . . sense . . . ."

Wan Meicheng was now blind drunk, reeling drunk, and she slumped to the table. Youyou called for a taxi and took her home with Tiao.

It was the first time that Tiao had entered Chen Zai's previous home, which was a mess, an embarrassing state caused by the mistress's neglect. They helped get Wan Meicheng into her bedroom and onto the bed. Tiao saw their large bed. Even though Chen Zai was long gone, two pillows still lay side by side. A crumpled bath towel was spread loosely over the right side of the bed, and the left side must have been reserved by Wan Meicheng out of habit. Man on the left side and woman on the right. Tiao knew Chen Zai preferred the left. It seemed Wan Meicheng would never sleep in the middle of the bed, even though Chen Zai was never going to come back. Now, even drunk, Wan Meicheng lay down on the right side of the bed. To look at this large bed that Wan Meicheng didn't want to be faced with made Tiao especially sad.

She and Youyou closed the door and went to the street. They stood in the summer evening breeze for a while and then walked together to the design academy. They hadn't walked side by side for a long, long time, and it felt like going back to old times, to their teenage years—on their shoulders, canvas backpacks with *Chairman Mao's Quotations* inside, which included the words, "Revolution is not inviting friends to dinner." It was when Youyou misquoted Chairman Mao that they'd gotten to know each other. At the time, inviting friends to dinner was their shared obsession. Farther and farther they kept walking into the design academy grounds. When they passed the awful manhole, they pretended not to see it. They finally entered the small garden and found a bench to sit down. Tiao said, "Youyou, I feel very sad."

Youyou said, "Is it because of Wan Meicheng?"

"Not exactly."

"When are you and Chen Zai going to get married?"

"Maybe in the fall, when he's finished the project he's been work-ing on."

"Of the three of us—Fei, you, and me—you've been the happiest."

"What do you think happiness is?"

Youyou said, "Happiness is when you feel happy."

Tiao smiled. This was the reason that she had liked Youyou all her life. Whether Youyou felt happy or not herself, she could always make Tiao feel happy and at ease. This was the most precious part of Tiao's life—her friends. This childhood friend of hers, Youyou, was always ready to help Tiao, and never judged her.

"Am I wrong?" Youyou asked.

"Someone said to me once, happiness is to be in your hometown, holding your sweetheart's hand, and eating your favorite food! By that measure, you're the happiest of us."

Youyou said, "I haven't read any books for a long time, but I think the lines that Wan Meicheng quoted were very true. It's human nature to pursue the intact, but the most intact thing in the world is nothing but a broken heart. Tiao, my heart has never been broken. I'm a pool of stagnant water. When we were little, when we set up our banquets at home, I believed the thing that would make me happiest was to become a chef. Now I own a restaurant, but I don't feel happy. Of course, I don't feel unhappy, either. That's what I meant by a pool of stagnant water."

A cool breeze blew and Tiao smelled the faint odor of grease smoke in Youyou's hair. She was not put off by the smell, because it was real, a reminder of the ordinary world.

As the wind stirred the leaves of the London plane tree, they both raised their heads simultaneously to look at it, perhaps thinking about the ring at the same time, too. Youyou said, "One year, Fei brought me here and asked me to help her get a ring that was in that tree. She said you threw the ring into the tree, and that it was a keepsake from

Fang Jing. But she was short of money at the time and wanted to get the ring and sell it. She took me to the tree and we did see the ruby ring caught in a branch. She said, 'Youyou, can you climb up and get the ring for me?' I said I was too fat, and Fei said, 'Maybe I can stand on your shoulders.' I said I was afraid it would hurt. Fei said, 'You don't really want to help me.' I asked, 'Do you really need the money?' Fei said, 'It's simple; if you feel you're short of money, then you need it.' In the end we didn't touch the ring in the tree. Tiao, are you thinking it's still there?"

"I'm thinking about something else."

"What is it?"

"There is nothing more broken in the world than an intact ring."

"Is that also from a book?"

"It's from me."

5

On Monday morning, Tiao walked into her office. The janitor had done the cleaning, so the desk, the chair, and the floor all looked very clean, and also the windowsill. The flowers had been watered, and the corn plant standing in the corner was growing vigorously. Tiao liked the corn plant very much, not because it was expensive—the plant might have been expensive when it first appeared in the north many years ago. Now it was commonplace, not expensive at all, which was precisely what Tiao liked about it. She saw the resemblance to a stalk of corn. When she felt tired of reading manuscripts and looked up from her desk to gaze at it across the room, she felt as if she were looking at a small piece of a cornfield, and that golden kernels were hidden under the fleshy leaves. Who said that the ripening corn was like little hands on the stalks? It must have been a poet. She didn't remember. She liked this sort of metaphor. Crops were more human than flowers or other plants.

She sat in front of her desk and started to open a stack of letters on the desk. There was a letter from Fang Jing:

Tiao, how have you been?

You must be very surprised at receiving this letter. I hesitated several times before I decided to write. Next Monday, I'll be at the premiere in Fuan of my new movie, Going Home Right Away. *The distributor there invited me. Will you be in Fuan then? We haven't seen each other for many many years, but I've never forgotten you. In Fuan, it's you I want to see, nothing else. I think if I go to your publishing house, it might be inconvenient for you. Would you mind coming to my hotel? I'll be staying at the Holiday Inn at Yunxiang Square, room 888. I pray to God that you receive this letter. I'll call you when I arrive.*

Tiao finished reading the letter and looked at the date and realized that the "next Monday" mentioned in the letter was actually that day.

Fang Jing's letter didn't cause too much emotional turbulence in Tiao. It just reminded her of the sixty-eight love letters that she had burned and drunk down. She didn't plan to burn this one or throw it in the trash can. There was no need. It was not a love letter, and she was no longer the Tiao who clutched the sleeve of Fang Jing's leather jacket and begged him to stay. She decided to go to Yunxiang Square to see him; she wanted him to see her as she was now, calm and confident.

She got Fang Jing's phone call before her lunch break. Because of the letter, she was emotionally ready, so she was fairly relaxed on the phone. He said, "Tiao, how are you?"

She said, "Yes, Professor Fang, I'm very well."

He paused briefly and then said, "Can we meet tonight? I'm fully scheduled for tomorrow."

"Sure, we can meet."

At eight p.m., she took a taxi to the Holiday Inn at Yunxiang Square, found room 888, and rang the bell. Fang Jing opened the door for her and there was gentle music in the room. She took the initiative to hold out her hand, as any polite guest who came to visit the host would do. But he didn't take her hand; instead, he opened his arms and suddenly embraced her. She immediately smelled the cigarettes on his body. Disgusted with his gesture, she turned her head and said quietly, "Please don't do this."

Her seriousness made him release her immediately. She rushed to the window, stood with her back to Fang Jing, and said, "Let me repeat it one more time. Please don't do this." He then came at her from behind and again tried to embrace her. She cringed at his sudden attack. She drew in her neck and bent her body, and her tone was very serious, "Let me go. Please let me go!"

He let her go.

He said with some emotion, "I don't know why I'd act like this as soon as I see you."

"I don't want you to."

"I'm sorry. I didn't think you would reject me. So, I see you still hate me."

"Not at all, Professor Fang, I don't hate you at all."

"I mean you don't love me anymore, right?"

"Yes, not at all."

They seated themselves on two small sofas near the window. He lit his pipe and said, "Yeah, I should have known. Do you think I really look old?"

She glanced at his cheeks, which seemed to have sunken, and at the gray hair on his temples, and said, "Yes, you do look a little old."

"Can you stop being so formal with me? Also, can you please not call me 'professor'?"

"I can't. I'm sorry."

He fiddled with the silver lighter in his hand and said, "Compared to Westerners, I look pretty young. Western women like Asian men very much. But to be honest with you, I can't stand them. Their skin is too rough. There's no real pleasure in touching or even looking at it closely. But the hotels abroad are pretty comfortable. You know, once I went to Spain and stayed in their royal hotel at Madrid. In my room, the sheets, coverlet, pillowcases, bath towels, and even the washcloths were all embroidered with my name. Tiao, do you understand this was the standard? An extremely high standard. There is also this lighter in my hand. Do you know who sent it to me? The queen of Denmark. Have you seen my movies in the last few years?"

She said, "I'm sorry, but I haven't had much of a chance."

"Yeah, I know that lately my movies in mainland China haven't been as influential as those made by the fifth or the sixth generation of directors, but there are people abroad who recognize my worth. Not long ago, the University of Chicago invited me to give a lecture. Over there I met your younger sister, Fan."

"I know. Fan told me about it on the phone."

"Then I don't need to go over anything, but I still want to explain. Whether you believe me or not, what happened with Fan in America was not just a fling. I seized her like I was trying to seize hope because there was some reflection of you in her."

She interrupted him. "Would you please change the subject? You probably don't know my current situation, do you?"

"I don't know and I don't need to know. Please don't tell me."

"All right, then let's talk about your new movie." She looked at Fang Jing smoking, and thought he was still a charming man who could attract women. But he was much less dashing than before. His bragging about how he was received abroad, and how the queen of Denmark sent him a lighter, actually suggested a comedown—not materially, but spiritually and psychologically. Apparently he wanted to pique her interest with this talk of "standard" and gifts; much farther down that road and he'd be making a living as a prostitute. Unfortunately for him, these things no longer impressed Tiao; she merely felt some sympathy about his need to boast. Yes, she felt sympathy for him, this man with whom she used to imagine spending her entire life. She wondered what made him look old. Certainly not his sunken cheeks or the gray at his temples, nor his slight stoop or the belly that was starting to show. What made him seem old was his eagerness to boast, which exposed his insecurity and weakness. The more insecure he felt, the more he bragged; the more he bragged, the more insecure he seemed. Tiao knew the man before her could no longer attract her; all she could give him was polite sympathy. Even though she encouraged him to speak about his new movie, nothing could change her feelings. Over the years she had watched only two of his movies, the same old stories about suffering, and the lectures, plus a little formula romance, which she didn't like. She didn't know what this new movie, *Going Home Right Away*, was about, so she asked him to tell her.

He said, "Right Away is a person, a migrant worker from the Henan countryside who works in Beijing. The movie tells the story of how he goes home during the Spring Festival. It's a very interesting story, it's . . . No, I shouldn't continue. I'm a little afraid to talk about art now around you. Are you coming to see the movie tomorrow? I hope you will, and I also hope . . ."

"What else do you hope?"

He put down the pipe and hugged himself with both arms. "Tiao, you're still not married, right?"

"Yes, I'm still not married."

"Well, I'm the same. I'm also not married."

She said, "Oh."

"Aren't you interested in my life anymore?"

"We all have our own lives."

"Don't you want to know why I'm single? My wife . . . she died, a brain tumor, a malignant brain tumor."

"I'm sorry. I didn't know."

He said, "Why do you think I came to Fuan? I made the trip almost entirely because of you. Tiao, if you're still unmarried, if you could . . . could recall everything between us before . . ."

"Professor Fang Jing, I'm not married yet, but I will be soon."

"Really? Who is he?"

"He's an architect. This Yunxiang Square where you're staying was his work."

He said, "Oh."

She glanced at her watch and said, "It's getting late. I should go. I have to work tomorrow, so I can't attend the premiere, but I'm sure it will be a great success. Please take care of yourself."

He stood up and stopped her at the door. He said, "I beg you to keep me company a little longer. If you think it's too late and it's inappropriate for us to stay in the room, how about going out? Can we go out to have something to eat?"

She smiled at him calmly. "Please let me by."

He moved aside to let her leave the room. Not quite in step, he walked her into the elevator and then down through the lobby. Knowing he would receive her polite but firm refusal if he continued, he stopped at the door of the hotel. He gazed at the back of her figure, so familiar to him but which he could no longer approach, and he remembered the first kiss she had given him, as light as a feather. Suddenly he wanted to return to Beijing right away, right then.

Sitting in the taxi and seeing Fang Jing's figure, which seemed a bit at a loss at the door of the lobby, Tiao's stomach started to gurgle. Those tiny black characters, long destroyed by her, seemed to emerge again, flowing around her body, inside her, and down her limbs. On her bare arms, the goose bumps seemed to be the bulges made by the letters. She confirmed to herself again that what she loved were the words, which would never disappear, not the person who wrote the words. Sympathy arose again in her heart and she wished Fang Jing's life would turn out happy.

She went home and Chen Zai was waiting for her in the light of the desk lamp.

He said, "I read the evening paper. Fang Jing is here."

"I just came back from Fang Jing's place."

"I knew you would tell me."

"Hold me, Chen Zai. Hold me."

He held her and kissed her eyebrows gently. "Try to be a little happier, a little happier."

She buried her head in his shoulder and said, "I'm happy. I'm very happy." But even then she couldn't explain to herself why there were so many undercurrents that wouldn't go away.

6

The experience of many women testifies to the power of shopping in relieving depression. Tiao didn't think she was depressed, but today she walked around the mall aimlessly. She intended vaguely to buy things for her wedding; she had already bought quite a bit on and off, but still felt as though she'd gotten nothing accomplished.

She went first to a small shop that sold light window curtains and saw many sample products from the Netherlands. Some were quite expensive, such as the pipe organ shade, wooden venetian blind, and a bamboo shade, but she liked them very much; others, like those metal blinds, didn't appeal to her. She was thinking that the soft-looking pipe organ screen might suit Chen Zai's study. As for the living room, she preferred a white shade, more classical and traditional, but peaceful. She'd always liked white shades.

After that, she went to the Fuan Famous Brand Department Store, which had opened recently. She took the elevator directly to the second floor to shop around in women's clothes. While she was there, an argument between two customers flared in the makeup section, maybe near the Christian Dior counter. The argument started small, but for some reason it got more and more heated. On one side were two young women with a child, and on the other side, the person who caused their anger and raised voices, was Tiao's mother, Wu.

Wu had been picking out mascara for herself, and the woman holding her child was also looking through the display in the case. The child in her arms was about two years old and growing increasingly impatient with his mother's meticulous browsing. He wriggled in her arms and kept hitting his mother, and as a side target, he hit Wu, who stood next to them. Wu didn't like the child next to her, and she expressed her feelings by staring at him, as if she were one child staring at another, and maybe this was the true flash point. As an adult, if Wu had reminded the mother that she should stop her child from hitting other people, what followed wouldn't have happened. However, stare she did, a sixty-year-old woman glaring at a two-year-old, which seemed immature and ridiculous. Even though the child's mother didn't notice Wu's rude stare, a seed of hatred had been planted in the child's heart. Children hold grudges. A two-year-old already has the ability to judge who's good to him and who isn't. This strange old woman next to him apparently was not friendly to him, so when she pressed against his pinkie accidentally with her elbow, the child suddenly started to cry.

The child pointed at Wu with an aggrieved expression through his tears. Although he couldn't describe to his mother Wu's stare of a moment before, he could let his mother know that the person who made him cry was this old woman beside him. It was this old woman who had bullied and violated him, in a manner impossible to bear! Shocked by her son's crying, the woman immediately seated the child on the counter with an air of entitlement and asked anxiously, "Sweetheart, sweetheart, what's wrong? Did someone hurt you? Tell Mom what happened." The child looked even more wronged. He kicked his little legs, pointed at Wu, and was choked with sobs. The woman glared at Wu and walked up to her. "What's the matter with you? Why did you make my child cry?"

"It wasn't me. I didn't make your child cry."

"Then why did he point at you? Why didn't he point at someone else?" The crying child pointed his little hand at Wu again and said through his sobs, "Hand . . . hand . . ."

Wu recalled that she might have accidentally knocked against the child's hand with her elbow a moment ago. She said to the woman, "I'm sorry. Maybe I accidentally hit your child's hand. I apologize."

As soon as the woman heard that this old woman had hit her child's hand, her anger flared. She first grabbed the child's hand, rubbed and blew on it, then blew on it and rubbed it again. She blew and rubbed it some more, and then grabbed Wu's sleeve and said, "Hmm, you hit my child's hand and didn't want to admit it at first. Why did you hit his hand? You've lived all these years and learned nothing. Don't you have eyes? What would you have done if you broke his hand? Not a single hair on his head has been touched since he was born, and now he has the misfortune to run into you. How could you treat a child this way? How could you? He's a baby, and what did he do to deserve being attacked by you?"

With her sleeve in the woman's grip, Wu was embarrassed. She was unprepared for an encounter with so difficult a woman. Yes, indeed, a very difficult woman, a horrid woman, with expensive but tasteless clothes, and at least two diamond rings on her hand. With her child such a treasure, the rest of the world was bound to become her enemy. Wu struggled to get free, but the woman grasped her even harder. Wu had never been good at fighting, and at this point she was more helpless and petrified than she'd ever been. How she had managed to get herself into such a fix was a mystery to her. She found it particularly unbearable to have her sleeve clutched by a total stranger. With a frustrated expression, she said, "What are you doing? What are you doing, pulling my sleeve?"

The woman turned even more fierce. She whirled back and forth from Wu to the customers who had started to gather. "Everyone listen: she bullies my child and then complains about me pulling her sleeve! So you know what an uncomfortable feeling it is to have your sleeve grabbed by someone? Did my child feel comfortable when you hit his hand? I've been talking for so long and you haven't even apologized. What else could you do if you've learned anything in all the years you've lived?"

Wu said, "What do you mean, I haven't apologized? Didn't I say I was sorry for being careless?"

"Did you say this to my child? Did you apologize to him?"

Wu said, "Why do you keep talking on and on like this? I've made it clear that I didn't do it on purpose and I was just picking my mascara. The saleswoman will tell you."

Suddenly a young woman next to the child's mother, with her hair dyed blonde and lips painted purple, cut in. She taunted Wu. "How old are you? Still painting your eyelashes with mascara? Look at the few you have left. What's there to show off? Why don't you go home and take a good look at yourself in the mirror? Come to the mall to give a two-year-old a hard time!"

Blond-Hair-and-Purple-Lips cutting in gave new energy to the child's mother. Judging by their looks, they seemed to be sisters. Blond-Hair-and-Purple-Lips was the child's aunt. They appeared to be people with money, the sort who got rich overnight and hadn't learned to conceal their essential vulgarity. They were eager to attract attention, to have people notice their money and the power

money conferred. Faced with an old woman like Wu, with her plod-
ding speech, what scruples would they have? So they couldn't stop.
The older sister chimed in with the younger, "Yeah, what strange
things happen these days. Whether the creature is human or not, it
always wants to dress itself up like a human being."

Wu was enraged. She shook the child's mother's hand from her
sleeve and said, "You've gone too far. Why are you insulting me?"

"Who's insulted you? Who?" the child's mother said.

"Both of you, together. Should I be insulted this way just because
I'm old?"

Blond-Hair-and-Purple-Lips said, "Yes, I insulted you. So what?
Shameless old bitch . . ."

It was at that moment that Tiao pushed her way through the
crowd and saw Wu. Her mother was standing alone in front of the
counter, her unrecognizable face full of agony and helplessness. She
looked weak and ashamed before the two vigorous young women,
at a loss to defend herself, not just in the current moment, but forever. She stood lonely in front of the cool perfection of the Dior
counter, a laughingstock. Her back was visibly stooped, and her right
shoulder was slightly higher than her left one, which made her seem
even more pathetic. This woman was Tiao's mother. Tiao had never
encountered her mother in such a situation or in such a condition,
and it evoked a care and protectiveness in her heart that she had
never felt before. No, she had never cared for or protected her mom;
her relationship with her mother was full of demands, resentments,
distance, and indifference. Her condemnation of Wu's betrayal of the
family had run through her entire life, and it was what argued loud-
est for Tiao's neglect of Wu. Wu accepted her indifference; they had
a tacit understanding. It took those two arrogant young women in
front of the Dior counter to awaken the maternal feeling in the depth
of Tiao's heart. She was certain it was a maternal feeling; a daughter
had to acquire the feelings of a mother in order to treat her mother
with kindness and care.

So when Tiao showed up while the two women were shouting
insults at Wu, she stepped between Wu and the women and con-

fronted them without the least hesitation. "Now, I apologize for my mother to your child, but I find your behavior a little shocking. You swear and shout insults right in front of the child like this, which will teach your child how to treat you in the future."

With that, Tiao took Wu's arm and said loudly, "Mom, let's go."

Wu stumbled along beside her. They left the mall and got into a taxi. As soon as Wu was in the car she couldn't help bursting into tears, like a child who had been bullied in the street and was finally taken home. Ah, your parents are your children. A heart must be big for that.

Wu said in tears, "Tiao, if you hadn't come, I really wouldn't have known what to do. I was really . . . I was really . . ." She kept blowing her nose with handful after handful of tissues. Ever since she had had the bridge of her nose raised, her nose ran, so she had to blow it constantly.

They got home and Wu said to Tiao before they went in, "Don't mention what happened today to your dad."

Fortunately, Yixun was not home, which immediately calmed Wu. She walked into the bedroom and lay down. Tiao took her a cup of water.

She lay in bed and closed her eyes for a while, and propped herself up to drink half a cup of water. She then lay back and said, "Tiao, come over and sit beside me."

Tiao got a chair and sat next to Wu's bed.

"I know none of you likes to see how I look now. I think maybe my plastic surgeries were a mistake, a complete mistake."

"Mom, you stay quiet for a while. After a while you'll feel better."

"Why do you think I had plastic surgery? To make myself look prettier? I wasn't sure in the beginning, myself. I was bored with my life. Later, I participated in the seniors' fashion show, and I think that got me into the plastic surgeries at first, and I convinced myself that this was the most important reason. But then I found it wasn't true. The real reason was for your dad, to please your dad. You know your dad doesn't like me, and for many years I didn't like myself, either. I fantasized that by changing my appearance entirely I could destroy the old me. By destroying the old me I would destroy my old memories. Most of the old memories were unpleasant. Your dad wasn't happy. You know."

"No, I don't know."

"You know."

"No, I don't."

Wu insisted, "You do know, no matter what you say. I wanted to please him, but that was another mistake. I don't know why there was always something that went wrong with my life. The old me has disappeared, but who is the person with this new face? Your dad can go without talking to me or looking at me for days on end, and I don't blame him. Only, he would never believe that I changed my face to destroy the past, to make him happy now."

Tiao looked at Wu's distorted, miserable face and believed what she said. She wanted to understand this strange and selfless wish, although all of it made her angry. Chen Zai's ex-wife came into her mind at this moment, and she remembered what Wan Meicheng had said about how she wanted to change herself into Tiao. They wanted to please their loved ones, but in an absurd way, and they were painfully misguided.

Chapter 10

❧ ❧ ❧

The Garden in the Depths
of the Heart

1

Autumn had arrived, and their wedding date was approaching, but
Tiao often lost her temper with Chen Zai for no reason. Once, when
he turned around, she discovered that the hair on the back of his
head seemed thinner than it had been; he was balding prematurely.
It wasn't as though she hadn't seen the back of his head before, but
why hadn't she realized that he was losing his hair? She mentioned
this to him, and he said, "I've been this way for ten years, Tiao. Have
you really never noticed?"

Tiao went quiet. If she hadn't noticed that the back of his head had
been like this ten years ago, then it simply proved she didn't know
him well enough. This made her nervous and unsure. And when she
was nervous and unsure, she became capricious. She stayed up late
and got up late, and Chen Zai had to try to wake her, calling her a
lazy girl again and again. Then she would lift off the quilt, sit up, and
say, "I know you think I'm lazy. I know it."

"I don't mind your being lazy, but if I didn't call you 'lazy girl,' you
wouldn't get up at all."

"Do you really not mind my being lazy?"

"I really don't mind."

"Then you have to say it in my ear."

So he said it in her ear.

Still unsatisfied, she said, "You have to say you love me."

"I love you."

"Am I the one you love most?"

"Yes, you're the one I love most."

She fell back, throwing herself onto the bed. This quick and careless gesture of hers Chen Zai found very exciting. The curtains were not opened yet, which tempted them into other activities. So he got onto the bed, held her tightly, and buried his head into her warm bosom.

As the evening came, she kept making demands on him, loosing a stream of obscenities, and also asking him to beat her. He didn't know why she would act like this, or why she was shivering as if with fever, frantic as if it were the last day of life on earth, and tender as if they were going to part forever . . . He didn't dare think about it any further. They were going to have a good life together, and nothing could stop him from loving her. During the night, late on this night with its bright autumn moon and light breeze, they drew the curtain open and let the moonlight flow over their big bed, and they made love in that moonlight, which melted Tiao's wildness into a soft coupling with Chen Zai; her gleaming body undulated in the moonlight like satin billowing in a light breeze. They were so naturally attuned to each other, what could it be, if not love? In his arms, she sank into a sleep so deep it seemed as if she would never wake up again.

For a while he gazed at Tiao in her sound sleep, then got off the bed quietly and went to the living room. He hesitated briefly in front of the telephone and picked up the receiver and began to dial. He was calling Wan Meicheng; he'd heard that she was going to Gabon. He didn't notice that Tiao in the bedroom had woken up and come to the living room in pajamas. She heard Chen Zai's conversation at the door. When he put down the receiver she turned on the light.

He looked at her standing at the doorway with some surprise. She returned to the bedroom and got his pajamas for him to put on. Then they sat down. "I heard your phone call."

"I'm sure you'll understand. She, their family, are southerners who like to sleep with their windows open at night. It used to be my job to close the windows. Now it's fall and the wind is chilly. I was afraid she wouldn't remember."

"Chen Zai, you don't have to explain. You haven't done anything wrong."

He stood up and said, "Let's go back to sleep."

"No. Listen, I have a few more things to say."

He reached out and took hold of her feet and said, "Your feet are very cold."

"I don't care."

So he lifted her feet and placed them on his chest.

"Chen Zai, you know when a person is planning to make an important decision he or she might feel frustrated for quite a while, as I have. I just figured out why I've been losing my temper at you and have been so unhappy with myself lately. It was because I wanted to make a decision but kept hesitating. Now I want to tell you, you should . . . you should . . ."

She couldn't go on; she was crying. Although she had made up her mind, it was still so difficult to let it out.

He said, "Tell me what you mean. What should I do?"

She calmed herself a bit and continued, "You should go back to Wan Meicheng."

"Tiao, don't treat our life like a children's game."

"If I treated our life as a children's game, I wouldn't be in such pain. Don't you know that? I wouldn't suffer so much. You think I want this to happen? Do you think I like doing this?"

"Is this because of a telephone call? A phone call isn't love. You know it isn't."

She said, "I know it's not love, but it's concern, something deeper than love. Ten years of marriage produces such concern. Because you understand this kind of concern I have to leave you; because you understand this kind of concern I respect you more. Chen Zai, I love you, but you should leave. You must leave."

"Tiao, listen to me. There are things you still don't know—"

She interrupted him and said, "I know. Wan Meicheng and I met a few times."

"You and she met? You two?"

"Yes, we met. So it's not because of the phone call you made today; it's because I was moved by her. She made me sad; she had the power to make me feel sad. I have to give you back to her. You might think you did something to hurt me, but you've done nothing wrong. You're a real man because you kept your promise of marrying me. In an era that despises promises, you preserve the old-fashioned innocence of a promise. But that's not how life is. Life demands that we be separate. Chen Zai, I want you to believe me, the farther away I'll be from you, the more I'll love you . . ."

The next day, Tiao called Wan Meicheng as soon as she got into the office. She told Wan Meicheng that she didn't have to go to Gabon anymore. Chen Zai had something urgent to say to her. She also told Wan Meicheng that she was not going to marry Chen Zai, and that Wan Meicheng could remarry him at any time.

To avoid Chen Zai, Tiao moved back to her parents' home for a while. She lived with Yixun and Wu again, in the midst of their quarrels.

One morning, when Wu heated up the milk, it began to spill over the sides of the pot. She immediately moved the pot off the stove and told Yixun that the milk was ready.

Yixun said the milk was not ready and she needed to heat it up again.

"The milk was already boiling over. How could it not be ready?"

"The milk has to boil in the pot. It has to really boil, like boiling water."

Wu said, "It already overflowed. How can it not have boiled?"

Yixun said with loathing, "Of course it didn't. It's very likely that some part of the milk is still cold."

Wu said, "So what? Pasteurized milk can be drunk cold."

Yixun said, "Are you trying to say it was a good thing to have the milk overflow because it can be drunk cold? I find it extremely strange that you can't admit to even a small mistake. Besides, it's not like I haven't found straw in this so-called 'high-temperature pasteurized' milk. You do know what straw is?"

Wu mumbled, "That was because you happened to drink the milk while you had your reading glasses on."

Yixun raised his voice and said, "Right, right. It's precisely because I had my reading glasses on that I saw the straw in my milk, which only proves I don't know how much straw I've swallowed when I'm not wearing them. What are you trying to say by pointing out that I drank the milk with my reading glasses on? What's the connection between my wearing reading glasses to drink and your lifelong ignorance of how to heat milk or to tell when water boils?"

Wu said, "I have not been making the milk overflow my whole life. Exaggerating other people's shortcomings is your favorite hobby."

Yixun suddenly laughed triumphantly. "Okay, okay, at last you admit that you have shortcomings. With your own words you yourself prove that I haven't been making things up out of nothing. And as far as exaggeration is concerned, it's your specialty."

Wu said, "I have never exaggerated your shortcomings, it's you who love to do that to me. Take, for example, time. I'm not very smart, so it does take me longer to get things done, but it's nothing like what you claim. Every time I wash vegetables, you watch me so closely and then say you don't understand why it takes me fifteen minutes to wash a tomato, but it doesn't take me fifteen minutes."

Yixun appealed to Tiao. "Listen to her, listen to her. Now you know who's exaggerating. Your mom said I watched her 'every time' she washed vegetables. 'Every time,' would that be possible? As if I had nothing better to do! I'd prefer to look at something more beautiful if I had that kind of time."

"I understand what you mean. So go find someone more beautiful," Wu said.

"If I want to, I will. I don't need you to tell me. Your disrespect for yourself alone would make me want to."

"How do I disrespect myself? Tell me, how do I disrespect myself?"

"You don't respect your own face . . . Do you want me to continue?"

Wu rushed toward Yixun; frustrated, she seemed about to push him, but turned instead to the embarrassing pot of milk, raised it to her mouth, and drank up the milk. The pronounced gulping irritated Yixun to the point that he had to shut his eyes. When he opened them, Wu had disappeared. She'd locked herself in her bedroom.

Tiao and Yixun were left sitting at the dinner table, face-to-face.

He said to Tiao, "Why didn't you say anything? How did you get so above it all?"

"It's not that I'm above it all. It's how extreme you are."

"Are you still holding a grudge against me for criticizing Chen Zai? Then you're being unfair."

"No, I'm not holding a grudge. I understand you."

"Then why didn't you speak up for me?"

Tiao went quiet. Yixun's fault-finding made his own flaws obvious to Tiao, but she didn't want to be the referee between her parents. She loved them, loved this man and woman who had been fighting all their lives. Today she loved them more than ever. Life owed them something and she owed them, too, and now she finally realized it. She realized strongly how they needed to be loved. From now on, she wouldn't demand that they understand her; she wanted to have a heart big enough to understand them.

The more they failed to understand her, the more she would attempt to understand them.

She received several phone calls from Chen Zai. On hearing his voice, she couldn't help the tears welling up in her eyes. He asked to talk to her again; he said he must. He asked her whether they could talk. He said that he had to talk to her.

So she went back to her own apartment, the place where she'd lived with Chen Zai, where they had made love. In the living room, she sat waiting for him, and he took her in his arms as soon as he walked in. Meekly, she snuggled into him, resting her head in the nest of his shoulder, which fit her perfectly. He bound her tightly with his strong arms as if he wanted to crush her. He kissed her crazily, saying, "Let me look at you. Let me look at you." But he couldn't care less about looking at her, because he had to kiss her. He kissed her and said repeatedly, "My little sweet gum candy, I can't leave you, I really can't leave you!" He sucked her tongue, and his strength forced her head back as if she were going to fall into an abyss. Then he suddenly grabbed her around the waist and lifted her head. Gasping, she said, "Come to me, come to me."

They made love again, to their hearts' content, more indulgently, more wildly, more sincerely than ever.

She held him and said, "Bite me. Bite me. I want you to leave your teeth marks on my body."

He held her and said, "Bite me. Bite me. I want you to leave your teeth marks on my body."

He bit her until there were bruises all over her. He reached out his large hand over her face and gently touched her eyebrows, nose, and lips. He said, "Tiao, Tiao. How can I not see you? You tell me, how can I not see you . . . ?"

They dozed for a while and then woke up almost at the same time.

He pulled her into his arms and she buried her face in his chest. He said, "I think you're too selfish, Tiao."

"Yes, I am."

"You don't care about others' suffering at all."

"Yes, you're right."

"You're also very cold and cruel. I can't move you even with my lifelong love."

She said, "Yes, that's right."

"Don't you want to contradict me? I was saying the opposite of what I meant."

"No, I don't."

"I really want to choke you to death."

"Choke me to death. Choke me now."

She grabbed his hand and placed it on her neck, squeezing his hand with hers. He freed himself from her grip and kissed the back of her neck. They made love one more time.

At daybreak, she said to him, "You should give me back the key to this apartment."

2

She thought about phoning Mike; she knew he had gone back to the States long ago. He had called her before he left China, hoping to come to Fuan to meet her. She refused to see him then; her heart at the time could only contain Chen Zai. Now she thought of Mike; she didn't want to consider this pragmatic. No, she was not that kind of pragmatist. She didn't know why she wanted to make the call, she only knew that she really wanted to.

She dialed Mike's home number in Texas, and an utterly unexpected voice struck her dumb—it was Fan who picked up the phone.

Fan said, "Older sister, I never expected it to be you calling."

"I didn't expect it to be you answering the phone."

"I knew I was going to surprise you. I planned to call home in a few days and tell all of you everything."

"Then you can tell me now."

"When you came to Chicago and called Mike, I wrote down his home number. And later we became friends."

"Can you tell me what kind of friends you are?"

"The kind who want to live together. David and I are divorced. He went back to that older German woman of his. I'll probably marry Mike soon; he's already proposed."

"Do you really love him?"

"I really do."

"Then what about David?"

"I didn't know anything when I married David."

"Fan, it's not that I want to stop you from marrying Mike. I just feel you get some kind of satisfaction from competing with me, and taking things from me. This mind-set can confuse the soul and prevent you from knowing who you really love."

Fan said, "That's what I should be saying to you. I just called Chen Zai and heard that you two are not going to get married. You're the one who wants to compete and take things away, right? You remember Mike when you have no one to turn to."

Tiao said, "If my agreeing would make you happy, I'd admit you were right. I apologize for remembering Mike when I had no one to turn to. It's weak and low of me. I should change my attitude and wish you happiness, wish that you and Mike be happy together."

Fan said, "Do you think I appreciate your sarcasm and insincerity? Don't use the Chinese way with me. I would rather you shouted."

Tiao's hand holding the telephone was shaking. How she wanted to scream at Fan through the receiver. Even though she had no relationship with Mike, she still felt the stab of a deep wound, and Fan was the blade. How busy Fan was, so busy that she didn't forget to pry into her and Chen Zai's business even when she was busy dating Mike. She was so busy, busily getting involved in order to spoil things, to get involved by spoiling things, to spoil things by getting involved. She couldn't be sure of her own existence if she didn't get involved and spoil things. Tiao held the phone, thinking. The strange thing was that she was no longer so angry. She felt like someone who had seen the final ending of everything, and understood that all the emotion of those who'd tried to change the ending meant nothing, suddenly didn't matter. She said into the receiver, "Fan, let's make up. I sincerely wish you two happiness."

"Older sister, I know you feel very bad now."

"When are you coming back to China together? I'll go to Beijing to pick you up."

"Maybe during the Spring Festival. Can we stay with you?"

"Of course you can."

"Can we use your bedroom?"

"Of course you can."

"Can we use your big bed? Mike and I have to sleep together."

"Of course you can."

"I really want to go home right away."

Tiao said, "Do you know that *Going Home Right Away* is Fang Jing's new movie?"

"He mentioned it when he was in Chicago. The movie was shown here a while ago. But Mike and I didn't see it; Fang Jing's generation is too old."

* * *

Tiao hung up without asking to talk to Mike. She sat cross-legged on her bed and cried quietly. She cried not just because she felt sad and misunderstood, nor because she wanted to relieve her sadness or allow herself to feel the gains and losses in her life. She was just crying, letting the tears run off her face and wet her clothes. The crying seemed to prepare her for another state of mind, and she entered into a meditation. She took herself into her heart, and only then realized what a mistake it was to think of her heart as the size of a fist; it was deep and wide—boundless. She led herself far down into her heart, spellbound by the flowers and fragrance that were everywhere. Finally, she reached the garden in the depths of her heart, and only then did she discover what it was like: the verdant green of the grass, the gushing springs, the flowers swaying joyfully on their stems, and the water dancing jubilantly in the streams. White clouds brushed lightly against the rippling water and birds called as they flew over them. Everywhere she went she saw familiar faces, people she knew so well, those who had been dearest to her, men she had loved . . . They were strolling the garden with smiling, untroubled faces. Those young girls who had passed from her life were also there, Fei, and that heroine of the war against Japan, and Quan. They glided over the tips of grass, wearing crowns of Persian chrysanthemums, bringing with them a light breeze. She moved through, full of wonder at being able to provide them a garden like this, with such breezes, with such a sense of love. When had she cultivated it? How did it come to be hers? Was it there naturally or had she planted it? It must be natural. There was a garden in every heart's core that each of us must enter. Everyone must discover it, cultivate, pull the weeds, and water it . . . and when we wear our crowns of Persian chrysanthemums and look back, we will feel blessed that the heart is the broadest place in the world and that we haven't let our love nest in weeds.

She kept walking, and her body and mind then sank into a profound stillness.

* * *

One day, Tiao received a phone call, a phone call from Yu Dasheng. She said, "Governor Yu, it's you. Governor Yu, what a surprise to hear from you."

"Don't call me Governor Yu. I'm already retired."

"What can I do for you?"

"Nothing in particular. But if you happened to have time, we could meet and chat. I read a book about the Jewish people recently and want to know what you think of it."

"Of course. You choose a time. Should we meet in your office?"

"No, I don't have an office anymore. Let's meet in a park, the new Rainbow Park by the river."

"Okay, let's meet there."

They sat on a green bench in the Rainbow Park and chatted, and Yu Dasheng brought his granddaughter along. The five-year-old was very polite, and she said, "Hi, Auntie," as soon as she saw Tiao.

Tiao looked at the girl and responded quickly, but she had a momentary vision of Fei. Didn't the child look a little like Fei? She really wasn't sure whether it was her imagination or not.

The little girl ran away and played on her own. Yu Dasheng put on his reading glasses, took out a book from his coat pocket, turned to a page, and said, "Let me read this paragraph to you: 'If a criminal were to commit arson, burning the temple, the most sacred and revered temple, he would only be sentenced to thirty lashes. Yet, if an angry person were to kill him, the punishment would be death because the temple and all holy ground are less important than a single life, even though it's the life of an arsonist, a blasphemer, the enemy of God, and the one who insults Him.' This is what the Jewish people believe, but what about the facts? The facts create irony for the Jews: 'We were driven from one country to another. Our temples were destroyed, our prophets assassinated, our children murdered, but still we sing the praises of the inviolable sacredness of life and spread that faith to all humankind.'"

Yu Dasheng closed the book and said, "I think this is a good book."

Tiao said, "Have you ever studied the Jewish people before?"

Yu Dasheng said, "Never. I haven't even seen *Schindler's List* yet."

Tiao couldn't help feeling surprised by this government official's ignorance, but soon excused him. Not all Chinese officials could pay attention to other peoples' troubles. Besides, she was rather touched by the way he sat on the park bench and pored over the book in his reading glasses: a governor reading passages from a book about the Jewish people . . . She said, "The paragraph you read is about the value of life."

"Yes, the value of life, the respect that one race has for life."

"Have you ever thought about committing suicide?"

"No, not even during the most difficult times."

"How about the urge to take someone else's life?"

"No. Why are you asking such a question?"

She said, "Because I had the urge—a long, long time ago. A criminal destroyed the sacred temple in my heart, and maybe all crimes only deserve thirty lashes, but I became that angry person. I am the angry one."

"I would rather get back to discussing the Jewish people with you."

"You haven't thought about killing yourself or taking someone else's life. Have you ever abandoned a life?"

He seemed to become alert—though maybe it was only Tiao's imagination again. He said, "No, never."

They both fell silent. She was about to mention Fei to him, but on second thought, what was the point? She had no right to force someone to admit to her assumption about him; she didn't even have the right to force him to comment on it. Neither Fei nor she had any right based on their own wishful thinking. Maybe he hadn't asked to see her because of Fei; maybe he just wanted to talk about the Jewish people because he had read a book about them.

The five-year-old girl approached her, and Tiao seemed to be seeing the baby Quan again. She was the two-year-old Quan, the green bud of the spirit. Quan was the first tender shoot in her garden, which she had trampled, and from which, in return, a garden grew.

As she stood up from the bench and gazed at the river, which had grown dirty, she caught the scent of a garden in the air. Fuan should be fragrant, she thought. Let me start over.

The little girl ran back and forth in front of her and kept turning her head to look at her. A voice floated to her from far away: "Child, what's the matter?"

Child, what's the matter?

She smiled and gazed at the child, her heart full of bitter sweetness.

About the Author

TIE NING came to prominence with a national short story award at the age of twenty-five and has won many other literary prizes since. She has published ten books—collections of short fiction, essays, and novels, including *The Rosy Gate* and *A City Without Rain*—three of which were made into movies and television series, including *The Bathing Women*. In 2006, at the age of forty-nine, she was elected president of the Chinese Writers Association, becoming the youngest writer and first woman to be honored in this way. Her works have been translated into Russian, German, French, Japanese, Korean, Spanish, Danish, Norwegian, and Vietnamese. This is her first work to be translated into English.